# BROKEN PARADISE

# BROKEN PARADISE

A Novel

CECILIA SAMARTIN

**ATRIA** BOOKS
New York   London   Toronto   Sydney

**ATRIA** BOOKS

1230 Avenue of the Americas
New York, NY 10020

Copyright © 2004 by Cecilia Samartin

Originally published in Great Britain in 2004 by Bantam Press,
a division of Transworld Publishers

ISBN-13: 978-0-7432-8779-1
ISBN-10:    0-7432-8779-7

First Atria Books hardcover edition February 2007

10  9  8  7  6  5  4  3  2  1

**ATRIA** BOOKS is a trademark of Simon & Schuster, Inc.

Manufactured in the United States of America

For information about special discounts for bulk purchases,
please contact *Simon & Schuster Special Sales* at
1-800-456-6798 or business@simonandschuster.com.

For all the cousins

Dear Alicia,

I'm told this letter may not get to you as the communists will cut it into shreds, but when I saw the picture of us together at Varadero beach I knew I had to write it anyway. I look at it every night and remember what life was like when I was alive. I do not belong to this place and every morning when I wake up and find myself still here I want to close my eyes and sleep forever.

All I have now are memories. I love them and hate them for what they do to me. I love them because when I'm lost in their vision, this hollow pain in my heart goes away for a while. I hate them because they are so beautiful, they fool me into believing I'm really home and then I must leave all over again.

I wish I were with you. I wish we were packing a suitcase for Varadero right now without a worry in our heads except whether or not it will rain before noon. . . .

## Sueño despierto

Yo sueño con los ojos
Abiertos, y de día
Y noche siempre sueño.
Y sobre las espumas
Del ancho mar revuelto,
Y, por entre las crespas
Arenas del desierto,
Y del león pujante,
Monarca de mi pecho,
Montado alegremente
Sobre el sumiso cuello,—
Un niño que me llama
Flotando siempre veo!


## Dreaming Awake

I dream with my eyes
Wide open, Day and Night
I always dream.
And over the foam
Of the wide and agitated sea,
And over the undulated
Sand of the desert,
And of the vigorous lion,
Master of my soul,
Joyfully riding
Upon the submissive neck—
A child that calls to me
I see always floating!
—José Martí

# CUBA

# 1

WHAT I LOVE MOST IS THE WARMTH, HOW IT REACHES IN AND spreads out to the tips of my fingers and toes until it feels like I'm part of the sun, like it's growing inside me. Have you ever seen the ocean turn smooth as a sheet of glass or curl upon the shore with a sigh? If you knew my country then you'd know that the sea can be many things; faithful and blue as the sky one moment and the next a shimmering turquoise so brilliant, you'd swear the sun was shinning from beneath the waves.

I often stand at the water's edge, digging my toes into the moist sand and gaze out at the ghostly gray line of the horizon that separates sea and sky. I close my eyes just a little so I can no longer be sure which is which, and I'm floating in a blue green universe. I'm a fish and then a bird. I'm a golden mermaid with long flowing hair that gets lost in the wind. With a flick of my tail I can return to the sea and explore the shores of other lands, but how can I leave this place that quiets my soul to a prayer?

Better to stay and lay on a blanket of fine white sand, gazing up at the royal palms for hours as we do. They sway in the ocean breeze, and I almost fall asleep if not for the constant chatter of my cousin, Alicia. She's hardly a year older than me, in fact for thirteen days out of the year we're exactly the same age, but for some reason she seems older and wiser. Perhaps it's because she's so sure of what she likes. She has no doubt that she prefers mango ice cream to coconut and that her favorite number is nine because nine is the age we were then and if nine were a person it would be a glamorous lady, a showgirl with long legs and swinging hips. I, on the other hand, have a hard time choosing between mango and coconut and if you throw in papaya, I'm completely overwhelmed.

Alicia squints up at the sun with eyes that are sometimes gold, sometimes green, and tells me what she sees. "Look how the palms move in the wind."

"I see them," I respond.

"They're sweeping the clouds away with their big leaves so we can look straight up to heaven and see God."

"Can you see God?" I ask.

"If I look at it just right, I can. And when I do, I ask Him for whatever I want and He'll give it to me."

I turn away from the swaying palms to study Alicia's face. Sometimes she likes to joke around and doesn't tell me the truth until she's certain she's tricked me. But I know her dimples show when she's hiding a smile. They're almost showing now.

"Tell the truth," I prod.

"I am." Then she opens her eyes as wide as she can and stares straight up at the sun and shuts them tight until tiny tears slip down her cheeks. She turns to face me, eyes sparkling and lips curled in a triumphant smile. "I just saw Him."

"What did you ask for?"

"I can't tell you or else He won't give it to me."

I too turn my face toward the sun and try to open my eyes as wide as Alicia, but I can't keep them open for even half a second, and I certainly don't see God or even the wisp of an angel's wing. I conclude that brown eyes are not as receptive to heavenly wonders as her magnificent golden eyes.

Alicia sits up suddenly and looks down at me, blocking the sun. "What did you ask for?"

"I thought you said we couldn't tell." I object, not wanting to admit I'd failed to see anything at all.

She settles back down onto the sand, while a full sun stretches over us once again. Soon we'll have to head back for our afternoon meal. These morning hours at the beach slip away so fast. I was hoping we'd get a chance to go swimming, but we aren't allowed in past our knees without a trusted adult nearby to keep watch. Ever since a little boy drowned at Varadero beach three years ago that's been the rule, and there's no use trying to change it.

"I want to go swimming," I say.

Alicia turns to survey the ocean. We see the waves lapping the white curve of the beach and know the sea is a warm bath. We'd float easily in the calm waters and maybe even learn how to swim more like the grown-ups, moving our arms like steady and reliable windmills. And maybe our grandfather, Abuelo Antonio, undoubtedly the best swimmer in all of Cuba, will come out with us and we'll take turns venturing into deeper water while riding safely on his shoulders.

"Let's go!" Alicia cries and we spring to our feet and run as fast as we can, leaving a wake of powdery white sand floating behind us.


All of the rooms in my grandparents' large house at Varadero overlooked the sea, and the dinning room was no exception. Abuela kept the windows open most of the time as she believed fresh air to be the best defense against the many diseases she worried about. Lace curtains fluttered on the incoming ocean breeze as Abuelo said the blessing over our meal. It wasn't until he lifted his head and took up his fork that we were allowed to do the same.

I was lucky to be sitting closest to the fried bananas, my favorite, and to have Alicia right next to me. At home, our parents knew better and always separated us so we wouldn't talk and giggle when we should be learning proper table manners. It seemed that Mami was more concerned with what fork I used for the salad than with my school work.

Most of the time, Abuelo and Abuela were amused by our antics and laughed at what our parents called *foolishness*.

"Look at how dark you're getting," Abuela said as she handed me a large bowl of fluffy yellow rice. "People will think you're a *mulatica* and not the white, full-blooded Spaniard that you are." Being a full-blooded Spaniard was also a very important thing, even more important than proper manners.

I helped myself to a generous serving of rice. "Look at Alicia. She's almost as dark as me," I shot back.

"Alicia's a Spaniard through and through," Abuela said. "With those light eyes and hair, there's no mistaking her heritage. She can get as black as a ripened date, and she'll still look like a Spaniard."

At these moments, the only thing that kept me from envying Alicia for her superior coloring, was that she always came to my rescue. "I think Nora looks beautiful, like a tropical princess," she said.

"That's right, Abuela. I look like a tropical princess."

Abuelo laughed. Having been born in Spain, he was more Spanish than anyone, but he didn't care as much as Abuela about where people came from or who their parents were. And even though he never bragged, everyone knew he was a real Spaniard because of his accent and eloquent speech, so different from the brusque Cuban style. "Would the princess mind passing the *plátanos* before she eats them all herself?" he asked with a slight bow of his head.

Later that afternoon, after we'd had our mandatory naps, Abuelo was easily persuaded to go out to the beach and continue his swimming lessons. I promised Papi I'd learn to be a good swimmer during this week's vacation, but I hadn't progressed nearly enough to impress him.

"Too much time playing around and not enough time practicing," Abuelo declared as he stood with us on the shore wearing dark blue swim trunks and a white *guayabera* shirt, perfectly pressed by Abuela that morning and every morning.

Alicia and I stood on either side of him, each clasping onto one of his big hands as we gazed out at the peaceful sea. Together, we stepped into the water and felt the waves caress our feet. We ventured in further and the silky blanket swirled up to our knees and then up to our waists, but we could easily see our toes wiggling in the sand.

We stood silent and nervous, waiting for Abuelo's instructions to begin. Perhaps he'd have us float on our backs as he usually did. Maybe we'd practice kicking our feet with our heads under water while he taxied us around by our hands that grasped at him for dear life when he dared to let go. Or he'd dive into deeper water while we clung to his neck, laughing and sputtering when he came up for air. "Not so deep, Abuelo!" we'd cry, hoping he'd go a little deeper still.

Instead, he pointed to the platform that floated a hundred yards from the shore. "You see that out there?"

We were quite familiar with the platform. This was the famous place to which both of our fathers had to swim as children in order to be declared real swimmers and allowed into the ocean without adult supervision. We'd heard the stories a million times and when our parents dropped us off we bragged that by the end of the week we would've conquered the platform.

On most days older kids were on and around it, diving into the water, lifting themselves easily on to the wooden planks, and jumping off again like loud happy seals, but on this afternoon the platform bobbed about without a soul upon it. In fact, except for a couple very far off holding hands, the beach was empty. Everyone still seemed to be resting after lunch.

"Well, do you see it?" Abuelo asked again, still pointing.

I felt the butterflies begin to stir. "Yes, I see it."

I detected a slight tremor in Alicia's voice as well.

He squeezed our hands. "Today you're going to swim out there all by yourselves. Who wants to go first?"

Neither of us spoke. "What? Nobody wants to go first?" Abuelo smiled down at us and then with an exaggerated expression of concern and surprise said, "You're not afraid, are you?"

"I think I'm a little bit afraid," I said.

Alicia thrust out her chin. "I'm not. I'll go first."

"That's my girl!" Abuelo dropped my hand and held Alicia's up in the air as if she'd won a prizefight.

"Now follow me and try to move your arms like this when you kick." Abuelo circled his arms over his head and Alicia imitated him as best she could while I stood with my arms glued to my side, aware that this lesson wasn't meant for me. Abuelo pulled his *guayabera* up over his head and threw it onto the sand before diving smoothly into the sea with hardly a splash. Three or four strokes of his powerful arms and in no time at all he was pulling himself up on to the platform and waving for Alicia to follow.

She began with more of a belly flop than a dive, but it roused a cheer from Abuelo just the same. Her head dipped in and out of the water with jerky motions as she swam slowly, but steadily toward the platform. She tried to swing her arms over her head like Abuelo instructed, but she floundered a bit and resumed her less than graceful, but reliable dog paddle. She'd never swum this far without stopping ever in her life, but she kept going well past the point where the water turned from a light green to an ominous deeper blue. And Abuelo kept cheering her on, standing on the very edge of the platform and reaching for her even when she was too far away. Her neck craned with the strain of her effort as she neared the platform and she was barely inching forward when Abuelo reached down and pulled her up easily by both arms. She collapsed on to the platform with a thud, panting and laughing and holding her sides. Once she'd caught her breath she stood up next to Abuelo, triumphant and glistening—a real swimmer.

She called out to me. "Come on, Nora. You can do it."

Abuelo turned his attention to me now that Alicia had proved herself. He wanted to be doubly proud. "Don't think about it any more. Just dive in like your cousin."

They looked so far away on that platform of champions, but I could see their smiles bursting out at me even from there. They believed in me. They knew I could do it too.

I dove in and felt the warmth that, for the first time, failed to calm my heart. My feet kicked and my cupped hands shoveled in a valiant dog paddle. Suddenly the water felt thick like jelly and it filled my ears, my nostrils, my mouth dulling my senses in an alien way. I filled my lungs with dry air in pockets and spurts between gulps of salty water as encouraging screams broke through the monotony of my labored breathing. I looked toward my goal and caught their smiles, their arms waving wildly against the bright blue sky. Momentarily blind and deaf, I tried desperately to find a rhythm for my arms and legs that would propel me forward. I had to make it. I had to prove I could do it too.

Listening for their calls, reaching for Abuelo's big hands that should be only inches away, I looked up again, but they were still waving, no closer than before. Could it be that I was actually farther away?

I pointed my toes toward the sandy bottom. If I reached it, I might push myself up and catch my breath, but the bottom was much further down than I'd thought. I knew suddenly there was no need to go forward any more, just up. Up to the sun that's a splash of watery light, up toward the birds watching me as they flew in gentle circles above my thrashing attempts to stay afloat, for even a bird would know that whatever I was doing, it wasn't swimming.

Somehow I managed to force my nose and mouth above water one last time, but the silky blanket covered my head and there was no sound, no sky, no wind, just the rush of water inside my head as I sunk deeper in the quiet blue. It was cool and dark, only bubbles, clear white bubbles spinning me around.

I awoke lying on the sand with the afternoon sun full upon me. I felt my chest rise and fall in shallow spasms, but when I tried to breathe deep I coughed up enough seawater to fill a good-sized pitcher. Abuelo's face was very close and I detected the sweet fragrance of cigar on his breath. Alicia was crouched next to him, but he held her away from me with a protective arm. Their mouths moved, but there was only silence. Finally the faint hum of their familiar voices grew into clear and understandable words.

"Nora, can you hear me?" Abuelo asked smiling, though his voice was firm as if directing me more than asking me. "Oh yes, you can hear me. She's OK now," he said to Alicia and then he chuckled nervously as he did when caught by Abuela in a white lie of some sort.

He allowed Alicia to peer in closer with instructions that she should give me room to breathe. I wanted to turn and smile and say I was fine, like I did when I fell off my skates, but I could hardly move.

"You almost drowned, Nora," Alicia said in wonderment.

Abuelo came in close again and they both dripped on me, forcing me to blink.

"Now, now, Alicia, that isn't true," he said. "I was watching her every minute. There's no way she could've drowned."

"But her hand went up like this, Abuelo," Alicia said, thrusting her hand up in the air like a claw grasping at nothing. "And she had that horrible look on her face."

"You were always safe, Norita. I would never let anything happen to you."

I tried to nod and felt my head shift in the sand, but this small movement caused their faces to start spinning, and I had to close my eyes just to settle my stomach which felt as if it was still sinking to the bottom of the sea.

In a few minutes, I felt much better and was able to sit up and look around. The world was still the same as I'd left it except that Abuelo and Alicia watched me as if I'd just hatched out of an egg or grown horns on my head.

Abuelo directed Alicia to bring me an ice-cold Coke from the house, and when she returned I drank it down. Soon I was able to stand and we sauntered back toward the house hand in hand. Just as we arrived, Abuelo reminded us that Abuela promised to welcome us back from our swim with a piece of her delicious rum cake.

"By the way, there's no reason to tell your grandmother what happened here today," he told us, "She'll only get very upset and worry for no reason."

We needed no convincing of the need for secrecy. We could well predict our grandmother's reaction, and we were quite familiar with her particular brand of worry. It was the kind that made the world stop until the worry was finished. And it usually involved complicated promises to various saints who made her cut off all her fingernails and eyelashes, or never wear lipstick again. Perhaps this time our eyelashes would be cut, and we couldn't risk the possibility of never wearing lipstick. We'd already chosen our colors for when we were old enough. At the very least, we'd never be allowed to go swimming with Abuelo again, of that much we were sure.

# 2

IT WAS A MYSTERY TO ME HOW THE NUNS AT EL ÁNGEL DE LA Guarda School in Havana walked about without making a sound. One might steal up behind you, and you wouldn't know until it was too late. Not that we had much to hide, and there was little trouble to get into except when one of the older girls was occasionally caught wearing lipstick. The sisters would march her straight to the bathroom to wash her face, and it seemed that she was redder than her lipstick for an entire week. That was the extent of our sinfulness.

Nevertheless, we filed into the chapel for prayers every morning at ten o'clock sharp to confess our sins and pray for forgiveness. Most of the other girls disliked chapel time, and I pretended to dislike it too, though actually, it was my favorite part of the day. I loved the way sweet incense drifted about in hazy clouds rising along multicolored streams of sunlight that filtered through stained glass windows high above. Hundreds of small white candles wavered at the bare feet of saints, their wax dripping like liquid lace as they carried their smoky messages to heaven. All the sisters, even the quick ones with eagle eyes, hung their heads low as they whispered their prayers with steady precision, lips hardly moving in quick spasms of half-formed words.

I was particularly fascinated by the Stations of the Cross

carved in white stone that hung over the closet confessionals. I gazed at the depiction of Jesus hanging with his arms outstretched as he looked up to heaven, asking God to forgive all the sinners. I thought of Abuela and her promises. Would it be wrong to ask Jesus to help me learn how to swim? Perhaps if I made a promise to him right now He'd fix it so I could go to the beach every day and practice. I could promise to cut off my hair like a boy's and give my new skates to my little sister, Marta. I could promise never again to ask Beba questions about the African saints; but surely this was asking too much? Our maid Beba was the most fascinating person I knew. As tall as Papi, and with shoulders just as broad, she had a deep golden voice, and laughter that could entice the sun to shine brighter. She told amazing stories about the black people who lived in the country and worshipped African spirits like Ochún and Yemayá. Because of her religion, she always wore white: white dress, white shoes, white stockings, even a white handkerchief. Mami told her it was OK if she dressed this way as along as she didn't bring any of that *Santería* business into the house. The thought of never talking to Beba again, about what I knew she loved most, brought tears to my eyes. And as I wiped them away I caught Sister Margarita watching me from the other side of the chapel. I immediately dropped my head. Interrupting prayer for anything at all was forbidden.

Sister Margarita was one of the most important and feared nuns at the school, and she rarely had time to talk to any student individually, addressing us in large formal assemblies instead. As we were filing back out of the chapel, she touched me on the shoulder and ushered me into a small vestibule away from the others.

In the semi darkness her round wrinkly face looked down on me. It was as sacred and fragile looking as the old Bible they kept behind glass in the library. A shaft of light that came in through the half open door illuminated fine dark hair sprouting over her lips, lips that were smiling when she should've been preparing to reprimand me for my misbehavior. I braced myself.

"Why were you crying during prayers, Nora?" I was surprised that she knew my name.

I could recite the Lord's Prayer, the Hail Mary, the Act of Contrition, and list the Ten Commandments and Stations of the Cross without blinking an eye. If she'd asked me to tell her about any of those things I could've answered confidently. But how could I tell her I was sad about the thought of not asking our maid about *Santería?*

I said the only thing that came to mind, the only thing that might save me and my family from the ultimate disgrace of expulsion I knew would surely follow. "I was sad because of what happened to Jesus. It must've hurt really bad when they put those nails in his hands." My face burned, and I thought I might start to cry again.

Sister Margarita smiled a knowing smile, as if that was exactly what she expected me to say. She bent her head closer to mine so that her dark robes brushed my cheek. "You know," she whispered and I smelled the aniseed on her breath. "We're called in many ways. I sense that a religious life may be in your future. Have you ever thought about that?"

"A religious life?"

She nodded gravely. "Yes, Nora. Have you ever thought about being a nun?"

My heart beat so fiercely that I thought I might have a heart attack. Was there a chance that Sister Margarita would sequester me to some secret chamber where I'd be forced to sign my life away on a ready-made contract from heaven? And how did a girl become a nun? I hadn't really thought about it, even though I'd been surrounded by nuns all of my life. Surely this was the way it happened. Right here, right now.

"Did you hear what I said?"

"Yes, Sister Margarita."

"I was about your age when I received the calling, and it scared me a little too."

"Yes, Sister Margarita."

"I think I'll talk to your parents about it." She placed the large hands that she kept tucked under her robes on my shoulders. "I am right about you, aren't I?"

I braced my knees to stay standing beneath the weight of her hands and took a deep breath. "Yes, Sister Margarita."

I lay on my bed staring up at the ceiling. My parents were devout Catholics. We went to mass every Sunday even when it rained as hard as a hurricane and the windows rattled in their panes. My mother looked like the Virgin Mary herself, in a black lace veil that draped over her shoulders as she lit many candles with a long tapering matchstick. I knew her prayers were for me and Marta and all the people she loved, and she let me light one, maybe two candles of my own. We followed all the Catholic rules like not eating meat on Fridays and making the sign of the cross whenever we passed a church. And Papi and Mami always agreed with the nuns. When they said I should take piano lessons, they agreed. When they said I needed a tutor for math, they agreed.

A holy life—what did it mean? I couldn't go to the beach ever again or learn how to roller-skate fast down hill without falling. I'd never wear lipstick and high-heeled shoes with smooth stockings. Instead I'd walk along darkened corridors, with hands hidden and head lowered, praying constantly as I practiced how to walk without making any noise. And I'd take baths in the dark just in case I saw my body by accident, because everybody knew that nuns weren't allowed to see anybody naked, not even themselves.

There was a soft knock on the door. I knew it was Beba wondering why I hadn't yet asked her to prepare my afternoon snack.

"What's wrong with you? Aren't you hungry today?"

"No. I don't feel too good."

"I heard," Beba said, opening the door wide and narrowing her eyes to a comical glare. "Your mother said you were faking something this morning to get out of going to school."

I turned away. It was easy for Beba to make me smile. All she had to do was stare for a while with mock seriousness. It worked every time, but any temptation to smile vanished when I remembered my dilemma.

"OK. Let's see if you got a fever." She placed her large hand on my forehead and I closed my eyes, comforted by her touch. Everything seemed better when Beba was around. She didn't take anything too seriously, and her solution to most problems involved a good dose of laughter accompanied by something sweet and delicious to eat. The only things Beba took seriously were her religion and politics. When she talked about Batista her eyes rolled in their sockets so hard, I was afraid they'd get lost in the back of her brain somewhere. She hated him with a vengeance and didn't mind who she told about it. Luckily for her and for us, there weren't any Batista fans in our household.

She removed her hand from my forehead and placed it on her ample hip. "Well, you don't got a fever. I'll make you some tea anyway. Maybe then you'll eat a little something."

Beba left and I clutched my pillow. When I became a nun, Beba wouldn't be there to make me tea or take my temperature. Nuns had to do all that for themselves.

Papi arrived home from work at the usual hour, just past seven. He sat in his chair with the evening paper until Mami called us all for dinner. I knew that sometimes Papi wasn't as agreeable as Mami, and there was a slight chance that if Sister Margarita talked to him alone, he might not agree that I should become a nun. But Papi and Mami rarely went anywhere without each other, and it was a sure thing he'd agree with whatever Mami thought because he loved her so much. He couldn't stand to see her upset even for one second. He told her she was beautiful all the time and ran down to buy sugar cane juice or fresh guava whenever we heard the little bells and calls from the vendors on the street. She'd just flutter her eyelashes at him, and he'd jump off his chair and rush to the elevator before the vendors made their way down the street.

He even told her she was beautiful on the day she tried on the polka-dot two-piece bathing suit. She stretched those two pieces of fabric so hard I was afraid they'd snap like rubber bands. When she was finally into it, her cheeks pink from all her hard work, Marta giggled and I stared at her in horror and pleaded with her not to show Papi.

"Why shouldn't I let your father see me? I had two children with him."

"Because you don't look like those ladies on TV, Mami. Maybe he won't love you anymore."

Mami ignored my warning as she evaluated her plump pale body in the full-length mirror. She looked like bread dough that had risen too far out of the pan. I grabbed her hand and pulled her away from the mirror and toward the bed where she'd discarded her dress. There was no doubt in my mind that her best physical attribute was her lovely face with large dark eyes and long eyelashes that curled just right at the corners like delicate fans.

"Put your dress back on, Mami. You look really pretty in it."

She snatched her hand away from me. "Don't be silly." Then she marched straight out to the living room where Papi sat reading his paper. Marta and I followed her wiggling behind into the living room.

"Well," Mami said in a seductive voice, as she struck a bathing beauty pose. "What do you think?"

His eyes opened wide and he let the newspaper drop to the floor in a heap. "You're an angel, Regina. A beautiful angel."

"Not exactly the young girl you married. I'm afraid these two babies changed my figure a little bit."

"You're more beautiful now than ever, my love."

Marta and I stared at each other in utter disbelief. This was yet another confirmation of Mami's amazing powers. All she had to do was look at me with those piercing eyes to know what I was thinking, especially if I was thinking something bad. And all she had to do was wink at Papi and smile a little to make him think whatever she wanted. The only people who had more power than Mami were the nuns, and this was the problem.

I hovered about the other side of Papi's newspaper waiting to be noticed. He lowered the paper and motioned for me to come closer so he could plant a firm kiss on my forehead. "How's my girl?"

"Fine, Papi."

"Will your mother be home soon?"

"Yes, she's visiting Tía María, but she'll be home soon."

He returned to his paper and I learned against the back of his chair and studied the dark gloss of his hair, the matching polish of his shoes. The gold watch Mami gave him for Christmas the year before peaked out beneath his white-cuffed shirt.

I walked around to face him. "Papi?"

He grunted without looking away from his paper.

"Do you think that priests and nuns are always right?"

"I'm not sure what you mean, Nora. Right about what?"

"You know, like about what to do in life?"

He lowered his paper again, intrigued. "That's an interesting question. Now that you mention it, I think that's exactly what they're there for—to help us live better lives. The answer is yes, they do know about what we should do in life. Absolutely."

I dodged Sister Margarita for the rest of the week, but everywhere I turned it seemed her brown steady eyes were hunting me down and trying to capture me into another moment of mysterious understanding. In the chapel, my head hung lower than anybody else's, and my lips moved rapidly in constant prayer. Glowing streams of rainbow colored light might have swept me off the bench, but I wouldn't have so much as blinked. The Stations of the Cross could've come to life, dancing and singing all around me, and I wouldn't have missed a bead on the rosary.

I began to feel some relief by the end of the week. I'd walked past Sister Margarita in single file twice without her noticing me. Being the head nun, she had many more important matters to attend to than my conversion to a holy life. I was convinced that the whole matter had been forgotten and by Friday my appetite returned.

"It certainly looks like you're feeling better," Beba said as she served me an extra piece of guava paste and cream cheese. How could I not? I had my life back. Alicia and I could dream once again about being nightclub performers with feathers in our hair and long tail capes. Anything was possible.

# 3

AFTER CHURCH ON SUNDAY WE ALWAYS WENT TO MY GREAT aunt, Tía María's house for lunch. I always looked forward to this, but never more than on this Sunday when I was still rejoicing in the glory of my escape from nunhood. All the family would be there, cousins, aunts, and uncles who gathered for the weekly feast of *arroz con pollo* and *brazo gitano* made by Tía María. More than anything, I looked forward to seeing Alicia and telling her about my near miss with a fate worse than death.

As the adults sat outside on the porch playing dominoes, talking over each other, laughing, and occasionally raising their voices about the "plundering Batista supporters" and the need for "democratic elections," we'd sneak off and wander about the big house, hiding in wardrobes filled with old clothes and pretending we were eluding an evil man who was trying to kidnap us. Marta followed us around with no idea that we'd cast her in the role of the evil bad man or witch. When she finally figured it out she'd start bawling at the top of her lungs and several adults would come to her rescue, with Mami leading the pack. If Juan, our oldest cousin was around, we'd allow him to lead us in a rousing, yet confusing game of baseball that he was happy to play with his girl cousins because he always won.

Alicia and I were hiding from Marta under the porch when we overheard Mami. "José, do you remember Sister Margarita?"

"I believe I do," my father replied. "She's the sister with the mustache."

"Seriously now, she called me yesterday and said she wanted to talk to us about Nora."

"Is there a problem?"

I clamped my hand tight over Alicia's mouth. "Did you hear that?" I asked her.

She nodded and I removed my hand. "Are you getting in trouble?" she whispered.

"Worse than that. They want to make me a nun!"

Horror registered on her face. "Why?"

"I don't know. But Sister Margarita thinks I should be a nun, and she's going to tell Mami and Papi."

"How do you become a nun?"

"They send you to a special nun school where they cut off all your hair and fingernails and eyelashes. All you do is pray and light candles and dust the statues of the saints."

We crept out to the far end of Tía María's backyard and crouched behind her biggest rose bush to think about what we were going to do. This was a real problem that required a real solution, and the adult nature of our discussion quickened my pulse. We almost sounded like our parents on the porch when they talked about the government problems in tones that alternated from exuberant to resigned.

"There's only one thing to do," Alicia said, as she tossed a stone from one hand to the other. "You have to run away. And it has to be today . . . before you go home."

Alicia and I had fantasized about running away for years. We'd join the circus and learn how to balance on the high wire and ride elephants like they were ordinary horses. We'd walk along the railroad tracks and live off of figs and bananas, our favorite food. We'd build a raft and go anywhere in the world we wanted, starting with New York, where we heard everything was bigger and brighter and better.

"Don't worry," Alicia said, sensing my fear. "I'll go with you."

"You will?"

"Sure I will. You need company."

Marta eventually found us crouching behind the rose bush. She sensed there was something different about our play and began to whine and beg to be let in on our secret, even after we'd banished her and threatened to feed her to the sharks next time we went walking on the *malecón*. She crept up one last time with an offering in hand: cookies hastily wrapped in a paper napkin. Suddenly, and quite unexpectedly, I felt sorry for her and noticed her large brown eyes were swimming in tears.

"Our parents will be worried when they can't find us," I appealed to Alicia. "After a week, Marta can tell them why we left."

"Can Marta keep a secret for a week?" Alicia asked, with hands on hips and doubt lurking in her golden eyes.

Marta jumped with every word. "I can, I can keep a secret for a week! For a whole week!"

We made space for her behind the rose bush and settled ourselves down in the stillness of the late afternoon as we whispered our plans into her ear. She didn't understand at first and giggled as we tried to whisper more loudly. Finally, after three more attempts, there was no doubt she understood because she started bawling again. "I don't want you to go away, Nora. I want you to stay with me and Mami and Papi forever." She threw her arms around me in a desperate display of affection.

I peeked around the rose bush expecting to see Mami's high heels marching toward us, but all was clear. Alicia rolled her eyes. "I knew we shouldn't have told her anything."

I patted Marta's back. "Marta, listen. You know all those times we fight because you want to play with my stuff? Now you can play with anything you want, and you'll have Beba all to yourself too."

This possibility seemed to calm her a little. "I still don't want you to go," she said more quietly.

"We have to," Alicia replied for me. "It's Nora's life if we don't. You don't want her to become a nun, do you?"

Marta shook her head and clasped my hand possessively. Normally I would've wriggled away, but it was very comforting to feel her warm hand neatly tucked into my own.

The three of us walked back toward the house ready to begin the first phase of our plan, and Marta pulled on my arm to indicate that she needed to whisper something meant for me alone.

Again, indulging her far beyond than what I was accustomed, I bent down and offered my ear.

She cupped her hands. "How long is a week?"

In the pantry we found an empty burlap sack that was normally used for raw sugar. We used it to pack the provisions for our escape. The happy sounds of conversation and laughter drifted in from the porch, along with the toasty sweet fragrance of cigars and strong Cuban coffee. Whatever hesitation I felt about our plan had quickly escalated into a quivering sensation, in the pit of my stomach, rolling like the sea before a hurricane hit. I stood paralyzed in the middle of the kitchen that still smelled of Tía María's *arroz con pollo* with Marta clutching at my hand, taking full advantage of my unusual kindness toward her.

Alicia hummed to herself as she tossed cheese, bread, and bananas into the open sack. "This should do it," she said brightly, wiping her hands on her skirt. "We can't make it too heavy, or we won't get far."

I helped her move the sack from the chair onto the floor. "Do you really think you should go? I mean, you're not the one they're trying to make into a nun."

Alicia grabbed my shoulder and shook me a little. "I won't let you go alone." Her cheeks were flushed and her mouth twitched as she tried not to smile for she knew it would not be seemly at such a serious moment. Then she turned to Marta who watched us with a glum expression, almost on the verge of tears again. "Now, Marta, when they start looking for us you have to tell them we're playing a hiding game. This will keep them from really looking for a while. You have to be strong, OK?"

Marta nodded and tightened her grip on my hand.

I squeezed my legs together for fear of urinating right there on the floor, wrenched my hand free from Marta, and ran to the nearest bathroom. Perhaps if I took long enough Mami would come looking for us before we had a chance to run away. But as I listened through the open window, I realized they weren't going anywhere soon. They were in the midst of one of those conversations that had grown more animated as the cigars were lit and little cups of cognac passed around. I hoped Papi and Alicia's father, my uncle Carlos, wouldn't start arguing again. Last time they did Papi fumed all the way home. He kept talking about "revolutions" and "free elections" and that "bastard Batista" as Mami shushed him to be quiet. I asked him what a revolution was, but he refused to explain and only became more irritated that I'd been listening as Mami shot him a knowing glance.

"This isn't anything you girls need to worry about," Mami had said in her overly soothing way that really meant I'd stumbled onto something only meant for grown-ups. "All you need to worry about is doing your schoolwork and being well behaved."

That was simple enough and sitting there with my cotton underwear around my ankles, I felt anything but curious. The next morning, as my fifth grade class was filing into the chapel there'd be a space between María Luisa and Carmen where I should be. Sister Roberta would wonder if I was sick, and she'd probably say a special prayer for me to Our Lady of Fatima. And instead of doing my arithmetic problems after lunch, I'd be sitting on the side of a dusty road in bare feet eating a banana or a few figs. Then I'd have to look for a place to sleep where the mosquitoes or the hairy spiders of the jungle wouldn't get me.

As I headed back to the kitchen, I ran into Mami. I'd never been so happy to see her in all my life, but when I glanced at Alicia, she was scowling with disappointment. "Get your sister. We're going home," Mami said.

"Why?" I asked, merely out of habit because I wasn't about to argue.

"Tomorrow's a school day," she said, but I knew she wanted to leave quickly before Papi and Uncle Carlos started to argue.

We drove back in silence, and Marta fell asleep with her head on my lap. I let my own head fall back on the seat, while I stared out at the darkness through the windshield. The lights bordering the *malecón* whizzed past like angry comets rising up from the sea as the motor's drone lulled me into a semi sleep. I heard the rush of the waves and distant voices calling me from the deep.

My parents spoke in hushed tones to one another. "Carlos doesn't know what he's talking about," my father said. "People wouldn't support a revolution right now. The economy is too strong, too many people are making money like they never have before."

"People like us are making money . . . but, Carlos wasn't talking about people like us. . . ."

"I'm not saying it's all perfect."

"Then what are you saying, José?"

"It's not enough . . . a few rebels in the hills making trouble. I want Batista out as much as anybody, but it won't happen like that. I just hope that crazy brother of mine doesn't do anything foolish."

"I hope not," Mami said.

A few more minutes of silence captured in the drone of the motor. Papi spoke again. "I think Nora spends too much time with Alicia."

"Oh, I don't know. Alicia's a good girl. She's very clever and pretty."

"Too clever and too pretty I'd say. I don't like the way Carlos and Nina are raising her, spoiling her the way they do. She's too free spirited for her own good, and I don't want her to influence Nora. Maybe that's what this meeting at the school is all about."

"Sister Margarita assured me Nora wasn't in trouble."

It was my father's turn to say, "I hope not."

Free spirited—what wonderful words. I closed my eyes and the lights of the *malecón* glowed against my inner eyelids, pink and purple and green bouncing balls, bouncing toward long sunny days at the beach with nothing to do, but swim, roll in the sand, and drink ice-cold Cokes. And there was the corner ice-cream stand, El Tropicream, crowded with laughing children who had ice cream painted all over their happy faces like clowns at the circus.

I was there too, hanging in a bird cage from the highest palm, somewhere between heaven and earth, wearing a black dress all the way down to my ankles, and praying that a swift wind would come and knock me back down to the sand where I belonged.

We passed under the gentle gaze of the Virgin. Her statue, holding rosary beads that light up at night, was perched on top of the main gate of El Ángel de la Guarda School and welcomed all who entered. After years of passing under her, this was the first time I prayed for her intercession. "Please, dear Virgin, let Sister Margarita be sick today. It doesn't have to be a serious illness, just something small that can only be treated in New York or Chicago, or some place really far away."

Marta kissed Mami and Papi good-bye, then ran off to her classroom, the red ribbon in her hair streaming behind her like a kite tail. "Remember to walk," a normally silent sister said when Marta whizzed by her. Marta slowed down to a brisk walk until she was inside, after which she raced to her classroom faster than before. The three of us were escorted past the formal salons where the piano recitals and graduation luncheons were held down a dark wood paneled hall. At the very end was Sister Margarita's office, the only office in the school with double doors. I imagined it to be full of wondrous and exotic things. Instead I was surprised to find a simple, yet spacious room filled with hundreds of leather bound books on shelves reaching from floor to ceiling. The only thing approaching magnificent was the enormous arched window behind a large desk strewn with stacks of papers and the occasional candy wrapper.

Through the beveled glass, students could be seen filing to class and for the first time I longed to be with them instead of sitting there on a straight wooden chair where my feet didn't quite touch the floor.

Mami and Papi watched me curiously as they pretended to carry on a conversation about our new neighbors that had moved in three floors down. They'd asked me several times what the meeting was about, but I didn't have the nerve to tell them. I wanted to stall my fate as long as possible. I'd lost the battle of the piano lessons and the math tutor, but I wasn't about to lose this one, and I needed more time to figure out my strategy.

Sister Margarita entered the office through a small door between the bookshelves and floated silently across the floor. She sat at her desk and folded her hands in a smooth and commanding gesture of sacred authority. With sunlight streaming in through the window behind her, she looked like an archangel guarding the entrance to heaven.

"Has Nora told you why I asked you to come in today?" she asked.

"No, she hasn't," my mother replied.

Sister Margarita turned to me. "Would you like to tell them now, child?"

My throat was tight and dry. I gripped the seat of my chair. I couldn't speak and could only shake my head and swing my legs back and forth.

"Would you like me to tell them?" Sister Margarita smiled down on me and I was momentarily awestruck. A smile from Sister Margarita was a gift bestowed on precious few and for a split second I thought I should just go ahead and become a nun so as not to disappoint her. I nodded that she could speak for me and felt an intense heat rising up from the furnace in my stomach.

She looked at my parents, glowing with pride. "It seems that little Nora has been called."

"Called?" Papi asked with a half smile.

Mami leaned forward in her chair and touched my knee lightly to stop me from swinging my legs. "We don't understand, Sister."

"I've been watching Nora for many months now, and I believe

she's been called to follow Christ in a holy life." Sister Margarita's words rang clearly like a bell striking the hour, and her eyes lifted toward the ceiling as if she were in ecstasy.

I dared not follow her gaze lest I see the face of God himself confirming my appointment. I felt dizzy and gripped the chair tighter and looked straight ahead, past Sister Margarita's smiling face and out the window toward the girls laughing in the sun. A bright beam of light hit my eyes directly, but I couldn't even blink as tears began to well in them.

All three were watching me. My parents appeared startled, as if they'd never seen me before. Sister Margarita looked as if she expected me to sprout wings and a halo.

Papi broke the silence. "Is this true, Nora? Do you want to be a nun?"

I blinked once and looked at him, then over at Sister Margarita whose smile had only intensified in sweetness. How could I disappoint her? She seemed so sure I wanted to be like her and not a chorus girl with bright pink feathers sticking out of my head or a wife and mother who dressed her babies in soft embroidered clothes.

Mami's neatly painted brows lifted in a curious arch, and she placed her hand on Papi's arm when he was about to speak again.

My bottom lip began to quiver. I tried to make it stop, but the more I tried the worse it became. No longer able to tolerate their probing gazes, I dropped my head and saw Mami's high heeled shoes press down on the floor as she moved to stand, but I jumped down from my chair and ran across the room before she could reach me. Flinging open the office door, I raced down the main hall (which was forbidden) and burst out the main doors, nearly knocking over Sister Roberta in the process.

"Nora, what's the matter?" I heard her call after me as I jumped down the stairs two at a time, not stopping until I reached the grassy lawn below. I stood with my back to the school, panting and staring at the slim sliver of ocean that peeked through the pastel collage of buildings before me. I could keep running past the gates and under the Virgin and never again return. I could find my way to Alicia's school and convince her to leave with me. The train tracks didn't seem so bad after all. A few nights in the jungle wouldn't kill me.

I heard spongy footsteps on the grass behind me. With his long legs, Papi could walk almost as fast as I could run. He turned me around by my shoulders and crouched down so we were at eye level. "No one's going to force you to do something you're not happy with."

I looked into Papi's dark eyes and breathed in the reassuring scent of his after-shave.

"Do you really want to be a nun like Sister Margarita?" he asked with a slight shake to my shoulders.

My answer came out with such force, that I almost knocked him over onto the grass. "No, Papi. I don't want to be a nun ever! I think Sister Margarita wants to steal me away to a secret nun school."

"Don't be silly. Even if you wanted to be a nun, you couldn't really begin to study seriously until you were much older."

By now Mami had begun her tiptoeing journey across the lawn, careful not to spike her heels in. Sister Margarita stood by in the doorway of the main entrance, but she didn't come down the stairs to join us, and although she was too far away for me to read her expression I knew she was no longer smiling.

Mami looked down on us, squinting in the morning sun and searching for her sunglasses in her purse. "Nora, running away like that was extremely rude. I want you to go apologize to Sister Margarita immediately."

A huge weight began to lift off my shoulders as we made our way back across the lawn.

"She doesn't want to be a nun, Regina," my father said.

"Of course she doesn't," Mami snapped. "Who ever heard of a nine-year-old nun?"

# 4

TÍA PANCHITA, MY GREAT-AUNT ON MY FATHER'S SIDE, HAD BEEN a widow for many years, and never had children of her own. She had a great head of silvery hair she pulled tight into a bun at the nape of her neck and she wore thick cat eye glasses that made her eyes appear so huge it was possible to count the flecks of green in the brown, like leaves floating on a murky river. She lived alone in a sprawling house on a sugar cane plantation in the heart of the island near a little town called Güines. I always knew we were getting close when the car rattled over roads that were either unpaved or rarely repaired. Marta and I sang and laughed as our voices bumped along making us sound like tipsy opera singers while Papi cursed and predicted the need for new shock-absorbers when we returned to Havana. Trees hung dreamily overhead, occasionally stretching out their limbs to brush the ceiling of the car in greeting.

In Güines everybody knew everybody and they liked nothing better than to lounge on wide porches for most of the warm days waving to friends and conversing with who ever decided to stop by for a cup of Cuban coffee or a cold glass of *guarapo*. The only problem with this was that Tía always insisted we look like we were going out for a party even if we were just relaxing and going no where at all. This way, she said, she could impress whatever visitors she had with her beautiful *sobrinitas*. Although we'd been visiting Tía Panchita since we could remember, it was only when I was twelve and Marta ten that we were allowed to spend the night without our parents.

Like everybody else, Tía Panchita had a black maid, but unlike anyone else, it was hard to know who was the maid and who was the *patrona*. Lola, a slight woman about Tía's age with wiry salt and pepper hair, came every morning before anyone was up and started the coffee. Sometimes she made bread, and sometimes she brought it already made from the bakery. Either way it smelled delicious, and Marta and I loved to sit in the kitchen with Lola and watch her make butter. First she skimmed the cream off the top of the milk, and then she'd add salt and stir it for hours.

Lola wasn't a talker like Beba. Mostly she liked to listen, which was great for Marta who'd chatter her ear off about silly things. But Lola always appeared to be interested, nodding her head and widening her eyes when Marta asked her, "And then guess what happened?" I'd lost interest long ago and figured Lola had too, but she really was listening because most of the time she guessed right.

Often Tía burst into the kitchen and snatched the spoon from Lola, and Lola would snicker and shake her salt and pepper head.

"Lola, I've told you before there's no need to make butter from scratch. I buy it already made, and you're too old to be working so hard." Lola would keep shaking her head and chuckling, complaining that store-bought butter wasn't the same. I agreed.

Both women would sit out on the porch together for hours, each in her own wicker rocker, talking and laughing and greeting visitors like a pair of old hens. They'd take turns preparing refreshments, and if they were too tired, they'd enlist our help and direct us through the open window leading to the kitchen. We'd emerge from the house, feeling quite accomplished, as we balanced trays of coffee cups, spoons, sugar, cookies, and guava paste. When night fell and most of the visiting was over, Tía Panchita and Lola always ended the day in the same way. Tía went inside and took the wooden cigar box off the shelf in the dinning room and placed it on the little table between their rocking chairs. She insisted that Lola select first. They'd roll the cigars between their fingers and tap it next to their ears. Then they'd light each other's cigars and puff and rock for at least another hour until the stars made their appearance in the blue black sky above.

On one of our visits, just as the cigar ritual was about to begin, Alicia's parents dropped her off to spend the rest of the week with us. Tía was delighted and together she and Lola moved the roll-away bed, *pin pan pun*, into the large bedroom that Marta and I shared. With her bed right next to mine, the mosquito netting could easily cover us both.

When it was time for bed and Lola had gone, Tía tucked us in, but before she arranged and inspected the mosquito netting for holes, she locked the doors leading outside. It took quite some time because every room in the house had an identical door that required bolting with a heavy wooden plank. Echoes sounded throughout the house every time she dropped a wooden plank into place. She secured the windows in similar fashion except for those that were locked with a metal latch that was easy to close. Once she was finished, she checked every door and window again to make sure she hadn't forgotten one. The entire process took almost half an hour.

"It looks like you're getting ready for a hurricane," I said.

Tía sat down on my bed and looked at the three of us with her magnified eyes. "It's worse than that. Listen."

At first I heard nothing but the chirping of crickets that always comes up as the sun goes down. Then I heard it—a quiet rhythmic thunder that seemed to emanate from the ground, all around us, everywhere and nowhere at once. My heart beat a little faster to the quickening sounds of what I knew to be the African drums, as they grew louder and faster.

Alicia jumped from her bed onto mine and scrambled underneath my covers. "Tell us about the drums, Tía," she begged, even though she, as I, had heard talk of these before. We knew the stories of people falling to the ground overcome by evil spirits and writhing like snakes. Those were the lucky ones. The less fortunate were turned into goats or even into rocks and trees. The most frightening stories were of the bloody sacrifices. They'd kill chickens and pigs and . . . and white children who'd misbehaved so badly that their parents didn't want them anymore.

Marta threw her covers off and ran over to sit on Tía Panchita's frail lap. She clung to her like a baby, and I rolled my eyes, although a chill had crept up the back of my neck as well.

Tía stroked Marta's hair. "Don't be afraid, little one. I was teasing you. Those are just the drums of the *Santeros*. They're playing loudly tonight. It's the music of Africa from long ago, and the black people believe it has special powers."

"What kind of powers?" Alicia asked.

Tía thought carefully. "They're powers I don't completely understand. But if you're afraid when you hear the drums you must say the Our Father and Hail Mary and pray for *Papá Dios* to keep you safe. You have to say it over and over again until you fall asleep. Come now, get into bed and we'll say it together."

Marta scrambled back into her own bed, and we pulled our linen sheets up under our chins and put our hands together. We prayed softly over the drums that sounded deep and full like one would expect the heart of the jungle to sound in far off Africa. We tried to ignore the intoxicating rhythm of the pounding that forced us to pray to its exotic cadence.

"Our Father," (boom) "Hallowed be," (boom) "Thy name," (boom boom) . . .

Our prayers had never sounded so beautiful before. I wanted to say them again and sing in a loud voice. For the first time, I wanted to dance to the Hail Mary and sing my Amens in keeping with the joyful and mystic glory of the drums. All at once, I was rushing through the green canopy of the countryside in bare feet, hungry for the wild spirit to take me and teach me the ways of the underworld. The place Beba had told me about had to be beautiful, and sleep must come easily in a place where dreams followed the rhythms of the night.

"Good night, my dear *sobrinitas*," I heard Tía Panchita say as she closed the mosquito netting and turned out the light.

Since I was a little girl I wondered what it would be like to become a woman. I imagined the transformation would happen gradually, in the same way a rose bud opens its petals one by one, until the fullness of its splendor is revealed. And when I asked Mami and Beba if this was so, they confirmed that it was, then quickly changed the subject. But that's not how it happened for Alicia. Alicia became a woman all at once before my eyes, and after that day she was never quite the same.

It was the next morning, and we sat along Tía Panchita's sun flooded porch, dosing and chatting in the warmth, watching the bees hover about the empty *guarapo* glasses that were still on the steps. Tía and Lola rocked in their chairs, drinking coffee and commenting on the unusual heat of the day.

"We won't get many visitors today," said Tía, squinting out at the road through foggy glasses.

"Anyone who has any sense will stay indoors," Lola agreed.

It was then that we saw the outline of a young man on horseback take shape beyond the heat of the dusty road. He looked like a wavering ghost, floating in a brown haze. At first we couldn't be sure he was riding toward us, but with a flick of his wrist he deftly maneuvered his auburn horse onto the narrow path that lead up to the house. As ignorant as we were about horses and as far away as we were from this particular specimen, we could tell that it was not like the other horses we'd seen. It was young and full of fire, the kind of horse only an expert should ride.

"Tony, hola, Tony!" Lola stood up from her rocker and waved both hands at him.

"It's nice he's come. It's been a while," Tía Panchita said, gathering the empty glasses together and tidying up a little for this new visitor, new to us at least.

The young man rode his horse up to the fence and in one

smooth motion, swung his leg over and dropped to the ground. The auburn horse raised his great head in protest at being tied up to the fence and not allowed to munch on the grass beneath his hooves. I was fascinated by the clean perfection of his muzzle and spirited precision of his every move, so fascinated that at first I didn't notice the amazing young man who'd been riding him.

But when I did, I no longer paid any attention to the horse. Tony was beyond beautiful. His skin was the color of burnished gold, and I imagined that if I touched the tip of my tongue to his cheek it would taste of honey. His light eyes were the color of the shallow sea close to shore where the water turns blue to turquoise to blue again, and they held a dreamy sort of gaze as though he were always contemplating pleasant thoughts.

He bounded up the steps of the porch two at a time, clearly comfortable with his body and unaware that his every move possessed a grace and strength beyond that of ordinary people, and kissed Lola and Tía Panchita warmly on the cheek. I don't remember what he said only that his voice was deep, but not deep like Papi's, for there was still a sweetness suggesting that boyhood hadn't completely left him. Yet the width of his shoulders, and the hint of the well-muscled body underneath his clothes left no doubt that he was not like our same-age boy cousins, who we could still push around with encouraging success.

He hadn't noticed us staring at him, and I preferred to watch from a safe distance, fearful that the strange sensations coursing through my body should become noticeable. An unusual warmth had collected in the very deepest part of my belly and floated down to create a tingling between my legs I'd never felt before. It was like the heat of being discovered in a fib but strangely pleasant and reminiscent of the intoxicating rhythm of the drums.

Alicia straightened her skirt, smoothed her long uncombed hair back with one hand, and walked straight up to the three without a word to Marta and me. Tony's back was turned to us when Alicia introduced herself, and we could see her above the broad curve of his shoulder.

Her face glowed and her lips were shining and red, as if she'd just eaten fresh strawberries and didn't bother to wipe her mouth. Several strands of hair had escaped her ponytail and framed her face like corkscrewed ribbons of gold. Her golden green eyes were swimming with allure and confidence as she rested one hand on her hip and played with a strand of hair that had fallen over her shoulder with the other. Never before had I noticed the swelling beneath her blouse or the way her hips flared when she put more weight on one leg like she was doing. Alicia had walked to the other side of the porch and become a woman.

"Come over and meet Lola's nephew," Tía Panchita called over to Marta and me.

Marta and I dragged ourselves over to the other side of the porch, but there was no similar transformation in store for me. I felt fantastically awkward when Tony stood and offered me his hand. It was firm and slightly callused and his touch and gaze rendered me speechless. Marta giggled and asked questions about his horse, while I attempted to strike the same sort of womanly pose as Alicia had, but my socks had fallen down to my ankles and my blouse, that Tía had reminded me to tuck into my skirt, billowed about, effectively hiding any semblance of a waist. And when Tony smiled at me and winked one of those incredible eyes in my direction, I felt my knees turn to jelly and my tongue to stone.

"Tony, why were the drums so loud last night?" Panchita asked.

Tony's eyes twinkled with amusement. "Were you scared, Doña Panchita?"

"I certainly was. I thought Satan himself was dancing on my bed. I could hardly sleep!"

Lola and Tony laughed and I noticed that Tony's teeth were perfectly straight and white. Mami always said that black people had the best quality teeth of any race. I guess she was right, although I knew that Tony was mulatto and not black. Mami also said that mulatto people are sometimes the most beautiful because they have the best features from both, black and white.

"Don't be scared. Satan was far away last night. They were preparing for the initiation ceremony tonight." Tony was still laughing as he said this and even though he was talking with Tía, he was turned toward Alicia.

"Oh dear Lord, that means there will be more drums tonight! I need some more coffee, good and strong this time." Tía left to prepare the coffee, and Alicia swiftly sat in her rocking chair.

She crossed her legs and fingered the hem of her skirt. "Will you be there tonight?"

Tony's smile was soft, and his voice softer still. "I'll be there."

"And what will you do?"

"I'll dance with friends . . . have a good time."

"I bet you're a good dancer."

Tony's smile lit up again and for a moment he seemed to lose his composure as his gaze quickly swept across Alicia from head to toe, lingering on her bare knees that pointed straight at him, ever so slightly parted so that only the finest writing paper could pass between them, but parted nonetheless. It all happened so fast that in a blink I would've missed it. But I didn't miss it, nor the slight trembling of Alicia's hand when she swiped an errant strand of hair behind her ear.

I felt suddenly guilty and turned to join Marta, who was slowly inching her way toward Tony's horse, when Tía Panchita returned balancing a tray loaded with cookies and three cups of coffee. Tony stood up and helped her with the tray, but then expressed his apologies, saying he had business to take care of in town. I was glad to hear it.

With hasty good-byes to all and a lingering smile for Alicia, he sprung back on his horse and headed down the path. He was almost at the road when Alicia snatched a handful of cookies and wrapped them in a napkin. She jumped down the stairs and ran after him, and even though his horse shied a little, she didn't hesitate as she reached up to offer him the cookies. When he took them from her she didn't release them right away, and their hands touched. I saw this too even though I pretended to be amazed and distracted by the horse dropping that Marta was pointing out to me and listening to her chatter about the hay sticking out of it.

I was glad to see the bronze shiny rear of the horse, its tail swishing like a broom as they headed out, and I was relieved when the strange sensations I'd felt since Tony's arrival began to fade. I was myself again. Alicia, however, seemed possessed, and alternated between melancholy and jubilation for the rest of the day. She ignored Marta and me, preferring to sit with Tía Panchita and Lola on the porch all afternoon, asking them endless questions about Tony. How old he was, where he learned how to ride horses so well, what kind of business he had in the city, what word would best describe the color of his eyes. She must've spent an entire hour pondering this one, finally concluding that his eyes were the color of the sky at twilight, just before the stars appeared.

Marta and I attempted to entice her with a walk through the sugar cane fields or a game of dominoes, but she turned us down, gazing out toward the road Tony had taken into town.

Eventually, when Alicia was convinced that she'd learned everything she could from Lola and Tía Panchita, she stood up from her chair, sighed loudly and wandered back into the house, smiling to herself and humming along to music only she could hear.

"I believe your niece is in love," Lola said as she helped herself to the last of the cookies on the tray.

Tía Panchita nodded and chewed her own cookie pensively. "No doubt about it."

That night we said our prayers over the drums again. They were louder this time and faster too. It was easy to imagine the dancers swirling around a huge bonfire, their giant shadows playing against the trees, the beads around their necks swinging and catching the light like miniature planets on a frenetic orbit. I imagined their heads wrapped in handkerchiefs, some all in white like Beba, dipping and swaying to the hypnotic rhythm. Even from such a distance, it was impossible to keep from moving my toes under the blanket to the delicious beat that pounded out its cry like a wounded heart, begging to be loved, trading life for the promise of seduction. Any price could be paid for a moment of bliss. That's what Beba said and even though I had little idea what she was talking about, I liked the sound of it better than anything else.

As soon as Tía turned out the lights, Marta's breathing grew heavy and regular, but I sensed that Alicia was still awake, waiting in the dark and holding her breath. I'd been angry with her ever since Tony left and refused to answer her when, posing in front of the mirror, she asked me which way I preferred her hair: up in a pony tail or loose around her shoulders.

I looked over toward her bed, but she was lying well below the only stream of moonlight that came through the window slats, and I couldn't see her.

I closed my eyes. The sound of the drums slipped into my dreams, and the anger began to melt away with the promise of a new day. Surely the next day things would be as they always were. After breakfast, we'd sit on the porch and invent a new game to play. Marta would follow us into the sugar cane fields, and Tía would warn us to not get dirty just in case visitors came by. A smile had already curled the corners of my lips when I heard Alicia speak to me. At first I thought I might be dreaming because her voice was so soft. But I heard it again, a desperate whisper, "Nora, I'm going there."

I opened my eyes, and she was sitting up in bed, her face glowing in a thin ray of moonlight, her eyes huge with excitement. She was wearing the white dress she normally wore to mass on Sundays.

"Why are you dressed like that?"

"I'm going to the drums. I'm going to see Tony."

I couldn't believe it. Going to the drums? Going to see Tony? The huge doors of Tía's house were locked and bolted, every one of them. And the drums . . . the drums were not for us.

I was about to protest when she placed her hand over my mouth, and I tasted the bitterness of Tía Panchita's expensive perfume on her fingers. "Be quiet and don't bother trying to talk me out of it. I have to see Tony. I know you don't understand."

She was right. I couldn't begin to understand what would possess her to go out into the night and risk her life to see this man, any man. She was still a child, a mere girl. Yet at that moment, wavering in the moonlight with her hair loose around her shoulders, she looked remarkably like a full-grown woman. It wasn't her face or the emerging maturity of her body, but the expression in her eyes: determined, self-assured, and glowing with a light from inside.

She removed her hand from my mouth. "You're going now? In the middle of the night?" I whispered.

"I know Tony will be there. You can come if you want."

I shook my head, horrified at the prospect of venturing out into the night. This was beyond the realm of forbidden, far worse than our plans to run away. It was lethal to the soul. "I . . . I can't go."

Alicia moved aside the covers, smoothing out her skirt and I noticed she was wearing shoes, but no bobby socks, her bare ankles reflecting in the moon light. Silently, she approached the door leading to the field. Placing her hands on the heavy wooden plank, she paused, lifted the plank, and leaned it against the wall without the slightest sound. Marta did not stir despite the creaking of the floorboards and the groaning of the door that Alicia slowly, almost imperceptibly, opened.

Sounds of the drums flooded our bedroom. Alicia stood breathless for an instant before stepping over the threshold and slipping out into the night.

Although it was warm and humid, I trembled beneath the covers for what seemed like hours. I stayed in bed, straining my eyes against the dark and praying as intently as any nun or priest could pray, abandoning the verses I'd memorized over the years and speaking to God with my own voice in a desperate plea for help. But mostly, I listened to the sounds drifting in through the slim sliver of night. Were those footsteps outside? Had Alicia come to her senses and returned, or were her captors searching out fresh victims?

I shut my eyes again. "Make this nightmare go away, Papá

Dios." I prayed fervently. "Please make it go away and let the sun come up over the ridge of the green mountains so we can have our *café con leche* like we always do and play dominoes on the porch."

But the drums grew louder to what I had no doubt was the rhythm of death. They'd captured Alicia and were preparing her for the sacrifice. Tony was smiling and his ghostly green eyes were gleaming at the sight of his perfect prey. How could I just lie there and allow this terrible thing to happen? I had to rescue Alicia. She would do as much for me. I knew she would.

I pushed back the covers and emerged from the mosquito netting, my knees quivering as I searched for my slippers under the bed. With excruciating caution, I walked to the door and stuck my nose out first. The air was cool and foreboding now that the wind had changed, and the sounds of the drums vibrated through the air, the trees, the ground, and every blade of grass.

Out onto the porch, I surveyed the shadows of the night. All was dark and misty green. Stars blanketed the tropical sky. I looked back into the room to make sure Marta hadn't stirred and proceeded to step slowly off the porch. I'd made it to the second step, knowing there were three more to go. And then what? The vast field lay ahead of me, then the grove of trees that were shadowed even in the daylight. Beyond these was San Nicolás, an all black village where Lola and Tony lived, no doubt. Alicia would have taken the dirt path through the woods, and if I wanted to find her I had to allow myself to be swallowed by the void of blackness before me.

Then I saw movement. Black upon black, moving and shifting. Was Alicia returning? My heart leapt with the possibility, and I almost called out. But what if it wasn't Alicia? What if it was one of the evil spirits of the night Beba told me about? Chopping onions and green peppers in the bright sunny kitchen I was never afraid, but here in the clutches of the night, while everyone slept, an evil spirit could easily devour me.

After several minutes of heart wrenching paralysis, I saw the movement in the blackness get closer, bobbing up and down in a familiar way that I would've found comforting if I weren't hysterical with fear. It was Alicia walking absent-mindedly, as if kicking shells on the beach. Her hair floated on the night air, catching the light of the stars. She didn't see me, and I would've yelled at her to hurry if I hadn't been frightened of waking Marta and Tía Panchita.

When Alicia finally did look up, she froze and gasped faintly until she realized it was me and then quickened her step. I looked behind her to see if anyone or anything was following her, but she was quite alone.

"What took you so long?" My fear had turned to anger.

She half smiled when she spoke. "I was with Tony. He kissed me."

Her lips were swollen, as if she'd eaten something that made her allergic.

"On the lips?" I asked incredulous. Only grown-ups kissed on the lips.

Alicia nodded and rubbed her eyes.

She walked past me and opened the door casually, as if she'd just returned from a long and relaxing day at the beach. She kicked off her shoes and pulled her dress up over her head, letting it drop to the floor in a heap. Then she fell into bed and was instantly asleep.

Taking care to re-bolt the door without making any noise, I hung Alicia's dress back in the wardrobe and tiptoed about the room arranging everything just as it had been when Tía turned out the lights a lifetime ago. She'd never know anything had happened. Alicia was back and everything would be all right.


When I awoke, I could tell by the way the sun shone full and bright on the wooden floor that it was almost half way up the sky. Marta and Alicia's beds were empty, and I heard the sounds of plates and spoons clinking over breakfast in the kitchen.

I kicked the mosquito netting open and ran out to the kitchen to find Tía and Lola fussing over the coffee and the bread and butter as usual. Marta had her elbows on the table and was munching happily on a steaming slice of bread dripping with butter.

"Where's Alicia?" I asked, noticing that a place hadn't been set for her.

Tía didn't look at me when she answered, and Lola simply pulled out my chair and started to butter a piece of bread.

"Your uncle Carlos came for her early this morning," Tía finally said.

I was shocked. "But she was supposed to stay for two more days. Why did she have to go so soon?" The possible answers to this question caused the hair on my neck to bristle, and I eagerly stuffed my mouth with bread and butter.

Tía Panchita stirred her coffee vigorously, then shoveled in three teaspoons of sugar when I knew she only took one. The clinking spoon silent, she studied me behind thick glasses, her huge eyes unblinking and calm. I knew there was no need to repeat my question, and I squirmed under her hot gaze.

She took a sip of coffee, then placed her cup down on the saucer with an audible clang. "It was time for Alicia to go home."

# 5

WEEKS WENT BY WITHOUT A WORD FROM ALICIA. EVERY TIME I asked Mami if I could call or go for a visit she turned away and mumbled something about Alicia being sick or the family being out of town, but nobody went out of town during the school year. I reminded her of this, and she looked at me like Tía Panchita did the morning Alicia left, as if she was able to determine my innocence or guilt by the way I held up to her stare. I passed these tests, but it was difficult, and I dared not attempt it often, so I silently worried about Alicia, and wondered when I'd see her again.

I felt more hopeful about our reunion when Christmas Eve arrived. On this day the entire family got together for a pig roast at Tía María's house in Havana. We roasted it in a big pit filled with hot coals and rocks. It was a full day of cooking that started first thing in the morning. The men stood around the pig in a circle out back, smoking cigars, laughing and talking about things not meant for women's ears. I wasn't a woman yet, but when I walked up to see how the pig looked all splayed out like a thick rug and to inhale the enticing aroma of pork fat sizzling on hot coals, they poked each other with their elbows and pretended they were coughing in the middle of their words. This served as some kind of code and prompted them to make polite comments about how tall I was getting and to tell Papi that he'd have trouble on his hands when I was older because I was so pretty that all the boys would come calling. I didn't listen much to them, I just inhaled deeply and asked if I could poke the pig with a stick like they did.

Alicia and her parents finally showed up well past noon, when the pork was already half cooked. I couldn't believe my eyes when I saw her because she looked as though she'd faded into an old black and white photograph, where the people just stare into the camera like they're already dead.

She wore a brown dress almost down to her ankles and her hair was drawn back in a stiff looking braid. Alicia hated brown. She liked pink and light blue and yellow. Perhaps Mami was right and Alicia had been sick. In fact, she still looked a little bit sick. We waved excitedly to her, and she barely lifted her hand in return.

When she approached the gathering on the porch, everyone crowded around her. I wasn't the only one who'd longed for her, and for a few minutes her old smile returned, and her eyes shone brilliantly, sometimes golden, sometimes green. She was just as beautiful as ever.

Once again I noticed her figure was more like a grown-up woman's with breasts that stretched the stiff fabric of her dress. And her fingers were long and graceful as she patted the heads of our younger cousins and accepted chicken croquettes from my mother, who planted a firm kiss on her pale cheek.

"We missed you," I heard my mother whisper.

After the meal Alicia and I found a moment to speak alone. We sat behind the rose bush, and reaching down into her sock, she produced a small white envelope. She was solemn as she held it out to me like a communion wafer. "If anyone sees what's inside this envelope . . . I'll be sent away forever. You have to promise complete secrecy."

"What is it?"

"Do you swear not to tell anyone?"

"Yes, I promise."

Alicia took hold of my hand and put the envelope in it. "This is for Tony," she said. "You have to give it to him next time you see him; next time you go to Tía Panchita's house."

"Why don't you give it to him yourself?"

"Because I can never go there again, or talk about what happened. That's part of my agreement."

"What agreement?"

"My agreement with God." Alicia's brows knitted together with such force that they produced a deep wrinkle in her forehead. I'd never seen a girl with lines like that on her face.

I folded the envelope twice and stuffed it in the pocket of my blouse, pressing it down hard on my chest so that it would show as little as possible. "Isn't giving this envelope to Tony against your agreement with God?"

Alicia wrung her hands and glanced nervously over the rose bush toward the house. "Yes," she whispered. "It is."

"Then tell me what happened."

She attempted to sit Indian-style but the narrowness of her long skirt prevented her, and she had to sit like a lady with her legs to the side. She folded her hands, looking more like a nun than ever. "Lola was there that night; the night I left to see Tony. She saw me, but I didn't see her."

"Lola . . . saw you with Tony?"

Alicia nodded. "The next day, very early, she called Tía Panchita and told her everything. It was probably still night because Tía called my parents, and they came right away to take me home, before anyone was awake. They had me checked by the doctor, this old man with bad breath and a red spotted nose. He made me lie on a table and open my legs wide so he could look inside me. After that, they sent me away to stay with a priest and some nuns. We prayed all the time and ate beans and rice with a little meat. We went to Church twice a day and they made me talk to the priest over and over again about what happened with Tony, but they didn't believe me when I told them he didn't do what everyone thought he did. He only kissed me on the mouth and told me that he loved me. He didn't violate me like they said."

"Violate you?"

"You know, like when a man and a woman make a baby. When they have sex."

I was stunned. How could Alicia be denying anything about sex, when I still wasn't exactly sure how the act was performed? Seeing my hesitation, Alicia sighed. "When they're alone in bed at night, and married, because they're supposed to be married, the man puts his *pito* inside the woman's hole down there. There's a hole down there where the blood comes out."

I knew about the blood from Mami. She'd blushed when I presented her with my blood spotted underwear one morning, convinced I was dying. But I was already well past thirteen, and there hadn't been any blood since that day even though I checked my underwear rigorously since she told me about it. I was glad it hadn't come again even though Mami told me it would, and that it meant I was officially a young lady.

"Did you get the period blood yet?" I asked, interrupting Alicia.

"Yes. How about you?"

I nodded, ashamed, but not sure why.

"They made me promise before God that I'd never talk to Tony again or be with any man, especially a black man." Alicia looked up, her eyes clouded with shame. "I can't really explain what I feel. It's a strange pain in my heart whenever I think of him or say his name. It makes me feel like I'm the luckiest person on earth just to have known him, and other times I feel like I want to die. I've prayed so hard for this feeling to go away so I can feel how I did before I knew him, but I can't stop thinking about him. That's why you have to give him the letter. Will you give it to him, Nora?"

"If they catch you again, then what?"

"I don't care." Alicia drew several quick circles in the dirt near her feet and smoothed her skirt leaving a light trail of dirt with her fingers. "If you don't give it to him, I'll have to run away and give it to him myself."

"No . . . I'll do it," I said quickly, helping Alicia to stand up in her narrow skirt.

As we walked back to the house, I asked, "Do you always have to wear those clothes?"

"I have to wear them for a year to make sure that God forgives me for my sins. I made a promise."

I shook my head in disbelief at the number of promises flittering about like fireflies glowing in the night and, like Alicia's vows, vanishing in the light of day.


It was several weeks before I managed to fulfill my promise to Alicia. I sat on Tía Panchita's porch like an anxious sentry waiting for Tony with the envelope, already crumpled and sweaty from weeks of continuous handling. This day alone, I'd moved it from my drawer to my pocket, from my pocket to my bag, and then back to the drawer again. I couldn't wait to get rid of it, and although I'd seen him ride by on his horse twice during our stay, Tía Panchita or Lola were always on the porch and would've seen me pass him the note. It was during his third pass that I had my chance. Both had gone inside to fix the afternoon meal, and I ran down the porch steps and down the path to the main road, pulled the letter from my shirt as I did so, waving it like a white flag.

Tony looked suspicious as he saw me running toward him. For a moment I thought he was going to urge his horse into a gallop, but he waited and looked down on me and my letter as if it were a gun instead of a simple white envelope.

"This is for you from Alicia," I said, panting and nervous.

Tony made no move to take it from me. A fine vein running down the smooth brown skin of his neck throbbed steadily, and his hands fumbled with the reins that rested on his thighs. He was without a doubt the most amazing boy I'd ever seen, and at that moment, I could easily imagine Alicia risking all to be with him.

Finally, he reached down and took the letter up to his lips and inhaled deeply. Then it slipped out of his fingers and fluttered down to the ground, settling on the dirt near his horse's hooves. "Tell your cousin not to write me any more letters, unless she'd like to see me hanged from the nearest tree," he said with sad resignation. He prodded his horse with his heels and started to ride off. "Anyway, I can't read," he added, turning back one last time.

I returned the dusty envelope to Alicia behind the rose bush at Tía María's the following Sunday. She implored me to recount every detail of my encounter, the exact words Tony spoke, the expression on his face, the clothes he wore, and then I had to repeat it all over again at least three or four times.

"Do you really think they'd hang him?" I asked.

The deep line in her forehead returned as she gazed at the rejected envelope. "Do you really think he can't read?"

# 6

I HEARD THE DRUMS IN MY SLEEP AGAIN. THE DREAD I'D FELT AT Tía Panchita's house settled on my heart with a heavy and star-tling thud. I was still waiting for Alicia to return from her en-counter in the forest with Tony. Time froze and I began to shiver as I struggled to breathe in the thin air around me. I'd lose her forever and have to explain through lying, rattling teeth what had happened. Worse than that, I'd have to live with the knowl-edge that I could've saved her.

But there was something different this time. The sound of the drums was deeper, and the enticing rhythm that made my toes twitch when I was afraid was replaced by a haphazard pounding that woke me with a start.

I was not at Tía Panchita's, but in my own room seven stories up in Havana. The drums were never heard in the city, only in the deep forests at the edge of small towns where the sugar cane grew thick. And the sound that made the windows tremble in their panes, they weren't like any drums I'd ever heard. Instead, a low blasting sound spread out across the silence of the city like electric rain. I bristled with fear and dared not get out of bed and peek through the window into the night.

The hall switch clicked on, and my room glowed by the faint light fanning under my door. Mami's slippers padded toward me.

She opened the door to Marta's room first and then closed it promptly. Marta could sleep through anything. We always joked that a hurricane could blow her windows open and swoop her out into the storm and she'd still sleep through it all, wondering what happened when she found herself lying amongst the trees in the street.

My door opened slowly. "Nora, are you awake?"

"What's that sound, Mami?"

"It's OK. It's far away."

"But what is it?"

Mami entered and sat on my bed. In the half-light the delicate crease between her eyebrows that appeared when she contemplated simple worries, like who to invite to her next dinner party or whether or not Marta and I should wear the same color dress for Easter, had grown into a cavern. She spoke with careful and measured words. "Somewhere in the city, angry people are setting off bombs."

"Why?"

"They want a different government."

I sat up in bed, feeling safer now that she was in my room. "Does it have to do with what Papi said yesterday about the people who were killed?"

"It might." The crease shifted and smoothed out slightly. "They were also against the government. You see, there are many who want Batista out. They want free elections."

I'd heard about this from fragments of conversation I'd collected throughout the years as adults argued on the porch, debated over coffee at the dinning room table, or when Mami and Papi were talking in the car. Everyone we knew was opposed to Batista and wanted a new and better government. There'd been talk about revolution and free elections as far back as I could remember, but nothing ever really happened. Now it seemed things were happening all at once, frightening things.

"Do you and Papi want Batista out too?"

"Not like this. Free elections like they have in the United States, that's what we want. Now go to sleep."

I could tell by the way she bit the inside of her cheek that she didn't want to talk about it anymore. "You have school tomorrow. You're safe here, and you'll be safe there too."

She kissed my forehead and closed the door behind her. I heard another distant boom, but it was no longer the sounds outside that kept me awake. It was the image of my mother's face, shifting and vague, a smile flickering on her lips as she tried to comfort me. She was pretending to be strong instead of just being strong like I knew she was, and this made me worry in a new way.

I closed my eyes and wondered if Alicia could hear the explosions from her house. Was she trembling in bed like me? No; she was probably hanging from her window, almost falling out on to the street below, as she strained to see what was going on. If Alicia were here she'd turn it into an adventure. We'd become underworld spies eager to save our country from Batista, beautiful heroines who snap our fingers and command the revolutionaries with our cunning and beauty. And after a night of death-defying adventure all would be still and calm in the morning. There would be *café con leche* waiting for us on the kitchen table and fresh bread and butter, and Beba would smile her expansive smile with teeth as white as sugar cubes, and tell us it was going to be another beautiful day.

Marta and I arrived home from school to find Alicia and her mother, Tía Nina, sitting on our living room couch. Never before had they visited on weekdays in the afternoon. Stranger still, Papi was home, and it was hours before he was due back from the office. And instead of her school uniform, Alicia wore a pair of white pedal pushers with her loafers and a yellow sweater, clearly weekend wear. Tía Nina looked ill. Her hair was in disarray and falling out of a hastily made bun. Her red-rimmed eyes darted about the room at nothing in particular as she puffed on an unlit cigarette. She fumbled with a lighter, then tossed it with the cigarette on the table and began to sob with her head in her hands.

Papi sat next to her on the couch, still and pensive. It was obvious he'd been watching her cry most of the day. Mami ran in from the kitchen when she heard Tía Nina's sobs. A cup of hot tea rattled in her hands, and she winced when it spilled a little over the sides and burned her fingers.

"This will help you calm down," she said, placing the cup in front of Tía Nina. Then she gave us her sit-down-and-don't-say-a-word look, and we dropped our books and sat right there on the floor. Marta and I became very obedient when we were scared.

Alicia's eyes were puffy from crying too, but she kept her hands neatly folded in her lap and smiled weakly when she saw us. She wanted to speak, but we both knew that we had to be quiet and still and simply listen, lest we be banished to our rooms. I was aware of Beba poking her head through the kitchen door while she prepared dinner, trying to hear what was going on. Her eyes were on fire, and she frequently shook her head in disgust and loudly grumbled her disapproval of the whole situation.

Tía Nina took a tremulous sip of tea. The cup and saucer rattled all the way up to her lips and back to the table. Then she told the story she'd been telling all day, but had to tell again and again as though she herself could hardly believe it. "The sun wasn't up when we heard them. I'm telling you, he barely had time to throw on his clothes." Aunt Nina glanced at Marta and me, and stopped talking as she noticed we were in the room, but then tore her eyes away, and continued. "The police came fifteen, maybe twenty minutes after that."

"What exactly did they say?" Papi asked, his face cold, his eyes dark with a fear I'd never seen before. Papi was never afraid; he was angry sometimes and impatient, but never afraid.

"They suspect he was involved in the bombing last night, but he was with me all night. He never left home. They wanted to know where he was, and I told them I didn't know . . . And I don't now, that's the truth."

Papi's trembling hands raked through his hair. "The less you know the better, Nina."

"My God, will they kill him if they find him?" Tía Nina threw herself on the couch almost landing on Papi in the process. He jumped and glared at Mami as if he expected her to do something.

Beba poked her head out of the kitchen door. "They're common criminals, and they should be shot," she shouted, before disappearing once again. I could hear her grumbling in the kitchen as she threw pots and pans around.

Mami kneeled next to Tía Nina and gently stroked her hair back into place. "Everything will be all right, Nina. We're all praying. Everything will be OK."

Alicia took hold of her mother's hand. "Papi knows how to take care of himself. Don't cry anymore."

"She's right, Nina. Carlos knows how to take care of himself, he always has," Papi said with a certainty that was reassuring. But I could see by the way his gaze turned inward and his jaw tightened that he was thinking about things he couldn't discuss here, things that would make Aunt Nina worry more.

We stayed in my bedroom for the rest of the day. It was a brilliant afternoon, the sky was as blue as ever, and we saw the ocean twinkling playfully as it always had. But an unusual stillness had settled on the street below. The constant drone of cars on the wide avenue had dwindled to an occasional whirl. Last night's bombing had kept many people home, and the merriment that was peculiar to Havana evenings was absent. It was so quiet that we heard the birds on the roofs and the occasional tinkle of someone selling *tamales* or sugar cane juice on the street. But even their cries were different. It was as if they weren't interested in making any sales, but in getting home to their families in case they were caught on the streets during the explosions.

"If Batista catches my father, he'll kill him," Alicia said matter-of-factly as she sat on my bed, her bare feet dangling. I detected the cracking patches of pink polish on her toe nails. When did she start painting her toe nails? It wasn't even close to a year since she'd made all those promises to God.

Marta gasped in horror as Alicia went on. "They'll kill him, just like they killed those other men. That's why he has to hide. Then when Batista's gone, he can come out again."

"Some people say he'll never leave," I said.

"Then I'll go and find Papi in the mountains and live with him there."

It was upsetting to think of Tío Carlos in such a predicament. I imagined him strumming his guitar and singing Cuban folk songs to his companions, telling jokes as everyone laughed and slapped him on the back and tucked cigars in his shirt pocket because he was so clever and fun to be around. It was hard to imagine him doing anything so serious that would cause him to hide from the police. Even when he was serious, which wasn't very often, his eyes smiled. He'd escape their capture, I was sure of it. He could slip through anything with his slick sense of humor that could charm a man out of his own shirt, not to mention a box of cigars. And Alicia knew this better than I did which is why she wasn't afraid.

But Tía Nina was not so confident. As the days went by without word, her desperation intensified and she lost so much weight that her nice dresses hung on her shoulders as though they were still on the hanger. She talked constantly in a shaky voice and smoked so much that the tips of her fingers started to turn a dark yellow. We'd sit at the table to eat the wonderful food Beba made, chicken and plantains, yucca with mojo, the best flan in all of Havana, and Tía Nina wouldn't eat a thing. Beba shook her head when Tía Nina passed on the meat and potato stew, her favorite, and muttered that she couldn't eat. Eventually it was decided that Tía Nina should go somewhere far from Havana so her nervous condition could heal, and Alicia would stay with us so she could continue to go to school.

We hadn't spent this much time together since we'd stayed at Tía Panchita's house. Now we'd gaze at ourselves in the mirror while listening to Elvis Presley records and pretend we were on our way to grand parties to meet the most wonderful boys who immediately fell in love with us because of our amazing beauty and dancing skills. Marta, who was still happy just to be included, often played the role of the matronly chaperone who'd accompany us on our dates and scold us when we allowed the young men to hold our hands or peck us on the cheek when she wasn't looking. Alicia and I took turns playing the young men's role, and I suspected that no matter how I played my part, she'd always cast me as Tony. It was always Tony who asked her to dance, and Tony who fought off the rivals when it was time to go home. Once when I pretended to have been thoroughly beaten by another boy and was lying flat on my back begging for mercy, Alicia corrected me. "Tony would never give up like that," she said. The game went on for hours and evolved into the most fascinating variations, the magic spell following us to the dinner table, out with Mami to run errands, even to school. I happily completed my lessons knowing that in the afternoon I'd be rewarded with the delight of Alicia's company.

Months passed and still Tío Carlos had not returned. We heard occasional explosions in the middle of the night and in the day, but by now we'd become accustomed to the booming. It didn't get in the way of our school, homework, dinner, and girl talk routine. Quite the contrary, it made us feel we were invincible. When we encountered the rubble produced by an explosion the previous night, we were intrigued not frightened, as if we were passing by the ruins of some ancient city and not the pharmacy we'd walked by for so many years. But Mami tensed up and began to walk very fast, so we could barely keep up with her, and behind her sunglasses, her eyes were moist with tears. I knew she didn't want Alicia to see her crying for fear that it would make her worry about Tío Carlos, so I didn't ask her what was wrong.

Alicia still talked to her mother on the phone every day, and one afternoon, almost four months after she'd moved in, she hung up looking rather somber. "Mami's coming back next week, and I'll be going home," she said.

I felt empty and lost to hear the news, as though a magnificent party were coming to an end.

Uncle Carlos reappeared a few weeks later, thin and easily startled, but in a very good mood nonetheless. Batista had left Cuba for good, driven out by a handsome man with a bushy black beard.

After that, Fidel Castro and the Revolution were the only thing anybody talked about. Of course, we'd all heard of him before. He'd been fighting in the mountains with a few rebel supporters for years, but nobody paid too much attention. Now whenever we turned on the TV, Fidel was there. If we changed the channel, Fidel was there. If we turned on the radio, Fidel was still there preaching about a new Cuba that would grow stronger and richer and take its rightful place in the Americas.

It all sounded very good and for the most part, the adults in my family liked what they heard, and Papi was so happy to have Tío Carlos back that I think it helped them finally agree on something. They stood around the TV during Fidel's speeches like soldiers standing at attention. Papi was particularly pleased about his promise to reinstate the process for free and democratic elections. Uncle Carlos was simply overjoyed that Batista was out, and that he'd had something to do with it, although he was very mysterious about just how much.

"Nothing could be worse than that bastard," he said over and over again, his eyes were smiling, and his shirt pocket was never without a cigar.

All the while Beba stood in the doorway of the kitchen surveying the scene with arms folded, shaking her white turbaned head in disapproval. "I've got a bad feeling about that man."

"About Castro? Why?" I asked.

She narrowed her eyes at me suspiciously like she did when she thought I sneaked a spoon full of freshly made flan she was saving for dessert. "Someone who can stand in one place and make speeches for that long—there's got to be something wrong with him."

All I knew was that the bombing had stopped and the only

thing to worry about was completing my homework, weekend plans, and whether or not Mami and Papi would allow me to shave my legs like the other girls.

"You're too young to shave your legs," Mami said.

"My legs are as hairy as Papi's, and all the other girls at school shave."

"OK, but only up to your knees, do you understand me? Only girls on the street shave their legs above their knees."

Here was yet another rule I couldn't understand. But I welcomed it along with Mami's usual attention to my grooming and manners. It seemed that things were finally returning to normal.

# 7

ALICIA AND I WERE TO ATTEND OUR FIRST FORMAL DANCE AT the Varadero Beach Club. Abuela selected our dresses and brought them home one afternoon as we sat with Abuelo drinking cokes frothing over with sweetened condensed milk. Marta scowled at the sight of the boxes; there'd be no dress for her as she was still too young to attend a dance.

"Don't be sad. We'll have fun together, Martica," my grandfather said, poking her in the arm. "While they're at that silly dance I'll take you out for a night swim. Have you ever swam in the ocean at night?"

Marta shook her head, intrigued, but still pouting.

"It's magical. The moon lights the water with a silvery glow and the. . . ."

"You're not going on any night swim with that child, Antonio," Abuela interrupted as she fumbled with boxes and shopping bags. "It's far too dangerous."

"I guess we'll have to settle for a walk and an ice cream then."

Marta gazed longingly at the boxes and tissue paper flying. Abuela produced a blue green dress, the color of the ocean at twilight and held it up against Alicia who batted her eyelashes playfully. Instantly, her eyes assumed the same misty color of the sea and her hair shone like the sun in golden waves across her shoulders. We stared at her silently, not gasping only because we were accustomed to her beauty that grew more alluring with each passing day. I had no doubt she'd be the most beautiful girl at the dance. She was always the most beautiful girl anywhere she went.

"I knew that color would be perfect for her," Abuela said, well pleased with her selection. "Now, let's see about Nora." She opened the second box that contained a delicate cream colored dress with an embroidered light blue sash. Next to Alicia's brilliant dress it looked horribly plain and child-like, more of a confirmation dress than a grown up dress for a dance. I wanted to cry at the sight of it, but I didn't want to hurt Abuela's feelings. I could see that she loved this dress as well.

I could already picture us walking into the Beach Club. We'd make our entry into the hall chaperoned by Abuela, and Alicia would be mobbed by every boy in the room. They'd step on my white patent leather shoes in a desperate attempt to get somewhere on her dance card, while Abuela pushed me forward, trying to entice the boys like a street vendor selling over ripe mangos.

"This light color will look beautiful on you," Abuela said, but there were no gazes for me as there had been for Alicia, no flash of time standing still for the appreciation of my beauty. Abuelo was already setting up the dominoes to play with Marta, and Alicia was busy examining the length of her dress. It hit right above her well-shaped calf.

"Try it on," Abuela said. "I wasn't as sure of your measurements as I was of Alicia's. There's still time to make adjustments if we need to."

"I'm sure it'll fit just fine." I dropped the dress back on to the tissue paper, eager to get it out of my sight. I needed to be out in the sun and the wind, away from this shameful stage where I always came up second. I didn't understand why all of a sudden these things mattered to me, but for the first time, I wanted to be beautiful and draw the admiring gaze of the boys and feel the powerful rush of my own femininity. I wanted to cross my legs and catch the world with the tilt of my ankle as I'd seen Alicia do while we waited for the bus downtown. I wanted to pretend not to notice how every man I passed held his breath in the hope of possessing me.

I mumbled a hasty excuse and left Abuela standing with my white dress in her arms. My feet dug deep as I marched across the beach toward the ocean. I kicked off my sandals and stepped into the warm water, wiggling my toes in the soft sand. I longed for a long cleansing swim, but that would involve going back to the house for my bathing suit and I didn't want to face anyone. The only thing more shameful than being second best was letting them see how much it bothered me.

Alicia's toes appeared next to mine, pink toes wiggling next to my brown ones.

"Why are you so mad, Nora?"

I continued to stare at my toes that were now covered under ten little mounds of fine white sand.

"It's because you don't like your dress, isn't it?"

Again, I remained silent.

"You can have my dress if you want. If you like it better, that is."

I stepped back and sat by the water's edge. "No. Your dress is beautiful on you. I just get tired of it sometimes . . . being the plain one."

Alicia sat next to me. "You're not plain, Nora. You're beautiful. You just don't know it yet."

I felt irritated by her lack of understanding. "But everyone always tells you how lovely you are with your green eyes and all. The only thing I'm told is to stay out of the sun, so I don't look like a *guajira*."

Alicia laughed. "Don't pay attention to Abuela. She doesn't know everything. Besides, some dresses look better when you wear them than they do on the hanger. I think yours is one of those."

"Maybe it is," I responded, feeling sleepy all of a sudden.

There's a spicy fragrance floating on the breeze today. Does it come from the vendors selling their garlic tamales or is the sea in a mischievous mood? My head falls back and the ends of my hair brush the sand. I let the full force of the sun hit me unconcerned that my tan should deepen, and that I will look like a shadow lurking about in a white dress. When I glance at Alicia, her face is also turned to the sun, like a sunflower smiling into her mother's face.

I don't need to go to the dance. I'm not a dance type of girl. I don't need to whirl about and be noticed and crooned over. I just need this moment on the sand. To know the ocean will always be blue or green or somewhere in between and that I can turn my face to the sky and find a moment's peace.

Alicia was right. My dress did look better on me than on the hanger. And Abuela was right too. The delicate cream color contrasted nicely against my dark hair and complexion.

Before we left for the dance, Abuelo stood before us and smiled proudly. "Two beautiful princesses," he said. "One as lovely and bright as the Cuban days, and the other as mysterious and alluring as the nights." Then he turned to Abuela. "And let's not forget the queen of them all, who graces us with her beauty, be it day or night, rain or shine."

Abuela laughed happily, and patted his cheek. She wore a navy blue polka-dot dress and her generous mane of gray wavy hair was molded artfully to her head. She smelled of soap and lavender and her black box purse hung neatly over her arm.

"How about me, Abuelo? You forgot me," Marta said, running in from the porch.

"You aren't merely a princess," Abuelo said, putting his arm around her chubby shoulder. "You're an angel from heaven, and your beauty is beyond description."

Marta smiled in spite of her bad mood.

We walked to the dance along the sidewalk that followed the water's edge. The sun hung low, wavering in the misty warmth of the tropics. The sea was a smooth silver tray that received its nightly offering of heavenly gold with unusual grace.

Tiny lights started to blink in mesmerizing patterns along the distant shore. They reminded me of the glamorous parties my parents attended, Mami in her swirling skirts and Papi in white linen, crisp and cool. They'd kiss us good night in a haze of perfume and tinkling bracelets and slip out into the night, gig-gling like children. They were going out into those beautiful lights, and even though it looked like a fantastic carnival, chil-dren weren't allowed in. But on this night we were entering that magical world for the first time.

I was surprised that so many boys had asked me to dance. I accepted, a little awkwardly, and allowed them to lead me to the dance floor with sweaty palms that trembled ever so slightly when we touched. Cologne and perfume were applied with such vigor that I felt I might be overcome in a forest of exotic flowers writhing erotically at times, hesitantly at others, to the mambo beat of the orchestra sway-ing on stage. The chaperones, mothers and grandmothers, chatted along the perimeter of the room, pointing to their daughters and granddaughters as they held their purses on their laps.

I hardly had a chance to talk with Alicia who was continually surrounded by a throng of young men who looked a bit older than the boys who asked me to dance, and Alicia wasn't awkward at all on the dance floor. She smiled and moved with the grace of a woman born to royalty, at ease with being the constant center of attention. She was the star of the ball, and she left a wake of turned heads behind her when she walked out onto the dance floor, her companion beaming as if he'd just been declared king of the world. Other girls shot envious glances and quickly turned to see if Alicia had caught the attention of their partners, which of course she had.

One of my dance partners, a tall pimply boy with sweaty hands, asked me if Alicia was my cousin, and his eyes turned glassy as though he was talking about Marilyn Monroe.

On the walk home, Alicia giggled about the boys who'd pro-fessed their love for her, how they'd gone on and on about the beauty of her hair and her skin and her eyes. I was able to share a couple stories of my own, but nothing like the volumes Alicia shared. At one point a boy even tried to kiss her cheek when she offered him her hand.

Abuela listened with a serious ear and slowed her footsteps considerably. Then she stopped in her tracks and turned to face Alicia, even though she was speaking to us both. "You're very beautiful, and boys and men are naturally drawn to beauty, but you mustn't be fooled by their flowery compliments."

"They're just trying to be nice," Alicia said, still smiling.

"Nice," Abuela barked as she pushed her glasses up her nose with a quick thrust of her finger. "A man would be nice to a mule if he were desperate enough. Never, never allow a boy who is not your father or grandfather to touch you or kiss you in any way. There are places men can go if that's what they need."

I knew Abuela was referring to the brothels in the Barrio de Colón where the prostitutes were said to saunter around the streets wearing next to nothing while smoking long cigarettes. It was well known that this is where young men went to learn about the arts of love and physical pleasures. It was also understood that young girls didn't require a similar education. They would learn from their husbands on their wedding nights. Chaperones were there to make sure that the education didn't begin before then.

We were almost home when I asked the question that upset my grandmother the most. "Abuela, who are those ladies, the prostitutes? Where do they come from?"

Abuela stopped dead in her tracks and stared at me with incredulous eyes. "How can you talk about such things? That is nothing that a young girl like you needs to worry about. You shouldn't talk about such things, do you understand me?" The color in her cheeks was clearly visible in the pale moonlight. "Those women have sold their souls to the devil. They're worse than dogs. That's all you need to know." She was walking ahead of us now, as if she'd suddenly become self-conscious about being out at night with such ignorant young ladies.

I dared not ask her about the men's souls, but I could well imagine her answer. The men checked their souls at the door along with their hats and claimed them unharmed at the end of the evening. Once a woman lost her soul it could never be regained.

# 8

THE EXPLOSIONS STARTED AGAIN. AND THIS TIME THERE WERE gunshots too. Sometimes it sounded like the shooting was right outside our window and not far away in some other part of the city. More than once the shots came in the middle of the day, and we dropped to the floor below the windows like soldiers in a war movie trembling and waiting for the silence to return. One afternoon Beba and I dropped to the floor in our kitchen, and on the way down, Beba knocked over the tomatoes and onions she was preparing for our meal, and we lay in them for several minutes. When it was over, we carefully collected every piece of onion and tomato that had fallen and washed it off. With the shortages getting worse every day, we couldn't afford to throw anything out.

We crowded around the television set at all hours of the day and night trying to learn some new bit of information that might offer hope or alleviate our growing despair. The prevailing mood was cold and suspicious as if we were at a funeral for somebody who'd been murdered and whose killer was still on the loose, maybe among us, maybe next door or down the street. It could be anyone in this shifting and unpredictable climate, but one thing was certain: Castro was no longer the redeemer; the man who could save Cuba and put her on a level playing field with the United States; the man who would clean up the corruption of

Batista and his superrich cronies, and paint the country new with a sparkling coat of democratic ideals. Suspicions and fear abounded that Castro's promises were false and that his sudden sweep to power was being supported by the least democratic people of all.

We knew that the explosions we heard in the day and night were caused by those against the Castro regime, and the discord between Papi and Tío Carlos began anew. Tío Carlos believed Castro's militant position was necessary during these uncertain times and that it would change once stability had been established. He believed there was still a possibility of a democratic solution. But Papi had lost all hope. He sat in his chair in his immaculate suits and polished shoes as he listened to the demolition on the streets and watched Castro gesticulating on the screen. His eyelids were heavy from lack of sleep. "It's only a matter of time," he said to Mami who had nothing to say herself, but who shared his vacant expression.

In spite of the sounds of war, and the intolerable tension that ensued during discussions of politics between the adults and the inevitable choices some were bound to confront, we tried to live our lives as before and, on most days, I managed to forget that there was any trouble at all.

Alicia and I returned to the beach as often as we could. And we talked about what would happen if we had to leave Cuba. We lay as we had as children on the white sands gazing up at the palms swaying in the wind. We swam to and from the platform like a couple of dolphins, and laughed as we shook the wet hair out of our eyes, always composing ourselves when good-looking young men came into view. As usual, most of the glances and comments were for Alicia, whose voluptuous figure was a beacon for any male nearby. I was happy with the occasional leftover remark or compliment when they noticed the dark girl alongside the beauty.

"I don't ever want to leave Cuba," Alicia said as we lay drying in the tropical sun.

"I don't, either."

"There could be no better place than this in the whole world. I could never be happy anywhere else."

If I hadn't been on the verge of falling asleep, I would've told her that "anywhere else" was an impossible thing to consider. We were Cuban and this was our country. Things would get better because they always did. If you couldn't count on the ground beneath your feet, then what did you have? But why say all this when the wind caressed our bodies with such perfect warmth? Why interrupt the chorus of the sea that said it all much better than I? We were home and this was where we'd always be.

Papi arrived home early from the office and didn't sit in his usual chair. Instead, he went straight to the bedroom without a word to anyone, not even a kiss hello for Mami who'd been anxiously waiting for him since early that afternoon. Mami followed him, and Marta and I went straight to Beba as we always did when we wanted to get the straight story about what was going on. Political issues weren't discussed at school, in fact they were avoided, and Mami and Papi still protected us from the truth whenever they could. But Beba had a special X-ray vision that could see beyond the complicated surface of things and understand the simple and bare bones truth without fancy explanations or excuses. She'd say, "Your mama doesn't want you to shave above the knees because no man should be looking any further than that. And if he doesn't like what he sees, he isn't likely to touch." Or, "Your figure will fill out when it decides to. Besides, some men like their women skinny. No use worrying about the Good Lord's plan. It's always best."

We went into the kitchen and found her chopping onions with such force that it looked as if she might cut right through the cutting board. Her eyes were dampened by the onions, and soon my eyes began to water too.

"What's happening, Beba? What's wrong with Papi and Mami?" Marta asked.

Beba dried her eyes with the back of her hand and then wiped her hands on her apron. She leaned on the counter, like she did when her knee was hurting her from standing too long, so I pulled a chair over for her and she sat down with an audible and weary sigh. "The world we know is changing. Some people think it should change. Some people think it should stay the same." She shook her head slightly, and I saw that the tears in her eyes were not caused by the onions.

"What do you mean?"

"While you were at school today that man gave a speech that lasted more than six hours. Holy Lord, how that man can go on for so long without losing his voice, I don't know." Beba had refused to say Castro's name for weeks now, believing that simply uttering it would give him more power. "He said what I knew all along; that he was a Communist and that he would be a Communist until the day he died."

Marta and I were silent. Although we weren't exactly sure what communism was, we knew from conversations we'd overheard that this was the worst outcome of all the possibilities debated during the past several months.

Mami and Papi emerged from their bedroom. Mami's face was tearstained and red. Papi sat at his place at the head of the table after placing a weary kiss on each of our foreheads. In the kitchen Mami whispered that we should refrain from asking any questions. "Your father is very upset, and I don't want him to get more so."

"Mami, is it true? Is Cuba communist?" Marta asked and Mami turned on her suddenly as if she might slap her across the face, although I'd never seen her slap anybody ever in my life. But she pushed the hair out of her face and turned to help Beba set the table for dinner. She gave two plates to Marta and two to me.

"Castro may be communist, but Cuba is not communist," she said with a conviction that was chilling. "Cuba will never be communist."

"May God hear you, Doña Regina. May your words go straight

to heaven," Beba said from the other side of the kitchen, and we all prayed the same.

Sunday dinner at Tía María's had become a somber occasion, but one that became more meaningful as we held on to what we knew of the world that was crumbling around us. There was no laughter on the porch, with clouds of cigar smoke being generated by a circle of happy, back slapping men in *guayabera* shirts, and no domino sets being arranged after dinner with good-natured banter about who was the best player and who was the cleverest cheater. Although there was much less meat to go around, the chicken and rice was as delicious as always, and Tía María received her compliments with a sad bow of her silvery head and no promises of the feast she planned to prepare next week. We cousins didn't separate ourselves from the adults like we usually did to make our own fun. Instead, we hovered nearby to learn about the state of affairs and about what would happen next. My cousin Juan seemed better informed than any of us, even Alicia.

"The government has taken over everything," he said authoritatively, "including the sugar mills and the banks."

I wondered how it was possible for a government to do such a thing. Did they simply stroll into all those hundreds of sugar mills and kick out the workers and assume control? Would they open all the giant bank vaults, where I imagined a little man with rolled-up sleeves lived counting money, and shove him off his chair so that someone else in green army fatigues could start counting where he left off? It seemed impossible and not at all real. And how about Papi? He was an important person at the National Bank. Surely they wouldn't kick him out? The bank couldn't run without him, of that I was sure. And he'd never wear one of those green uniforms. He'd die first.

"I think we're going to be leaving," Juan said, as he took a big spoonful of flan.

"Leaving where?" I asked.

"To the United States, of course. New York or Miami. You'll all be going too, sooner or later, I bet you."

We all looked at one another, shocked, some more horrified than others, but Alicia was calm and she smiled serenely. "I won't ever go. If they try to make me go, I'll run into the hills and hide like my father did."

"You're crazy," Juan said as he scraped up the last of the sweet caramel sauce with his spoon.

I thought a lot about what Juan had said about going to the United States, and I listened carefully to everything Mami and Papi discussed and was relieved to hear no word of leaving Cuba. In fact, they seemed more hopeful that things would change. Everyone seemed to agree that the United States would never tolerate communism so close to their democratic shores now that it had been so clearly spelled out by Castro himself. They'd consider it a disease that could infect their capitalistic ideals. Everyone knew that Russia and the United States were the worst of enemies, and rumors had already been confirmed by Castro himself that he was collaborating with the Russians on his new socialist state. There were too many reasons to believe that Castro's days were numbered, and we'd be back the way we were; too many days and nights spent glued to the television set as if our lives depended on its eerie glow. For the first time in my life, I'd grown pale from lack of sun. At least Abuela would be happy with my lighter complexion.

Mami cried every day. At first she didn't want us to see her, and she'd withdraw to her room and return to the business of her day with swollen eyes and a tremulous smile. But as the days went on she lost all concern for appearing weak, and openly sobbed whenever and wherever the feeling took over: on the couch while watching the news, in the kitchen while helping Beba put together a meal with scant provisions, or out on the balcony as she watched the sun disappear into the wide stretch of ocean before her. She avoided shopping as much as she could, and if she did venture out she'd return worse than she left, the sour mood of her experience causing her face to wrinkle with disgust and her unpainted lips to pucker as if she'd been forced to suck on a bitter lemon all day.

One afternoon, she came back from her marketing with a small bag of rotting potatoes and dropped them on the dining room table with a thud. "I stood in line three hours for these," she said and then locked herself in her room for another long cry.

Eventually she refused to do anything but stay home and talk to Beba. It seemed Beba was the only one who could calm her down with her straight no nonsense talk about government and society and the way things should be. All of this would go down very well with a cup of strong cinnamon tea. Mami sat at the kitchen table bobbing her head as Beba talked to the rhythm of her knife coming down on the chopping board. Sometimes Mami laughed through her misery when Beba said things like, "That man should be taken to the deepest part of the shark-infested ocean and sunk with a weight around his neck. Then we'll pass out his bones, picked clean, and use them to play the drums during the big party we're going to have because Cuba is free."

But there was one day when even Beba wasn't able to calm her down. We were driving to one of the few restaurants still serving dinner, for many had closed due to the shortages. The string of lights that always blinked merrily along the malecón were blowing out one by one, leaving a silent gray sweep of ocean front. Where once music and singing could be heard, there was now an empty and silent stage strewn with the garbage of happier times.

Papi said we had to spend as much cash as we could because it would soon be worthless. He spent it on anything he could, two full boxes of corn oil we could use for trade on the black market along with ten pairs of expensive women's shoes of all different sizes he bought from an old toothless man in an alley of the oldest part of Havana. He also paid Beba twice her usual salary, which she accepted sadly while clucking her tongue and shaking her head. "I'd trade all the money in the world for that man to leave. Lord knows it's true."

We drove a roundabout route that passed by our small parish. We knew it well, the little fountain in front where we'd thrown our pennies, and the corner where the man usually sold ice-cold mangos we enjoyed after mass on Sundays. "You're going to stain your Sunday dresses with mango juice," Mami would say.

"We'll be careful, Mami. We're not little girls anymore, you know."

We drove by the church and Mami was raising her right hand to make the sign of the cross as she always did, when she choked on an agonizing scream. Papi slammed on the breaks with such force that Marta and I flew against the back of the front seat. I looked to see if we'd run someone over or if we'd hit a dog. They sometimes ran loose through this part of the city.

"No! Dear God!" Mami wailed, her hands flying to her face. At first, I didn't understand what I saw. The black people in the church courtyard looked so happy, and they danced and laughed as though they were having a big party, the kind we often saw in the country when the drums pounded their infectious rhythms and smiles flashed like beautiful crescent moons. Perhaps they were happy because Castro was gone and Cuba was free again. My heart jumped at the possibility.

I hung out the window to get a better look. Young men swung on the carved wooden doors wearing the rich colored robes of the priests and tossing them up into the air and pulling them off of each other in a frenzy. One man in bare feet pretended to be a matador as he waved the drape used on the altar during communion at his companion who sported two crucifixes on his head like horns. Several women wrapped their bodies in embroidered capes and gyrated their hips to the sound of the congas being played from the sacristy so that the pounding, spilling out onto the street, echoed with mystical and evil enchantment.

My own heart beat with rage at the sight. This was our family church, the place where my parents were married, where Marta and I were baptized. This was the place where I'd learned about God and his benevolent and unchanging ways. I expected a lightening bolt to rip open the sky and incinerate these blatant sinners for their blasphemy. But the sun was out and the breeze was as warm and sweet as always.

Marta's face was streaming with tears. "Where are the priests, Papi?"

"They left," he answered shaken, but composed. "Some of them went back to Spain. I don't know where the others went, but they're not here anymore."

"Why can't there be any religion? It doesn't hurt anybody," Marta asked.

"A communist state is an atheist state," Mami whispered with spit and venom in her voice. "The only thing that can be worshipped in this country now is that man."

# 9

SCHOOL HAD BECOME OUR SANCTUARY, THE ONLY PLACE WHERE we could pretend things hadn't changed. Whenever we passed underneath the Sacred Virgin clutching her rosary, I knew I could look forward to a few hours of peace and sanity. We went to the chapel at the same time every day and ate lunch at the same time. The sisters expected behavior and academic performance to be absolutely perfect as if the world weren't falling apart outside the school's wrought-iron gates. We all pretended together, and when the large paned glass rattled with the explosion from somewhere deep in Havana while Sister Roberta read Shakespeare to the class, she didn't flinch. She just kept reading in her sweet even voice, and we all listened harder than we ever had before.

The prayers in the chapel were heavy and long, and for the first time it seemed everybody was truly praying for something that mattered. I prayed that life would return to the way it had been before, that I could graduate from El Ángel de la Guarda, that Alicia and I could go to the University together, and go shopping by ourselves for the first time at El Encanto. I prayed that my mother would stop crying everyday, that Papi would come home and read the paper in his chair like he always did and not just sit there silently as if he was waiting for his own death. I prayed that we could buy food at the market, fresh beautiful food, enough to feed an army of friends and family so, that Papi would never have to go to the black market and secretly trade for food and risk being arrested. Most of all, I prayed that my home would always be right here and that I could be close to all the people I loved.

Within the solid walls of El Ángel de la Guarda it seemed right that God should answer our prayers and that our previous way of life would continue as it always had. It was only when Papi came to pick us up at the end of the day and we passed under the gates of the Virgin back out into the world that I'd begin to feel the cold dread creep into my body again. Outside of the gates there were no longer any rules we were familiar with. We had to be watchful constantly and scramble from school to home in case the unforeseeable should happen while we were out.

One morning as Papi drove us to school, I was beginning to feel the reassuring calm of the day come upon me when Papi stopped just outside the gate, underneath the Blessed Virgin. He cocked his head to one side, and his eyes filled with an unspeakable torment.

"What's wrong, Papi?" I asked.

His face had turned from a light tan kissed by the sun to a chalky white, and his jaw was clenched tight, but he said nothing. I looked out toward the simple two-story structure of our school, the broad green lawn split in two by the path leading up to the double doors of the main hall. At this hour the doors should've been open, and girls of all ages wearing the same beige and brown uniforms would be buzzing about the lawn and steps waiting for classes to begin, but the doors were closed and not a soul could be seen anywhere.

"Are we early?"

Then I turned again to see that Papi wasn't looking toward the school, but upwards. I followed his gaze, heard Marta's weeping, and then wept as well. The Virgin with her rosary was gone. We saw her later on the side of the entrance road, broken in pieces, her severed hand still clutching her rosary. In its place, piercing the blue topical sky, was a strange angular metal crescent with a hammer in the center of it, looking heavy and ominous.

Papi reversed the car with a screech of the tires and headed back for home. El Ángel de la Guarda was gone along with every Catholic school in Cuba. There would be no more sanctuaries.

Every day we listened to Beba's powerful golden voice defame the man who'd become synonymous with the devil. "He's a lying pig who deserves to be shot in the head. He says he wants to take care of the black folks. Do you see any black man standing next to him up there? I sure don't, and my eyesight's pretty good. He says we were enslaved before and now we're free. Shit, if this is freedom, then give me slavery any day of the week. I can't even buy a piece of bread for my breakfast with all this freedom I got."

Papi was no longer able to work after he applied for our visas, but he was glad and said that he no longer worked in a bank, but a circus run by clowns who were controlled by the communist party. And we were glad he was out of the bank too because several employees had been imprisoned for counterrevolutionary activities. Papi described how one of the clerks entered the bank one morning with a Castrista soldier at his side. Slowly he made his way through the offices pointing his finger at those he suspected to be actively against the revolution. Each one was lead away for questioning and several had yet to return home. The jails were full of political prisoners, and everyone was a suspect.

With our visa application in process we'd literally thrown off our red revolutionary bandanas and become "gusanos", worms betraying their homeland and the revolution of their people for their own self-gain. "Gusanos" were publicly derided, and it was not unusual, if you were lucky enough to find a few precious gallons of gasoline for your car, to discover you could not drive it because your tires had been slashed or your windshield smashed. In this beautiful land where the sun shone everyday and the breezes called you to walk the shore at any time of day or night, we were forced to stay inside our apartment and avoid taking any unnecessary risks.

"If we're worms," Mami said with her fists clenched and her eyes watering with fury, "then the idiots who support this godforsaken revolution are cockroaches, and may they rot in hell!"

Juan and his family were the first to receive their visas. They had plans to move to Miami, and they were already taking English classes to be as prepared as they could to succeed. But it was harder for the older people to consider leaving. We visited Tía Panchita at her house and tried to persuade her to apply as well. A few months earlier, the government had given her plantation to Lola's brother, Pedro, saying that he worked the land, he should be in charge.

Mami and Papi begged Tía to apply for her visa as well. Marta and I sobbed when we imagined her here by herself, but Tía wasn't moved by our arguments or our river of tears.

"I won't leave my home," she said resolutely. "I won't spend my last days in some foreign place where they don't speak my language, shut away in a one-room apartment where I can't look out on my fields. I'd rather go hungry at home."

Then she poured herself another cup of weak coffee and stared out at the dusty road, rocking on the porch and blinking behind her thick cat-eyed glasses.

Lola reached across from her rocking chair and patted her hand kindly. "Maybe you should think about it, dear. Don't you want to be with your family?"

"I have thought about it. I'm staying here with you."

One afternoon, Tony came by while I sat on the porch with Tía Panchita and Lola. He'd grown to well over six feet and was more handsome than ever. All that had occurred between him and Alicia seemed to have been long forgotten by the adults, but Alicia had never been allowed to return to Tía Panchita's, in case memories should become inflamed. And I knew that Alicia still compared other men she'd see to Tony and invariably conclude that he was the most beautiful man of all. I could hardly disagree and when he bounded up the porch, two steps at a time, with that sparkling smile, my breath still caught a little bit in my throat, and my heart pounded a little more vigorously as it had on the first day I saw him.

Under his arm he carried a thick book and his wide eyes danced with light and amusement. "I'm learning how to read," he exclaimed proudly, holding out his book for our inspection.

Tía put down her needlework and repositioned her glasses to get a better look at the kind of book communists would use to teach reading. Her face betrayed nothing, for she already knew as we all did that Tony fully supported the revolution. "You're a smart fellow. You'll learn fast," she said severely and promptly returned to her needlework.

"You'll only learn what they want you to learn, boy," Lola said to her nephew.

"I want to learn how to read. This is my chance to do something better than just work the sugar cane."

"Sugar cane?" Lola laughed a dry throaty laugh that ended her up coughing more than laughing. "You don't have to worry. Pretty soon there won't be any sugar cane left to work."

"That's the problem with you old people," Tony said, inflating his muscular chest. "You've already decided the revolution is a failure. Maybe for those who never wanted anything to change it is, but for me, it's a chance to better my life."

Lola got up slowly from her chair to go inside. "I'm just a stupid old woman. What do I know?"

Tony turned to me with eyes pleading for sympathy. "What do you think, Nora?"

I struggled to find the words to respond. I couldn't imagine a life without books, and my heart went out to him. "I'm glad you're learning how to read, Tony. That's a good thing, if you're happy with it."

Tony cocked his head to one side and smiled sadly. He was hoping for more support than this, and his eyes searched my face, causing me to blush and squirm. Then he jerked his head away as though ashamed for my lack of courage and stepped off the porch slowly this time, each step representing yet more miles between his world and ours.

Lola came back out in time to see him leave, on foot this time, as his fine horse had been commandeered by the government almost immediately. None of us waved to him or called out, wishing him a good day. Never had there been such silence on the porch.

Mami developed a bad case of nerves. She jumped if there was a knock at the door, convinced that soldiers stood behind it ready to search our apartment and take us all to prison because of our black market dealings and desire to leave the country. We heard that our downstairs neighbor had been recruited to spy on the other tenants for just that purpose, so Mami persuaded Papi to pour the entire box of cooking oil he'd bought down the toilet. Executions were also aired on television, but Beba was directed to scurry us away to our rooms when questionable television programs aired. She placed one strong hand on each of our shoulders and escorted us there while we complained. Then she'd rush back to the living room so she could watch it herself.

What nobody knows is that, on one occasion, when passing from my bedroom to the kitchen in search of Beba, I saw that the rumors were true. Papi and Uncle Carlos didn't notice me standing behind them, and in the gray light of the television I saw it all, the skeletons, already half dead, lined up against the wall, wearing prison uniforms, stained and torn. They were blindfolded, with their hands tied behind their backs even though they obviously lacked the strength to take even one step toward freedom. Gunshots sounded like a huge firecracker echoing on and on, and the men collapsed on their knees before spilling to the ground like half-empty sacks of potatoes. The revolutionary music played; the flag was flown, and Papi's face was ashen when he turned around and saw me standing there.

"Why did they shoot those men, Papi?"

He took a moment to answer. "Because they're suspected to be counterrevolutionaries. They're martyrs, and they have their place in heaven." Papi sat down in his chair, his eyes red and pained. He put his face in his hands. "Go to your room now, Nora."

I spent many long afternoons lying on my bed waiting—waiting for the visas to arrive, waiting for someone (especially Alicia) to come and visit, waiting for the silence and the dread to be interrupted by anything. One day I spent an hour watching a spider in the corner of my room spin its web. Where once I would've felt the immediate need to scream and have Beba squash it with her bare hands as she often would, I now felt peaceful watching it spin to and fro, up and down, swinging on its invisible tether. The revolution didn't bother the little spider. It continued spinning and crawling around as it always had. Watching it, I could make myself believe that things weren't really so bad. Even if the explosions continued to sound throughout the day and night, maybe it would all soon be over. Even if the Bay of Pigs invasion had failed and everyone had given up hope that the Americans would save us from communism, I still prayed that they'd try again. I prayed that the next bullet I heard would shoot straight through that man's head, blowing off his green army hat so that it landed in the mud and was trampled by every man, woman, and child in Cuba. Spin, little spider, spin your web of dreams and hope.

Months passed and we heard nothing of the visas. Food was getting scarcer, and lines formed all over the city for milk and bread and even toilet paper. Mami forced herself to stand in them with the hated ration book in her purse, and Beba still came over every day, even though we were only able to pay her in *pesos* that were worthless even if there was something to buy. She was willing to come for food and company and for something to do. We were grateful for her presence.

Beba had just arranged the silverware on the table when there was an unexpected knock at the door. Mami nearly dropped the plates she held. When she set them down on the table and faltered on her feet as though she was drunk, Beba answered the door, and we all stiffened at the sight of a severe looking woman carrying a clipboard.

"Are you the domestic?" the woman asked.

Beba wiped her big hands on her white apron and eyed her suspiciously. "I am. I've been working for the García family for almost twenty years."

The woman was unimpressed. "I'm here to offer you reading lessons."

"Reading lessons?"

"Yes. Don't you want to learn how to read, so you can improve your station in life?"

Beba placed her hands on her wide hips and glared at the woman without shame. "What makes you think I can't read?"

The woman appeared shaken, but quickly regained her composure. "Well . . . can you?"

"No, but that's none of your business," Beba replied in a voice loud enough to echo throughout the entire building.

The woman's face dropped, but once again she resumed her purpose with resolve. "The party is offering this opportunity. . . ."

"I don't care what you or the party is offering me. I do what I please, and I don't want to learn how to read. And when I decide I do, I'll find my own teacher, and I'll read the books I want to read." And Beba slammed the door in her face and sauntered past all of us chuckling to herself and humming a tune. I imagined that she'd be able to render Castro a helpless little boy given an hour alone with him, and I would've let out a cheer if not for Mami's slumped body on the couch.

"What have you done?" she whispered. "What have you done?"

"Don't worry, Doña Regina," Beba said, setting out the plates Mami had abandoned at the table. "They won't do anything to me. They don't do anything to colored people."

It was late Sunday morning when Papi managed to find a leg of pork on the black market. It was a bit scrawny and said to come from a pig that was too old to eat, but it was meat and we'd had precious little of it lately. He wrapped it carefully in many layers of newspaper and placed it in the bottom of a shopping bag, as he prepared it for its journey to Tía María's house, where most of the family was assembled. Even though everyone did it, buying on the black market was considered a counterrevolutionary crime and Papi could've been arrested. But the gnawing in our stomachs made us courageous, and I felt like an underworld spy as we drove the five minutes or so it took to get to Tía's house.

The pork leg was cooked indoors and all the windows were closed, lest the wonderful aroma escape and proclaim our find. No neighbor could be trusted. You could never be sure about who had aspirations to join the party, and the fear and the greed for power motivated many to point their finger at friends they'd known all their lives. And it wasn't just neighbors. Children denounced parents, and parents denounced children. Everyone had a heartbreaking story to tell about a child who'd turned his own parent in for a crime against the state, often considered less horrendous than Papi's delectable purchase on the black market.

The aroma of pork skin sizzling with lemon and garlic almost brought tears to our eyes and fear of being caught didn't dampen our delight. On the contrary, this was our secret way of snubbing the party and all its informants. With each delicious bite of pork we were declaring our hatred for Castro and the communist party, a private gastronomic counterrevolution.

Alicia and I sat together on the porch, savoring our few pieces. (One leg of pork didn't go very far.) All of our conversations of late had been clouded by our inevitable separation. Alicia's parents wouldn't be applying for visas because Tío Carlos was convinced that the present circumstances were only temporary, and Castro would soon be ousted. Many agreed with him, but Papi considered Tío Carlos to be as stubborn as he always was and too proud to admit that the man he'd once supported into office had ruined our lives.

"Maybe the visas will never come," Alicia said, as she mopped up every last bit of pork juice with a stale crust of bread. "And even if they do, you don't have to go, Nora. You're already fifteen. You can say you want to stay here and live with me and my parents." She offered this possibility even though we both knew it was inconceivable that I should do anything but go with my family. I nodded glumly and watched the fireflies dance and flicker.

We remained out on the porch after we'd finished our meals and wondered if this might be the last time we would be together at Tía María's house. Lately I'd been wondering if everything I did was my last time: my last time walking around the corner with Marta to buy a loaf of bread or an ice cream; my last time waking up to the sound of Beba singing in the kitchen, and banging plates and dishes around as she did when she wanted us to wake up; my last time standing outside on the balcony waiting for the sun to go down, so I could see the city glow pastel pink in the twilight.

But how could I measure a week without Sundays at Tía María's house? It was as central to our existence as the rising and setting of the sun. No matter what happened during the week, there was always dinner at Tía María's house on Sunday. Our difficulties would be sorted out, the harsher edges of life softened by the laughter and music on the porch, and the promise of a delicious *brazo gitano* to come after dinner.

And how could I live without Alicia nearby? She was my mirror, my inverse self. She had secrets of mine in her heart that I could never share with anybody else. And living any place other than Cuba was tantamount to saying I was going to go live on the moon. How could people survive in a place where it was cold; where the tropical breezes didn't warm your soul on a daily basis? How could people live in a place that was so enormous? Cuba was small and cozy. Like my bedroom, I knew where everything was. The United States, spanning three thousand miles across an entire continent, would be like sleeping in an auditorium, my tiny bed miniscule and insignificant in the corner. This I could not imagine. Even less could I imagine speaking English, even though I'd studied it in school. It seemed right that this strange and complicated language with its thick "th" sound and irreverent vowels should come from an icy place where everybody was shivering and hurrying to get somewhere.

We spoke very little about our impending separation, almost not at all, as if fearing that talking about it would somehow make it happen. Perhaps Beba was right. Better to talk about the strong Americans and their hatred of communism and about a thousand planes buzzing over our heads like a swarm of angry bees aiming their stingers at the capped and bearded head of that man. Better not to talk about anything at all.

# 10

"TAKE ME WITH YOU," BEBA CRIED, KNEELING ON THE FLOOR AT Mami's feet. Mami was sprawled on the couch weeping with the same agony Tía Nina had unleashed earlier. Marta and I were speechless and numb at the sight of Mami and Beba in such condition. We couldn't comprehend the reality that, with our visas granted, we'd be leaving our home very soon.

Papi stood apart from us, hands stuffed in the pockets of his linen trousers as his black shoes tapped out an erratic rhythm on the tile floor. He was somewhere else, way ahead of us and unable to offer any consolation to the wailing women before him.

He walked to the center of the room and spoke only to Mami. "Beba isn't the only one who won't be leaving, Regina." The wailing stopped and silence spread over us like death.

Mami straightened up and wiped her eyes with the back of her wrist. "José, what are you saying?"

For a moment Papi couldn't speak.

"For God's sake, tell me!"

"Regina, calm down. There's a solution for this, I'm . . ."

"What is it?" she screamed and she sprung up from the couch to lunge at Papi.

Gently, he placed his hands on her shoulders and eased her back down to the couch. "My visa will be granted shortly, I'm sure."

"Your visa wasn't with ours?"

"No, but it'll come."

Mami stood up again, clear-minded and chipper. "Then we'll wait until it comes, and we'll all go together. That's what we'll do," she said in her most reasonable voice. Her solution sounded logical enough and perhaps while we waited for Papi's visa, Beba's would come too, and if we waited longer still, the government would change again and we wouldn't have to go at all.

We patted Beba on the back and told her, with voices trembling, that it was going to be all right, but she stayed on the floor quietly weeping, her face covered by her hands. Beba never gave her grief up easily, and she wasn't prone to hysterics. My dread returned at once.

Papi took slow steps to the window and gazed out at the glittering Caribbean in the distance. He kept his hands in his pockets, but I saw them ball up into fists and expand the linen. He walked back and spoke strong and clear. "You have to leave with the girls as soon as possible. If you lose these visas, you'll lose your chance forever."

"But it could be years, José. We might be separated for years."

Papi was silent. A fine mist of perspiration glistening on his forehead. "It won't be years. Don't you see?" He turned to Marta and I, attempting a smile that looked more like a half-hearted grimace. "This is their ploy to make us stay. They think you won't go without me. But it won't work. You three will be on that plane if it kills me. And if my visa doesn't come, I'll swim to Miami if I have to. I promise."

Mami collapsed on the couch once again. "You can keep your promises to yourself. This is too much for me to bear."

Beba collected herself and retreated to the kitchen without another word.

We were scheduled to leave in a week, which was the same as saying tomorrow, in an hour, this very second you'll walk out the door and leave the life you know forever. There were no elaborate preparations for our departure, no packing to be done because we were only allowed to take one change of clothes, no pictures or books or jewelry or anything that might remind us of the home we were leaving behind. We simply floated about the rooms of our apartment like ghosts wandering through a museum of belongings that were no longer ours. Our heartache settled like fine dust on every stick of furniture, every corner of tile. It blew, like a silent storm out of the windows and blended with the moisture of the sea that seemed to be weeping with us. We took pictures with our hearts and minds, and the little time we had expanded into an eternity of tomorrows we would never have. I found myself gazing at the Caribbean in the distance for hours at a time trying to make up for a lifetime of lost memories.

Mami and Papi were more inseparable than usual, and Mami cried constantly while Papi held her. When her head was on his shoulder so she couldn't see his face, he looked like his big heart was rotting and shriveling up into a small dry raisin. I tried to interpret the despair I saw in his eyes, for I knew better than to ask directly. Did it mean we'd never see him again? That he couldn't bear being apart from us? Was he keeping a secret too dangerous or painful to share?

Marta and I stood around the apartment, too weak from the shock of what was happening to do anything else. We hovered about Beba who'd regained her composure, but her strength was no longer warm and familiar; it was cold and resigned. She stopped singing and telling stories. Her pure white clothes appeared crumpled and occasionally stained. We sat together in the kitchen with no food to prepare and waited for the days to pass and the world to end.

Alicia and I were together at Varadero beach two days before we left. Even here where the breeze had always floated light and fragrant through our childhood dreams and scattered our fears into the brilliant sky, the air felt heavy and difficult to breathe. I could feel the sun pulsating angrily as it looked down upon its favorite island falling into ruin.

Alicia's parents had still refused to apply for visas, certain that the political climate would change. Although I didn't dare say anything, I secretly believed that they were right. Why should we leave our home because of the capriciousness of one man? It seemed like an incredible overreaction to leave our lives, our families, everything that made us who we were, when so many other proud Cubans were willing to wait and pray for change. Wasn't that the most reasonable thing to do? Hadn't Papi and Mami and the sisters at El Ángel de la Guarda always told us to be patient? Didn't the Bible say that patience was a virtue? Why were we willing to abandon our home when there was still hope?

All of these questions I longed to ask, but dared not when I saw the anguish in Mami and Papi's eyes. I didn't want Mami to go weak and crazy like Tía Nina had when Tío Carlos went away. I knew that it was better to remain silent and hold my breath and pray that things wouldn't get any worse.

Alicia and I sat on the white soft sand, resting our eyes on the turquoise blueness spread out before us, allowing the tepid water to moisten and tickle our toes.

"We learned to swim together here," Alicia said, still staring out at the sea. "Remember the day Abuelo made us swim to the platform?"

The platform was still out there bobbing peacefully, unaware of the grand role it had played in training generations of swimmers in our family and other families as well, no doubt.

"As I remember, you were the one who learned how to swim. I learned how to sink to the bottom like a big rock." I laughed at the memory, but I wanted to cry.

"You were brave, Nora. You tried even though you were afraid."

"I was definitely afraid."

"How about now? Are you afraid?"

I buried my toes in the soft sand and studied the thick drips of sand and water that spilled over my feet like hot fudge. "Yes, but I don't feel like I did when I was little. I just feel this frozen kind of sadness that doesn't let me cry."

Alicia nodded in the way that let me know she knew exactly what I meant. "It doesn't seem real. We've grown up together our whole lives. How can we just keep growing up apart?"

"Maybe we won't. Everybody says this can't last much longer. I think we'll only be gone a short while."

We lay back and gazed up at the palms, sweeping the sky as they had since we were little girls and before that . . . forever as they do.

"Can you see God today?" I asked, and Alicia took hold of my hand and the warmth of her love and sadness filled me like the sun overhead.

"Oh yes," she whispered. "He's looking right down on us at this very moment."

"And what did you ask him?"

"Well, you know I can't tell you that, Nora," she said and we both smiled through our tears.


José Martí Airport was a confusing throng of young soldiers with enormous guns slung about their bodies as they surveyed anxious and miserable people of all ages running around with their one mostly empty suitcase, bawling like babies as they hugged family members they might not see for years, if ever again. Children looked up at the adults with wide eyes, curious about this sudden reversal of roles.

"Don't cry," we heard an irritated soldier instruct a woman old enough to be his grandmother. "If you cry like that, it means you're against the revolution, and that's a crime, or haven't you heard?"

The old woman wiped her eyes under her glasses with her handkerchief and turned away from the soldier, her bottom lip trembling. "*Cabrón*," she muttered as she walked past us.

The four of us waited against the wall as Abuelo went to check on the status of our flight. Mami was a zombie, which was quite a change from her usual hysteria, but I preferred her hysteria to this death mask. Papi whispered into her ear and she nodded as she listened, blinking slowly like a child who's learning the rules for hide and seek. I imagine he told her what he'd been telling her all week, that everything was going to be fine, that we'd be together soon, and that nothing could keep our family apart.

Arrangements had already been made for our arrival in Miami, where we were to stay with friends until we reunited with Papi. The longest he'd wait for his visa was one year, and if it didn't come, he'd start looking for other ways to get out. There were many reports of people who were stowing away on boats and planes. And the United States was accepting anyone from Cuba, with or without a legal visa. It seemed a reasonable plan; a year wasn't so long. But Papi might as well have been talking to the wall that Mami leaned on.

She mumbled what she'd been saying for two weeks. "I can't believe this is happening to us."

As I looked at Papi, tall and strong, his eyes bright with emotion, I had no doubt our separation would be a brief one, but what would we do until then? At fifteen, I was already taller than Mami, and when I took her hand she let her head drop on my shoulder. "You have to help me, Nora," she said in a voice weakened by pain. "I need your help to get through this."

"I'll help you, Mami, don't worry," I said, trying to sound strong, although I too wanted to break down and weep like everyone else. I wanted Papi and Mami to take me in their arms like they did when I was a little girl and tell me it was all a bad dream and that things would be fine in the morning. I'd wake and see the light streaming through my window. I'd smell the coffee brewing, and I'd hear Beba singing merrily from the kitchen in her beautiful golden voice.

"We're planning a trip to the beach," my mother calls brightly. "Get up before we lose half the day."

"I'll get up right now," I want to call back, but I can't because I'm leaning against a gray wall with her head on my shoulder, holding an empty suitcase and wearing three pairs of underwear.

"I'll help you too, Mami," Marta said as she took the suitcase from me.

"You see, Regina? You have two wonderful daughters to help you be strong. And I'll be there soon."

"I don't think we should go," Mami said. But the strength had gone out of her argument, and it was only a hollow whisper.


Abuelo was weaving his way swiftly through the crowd. His face twitched when he neared, and his desperation swept over us like a furious wave. We were no longer sad and contemplative, but energized with the need to get on with it: this business of saying good-bye, to our home, to Papi, to everything we were.

Abuelo was so nervous he could hardly speak. Since sweet calm Abuelo was never nervous, the pit of my stomach fell to my feet. Everything was falling down around me, but I still wanted to stay with all my heart.

He pressed Papi's shoulder. "The plane is boarding."

Papi looked at his watch. "They shouldn't be boarding for another hour, Papá."

"Look at this place. Does it look like anyone knows what they're doing? This is a mad house, and I'm telling you that your plane is boarding now!" Abuelo never yelled, but he did so now and his face assumed a tightness that pulled the corners of his mouth down taut.

Mami straightened to attention and her eyes cleared. She shook herself. "We can't miss the plane, you heard what he said," she snapped, looking straight ahead. We almost ran behind her and Abuelo to keep up.

We arrived at the gate out of breath, with our hearts in our throats as we joined the end of the line trailing through the door out to the plane that reflected the tropical sun like Beba's pot and pans after she polished them. A middle-aged lady in front of us wept as a female official inspected her suitcase. The official took great pleasure in ripping the photographs she found, one by one, and tossing them on to the floor. She had a full mouth and wide-set almond eyes. She would've been considered very pretty if not for the sneer that cut across her face.

"Get in line right there," Abuelo commanded, unmoved by the scene before us. "Give me your visas." Papi handed him the three visas and stood with Abuelo outside the rope.

We looked at the flight number on the board. This was not our flight, but we got in line anyway when we saw the look on Abuelo's face. He wasn't confused at all. He knew exactly what he was doing.

When it was our turn to give the clerk our tickets, Abuelo stood close to him and passed him our visas so that his body blocked what he was doing, but I saw him slip several dollars into the front flap of one of our passports and remembered that Abuelo had money invested in an American bank account.

The clerk examined the passports and visas, then glared at Papi. "Sir," he said. "Didn't you read the sign? Passengers boarding the plane must stand inside the rope."

Papi looked confused, but when he saw Abuelo nod and lift the rope so he could pass underneath, he scrambled under without a word.

We knew we had to look natural and normal in every way. We couldn't risk calling any attention to ourselves when we wanted more than anything, to leap out of our skins with joy. The uniformed boys with machine guns strapped to their fronts and backs were everywhere. Anything could lead to an arrest. And this was much more serious than buying meat on the black market.

Together the four of us walked out the door in single file with our heads down, lest anyone read the apprehension in our eyes as something more than the sadness of leaving our homeland. I realized, as we almost ran across the tarmac to the plane and climbed up the stairs, that in our haste we'd forgotten to give Abuelo a hug and a kiss good-bye.

I turned around to see if I could catch a glimpse of him at the window and he was there, standing as straight as a royal palm, his hands stuffed in his pockets and his *guayabera* crisp and white in the sun.

We had all been dreading this moment, but now we couldn't wait for the plane to lift off the ground so there could be no doubt that we'd made it. The plane was full of screaming children and sobbing women and walking corpses and nervous bug-eyed young people paralyzed with shock, but we couldn't relate to their misery or their fears. We had our Papi back. Does anyone have some champagne? How about a cigar?

There were more passengers than seats, and several people had to sit on the floor during the short flight to freedom. Mami and Papi sat near the back huddled together with their hands intertwined. Mami wept and laughed and then wept some more while Papi held her close to him. Marta and I held each other too, as we heard the faint and mumbled prayers of the other passengers hum all around us.

"Please Heavenly Father, let us return soon. Blessed Mother, have mercy on us and keep us safe. Dear Jesus, don't forget our brothers and sisters who stay behind. Let us be together again soon."

The roar of the engine silenced the prayers and the sobs and the complaints of the children who weren't really sure what was happening to them. In the next few minutes over two hundred hearts would be ripped from their homeland. Who might survive the trauma, nobody knew. And who might be lucky enough to return and feel the warmth of the Cuban sun course through their veins once again, even fewer could say.

The plane charged down the runway, rattling and skipping as it went, and lifting it's beleaguered cargo up into the Cuban sky. Our swollen eyes peered out of small windows and watched the green of our island home become like a jewel embedded in a glistening sea. It grew smaller and smaller until it was barely a twinkling mist, a memory lost to the harshness of the glaring sun.

And then it was gone.

# THE
# UNITED
# STATES

# 11

Dear Alicia,

We haven't landed yet, but already I know . . . I will
never be American.

Everyone around me on the plane is happy and talking
about how much they can't wait for their first American
meal with plenty of American meat, and how they're going
to drink American beer until it comes out of their ears,
when the only thing I can think about is my last conversation with Beba.

She slipped into my room while we were waiting for
Abuelo to take us to the airport. As long as I live, I will
never forget what she told me. "When my people came to
this country from Africa, many lost their souls, but some survived, Norita. They never forgot who they were and where
they came from. They were the strongest ones, and I know
you'll be strong like them."

I told her I felt as weak as a baby, and I was crying like
one too, so she took a white handkerchief from her apron
pocket and wiped my eyes. "You aren't weak, Norita," she
said. "You're strong and you have a beautiful heart. But people in America will try to steal it from you, and you must resist or you'll lose yourself."

I asked her how I could keep them from stealing my heart and she said, "Just as my ancestors did. Give them your ghost heart, for they'll insist you give them something, but keep your real heart for yourself . . . always."

If I'd had the time I would've asked her a million questions about what a ghost heart was and where it came from and how to tell it from my real heart. And she would've explained it to me in her way that helps me understand just about anything. But just then Papi burst through the door, and announced that it was time for us to go. We barely had a chance to say good-bye to Beba, but as I'm writing this letter, I see her face in the clouds, and I'll be thinking about her and you when I catch my first glimpse of the land that might steal my heart if I'm not careful. It won't be long now.

I never thought I'd do this, but I made a promise to God like Abuela likes to do. I promise that every day I wake up in this place, the first thing I'm going to do is get on my knees, and ask God to end the revolution so we can go home. I won't cut off my eyelashes the way Abuela does, but I'll cut my nails very short and keep them that way until we're back. If you make a promise too, then maybe soon we'll be listening to our Elvis albums in my room and walking the beach early before the wind picks up. We'll go shopping to buy new dresses because there should be many more dances when the revolution is over.

Once we find a place to live, I'll write again on proper paper, (these immigration forms were all they had). And, I will keep my heart safe, just like Beba said.

Nora


When we stepped off the plane and onto American soil I hoped the ground would quiver and bolt me off like an angry horse, but I wasn't so lucky. We were immediately directed to form a line against the wall in a large building away from the main airport.

For a moment I felt like the poor souls lined up against the wall at La Cabaña waiting to be executed.

I whispered this to Marta, but Papi overheard and shook my shoulder roughly. "You listen to me," he said. "This is your country now. It's gratitude I want to hear from you and nothing else."

Poor Papi. There was such fear in his eyes. And it didn't go away even when we found ourselves in Little Havana in the heart of Miami the next day. We were surrounded by Cuban refugees everywhere, eating Cuban sandwiches and drinking Cuban coffee and listening to Cuban music blaring from speakers onto the street. Mami and Marta and I would've been happy to stay in this place as close to Cuba as possible, but Papi's fear grew worse. He told Mami about his friend at the National Bank who found a good job in California. His friend said that in California it wasn't like Miami where compassion for refugees was wearing thin and opportunities were getting harder to find. And in California there weren't any Cuban ghettos.

A few days later we boarded another plane for California, and the only thing that kept me from complaining along with Marta and Mami was the look in Papi's eyes. They sparkled like I hadn't seen them do since before the revolution. It was a comfort to see even though I knew that in this new place there'd be no mini Cuba to welcome us when we arrived.


Our new home in California was an apartment, even smaller than Tía María's shed out back. Marta and I slept in the living room on a couch that folded out into a lumpy bed, and Mami and Papi slept in the only bedroom. Every day for a week after we arrived, a lady from the church with an amazing head of blonde hair that looked like a stack of hay piled high on her head, brought us a meal. In broken Spanish she explained that the ladies at the church were taking turns making us special dinners so we wouldn't feel homesick.

The first time she made this announcement, we excitedly uncovered the casserole dish and peeked underneath the foil to discover layers of cheese bubbling over brown beans and meat. We'd never seen food like this before, but somehow it was supposed to ward off homesickness.

"Enchiladas," the blonde lady said. "Mexican food to help you feel at home."

Nobody had the nerve to tell her that we'd never had this strange food in our lives, and that Mexican food was very different from Cuban food, but the enchiladas were pretty good and we ate them around the small kitchen table barely big enough for two people. Our knees bumped into each other, and we tried to make light of it and focus on how lucky we were to have enough food to fill our stomachs. I tried to feel grateful, but everything seemed odd and disjointed; the food, the weather, even the way the leaves fell from the trees one at a time, as though to remind me that I was dying a little every day.

Sometimes after dinner, Papi and Marta and I went for walks while Mami did the dishes. She told us she didn't need our help cleaning up, but I knew she didn't want us to see her crying. All of a sudden, she'd become private with her tears.

During one of our walks, I detected a burning smell in the air, similar to the burning of coals before a pig roast. I knew it was impossible, but the mere thought of it warmed my heart with thoughts of home.

"What's that smell Papi?" I asked. Marta and Papi sniffed the air, puzzled too.

"Maybe they're burning trash?" Marta suggested.

We walked a bit further and Papi pointed toward the window of a big two-story house standing in the middle of a green yard with a white fence all around. There we saw the source of the smell; a fire burning inside the house, right in the middle of the living room. I'd heard and read about this in books, but to see it in real life was strange. How can a country this big and modern still use wood fires to keep houses warm? It seemed illogical when everybody knew that the United States was the richest and most powerful country in the world.

Not that the heater in our own little apartment made me feel any better. For a whole week Mami refused to let Papi light it because she thought it would blow up in the middle of the night. We didn't have enough blankets to ward off the cold, and when she finally allowed him to turn it on, she sat vigil next to it all night, watching the blue flame flicker behind the grate.

I could tell Papi liked the house with the fire inside because every time we walked by, he slowed down a little and gazed at it. "How would you girls like a big house like that some day?" he asked us. I wanted to remind him that we already had an apartment in Cuba overlooking the sea that was just as big, and that Tía María's house was twice as big, but I stayed silent.

"I don't want a big house," Marta said on the verge of tears. "I just want to go home."

Papi gave me a knowing look. Now it was just he and I left to be strong. I swallowed my own tears as best I could. "That big house would be nice Papi. I'm sure Mami would like it too."

Dear Alicia,

I dreamed of you for the first time since we left. You were walking along the rim of the island, dragging your feet on the sand, and wondering why I hadn't come home yet. You didn't realize I was sitting at the top of the tallest palm tree watching you. I tried to yell down to you, but my throat was stuck and I couldn't make a sound. My only chance was to throw myself down. I was getting ready to jump, but I wasn't afraid. Even in my dream I could feel the warmth that rescued me from the nightmare of this cold country.

When I woke up and realized where I was, I shut my eyes, hoping that if I didn't move a muscle and went back to sleep, I'd be able to talk with you before the dream ended. But I couldn't do it.

I hadn't cried since the day I left home. I've been trying to be strong for Papi and Mami and Marta, but on that morning before anyone was awake I buried my head in the pillow and sobbed so hard, it was difficult to breath and my lungs strained with the hurt I'd kept inside since we arrived. Beba would be disappointed to know that in so little time I've allowed my heart to become as brittle as the crunching leaves beneath my feet.

Marta and I started school last week. Here, boys and girls go to school together. The girls streak their eyes in thick, black liner and paint bright frost on their lips, making them look like voodoo dolls, and the boys wear their hair longer. Even the teacher's assistant, Jeremy McLaughlin, wears his hair long and he has a beard as well. All the girls think he's handsome. I suppose he is, if you don't mind that he's probably never once put a comb through his hair because it's so curly. But I shouldn't criticize him. He's been very nice and takes extra time to explain things to me without making a big fuss and drawing attention to the fact that my English is not so good. Everyone here is American, and we are the only Cubans in the entire school.

I try to say as little as possible while in class. But one day my teacher decided to begin the day's lesson with a discussion on current events. She showed the class the front page of the newspaper and the headline that read, "Trade Embargo: The US responds to Castro." Then she asked me to tell the class what I thought about it.

I couldn't think of what to say right away. For me this is more than a current event, it's my home, my heart, and my life. Finally, I stood up to speak even though my teacher said it wasn't necessary. To practice, I will write what I said in English.

"The Trade Embargo with Cuba . . . it is not enough to make change. Castro does not have hunger even though the people have hunger and much fear. They go to jail if they are against the communism. I miss my country and I pray every day I can go back home. There are some things worse than hunger." Nobody said a word and when I looked over at Jeremy, his eyes were red.

It's so strange to hear myself say to strangers what I can't say at home. I miss being home, and I miss you.

Nora


I wasn't ready to admit, even to Alicia, that I looked forward to school for one reason and one reason only. Jeremy would be there sprawled behind his desk wearing his blue jeans with a shirt and tie, diligently grading papers and answering questions asked by mostly female students who found any excuse to be near him. I could hardly blame them. His quiet gaze and unpretentious good looks were irresistible, and I too found my eyes wandering toward him from my front row desk several times an hour. More than once I caught him watching me, but he didn't look away, embarrassed to be caught as I was. He smiled sadly, probably pitying me in my starched clothes and knee high socks, studying me as though I were an odd creature from another world. It was painful to see my awkwardness reflected in his eyes.

I was leaving campus that first week when I heard him call my name the way he did, forcing himself to use proper Spanish pronunciation. As I watched him approach, my stomach tensed and I'm sure he noticed the redness gathering about the borders of my face and spreading like a storm of infatuation all over me. He was used to it of course, used to being adored by every girl who saw him. And so he had many opportunities to practice how to pretend not to notice. He was doing a very good job of pretending with me.

Slightly out of breath, he said my name again. "Nora. I hope you don't mind if I ask you something."

"I don't think so," I replied, rather stunned to be talking to him at all. I couldn't help but notice Cindy, the pretty blonde girl in my homeroom class, staring at us from her locker:

"What's worse than hunger?" he asked, and then expelled a sigh he seemed to have been saving for a week.

Nothing came to mind right away, and I became distracted by

the intense expression in his eyes, as though he was trying to read my thoughts as they formed.

"I'm sorry to catch you off guard like this. It's just . . . I've been thinking about what you said and I was just wondering . . ." His words trailed off.

"It is easy to find food," I said cautiously. "Maybe you don't like it, but you eat it and the hunger goes. When you lose hope," I looked into the soft palette of his hazel eyes once again . . . "You wait and hope finds you, but sometimes it doesn't find you."

Jeremy thought about my answer and slowly nodded his understanding. "You know something?" he said. "I'd like to improve my Spanish a bit. If I tutor you in English, will you tutor me in Spanish?"

"You want to learn Spanish?" I asked, smiling now.

"Oh yes," he said seriously. "I'm planning to join the Peace Corps and live in South America some day."

It was impossible to get to my classes without passing Cindy's locker. I wondered if she requested a centrally located one, so it was necessary for every member of the student body to notice her at least once during the day. And she took full advantage of her exposure too. She kept herself surrounded by friends who laughed incessantly as they looked out of the corners of their lavishly painted eyes to see if they were creating enough of a spectacle, sharing conversation and gossip without concern for who should hear them. I never paid attention myself; it would've been difficult to capture their words and phrases and put them together in a way that made any sense. The only reason I took half an interest was because more than once I'd seen Cindy strolling with Jeremy as he headed for the teacher's lunchroom. She chattered away while walking absent-mindedly so that she bumped into his shoulder as though by accident, but I could see by the sparkle in her eye it was not.

"Greasers!" I heard her scream from her locker to the semicircle of friends gathered around. "He likes greasers!" and she convulsed with a series of high-pitched giggles that infected the rest of the group.

I had almost slipped by, invisible and silent as always, when she addressed me for the first time. "Hey, your name's Nora, isn't it?"

"My name is Nora García."

More giggles from the rest of the group.

"Now, why do you suppose a fox like Jeremy likes greasers?" She cocked her head to one side and studied me from head to toe, as I tried my best to understand the unusual context in which she used the familiar words "fox" and "grease."

I shook my head, confused and red-faced.

"I thought you'd know, since you're a greaser." She smiled prettily while her eyes glared.

This sparked another burst of hysterical giggles and incoherent commentary from the others. I remembered Beba and her cold stare that could silence the worst of storms. I felt it surging up from the center of me and filling my eyes, hot and clear. It captured Cindy's watery gray eyes and she blinked curiously once and then twice, flustered to see I hadn't blinked at all.

"What are you staring at?" she mumbled.

I waited a few moments longer and then released her, and walked away without saying a word.

After a brief silence, I heard one of her friends call after me. "The greaser doesn't understand. Hey, you're in the U-S- of A now, so learn English, why don't you."

I kept walking until I reached my homeroom class. Jeremy sat at his desk and smiled up from his work when he saw me enter. I set my books down in front of him and wasted no time. "Am I a greaser?" I asked.

He seemed confused and a bit annoyed. "I hate that word."

"Some people just called me greaser."

Jeremy's concern became tinged with shame. "It's an insulting term fools use to describe people with a Spanish heritage."

"Then I am a greaser," I said delighted and smiling with the warm knowledge that Cindy said Jeremy liked greasers. I was almost positive that's what she said.

"I don't like hearing you say that, Nora."

"I am a greaser," I replied quiet satisfied. "I am Spanish like you say. And Spanish people are greasers, so I am a greaser."

Jeremy shook his head, half smiling at me and swallowed his amusement. "OK, if you say so, but you don't have to keep saying it over, and over, do you? How about referring to yourself as Latina or Hispanic or just . . . Cuban?"

# 12

Dear Alicia,

Papi finally found a job at a bank in downtown Los Angeles. He has to get up at four thirty in the morning to catch the bus and make it to work on time. It's not a prestigious job like he had in Cuba. He's a low-level accountant, and I heard him tell Mami that he reports to a man with a fraction of his education and experience, but they say that's no reason not to be grateful. When he came home with the news Mami was outside hanging laundry, and she got down on her knees to thank God as the wet sheets flapped in her face. Later she told me that if Papi hadn't found this job he would've had to take another job in construction laying tiles with someone he'd met on the bus who offered to teach him how. I wanted to ask Mami if she considered chopping sugar cane in the fields to be more dishonorable work than laying tiles, but it took me several days to get the courage. When I finally did she answered without getting upset or breaking down as I feared she would. She said, "Neither type of work is dishonorable, but if your father's going to break his back for a living, it should be to feed his family and not for that man."

I must begin my homework before it gets too late, as I have an early morning English lesson with Jeremy.

Every day I check the mail hoping there will be a letter from you, and every day I'm disappointed. Please write soon.

Nora

"What are you doing?" Mami asked me early one Sunday morning. I was settled on the kitchen table, the only writing surface in our tiny apartment.

"I'm writing to Alicia."

Mami raised her eyebrows in surprise. "You can write if you want, but she probably won't get it. They're intercepting the mail, cutting it up, and censoring it so that sometimes there isn't anything left." She yawned and shuffled across the kitchen, two shuffles would get her to the coffeepot. I shuddered to think she was starting to get used to the watery American coffee that she claimed helped her digestion.

She beckoned that I follow her back into the bedroom where Papi was snoring peacefully, and pulled out a large cardboard gift box from under the bed. Inside was a disorderly array of photographs and envelopes. I took one, held it to my nose and the homesickness I'd been feeling since we left rolled over me like an enormous wave. I could smell garlic and onions and sweet tobacco and lilac perfume and the sea itself. I felt I might stumble, so I sat on the bed with the letter still held up to my face. How could our home, be over there and we be over here? How did this absurd thing happen?

"I thought we weren't allowed to bring photographs with us?"

Mami sat down next to me and lowered her voice. "Your father got so mad at me when he saw them. I smuggled them inside the lining of the suitcase." She shook her head. "I know it was a risk, but I couldn't leave without taking some memories with me." She reached for a photograph and showed me. It was their wedding picture that had always lived in an elaborate silver frame on the shelf by the window. The line where the sun had faded the picture was clearly visible. Their smiles, once innocent and beautiful now inspired sadness.

Then I found the picture I'd been looking for. I could kiss Mami's feet for including it. It was of Alicia and me, hand in hand, the ocean swirling about our ankles on the day we celebrated Alicia's twelfth birthday. The whole family had gone to Varadero beach for the day, and we'd just completed our swimming lesson with Abuelo. We looked exhausted, but elated as we smiled into the camera. I looked closer: our skinny limbs were still shiny from the sea, my hair was plastered against my cheek in an unflattering mess, but Alicia looked beautiful, as always, chin up and golden hair lifted by the wind. I wished I could dive into the picture and never come back.

"You can keep it if you like," Mami said softly.

"I'd like that, thank you."

"Actually, this is what I wanted to show you," she said, holding an envelope out for me to examine. I could see by the signature that it was a letter from Tía María, but it was peppered with square cutouts all through out so if you held it up, it looked like the snowflake decorations I'd seen hanging in the American classrooms. I tried to read it, but it was difficult to understand and I kept falling into those little holes. The only message that came through loud and clear was that Tía's arthritis was getting worse.

"The Communists are censoring practically everything," she said with palpable disgust. "Even letters from little old ladies who complain about aches and pains and not having enough coffee for their breakfast."

I placed the photo in the drawer of my nightstand, and looked at it every night, wondering how long it would take for Alicia to receive even one of my letters. I planned to show this photograph to Jeremy. We'd been meeting regularly for our tutoring sessions, and I knew he'd be fascinated to see Alicia, whom I'd told him about, and to see us at the beach that I tried to describe with my limited English. "It is so beautiful and warm and my words are not enough. I can only say it is the place where my heart belongs."

Dear Alicia,

Of all the letters I've written so far, I hope this one reaches you more than any of the others. Perhaps that isn't quite true, but I'm so upset right now that it feels true and the only thing I can think of is to write to you, and pretend that you're here, or better yet, that I'm there.

There's serious trouble with Marta. It started when I noticed her leaving for school a good fifteen minutes earlier than necessary saying that she wanted to get to school early so she could get a "jump start" on her studies, whatever that means. She likes using American phrases like, "get off my back," and "see you later, alligator," and she tries to act as if she was born here which I believe only makes her look foolish.

I always walk the same route to school, but one morning they were digging up the road so I had to take another. That's when I spotted Marta sitting on somebody's porch, and she wasn't alone. She was with a boy. In fact, I'd seen him at my school, so I knew he had to be at least a couple of years older than Marta.

They didn't see me even though I was stomping so hard I could feel the soles of my feet tingling. I can't begin to imagine what Marta was doing with that boy. She knows she shouldn't ever be alone with a boy. But I could see by the familiarity in their eyes that this was not their first meeting.

I called out her name just as he was bending down to kiss her, and she jumped, obviously horror-stricken to see that I'd caught her in the act. But when she stepped off the porch and walked toward me, she looked just like the little girl I'd known in Cuba. I wanted to whisk her away back home and hide her under the bed and slap her cheeks until she came back to her senses.

She told me his name was Eddie and that he was her boyfriend. Can you believe that? And then she told me that things were different here and that people don't follow strict rules like they do in Cuba.

And I said, yelling right in the middle of the street, "I don't care what people do here. You can't change the fact that you're Cuban even if you change your hair and clothes, kiss every boy you see and eat hamburgers for breakfast, lunch, and dinner. You can't change it."

Marta stared at me for a few seconds, and I thought she might cry, but I know she was only worried that I'd tell Mami and Papi about what I saw. I thought long and hard about what I should do. And I finally decided not to tell them because I didn't want them to send her away like your parents did to you, but I might change my mind.

We walked wordlessly the rest of the way to school. And when we parted at the corner, I didn't answer her when she said good-bye. And I refused to speak to her after school as well.

Perhaps you will read this and think I was too harsh with Marta. But the way I see it, she's betraying who she is, and for what? An American boy whose life revolves around football. I bet he doesn't even know where Cuba is on the map. If you were here and living in this place, I know you'd understand. I miss you now more than ever.

Nora


I mailed the letter to Alicia the next morning and arrived to class one or two minutes late, to find Jeremy not waiting for me as usual, but talking with Cindy. She glanced at me, then at the clock on the wall, annoyed that I'd interrupted them. But she was the one interrupting us. Jeremy and I met daily for our Spanish/English lessons, and he was learning quite rapidly. He always told me what a good teacher I was and that I should considered taking it up as a profession. He said this while his hazel eyes softened with appreciation and his hand seemed to move just a little closer to mine. Our hands had been accidentally touching quite a bit lately as had our knees when we fumbled to get comfortable around the little table we shared during our lesson.

But Cindy was leaning on our little table and sticking her backside out while she continued chattering and laughing away, oblivious to me and my heated glances. I sat at my desk and pretended to be absorbed in my books and papers, turning the pages of my notebook this way and that. How long was I expected to wait? Jeremy hadn't even said hello to me yet.

I glanced at him once again and my heart broke, just like that. The softness in his eyes when he looked at me had intensified into a smoldering heat and he was slightly flushed. She probably didn't notice because she hadn't memorized the creamy tones of his face as I had. She didn't know that when he didn't shave in the mornings there was a delicate bridge of hair that appeared just above his jaw line and that it rippled like the sea when he chewed gum. And he loved to chew gum in-between classes, the only time it was allowed. Spearmint was his favorite. And he'd probably treated me to three or four packs during our lessons.

Still, I couldn't deny that Cindy was beautiful in the way American girls were considered beautiful. She always wore her hair loose around her shoulders, like a golden shawl. It glistened spectacularly in the sun as well as under the glare of florescent lights, and she swung it around as often as she could, under the most unnatural of pretenses. When searching for a book under her desk she'd have to swing her golden mane. When raising her hand in class, when entering a room and deciding where to sit, swoosh would go her hair and the effect was like a red cape on a mad bull . . . all the boys were transfixed, just as Jeremy appeared to be at that moment.

Yet, if you examined her closely, you'd see that her nose was slightly ill shaped so you could see into her nostrils and although her smile was cute and her laugh infectious, her lips were thin and her teeth tinged yellow gray from the cigarettes she liked to smoke when she walked home from school. Had Jeremy noticed this?

He must have whispered that he had to help this Spanish girl with her English, and I noticed him glance at her rear end, tightly packaged like a pair of oranges when she left. That was another thing: American boys preferred skinny women, while in Cuba Cindy's figure would've been rejected as unwomanly. They even had butt pads for people like her, I heard Beba telling Mami one day when they were chatting in the kitchen.

I focused on the English lesson that followed more intensely than ever. I made absolutely certain that our hands and knees never touched accidentally. I had planned to show Jeremy the photograph of Alicia and me at Varadero beach. I'd told him about it the day before and how dangerous it was for my mother to smuggle it out of the country the way she did. He was very interested to see it, as I knew he would be.

"So where's that photograph you were going to show me?" He asked once we'd settled in for our lesson at the little table.

I avoided his gaze and pretended to look for a particular page in my book. "The photograph . . . I forgot to bring it."

He cocked his head to one side. "How could you forget, Nora?"

I felt a surge of indignation. The photograph was tucked into my Spanish/English dictionary. I could've opened up to the page and shown him the splendor of my previous life just as I longed to open my heart, but I quickly dropped the dictionary into my bag instead.

"I think I may have lost it, because it wasn't where I left it."

"So you didn't forget it?"

For the first time since I'd met Jeremy I wanted to run away with my books and never return. These Americans can't get a subtle hint to back off. They hunt you down with their questions and wide-eyed curiosity as if they have a right to know everything.

"I just didn't bring it," I muttered. "That's all."


The next day I was relieved to find Jeremy alone, but I felt my mouth and eyes tighten as I avoided his gaze. He was watching me with certain concern. Even out of the corner of my eye I detected a smile playing about his lips and this unnerved me even more. He hadn't even opened his book, and we'd decided to begin with his Spanish lesson for a change as I'd concluded I was moving along with my English more quickly than he was with his Spanish.

"Something is wrong?" I asked as he sat twirling his pencil in his fingers.

"I was going to ask you the same thing."

I felt my ears go hot and a flush spread towards my cheeks. Once again, I had to fight the sudden urge to run out of the room.

He placed the pencil on the desk and leaned forward so he was near me, so near I could count the fine gold stubble on his upper lip. "Nora, I may be only a few years older than you, but I'm still a teacher here and there are certain things a teacher shouldn't do. . . ."

"I know what you do here."

Jeremy appeared flustered too now, and he pushed his long hair out of his eyes. "The girl you saw me talking with yesterday . . ."

"Cindy."

"Yes, Cindy." He nodded. "She's a student, and I'm a teacher. And you're a student. . . ."

"And you're a teacher," I said, acting as if we'd just begun our lesson. "We learned the words last week."

He smiled with me, but placed his hand on the dictionary I was preparing to open. "If I wasn't a teacher . . ." His eyes searched my face as he summoned the courage to say something, but then thought better of it and sighed. "I think we understand each other, don't we?"

I matched his smile and nodded. "You are a very good teacher, Jeremy."

# 13

Dear Alicia,

The other night, I heard Mami and Papi talking when they thought I wasn't listening. Our apartment is so small that the only place for privacy is in the bathroom or outside the kitchen on the back step. The window over the sink was open, so it was easy for me to hear them. Papi said that he'd heard your father had disappeared, like he did before. He was trying to keep Mami from worrying and I was worried too for a moment, but I felt better as I kept listening.

Papi also said that he was certain whatever happened with Batista before would happen with Castro now, and there was such hope and affection in his voice. Papi has always been very realistic about the revolution and the possibility of our going home and not at all like the rest of us who constantly wish for the impossible. If Papi says that things with Castro are going to change then I believe him, and I salute your brave Papi for helping this to happen. You must be very proud to be his daughter.

I have a wonderful feeling that this Christmas we'll all be together again. Don't be surprised if the next time you hear from me, I'm standing at your front door with a car waiting at the curb to take us to the beach. I suggest you tell Abuelo that next time we go swimming I'm going to beat him to the platform and back again.

It's late and I must get up early for my English lesson with Jeremy. I never thought I could like an American boy as much as I like him, and if I let myself, I could even fall in love. But Jeremy, as all American boys, prefers skinny girls with blonde hair. I'm still skinny, but last time I checked my hair was blacker than coal. Nevertheless, I'm learning English very quickly, and I'll put it to good use when I return. I'm certain the new government will need plenty of translators. Perhaps you can investigate this for me when you have time.

This is the happiest I've been for a long time.

Nora

"Eddie and I broke up," Marta announced on her way to school a few weeks later.

I was so surprised to hear her speak his name so casually, that I didn't say anything right away.

"Don't you want to know why?" She kept her eyes on the sidewalk. "He told me I was a prude, and he didn't want a prude for a girlfriend."

I searched my memory banks for the word *prude*, but it was nowhere to be found. I hated to ask Marta what it meant; it made me feel small and unworthy to show her she was learning better English than me. Anyway, I could ask Jeremy what it meant later.

"I thought I should tell you, so you could stop worrying about me," Marta added.

And so you don't have to worry about me telling Mami and Papi any more, I thought.

We were almost arriving to school and I held on to her arm for a moment. "Marta, please don't do this again. It'll be so much harder when we go back. . . ."

"What makes you think we're going back."

"I heard they're trying to get rid of Castro and . . ." I stopped myself. "I just know it, I feel it inside."

Marta shook her head and rolled her eyes, "Don't fool yourself, Nora."

Jeremy looked startled to hear my question, and he turned the same rosy color he had when talking to Cindy. He tapped his pencil on the desk. "Let's see, it's kind of like . . . Well it sort of depends how you mean . . . or . . ." Then he turned to me boldly. "Why do you need to know this?"

"My sister broke up with a boy who said she is a prude. I don't know what it means, but she should not be with him and I have to be careful for her because I can't tell my parents because they might send her away and . . ."

"Wait a minute . . . What happened with your sister and this boy?" Jeremy looked serious, and although I had forgiven him for his attraction to Cindy and decided that a trusting friendship with him would be better than nothing, the way he stroked his beard and nodded his head made me reconsider how I felt about him all over again.

"I don't know what happened. She is not supposed to have a boyfriend."

"How old is she?"

"Almost fifteen."

"It seems to me . . . Why isn't she supposed to have a boyfriend?"

"She is too young. She has not even introduced the boy to my parents."

Jeremy's eyebrow's lifted. It seemed as if there were many things he wanted to say.

I inched closer to him and lowered my voice. "In Cuba a man and woman are not ever alone until they get married."

"Are you serious?"

"It is true. Everywhere they go before, they are chaperoned to make sure."

"To make sure of what?"

"That nothing bad happens between them."

"Oh, man," Jeremy said, shaking his head in amazement. "I never knew that that stuff still went on."

"If a woman is caught alone with a man who is not her brother or father, people will think she is bad, like a prostitute and then no man will marry her."

Jeremy almost jumped in his seat at the word prostitute. "I can see why you're so worried about Marta then."

I nodded, glad that he'd understood. "So what does it mean . . . prude?"

Jeremy readjusted himself in his seat and faced me, his eyes sincere and open, but once again there was a smile lurking. "Before I tell you, would you answer a question for me?"

I nodded, eager to get on with our lesson.

"Do your parents know about our meetings?" While he waited for my answer his eyes positively sparkled. He seemed to enjoy the dilemma he'd created for me.

I tore my eyes away from his. My hands were hot as I fumbled with my books. "It's different for us."

"Why? I'm not your father or your brother, am I?"

I felt as though he was playing with me, using his knowledge of my attraction for his amusement and it maddened me. "You are the teacher and I am the student. Your words."

"I remember them."

"And," I looked him straight in the eye this time, unconcerned with whether my face was on fire or not. "You are not how Eddie is with Marta."

"You mean I'm not your boyfriend. How do you say boyfriend in Spanish again?"

"You know how." I felt flustered.

"Tell me anyway. I like how you say it."

"*Novio.*"

He said the word to himself several times, perfectly imitating my accent and not removing his eyes from my face.

"So are you going to tell me what it means this word? Prude?"

His eyes fell away from my face, and he cleared his throat while searching for something amongst his papers. "Well it's . . . Let's just say it's the opposite of a prostitute."

I heard him calling my name a few days later when I was walking home from school. He ran to catch up with me, his long legs and arms pumping like an athlete's. I rarely saw him outside of the classroom, and he was panting slightly and squinted in the bright sunlight. He was so different from any boy I'd known in Cuba. I'd have to find a way to describe him better in my next letter to Alicia.

"Nora," he said, laughing a little and shaking his head so that his curls bounced and bobbed. "I thought I'd have to call you tonight, and I don't have your phone number."

"What's wrong?"

Jeremy grabbed my arm. "I got my assignment. I'll be going to Peru in a few weeks, but I have to leave immediately for the training."

"I don't understand."

"The Peace Corps. Remember I told you?" Jeremy spoke with such enthusiasm and delight that it looked as though his eyes were going to pop out of his head.

I smiled and congratulated him and said all the things I knew I had to say to make him believe I was happy. I couldn't let him see that with this news he was taking away the only thing that made getting up in the morning and going to school worthwhile. How could he know that I'd come to depend on him in the way that I'd depended on Ángel de la Guarda during the early months of the revolution? He was my sanctuary. And now, once again, there were no more sanctuaries.

"I'm going to miss working with you . . . and seeing you . . ." He was still smiling and looking into my eyes. My sadness intensified. I was at the airport leaving my country all over again and there was a deep pain in the pit of my stomach that left me fluttering and vulnerable and lost.

Jeremy cocked his head to one side as he did when he didn't understand my English or Spanish, depending on who was teaching who. His smile faded and he seemed to be a little lost as well. He placed an awkward hand on my shoulder and left it there so the warmth penetrated through three layers of clothing and stamped my shoulder with his touch. "Thank you for being such a good teacher," he said.

I was about to thank him too, when she swept down upon us. Cindy, with her turbulence of blonde hair, her yellow smile, and exceptional energy. She circled Jeremy prodding and touching him repeatedly so he had to remove his arm from my shoulder.

"Hey, that's great news. I just found out," she said, and Jeremy smiled and turned that amazing shade of red. "Come and tell me all about where you're going." She pulled possessively on his arm. As always, I was invisible to her.

They were already across the street and Jeremy kept turning around and waving while Cindy jumped all over him, like the aggressive cheerleader she was.

"I'll look for you when I get back," he called out, holding Cindy at bay, causing her to freeze for a moment.

"How long will that be?" I called back.

"Two years, give or take a few weeks."

I smiled and waved. We'd be back in Cuba by then. I'd be walking on the beach and attending chaperoned dances by the dozen. Abuela would buy me dresses that accentuated a figure beginning to fill out quite nicely. Not as dramatically as Alicia's, but soft and feminine just the same.

I wrapped my coat around me tighter and wondered if the Peace Corps ever sent people to Cuba. I should've asked Jeremy this before when I had a chance. I should've suggested that he consider going to Cuba when he talked to me about joining months ago, but I didn't like talking about the possibility that he would leave, and it was too late to worry about this now.

I'd never see him again. Of this I was certain.

# 14

IT WAS HARD TO BELIEVE WE HAD BEEN AWAY FROM OUR COUNTRY for almost two years. In some ways, the time had gone by quickly in our struggle to adjust. In others, it felt as if we'd been gone for decades and I feared, that in spite of my promise, I was forgetting how to be Cuban. Even my English was getting better, and although I still had an accent, I was completely fluent. Marta and I almost always conversed in English now, but when we argued or confided our most secret feelings, we switched back to Spanish.

We'd saved enough money to move out of our one-bedroom apartment and into a two-bedroom house complete with a little yard in front and back that Mami wanted to transform into a beautiful garden even though she'd never touched earth in all her life. She was true to her word and the garden of our little house flourished. Almost every afternoon when I came home from school I'd find her digging the flower beds, pulling out weeds, pouring in plant food, or selecting roses for the table. She was happiest when gardening, but it was disturbing for me to see her hunched over in the dirt with a handkerchief tied around her head and her face smudged. She'd long foregone the habit of dressing well even if she was staying home and adopted her own version of American casual: a stretched polyester pantsuit, the church lady had given her when we first arrived, and tattered house slippers. This was something a respectable Cuban woman would never have done, but Mami happily waved her gardening tools at passers-by without the slightest concern for her appearance. And if it was Mrs. Miller, the little old lady who lived next door and who reminded Mami of Abuela, she'd find a perfect rose to give her as well.

I liked Mrs. Miller too. She always told me I was an elegant young lady and too smart for the crazy boys of today. Perhaps she'd seen Marta walking home with different boys who'd disappear the minute they turned the corner, whereas I was always alone. Or maybe she just said those nice things because I put her newspaper on her porch when it landed out on the grass, as I knew she had arthritis in her knees and going down the front steps was difficult. Whatever the reason, I felt good in her company and found the smell of soap and baby powder that lingered about her comforting, and the slow deliberate way she planned all of her movements, like opening her purse for a cough drop.

The cold autumn winds warmed steadily through spring and, if not for the dryness in the air, by summer I could almost imagine I was in the tropics again. Mami was especially proud of the way her roses were coming along, but one afternoon when I arrived from school, she wasn't in the yard, although her gardening tools were scattered on the ground and a bag of topsoil had fallen over making a tremendous mess on the steps. The front door was open and when I entered I heard Mami's low mournful wails, and Mrs. Miller's frail voice trying to console her. I threw my books down and ran into the kitchen to find Mami with her head on the table and Mrs. Miller stroking her back with a trembling hand.

"Your daughter's here, Regina," Mrs. Miller said, obviously relieved to be sharing this burden. But Mami didn't look up. She simply stopped sobbing and became very still.

My heart froze with fear. "What happened?"

Mrs. Miller reached for a yellow paper from the table to give me, but Mami snatched it back. "I don't want you to see this. Your Tío Carlos is gone. That's all you need to know."

"Gone?"

"Dead. He's dead." Mami's eyes challenged me to keep my distance. She was lying, I knew she was. How could Tío Carlos be dead? He was younger than Papi. Handsome and smart and strong. He'd never been sick a day in his life. Why would Mami make up such a thing?

I took a step closer. "Let me see the letter."

She clutched the envelope tight in her hand and shook her head.

"Mami. You can't protect us from everything. We're not little girls anymore. Please."

She dropped her head and began to sob silently once again. Without looking at me, her hand released the yellow paper on the table. It was a telegram and the Spanish words read, "Carlos Alejandro García died—stop. Executed by firing squad—stop. A traitor to the Revolution—stop."

A trembling pain overtook me. I sat next to Mami and felt Mrs. Miller's hand on my back this time. I read the telegram over and over. *Executed by firing squad.* I saw his sweet smile, and the way he played his guitar, taking requests while relaxing on Tía María's porch. *Executed by firing squad.* He was never angry, and even when he and Papi argued about politics, he maintained a hint of a smile and he'd end the exchange with a friendly slap on Papi's back. *Executed by firing squad.* Alicia was his princess. His eyes lit up whenever she came in the room, and he used to tell her to stop growing so fast, that he wasn't ready for a big girl yet. *Executed by firing squad.* Alicia, oh my God, Alicia. I still hadn't heard from her, and by now I feared that I never would. How could she find the strength to live? Tía Nina could never survive it.

Mrs. Miller sat down at the table beside us. "What's wrong, dear?" Poor Mrs. Miller. The telegram was in Spanish and Mami and I had been talking in Spanish too. She had no idea what was going on.

Saying the words out loud made it real in a way that burned through my soul, a branding of hatred and pain that I knew would never go away.

"They killed my Tío Carlos. They murdered him, because he stood up for what he believed in, because he had the courage to speak against injustice, because he loved his country, our country. They stood him up against a wall and shot him like a dog because they knew that as long as he lived, their lies would be discovered. They murdered him because he was too strong for them."

Mrs. Miller gasped. She may have expected a death in the family, but nothing like this. The fine trembling in her hands grew more pronounced, and her touch was jittery and warm on my arm. "Oh my. I'm sorry, I'm so sorry."

She made us tea and we sat silently in the darkening kitchen for some time. Marta should've come home an hour ago, and Papi would be home soon. I knew this was Mami's primary concern now.

At last, we walked Mrs. Miller to the door and thanked her for her help. Then we turned on one light and waited in the living room.

The phone rang. It was Marta asking if she could stay for dinner at Debbie's house. "You need to come home," Mami said.

"No, you need to come. Something's happened and we need you here. I can't tell you over the phone."

We heard Papi's car in the drive and looked at each other knowing the worst was yet to come, wishing we could do anything to spare him this pain.

He saw us sitting in the semidarkness waiting for him with swollen eyes. Mami stood up, the telegram in her pocket. Her lips began to tremble. "José, something has happened."

He drops his briefcase to the floor, and together they walk to their bedroom. The door closes and with a pillow pressed to my belly, I wait. I hear his scream in the very core of my soul, in a place where the worst of humanity can be imagined and where the idea of hell was conceived. My own sobs explode from the back of my throat and I can't stop them and I almost stop breathing in the pillow when I realize I've been suffocating myself in an effort to stop crying.

I hear him again, "Dear God, oh Dear Blessed Mother . . . Not Carlitos . . . please God . . . not my brother . . ."

I want to go in and help comfort him, but I know Papi will only allow Mami to see him like this. For everyone else, he must be strong and in control. I must respect this.

Then Marta comes through the front door ready to offer excuses for her lateness. I tell her what's happened, and her face twists in agony. She hears Papi scream from the bedroom, drops her bag, and runs to their bedroom.

"Marta, you can't go in," I say, running after her. I grab her arm, but she wrenches it free and bursts through the bedroom door. Papi is lying on their bed in his suit, his knees up to his chest, sobbing as Mami strokes his hair, talking softly with a gentle strength we only see when he is unable to be strong.

Marta throws herself on the bed and curls up next to him with her arm around his shoulder. He doesn't seem to notice her at first, but then his hand comes around and touches her cheek. Mami sees me standing in the doorway and motions for me to enter too.

"We need to pray," she whispers, but only Mami and I are able to say the words of the Our Father without sobbing.

"Tell your father what you said to Mrs. Miller today," my mother says. And so I try to remember and to make it sound eloquent and real, but I stumble a bit so eager to make it somehow better.

As I talk of Tío Carlos's courage and strength, Papi gazes up at me innocent as a child and nods slowly. He takes my hand and presses it to his lips. "Thank you, Nora."


After a few weeks, we stopped speaking of Tío Carlos's death. It was like talking about the air that we breathed, or the ground beneath our feet. It was always with us, and the sadness we felt pushed us deeper into the American way of life. Even I had to give in a little and concede that my dream of returning home was fading past the point of recognition. But, sometimes as I walked to and from school the realization of what was happening came upon me like the sudden rainstorms of the tropics. I used to love the rain and the way it washed the world clean. But these storms were of a different sort. They were filled with the tears I was too tired to shed myself, and they fell upon soil I could no longer feel beneath my feet. But the more I sunk into my cautious understanding of survival, the more Marta seemed to bloom. She flourished in this strange weather, and I watched her unfold as though she were not my sister, that little girl that scuttled after me and Alicia in my other life. She was changing as surely as if she'd shed her old skin and slipped into the pale freckled hide of the *americanas* who were her friends.

Sometimes when she talked about her friends and the boys she liked, I felt a deep sorrow in the pit of my stomach. But at least with Marta I wasn't forced to pretend, and I scowled fiercely at her.

"You're such a drip, Nora," she'd say with her crisp American pronunciation that was a marvel to my slow tongue.

I'd answer her in Spanish. "I'm not what you say. I keep my real heart safe. I don't give it away so easily like you do."

"That's a really strange thing to say. Have you taken a good look at how weird you're getting? I'm embarrassed that people know you're my sister sometimes. I feel like telling everyone my sister is a nun or that she's dead."

"Maybe that's exactly what you should tell them; that I'm dead."

I couldn't explain very well in any language this peculiar pain that refused to heal. It was always there, and I had eventually grown to love it as the only reminder I had left of who I was, the only certitude that I had once belonged to my life and my world.

Marta's eyes filled with tears, and she switched to Spanish. "Nora, don't talk about being dead. It makes me sad, and I hate feeling sad."

I waited for her to wipe her eyes. The sun had started to set and because the window of our room faced west, for just a few minutes every afternoon, the walls were bathed in golden light and we became translucent.

Marta's dark eyes opened wide as she absorbed the golden light. "I miss the way you used to be, Nora. You were so happy and fun, and all I wanted was to be with you. Remember?"

"I remember."

"Why can't it be like that again?"

I couldn't think of an answer to this question that would make any sense, so I stayed silent and we watched the golden light slip from the room, and the quiet gray of twilight fill the space of our dreams.

The envelope, worn and creased at the corners from its long journey, was propped on my pillow when I arrived home from school. I immediately recognized the writing on the outside, always graceful and neat, but slanting to the left instead of the right. My fingers trembled as I eased open the seal, and Alicia's voice floated up from the pages like a beloved melody from long ago.

Dear Nora,

I finally found the strength of heart to write you back. I also found a way, through an old friend of Papi's, to send you this letter so that words aren't cut out here and there as the government does. And believe me, if not for that there'd be only one big picture window, a frame for your beautiful face that I miss so much.

It's been nine months since they killed Papi. We were allowed to send one telegram after his death. Those words, "Traitor to the Revolution" were not our words, but considering the choices we were given, "Traitor to his country and his people" and others just as bad, it seemed like the best option. The truth is that Papi would've been proud to be considered a traitor to the Revolution. Soon after you left, he came to understand that Castro was never going to allow for free and democratic elections.

Papi was gone for weeks at a time when things got bad. He wouldn't tell us what he was doing, or where he was going, but we knew it was more dangerous than before. Mami became very sick during this time. She had to go to Abuela's again. We both went. Toward the end we hardly ever saw him anymore. We'd hear how he was doing through friends who'd come to our door in the middle of the night and leave us whispered messages or scribbles on scraps of paper. Mami burned them in the ashtray right after she read them, crying all the while. She was unable to get out of bed after we heard Papi was captured.

I couldn't help but imagine his execution. He must have stood together with the others, so thin, I wouldn't have recognized him. During that last moment of his life, he turned his face to heaven and called out, "*Viva la libertad, viva Cuba!*"

I screamed it with him and for hours after they killed him. I screamed until my voice was hoarse and I could hardly breath. Abuela closed all the windows for fear of the spies that are everywhere, but I didn't care then and I don't care now. Even after so many months have passed my heart is still screaming with him, Nora. They're silent screams that become great hurling sobs in the middle of the night when no one can hear. Every day I have the feeling he'll be home any minute and then I realize I'll be waiting for my father the rest of my life.

I can't explain the sadness that's lodged itself in my heart. I no longer feel the need to function as a human being, to bathe, to eat, to brush off the flies that land on my face and arms. I'm a paper doll, flat and empty, pretending to be like everybody else only because I'm tired of explaining why I'm not.

Mami stopped speaking altogether after Papi died. The

doctor sent her to a Sanitarium, but I'm not sure there's any cure for what she has or that she wants to be cured. Tía Panchita sent for me after Mami went away. She thought it would be better for me in the country, away from the madness of the Revolution, but there's no getting away from it. This disease has infected every person, every bird, every grain of sand. The island has detached from its usual place and drifted to some other spot on earth where life means something different from what it used to mean.

I have read your letters, each one a thousand times, and pretend all the while that you are here with me still. Please keep writing and don't interpret the length of time it took me to write back after Papi's death as anything other than the weakness of a frail heart.

Alicia

I refolded the letter and tucked it underneath the picture of Alicia and me in my nightstand drawer. Every night for weeks I took a moment to visit it. It was no longer necessary to read the words, for I'd memorized every one. Instead, I studied Alicia's script and felt the pain in every curve of the line, every tenuous crossing of the pen. Although thousands of miles away, we were together again and the understanding between us was stronger than ever.

I began to feel more like myself, and more alive than I had since leaving my country. And with every letter that arrived, I thanked God for granting me the peace of yet another sanctuary.

Dear Nora,

I'm going to write to you about the day I came back to life. I pray with all my heart you understand how close to death I actually was and that my will to live goes beyond

politics and fear and even the memory of my father, may he
rest in peace. I don't understand all that is happening to me,
but writing to you about it and imagining your quiet way of
listening helps me beyond what I can express.

I hadn't been outside of the house for weeks. I feared
that if sunlight touched my skin I'd be turned to dust, or if it
hit my eyes I'd go blind. I was so weak that even thinking
about whether or not I should eat made me tired, and often
I'd go back to bed for the rest of the day when I'd only been
up for an hour or two.

I was sitting in the shadows of the kitchen when Tony
came in. He was even more beautiful than I remembered
him. His manhood is full upon him, and he wears it like a
splendid cape of gold. The tropical skies live in his eyes, and
I felt my heart move the instant I saw him. For the first time
since Papi died, I became aware of the breath entering my
lungs and the mild aching in my legs that were folded underneath me.

He sat down and told me Panchita and Lola were worried about me and that I needed to eat and get well for many
reasons. His voice was like warm honey and right away I felt
the rumbling of hunger in my stomach. He took a loaf of
bread from the cupboard, broke off a piece, and handed it to
me. I ate it completely and the next, and the one after that.
Then he peeled the last banana Tía had, and I ate it straight
from his hands. A delicious energy coursed through my
veins, and I felt how a little baby must feel when he's born
fresh into the world.

He came to see me every day after that, and every day I
got stronger. We went for walks into the forest, he read to
me from his revolutionary books, and I listened to his voice
and tried to ignore the words. Tony believes in the revolution with all his heart and soul. He's taken me to his village
and I've seen the way the poor children live, without shoes,
without food and clean water. Most of them can't read or
even write their own names. Tony believes all children

should be taught how to read and have the chance for a decent life.

He tells me these things while we rock on the porch or walk through the sugar cane fields, hand in hand. He also says that he's loved me since the first day he met me and that I'm the most beautiful woman he knows. He doesn't say this as I've heard other men tell me, Nora. I can just see you shaking your head. He says it with true light in his eyes so I know he sees beauty in my heart the way I see it in his. And because of this, when we stroll beyond the grounds of Tía's house and wander behind the trees, I let him kiss me on the lips like we did so many years ago. I press my body against him so that my chest melts into his, and I feel the strength of his desire for me right on my belly. The only nourishment I need is to drink from his lips and to feel his arms around me. I'm not ashamed to say that I want nothing more than to lay with him and give him all that I am. I never knew I could love a man or any one the way I love Tony. He has become my life Nora, and I have become his.

He wants me to go with him to work the sugar cane fields when I'm stronger. The party is asking people to sign up in support of the revolution, even pregnant women and sick old people. I can't imagine supporting anyone or anything that killed my father, but I can't bear the thought of being away from Tony even for one day. I haven't told Tía Panchita yet, but I'm sure I will go with Tony to the sugar cane fields or to the ends of the earth; it's all the same to me.

Do you suppose Papi would forgive me? Sometimes I imagine him up in heaven watching me and weeping for the decision I've made to love Tony. At others, I believe he's happy that I'm alive again and able to love when I was sure my heart and soul had died. Perhaps he can see from heaven that right and wrong isn't as important as happiness and love. Or perhaps I'm simply a fool, too weak and shallow to care about anything but my own survival.

You wrote before that you didn't think me capable of

betrayal. Yet, isn't this the worst betrayal of all? Do not spare my feelings. I've always been able to hear the truth from you if from no one else. Please write me again soon. I'll be waiting.

Alicia

# 15

MAMI TOSSED THE PAMPHLET I GAVE HER TO REVIEW BACK ON the kitchen table. "What's this Peace Corps business?" she asked, pronouncing Corps as if it were a dead body and with the same disdain as if she could smell it rotting.

"It's a government organization that trains people, mostly young college-age people to go to other countries and help with. . . ."

"Oh yes, I remember hearing about this now," she said, getting up from her chair to attend to the stew she had on the stove. "Kennedy started all this, didn't he?" She nodded severely like a detective who just figured out who committed the murder.

"There's nothing wrong with it, Mami. It's a very good cause, and poorer countries benefit from the help."

She stirred with one hand and the other she placed squarely on her hip. "When do you go to college? What happens to your scholarship?"

"I won't lose my scholarship if I wait a couple of years and then I'll have more life experience. When you have life experience, it helps you do better in college. That's what my counselor told me."

She started to mutter which I knew wasn't a good sign. It meant she was trying to keep the kettle of anxiety she always had simmering in her heart from overflowing. "Life experience, eh?

Why don't you go down to skid row and take a good look at what life experience can do for you?" She waved her spoon in the general direction of where she thought skid row would be.

"That's hardly a fair comparison."

She turned to face me, her cheeks flush from more than the steam rising from the stove. "Don't talk to me about what's fair because I know better than anyone that nothing's fair in this life. Is it fair that you have an opportunity to go to one of the best colleges in this country and that you'd rather go traipsing through the jungle instead? Is it fair that you sleep on clean sheets every night with a full belly, when other young people your age can't be sure where they'll sleep for the night or where they'll get their next meal? They make it sound real glamorous," she said with that all-knowing roll of her eyes, something she'd recently picked up from Marta. "Taking young people from their comfortable lives and out to the sugar cane fields, putting *guajiro* hats on their heads, machetes in their hands, and making them believe they're supporting some great cause for humanity."

"I never said anything about going to Cuba, Mami." I could hear my voice rising, in spite of my effort to remain calm.

"Maybe not, but those young people go there too. I saw them on TV not long ago, and it made me sick to my stomach to hear the reporters talk about sugar cane production and increased profits when everybody knows the people are hungry enough to eat their own shoes if they had any." She pointed the spoon directly at me this time. "If you even think about going back there to help that man, then you're no daughter of mine. Do you understand what I'm telling you?"

"I understand perfectly," I said, almost yelling. "But you don't understand that I'm not going to Cuba. This has nothing to do with Cuba."

She held the spoon steadily at me. "Don't you forget who you're talking to, young lady. I'm your mother and you need to show some respect." I lowered my eyes and she lowered her spoon. After some more muttering, Mami put the lid back on the pot and forced herself to sit back down at the kitchen table to take another look at the pamphlet she'd dismissed so easily before. She turned each of the pages and squinted at the pictures of people raising livestock and digging ditches next to the natives and smiling all the while as if comforted by the knowledge that they were single-handedly saving the world.

She was making an effort to be reasonable, and she'd made some progress when dealing with Marta lately, but she never expected any trouble from me. "Now tell me honestly, Nora," she said, studying me with sincere curiosity. "What do you want with all this? I could understand if you always enjoyed camping, or if you had a great love for cows and dirt, but the truth is you won't even help me plant a rose bush out in the yard when I ask you to."

Encouraged by the disappearing crease between her brows, I made a brave attempt at explaining my humanistic sensibilities. I'd even managed to speak for three or four uninterrupted minutes, when Marta came home from school, sniffing about for a preview of that evening's meal. She only needed to listen for thirty or so seconds before folding her arms and making her declaration.

"Oh, I know what this is all about," she said with a self-satisfied smirk. "It's about that guy who used to tutor you, isn't it?"

"What are you talking about?" Mami asked, suddenly alarmed at the mention of some guy she knew nothing about.

"This has nothing to do with Jeremy," I shot back.

"Jeremy? Who's this Jeremy?" Mami's cheeks were reddening once again.

"Oh no?" Marta replied, ignoring Mami's question. "He's the only person you know who ever went to the Peace Corps. You wouldn't admit it, but I know you were in love with him. Not that I blame you. . . ."

Mami threw the pamphlet on the table for a second time. "Do you mean to tell me that you want to put off your college education for a boy? Is that what this is about, Nora García?"

I sat red-faced and silenced by my shame. I hadn't stopped thinking about Jeremy since he left, and I couldn't deny I'd been nurturing visions of finding him in the steamy jungles of Perú ever since reading Alicia's letter and about her plans to follow Tony to the ends of the earth, if need be.

"Really, Nora, I thought you were different. If Marta came up with something like this I'd understand, but you . . ."

"Hey, what's that supposed to mean?" came Marta's half-hearted complaint, but she was far too satisfied to see me squirming in her usual role to take it any further.

With head hanging low, Mami placed both hands, palms down on the table as if ready to conduct a séance. Then she raised her head slowly and glared at me. "I'm not going to tell your father about this, Nora. Because if I did, the disappointment would surely kill him. I don't have the heart to do it, and I certainly hope you don't, either." She turned to Marta, her tone somewhat fiercer. "And that means you too, young lady."

University life was as comforting as it was desolate. I sat in huge auditoriums with no fewer than 150 students and took feverish notes, barely raising my head to look at the professor for fear that I might miss an important point. Once again, I was invisible, like the black hole in space described in my astronomy class, absorbing and sucking in everything around it without ever revealing itself.

And yet, there were some definite improvements in my life. Something about the anonymity of the place made me feel freer than I ever did in high school. Since I was never required to speak in class, nobody heard my accent. I could be whoever I wanted to be. I took to wearing jeans and Mexican sandals every day, varying only a sweater or shirt. Even when it rained, I wore socks with my sandals and carefully avoided puddles. I let my hair go loose around my shoulders without brushing out the waves. One day I caught sight of my reflection in a window and actually liked what I saw. I looked again. Was it really me? It was the same narrow face and serious expression, but there was another presence behind the eyes . . . my shyness was replaced by a self-satisfied independence that went very well with my appearance. I fancied myself a wild and exotic creature, from nowhere and everywhere. Mami wasn't much too concerned with my change in style and even purchased a few oversized sweaters for me. She'd seen Marta transform herself so often that my evolution was like the receding of the ice age in comparison.

My vague dissatisfaction with life coupled with the lack of social distractions gave me a distinct academic advantage, and I managed to land on the Dean's List at the end of my first quarter. I even received an invitation to attend a Chancellor's reception at Royce Hall, along with other honorees. Instinctively, I hid the invitation from Mami and Papi aware that my anonymity would be challenged at such an event. I'd have to talk about where I came from and falter in English while my listeners nodded and smiled that obligatory smile of feigned understanding. They'd ask me if I was Iranian or Egyptian because they couldn't place my accent and they weren't accustomed to *Latinas* in their circle of academic excellence.

There was no doubt in my mind that this was an event to be avoided at all costs and on the day and hour of the reception I ensconced myself in the most remote corner of Powel Library to read Alicia's most recent letter. I had already planned to reward myself with it if I could get through a third of my reading for Medieval European History class. As it turned out, I finished with enough time to read Alicia's letter and respond with one of my own as well.

Dear Nora,

I'm starting to believe that God purposely partners good with bad, so we can understand that life is never simple and sometimes more confusing than a Chinese recipe for *quimbombó*.

I'm writing this letter from a small hut Tony and I share with two other couples in the heart of the countryside in

Matanzas. We've been living here for about five months ever since we were married. That's the good news; Tony and I are married, and we'll be blessed with a child in six months. Can you believe it? I'm going to be a mother, Nora! And I pray that our baby will have Tony's pure heart and strength. He's already begun building a sturdy crib from straight pieces of wood he collects in the jungle around the village. He wants to finish it as soon as he can because (and this is the bad news) he'll be going away to Africa soon. They're putting together troops of the strongest and most intelligent men for the cause in the Congo.

I love him more every day. With this life we made growing inside me, I feel I'll go crazy with love for him. Every night since I found out he was leaving I cry myself to sleep. It's almost as bad as when Papi died, that dark pain gripping the very center of my heart and squeezing it until I can hardly breath.

Tony tells me I have to be strong for the baby and that it'll sense my sadness and be born cranky and weak instead of happy and strong. I try, Nora, believe me I try to hold back the tears, but whenever I think about being alone again, I can't help myself. The other night I was glad when a small storm blew through the village so Tony wouldn't hear me sobbing again. I don't want him to think I'm weak, but I'm afraid I am. I can no longer put on that face I used to have. Remember it? I could make anyone believe I wasn't afraid of anything and that I could calm a hurricane by shaking my finger at it. All of that stubborn strength has now left me, and I feel more lonely than I ever have before.

Lola and Tía Panchita were happy to hear about the baby, but no one else in the family is, I'm afraid. They still believe a white woman has no business with a man who isn't as white as she is. It doesn't matter if he's kind and intelligent like my Tony. I thought Abuelo and Abuela would be different so I took him to Varadero to show him the house where we spent so much of our childhood, our beach and our palm trees. We knocked on the door and when Abuela saw Tony standing next to me, she slammed it in our faces, but not before saying that I shamed the whole family and the memory of my father by this marriage. I don't think Abuelo was home, but it's too painful to think of going back. I won't put Tony through that again, and I wouldn't hurt him for a lifetime of conversations with people who've turned their backs on me.

Tony's greatest hope is that he'll be invited to join the party. Even as I write these words and feel the hot wind of the jungle surrounding me, I shudder. How can I forget that the party killed my father? I don't forget and I'll never forgive them . . . yet, I see goodness here. I see people working harder than they ever have in their lives to improve a village where there was never running water. I see a medical clinic being built next to a schoolhouse, and if all goes as planned the children and adults in the village will be immunized against major diseases and be able to read in one year's time. It's happening all over Cuba.

Sometimes I wake up in the middle of the night and wonder what's happened to this world. It's as if God and the Devil are the same man depending on how you look at him, and so I try not to look too hard or else I will go back to how I was, a hopeless and pitiful woman.

The sun has gone down and Tony will be home shortly. We don't have much for dinner, a little left-over beans and rice. It's amazing how a bit of food can seem like a feast when you're sharing it with the one you love. After we eat, I'll settle myself into his arms and watch the stars come out over the treetops. If my life never changes from this moment on, I'll be the happiest woman on earth. I hope and pray that someday you can say as much and more.

Some of my new friends say I shouldn't write to you anymore. They say you and your family are traitors for leaving, but I defend you most of all. You had no choice but to leave, and now your life has changed as much as mine.

I miss you, Nora. More than ever, I miss you now. I promise you as I promise Tony to be strong. I hope you do the same. May I hear from you soon.

Alicia

# 16

"HOW DO I LOOK?" MAMI ASKED WHILE SURVEYING HERSELF IN the full-length mirror in the bedroom. "Your father said he wants me to wear something youthful."

I studied her with an objective eye. Red was always a good color on her and although she'd put on a few pounds, the overall effect was very flattering and I told her so.

"You're not just saying that?"

"You look great. Papi will love it."

For some time now, Papi had been able to budget for the occasional dinner out at a restaurant, and they'd been looking forward to this date all week while reminiscing about how it was in Cuba before the revolution. Their plans to try a small Italian place in town could hardly compare to the opulent night clubs and seaside resorts they'd frequented, but they weren't complaining.

"Do you ever think of going back?" I asked Mami as she stepped into her new red shoes. She wavered a bit and reached out toward the bed for support.

"Going back where?"

"Home, of course. To Cuba. I hear a lot of people are visiting now."

She turned to me, her eyes more fiery than her crimson dress. She kicked off her shoes and padded across the thick carpet in her stocking feet. "Cuba isn't home anymore, Nora. And those fools who go back to visit forget they were called traitors and *gusanos* when they left. They forget everything to set foot on their homeland again before they die." Her eyes spun in their sockets. "They want to look upon their green island and pretend they never left." She turned around. "I will never go back while that man is there. Do you understand me?"

"Alicia says it's not so bad. That good things are happening too."

Mami spun around again. "Alicia? What does she know?"

"She lives there. She sees it all with her own eyes."

"I'll tell you about Alicia. She's taken up with that black boy. And if that weren't bad enough, he's a Communist. He's brainwashing her to think the way he thinks and to do the things he does. Next thing you know, he'll turn her into a *Santera*. He probably already has."

"How do you know about Tony?"

"Alicia's not the only one writing letters. Your Abuela wrote all about the disgrace Alicia's made out of her life, and she and Abuelo can't wait to leave. Just pray their visas come up soon." Mami continued to mutter as she looked for a pair of earrings in her drawer. "The only person who's seen that girl lately is Tía Panchita. But everyone knows she's a little crazy and doesn't understand the problem between black and white people. Black people don't believe in interracial marriage either, let me tell you."

There was no use arguing with Mami when she got on to certain subjects and racial relations was certainly one of them. I dared not tell her that Alicia and Tony were married and expecting a baby for fear of invigorating her arsenal of criticisms.

"Is Abuelo coming too?"

"They're both planning to get out of Cuba as soon as their visas are ready."

My heart jumped at the thought of seeing Abuelo again. I pictured him with his soft smiling eyes staring out at the sea, studying the rolling surf and undercurrents to determine if it was a good day for swimming. We'd walk into the warm clear water side by side and swim with an easy pace to the platform. We'd pull ourselves up and wait until the sea has dried like flat crystals on our skin before we dive in again and head for shore. I'd hear him next to me, breathing steadily, his arms arcing in perfect smooth circles that slip in and out of the water without so much as a ripple. We'd walk back on the shore, and I'd marvel at his youthful physique. He's almost seventy, but his back is as straight as a board and his chestnut hair, barely frosting at the temples, falls full and thick on his forehead.

"That was a good swim, Abuelo."

He'd turn to me and smile with a warmth that outshines the tropical sun beating down upon our shoulders. "Yes, the water was fresh and smooth today. It was a good swim." I'd follow him back to the house where Abuela is waiting with our afternoon meal.

Just a splinter of this memory fills me with a quiet joy for what was, and a deep sadness for what will never be again.

In a crazy way, even Mami's outdated and glaring racism touches me in a tender way. I don't agree with it, but the fact that I remember her expounding those same views while standing out on our balcony in Havana with friends and family, not at all concerned that Beba was in and out freshening drinks and emptying ashtrays, makes me love it a little bit. Beba often agreed with her on the subject.

"Black folk get along better with black folk," she'd say with a swaying nod of her turbaned head. "Nobody can argue that. I don't see any reason why it should be different with white folk."

Mami applied the hairspray with quick bursts about her head. "I always thought Alicia was a little crazy," she said, her mouth taut across her face, her eyes squinting against the fumes. "She's crazier now than ever, I think." She applied her lipstick in one tidy sweep across her lips. "Keep your head on straight, Nora."


Dear Nora,

Everything you heard about childbirth is a lie. It's much worse than they say. I felt my body ripping open from the inside out and all of my parts falling out of place. After the baby was born I asked Tony to look and see if my legs were still attached, and if my navel was where it had been before, because I was sure I looked like a rag doll pulled apart by an angry gorilla. Tony laughed so hard he cried huge tears as he held Lucinda in his arms for me to see for the first time.

Isn't Lucinda a beautiful name? I think of the soft light that reflects off of the ocean when I say it. Tony says she looks like me, but there's no doubt that Lucinda is his daughter. I prayed our baby would have her father's eyes, and my prayers were answered.

Today is the kind of day I'm sure you treasure in your heart. The breeze is lifting the trees and carries a fragrant warmth you can taste, like honey and mint. The sun sparkles off every particle of dust, and the stillness reminds us that days like this should never change. We've come to stay with Tía and Lola, and sometimes I sit on the corner of the porch where I first met Tony and pretend nothing has changed. But it has, Nora.

Six families have come to live with Tía and Lola. They had to share the kitchen and the bathroom and don't even have one of the bedrooms to themselves. They lived in the little pantry room off the kitchen where Tía stored sacks of sugar before. There's just enough room for a cot and an old mattress beside it. Thank God there's a window, but the screen is broken and Tía and Lola's legs and arms were covered with mosquito bites. I couldn't stop crying when I saw them.

In less than an hour after we arrived, Tony selected two of the least dilapidated slave shacks behind the fields and was out there with an ax, a hammer, and a huge broom that he used to kill the rats before he could get to any sweeping. He said there were hundreds of them as big as little dogs, not to mention scorpions and spiders of every size. Every time he talked about it Tía and Lola gave out little screams that made him laugh like a schoolboy. I laughed too. Living in the jungle has cured me of these girly fears.

In a week, we moved into our new houses. Tía and Lola's house is right next to ours. They're simple, but clean and a definite improvement over where Tony and I spent our first year of marriage. All the windows have little shutters we can close at night to keep out most of the pests, and when I look outside I see Lola and Tía on their new porch, rocking away in their chairs.

The family that took over the pantry was so grateful for the extra space that they gave us a mattress they weren't using. Tony placed it right under the window, so when we lay together at night we can still see the stars like we did in the jungle. Tía found a roll of mosquito netting, and we fixed up our little bed so that it's actually quite pleasant. We enjoy quite a bit of privacy because the sugar cane stalks block the view from the main house and hardly anyone bothers to cross the field unless they need to go to the river, which isn't very often.

This is where I gave birth to my beautiful Lucinda and where Tony and I spent the first few weeks of our life together as a family. She slept between us as we watched the stars and with each one that appeared we whispered a new blessing for our daughter and fell asleep with such love in our hearts.

But the dream is over, Nora, at least for a while. Tony's been gone for weeks, and I don't know how much longer it'll be before he returns. I could say I miss him, but that's like saying I can live on a single breath for the whole day. Tony has taken my soul with him to Angola. It is somewhere in Africa, sailing out of his back pocket like a handkerchief forever moist with my tears. I spend most of my day praying for him and imagining what expression is playing on his face at that moment. Mostly, I imagine the look in his eyes when he wants to make love to me. His eyes caress me first with such longing that my heart flutters and my knees go weak. Then he smiles so slightly that I can't be sure it wasn't just a shadow brushing his cheeks. That's all he needs to do and I'm his, however and whenever he wants me.

I try to stay strong by reminding myself of the process of change, that with a revolution challenging the philosophy of a whole country, things always get worse before they get better. There are great agricultural plans in the works. Rivers are being damned all around the island to harness power and soon they tell us there will be prosperity for all, not just for a few like before.

There's a place for Tony and Lucinda and me in this future. We'll be together again and live in a house right on the shores of Varadero. I dream that someday you'll come visit us, and we'll sit on the sand under the palms for hours and watch our children play.

Alicia

We rarely ate dinner as a family anymore. Papi frequently arrived late from the office and sometimes I didn't get home from the university until well past seven, depending on traffic, and Marta always had something going on. I wasn't surprised, therefore, to find Mami sitting alone at the kitchen table eating left over stew from the previous night.

I took a plate from the cupboard, served myself, and sat next to her. She was moving the chunks of meat around on her plate without eating.

"I talked to Marta today," she said not looking up from her plate. "Or rather, she talked to me."

I began the painstaking task of separating the raisins from the rest of the meal and waited. Mami often complained to me about Marta. She'd describe her latest antics in colorful detail and defame her latest boyfriend who was always unworthy of her. Her latest concern was that Marta wasn't interested in continuing her education after high school at all. "Can you imagine?" Mami had said. "What's she going to do? Flip hamburgers for a living?"

I looked up at her from my plate, and I noticed her red-rimmed eyes. "What is it?"

Her tears flowed. "I don't know what your father's going to do. Marta says she's getting married to that boy—that boy with no education, and no way to support a family. She hardly knows him, for God's sake. How long have they been seeing each other? Six months?"

"I believe it's been three years, on and off."

Mami grabbed her napkin and blew her nose loudly. "Anyway, she's still a child. I don't care if the law says an eighteen-year-old is an adult. Everyone who knows Marta knows she's still a child."

"I thought you and Papi liked Eddie better than the others."

"We do. It's not that he's a bad boy, but he's a boy," Mami said leaning toward me on her elbows.

"And didn't he get accepted at USC?"

"Yes. But does he have a job? No, he doesn't. You know what Marta says? Just listen to this." Mami waved her napkin in the air. "She says that she'll support Eddie while he studies and then he'll support her when he's finished. Have you ever heard of anything so preposterous?"

"That sounds kind of nice to me."

"I can just see Marta working her fingers to the bone. Once he's got his degree hanging safely on the wall, he'll find somebody else, and leave her planted."

Mami wanted nothing less for us than the fairy tale of her own courtship and marriage. Tucked in for the night behind a cloud of mosquito netting, we'd beg her to tell us the story.

"Again?" she'd ask, laughing with pleasure. "I've told you that story three times this week."

"We want to hear it again," we'd wail.

She'd be a cameo silhouetted in the moonlight as she spoke. "I was very young when your father and I met, no more than nineteen and I was tiny, but I had a very nice shape!" We'd laugh and giggle our approval as ritual demands. "Your Abuelo made arrangements for a grand party to be held in the honor of your

Tía Griselda, who'd just returned from Europe. There were tables set on the sand and boleros sung by a trio and bright flowers everywhere. Of course, I was excited to see Tía Griselda and hear about her trip, but I was especially excited to meet the young man I heard so much about from my cousins. This young man, who's name you already know," (more giggles) "was the good friend of my cousin Alberto. He came from a well-established family in Havana. They had a beautiful house in Varadero and if that wasn't enough, he was already a rising star in the National Bank. You better believe all my cousins and I were carefully selecting what to wear that day."

"What did you wear, Mami?" we'd ask.

"I decided that whatever I wore, it had to be white. I wanted this young man to notice right away what a good color it was for me." It took us a few years to get this joke, but we'd laugh along anyway.

"When I first saw your father he was wearing a linen suit and a Panama hat as he looked out at the ocean. He didn't have to turn around for me to know he was handsome. I could already tell by his posture and the breadth of his shoulders. But when he did turn around. . . ."

Marta and I would sit up in our beds and poke our heads through the mosquito netting so we could clearly see Mami's eyes light up brighter than the moon floating outside the window.

" . . . I almost fainted."

"Why did you almost faint, Mami?" we'd ask, already having memorized the answer.

"Now, I don't just say this because he's your father, but he was the most handsome man I ever saw in my life! All my cousins fell in love with him instantly, but . . ."

"We know, we know. He only had eyes for you."

"That's right. And he didn't leave my side the entire afternoon. Every weekend after that, he invited me to go somewhere, the movies or to see a beautiful show at the Copacabana or to a magnificent dinner. Six months later, he asked your grandfather for my hand, and we were married at the Church of the Sacred

Heart, the same church where both of you were baptized. I was the happiest woman on earth and I have been ever since."

Mami would close the blinds so the moonlight entered in luminous bars across the floor and wall around us. "Now I don't want to hear any talking, just sleeping," she'd say before kissing each of us good night.

Now Mami twisted her napkin so that it fell to pieces on the kitchen table. "What am I going to tell your father?"

I stilled her unsteady hands. "Weren't you just a little over nineteen years old yourself when you got married?"

"Yes, but a girl didn't need an education like she does now. A pretty face could get you a lot in those days, but it's a different world here."

"That's exactly right," I told her. "It's a different world."


Heated arguments followed, some lasting well into the night and concluding with the slamming of doors and a few threats thrown in for good measure. "If you think we're going to spend a fortune on your wedding when we should be paying for your college education, you're crazy," Mami would yell.

"Then I'll elope," Marta countered. "And we'll move away and have many children—your grandchildren, whom you'll never know."

This was usually followed by Papi's more reasonable plea. "Now let's not talk this craziness, both of you. Let's calm down. . . ."

I was impressed with Marta's fortitude. She had to endure both Papi and Mami's onslaught for days. They made a formidable team: Mami, a volcano of emotions erupting and spewing with an irregular, but agonizing rhythm; Papi, like the constant drip of a faucet drip-dripping its pristine arguments that were collecting with the force of millions of gallons behind the Hoover Dam. I tried to intervene once or twice, but was quickly put in my place.

"Nora," Papi said, his anger controlled. "You may be in college and getting good marks, but you don't know everything yet."

I was ready to turn out the light after a particularly tense day when Marta came in and sat down next to my bed. She looked like a wounded puppy as she scrambled up next to me. We could've been in Cuba watching the stars through our bedroom window, feeling the warm breeze wrap itself around us one last time before we retreated to our tented beds.

"Thanks for trying to help with Mami and Papi."

"I'm afraid I wasn't much use."

Marta punched the bed with both fists at once. "They think we're supposed to do things their way until we die. It's my choice who I marry and when I marry him, not theirs."

"Of course it is."

"But it's so hard because as much as I want to say, 'the hell with you, we're not in Cuba anymore', I can't. It feels like I'd be cutting out my own heart." Marta buried her face in her hands and began to sob for the seventh or eighth time that day. She reminded me so much of Mami.

"Have you talked to Eddie?" I asked gently.

"I don't want to hurt him. He thinks Papi and Mami like him so much and everything . . ." Marta looked at me with her saucer brown eyes swimming in tears. "What should I do?"


Two days later, Eddie showed up at the front door wearing a suit and tie. His freckled face was flush and his hair slicked back with the broad stroke of a very wet comb. I hardly recognized him. No one had ever seen Eddie in anything but a pair of faded jeans and a football jersey. With barely a hello to anyone, he asked to speak with Papi.

Mami threw a glare at Marta who was curled up on the couch leafing through one of the many bridal magazines she enjoyed flaunting. We followed Eddie into the kitchen where Papi sat reading the evening paper.

"Excuse me, Mr. García. . . ." Eddie shoved his hands in his pockets and then pulled them out as if he touched something hot.

Papi lowered his paper. A slight redness began to glow about his ears as he surveyed the scene before him. I was afraid he might throw Eddie out of the house or explode in his face. He said nothing.

Eddie cleared his throat. His voice wavered, stringy and high. "I owe you an apology sir, and I hope that you'll accept it."

"I don't understand."

"I love your daughter, Mr. García . . . Marta." He coughed. "I asked her to marry me because I want to spend the rest of my life with her, but I didn't ask you first. I didn't realize. . . ."

I glanced at Mami who was smiling with tears streaming down her face. Papi stood up from his chair, his eyes also brimming.

"Mr. García . . . I'm asking you for permission to marry your daughter."

Marta slipped up next to me and squeezed my hand. "Thank you," she whispered.

# 17

Dear Nora,

So much has changed since my last letter to you. Some of the changes I saw coming, but other's fell on me like a wall of bricks, and each brick has inflicted its own particular pain.

Lola died last month, and Tía didn't speak for days. She just sat in her rocking chair with Lola's empty chair beside her. For a long time she wouldn't let anyone sit in it except for me when I needed to feed Lucinda. She hardly ate and never cried in front of me, but at night I heard her. She sounded like a little girl sobbing and suffering from a kind of pain she's too young to understand.

The government's plowing over many of the older sugar cane fields and planting a new kind of crop for cows. What that means is that we had to move out of our houses in the field and are now living in a little apartment in Havana, near the *malecón*. The rains have come, and they haven't stopped for days. Tony's not back yet, and the aching in my heart has spread out over my entire body so that I'm just one giant ugly sore of a person. Some days, I don't think I smile even once. Tía says my sadness is affecting my little Lucinda because she hardly smiles like other babies do. She doesn't play with little toys we make her or the brightly colored flowers I show her. All she likes to do is sit and stare at the sun.

But I wish you could've seen her the first day I took her to the sea. It was one of those days when the sun explodes in the sky and lights everything up to ten times its usual brilliance. The greens were greener, the blues were beyond heavenly, and the sand whiter than I imagine snow to be. Tía sat on the sand as I took Lucinda down to the water. As always she raised her head to the sun and would've been happy to do just that, but when we entered the water she splashed and jumped up and down with such happiness, that I cried and cried as she laughed and laughed.

I've had this secret fear, Nora, and you're the first to know. Sometimes I wonder if there's something wrong with my little Lucinda because she's not like other children. She's so serious all the time, like she's thinking these important thoughts instead of exploring with her little hands and her feet the way I see other babies do. But when I took her to the village doctor in Güines, he told me she was fine and very healthy and that I shouldn't worry, but I still do. When I saw her frolicking in the ocean, all the fears I had lifted from my heart, and I felt light enough to fly to the top of the palm trees.

I received a box of letters from Tony last week. He's been writing to me regularly but with mail backed up the way it is, they all came at once. It was like a feast for my heart, and I was most overjoyed to read that he'll be coming home soon.

You may have heard that Abuelo and Abuela's visas finally arrived. What you don't know is that tomorrow, Lucinda and I will take the train to Varadero where Abuelo will secretly meet us at the beach where we used to go swimming. I haven't been there for years. Do you think it's changed?

I must bring this letter to a close. Tía's waiting for me. She's better now, even stronger than she was before. It's as if she swallowed up all of Lola's strength so that now she's as strong as the two of them put together. We go out every afternoon before the markets close to see if we can find a few bananas or maybe a bag of rice at a lower price. I've managed to get a few things free. Tía says it's because of my looks, which still aren't too bad even though I don't have a proper dress to wear. It's almost an adventure. We take our ration books and even if it's not our day we show up and stand at the end of whatever line we find that sometimes wraps around the block. When we get to the front, (this only works with men) I ask in my sweetest voice if there's anything left. Everyone knows that even when the shelves are empty there's always something left. So, I bat my eyelashes, I toss my hair this way and that and even smile seductively. In this way I've been able to get three cans of milk, a loaf of bread, half a bag of rice and once, when this man told me that I looked like Botticelli's Venus, a whole chicken. Most days though, I don't get anything at all, and I'm afraid that soon I'll have to jump on the counter and dance like a show girl. I'm a little ashamed to admit this even to you, but hunger can lead a person to do things they would've once considered impossible.

I'm afraid that I'm not much of a revolutionary. I think too much about myself and my needs and not enough about what's good for the country. Perhaps it would've been better had you stayed and I left. But you are still here, Nora, I can feel it in your letters. You never left.

Alicia

When Abuelo and Abuela descended the steps of the plane I hardly recognized them. They looked as though they'd lost 100 pounds between them. Abuelo wore a faded suit somewhere between green and gray that was obviously made for a man twice his size and Abuela's normally plump cheeks were sunken, giving the impression that she'd lost most of her teeth. We managed not to gasp at the sight of them, but inside we were flooded with tears. For years we'd comforted ourselves with the thought that perhaps things weren't as bad in Cuba as we heard. After all, when people are missing their loved ones and adjusting to great social changes they can be prone to exaggeration, and Cubans love to tell their stories with a flare for the dramatic. We only had to take one look at the hollow sadness lurking in both Abuelo's and Abuela's eyes to know that even our worst fears couldn't compare to the reality of their suffering.

We hugged them cautiously, as if they might disintegrate in our arms if we weren't careful, and they looked upon us as if we were strangers. Was it the shock of it all? Was it like opening your eyes and realizing that the dream and the nightmare have suddenly reversed?

When we got home, Abuelo sat on the white couch and moved his rickety hands up and over the soft cushions. He gazed about at the art on the walls and stared at Marta and me with the same vacant appreciation.

"We missed you, Abuelo," we said. But this old man sitting in front of us wasn't my Abuelo who taught me how to swim. Those weren't the tranquil eyes that surveyed the ocean, the solid arms that cut easily and steadily through the crystal blue waters. Abuelo had sloughed off his skin like a snake and sent the body on the plane without him.

Abuela picked at the cheese plate on the coffee table and chattered nonstop like an angry bird, her boney ankles crossed and her panty hose rolled down below her knees because of her bad circulation. The red crease across her forehead created by her hair net turned redder as she talked about the plane trip, how it pitched and how she feared Fidel himself would shoot the plane out of the sky just because he could.

For days they wandered about our house as though searching for something they weren't sure they wanted to find. It wasn't unusual for Abuelo to walk into a room and just stand there watching us, as if he couldn't be sure whether we were real people or ghosts playing with his imagination. They didn't like to go out much, and Abuela contented herself with making Cuban dishes she hadn't been able to cook for years due to the lack of ingredients.

One evening she presented us with a giant roasted leg of pork on a silver platter. She placed it in the center of the dinning room table, sat in her chair, and began to weep.

"What is it, Mama?" Papi asked.

"For years I prayed that one day I could cook a leg of pork like this for my children again. Now I'm crying with gratitude. Forgive me."

The pork was unusually delicious that night, the way we remembered it in Cuba. Abuelo said it was so good because it was seasoned with our tears.

Summer turned into autumn, and Abuelo began raking the leaves on our front lawn in the afternoons. He marveled, as I had once, at the falling leaves, the russet and yellow carpet crunching beneath our feet. Abuelo told me that raking the leaves and smelling the earth on his hands reminded him that he still belonged to the land even though he was so far from his home.

"Are you sorry you left, Abuelo?"

He laughed a little at this question. He was looking much more how I remembered him, robust and confident, and he didn't slow his brisk pace with the rake. "I'd be lying if I told you that I didn't go to sleep every night with the sounds and smells of my country pulling at me like a stubborn dream. But I'll tell you this, it's much easier to sleep with the pain of nostalgia in your heart than the pain of hunger in your belly."

We played dominoes after dinner almost every night. I looked forward to this ritual and imagined we were sitting in the porch at Varadero gazing out at the Caribbean rather than on the redwood deck overlooking the valley filled with a sea of smog. It was at these moments, when we were alone, that I dared ask him about Alicia and Lucinda.

"Oh yes, we met at the beach," Abuelo whispered, casting a wary eye over his shoulder in case Abuela should hear him. "Alicia is as lovely as ever, but thin like everybody else. She's doing better than most," he added, when he saw my concern. "And Lucinda is a beautiful child. Her eyes are more captivating than the ocean and sky put together, but so sad. I've never seen anything quite like it. When I held her and tried to make her smile, she looked through me straight to my heart." He shook his head sadly and turned his attention back to the dominoes.

"Do you think Alicia will ever leave Cuba?"

He clucked his tongue with certainty. "She still believes in the revolution, that child. And Tony's a good man. He saved her after Carlitos died, but he brainwashed her in the process. She's forgotten all about her father and her mother who's still locked up in the hospital. She doesn't seem to see the country falling to pieces around her. I don't know if it's the revolution or the obsession she has for her husband, but there's no talking to her about emigrating. She looks at you in much the same way Lucinda does, and says she'll never leave her home."

The North Campus Café was a crowded blur of commotion, but I managed to feel peaceful in the midst of such frantic activity. As always, I sat in the far corner table and sipped my coffee until almost nine o'clock, depending on the time of my first class. It was a strange place for an education major to spend time because all my classes were at the extreme opposite end of the campus, but that's precisely why I preferred this spot. It was a small reminder that I had choices and space and freedom.

I'd been on a couple of dates since starting at the university but managed to end the exchanges efficiently enough. Perhaps Sister Margarita knew what she was talking about all those years ago. It seemed that the religious life was a pleasant one with few worries. Mami and Papi might be proud to have a daughter committed to the church, Mami could write to the family and brag as if now her place in heaven was secured.

"Nora, is it you?"

Startled, I spilled coffee over the table, creating a hot water-fall onto my jeans in the process.

"Oh no, I'm sorry . . . I . . ." Jeremy rushed to grab a handful of napkins from the dispenser, and I stared after him with hot coffee dripping off my thighs. Time suddenly spun around and did a flip. Jeremy was no longer real to me, but a legend from some distant time and place. Now here he was blotting the table with a wad of napkins, laughing, and shaking his head just like I remembered.

I placed my hand on his shoulder "Jeremy . . . you're here. I mean, what are you doing here?" A flutter in my throat made it difficult to swallow, let alone speak.

He laughed again and gave me a warm and friendly hug. "Nora, my God it's good to see you." He held me out at arm's length. "You look different than I remember you . . . but the eyes are yours." He gave my shoulders a squeeze. "May I sit with you awhile?"

"Of course."

I moved my books off of the table and blushed when our knees touched by accident like in high school. He explained that he was considering an assistant professorship in the anthropology department. He'd been traveling for the last couple of years, mostly in South and Central America.

"I dare say my Spanish is as good as your English now," he bragged with an impish grin.

"Show me," I challenged in Spanish.

Jeremy's eyes sparkled, and he began to chatter about the weather and about the different countries he'd visited and his hope to return soon. I listened politely and nodded with genuine approval at his fluency and accurate accent. Some words he spoke almost like a native.

"I was looking for you," he said, reverting back to English.

"You were?"

Jeremy finished his coffee and tossed the empty cup in a nearby trash can. "About a year and a half ago. I saw your name on the list of students invited to a reception of some sort, but you didn't show up." He looked past me as if trying to remember a dream, then shook the fog out of his head and laughed. I held my breath and waited for my life to change in the instant it took for his eyes to flicker and his chest to fall. "I remember that reception well."

"Really? Why?"

"It was just a few days before I got married." Long seconds passed before I was able to congratulate him and smile, but it was far from a convincing smile and best attempted while sipping coffee and hiding behind my cup. "Any kids?"

"No, not yet. Jane has a few health problems. She came down with malaria on our travels and it's weakened her a bit."

I tried to express my sympathy, while concealing the fact that I was quite pleased his wife's name was Jane and not Cindy.

"Do you have a class now?" he asked.

"Yes, I'm late."

"Come on then," he said grabbing my backpack and making a show out of how heavy it was. "I'll walk you."

We chatted about academic life and how much he preferred travel and field work to the office. He asked about my family and my studies. I told him I was planning to be a teacher, and he was delighted to hear this. There was so much more I wanted to say, but we arrived to the lecture hall and he handed over my backpack. "You didn't mention if you were married or anything like that."

As he waited for me to respond, I felt the spinning truth of the moment. It could be years before I saw him again, if ever. I had to seize the moment. What would Alicia do if Tony were about to slip through her fingers? She'd throw herself at his feet and declare her undying love for him. She wouldn't care if he was married and had children and grandchildren even. She'd just look him straight in the eye and say what she had to say.

"I'm not married," I answered.

"Of course, I forget how young you are. There's a seriousness about you that fools me sometimes. It always did."

"My mother married my father when she was barely nineteen. I'm older than that."

Jeremy nodded politely and took a step back. "That's right. I remember you told me before." He raised his hand to say good-bye.

"Maybe we could have coffee again when . . . when you're not too busy," I blurted out.

His face lit up. "I'd love to, Nora."

When I got in, I found Mami and Abuela in the kitchen hunched over their coffee in the classic gossip pose. Mami straightened up. "Have you heard from Alicia lately?"

"Not for a while."

Mami nodded her head in her solemn all-knowing way. Abuela folded and unfolded her napkin and added more sugar to her coffee, her eyes dripping with unspoken emotion.

"What is it?" I asked.

"We called your Tía María in Cuba today. She told us she had a visit from Tía Panchita recently. She lives with Alicia you know, and her baby . . ."

"What's wrong with Alicia?"

"It's not Alicia exactly, it's her baby. I forget her name . . ."

"What's wrong with Lucinda?"

"They're not exactly sure, but they're fairly certain the baby is blind. They don't know why . . ."

I felt dizzy and sat down at the kitchen table. A heated anger surged within me when I thought of the way Alicia had been ostracized by the family for marrying Tony, the suffering she had endured, and now this. I pictured her wandering the dilapidated streets of Havana carrying her blind baby on her hip, looking for a left over crust of bread that some shopkeeper might give her for a smile. I winced at my own helpless frustration. It could take weeks for her to receive my next letter.

Abuela shook her head sadly. "I knew nothing good would come of this marriage. It wasn't meant to be, and when things aren't meant to be and you do them anyway, this is what happens."

I swallowed my rage. I couldn't be disrespectful to Abuela, but at that moment I felt as though I was being forced to be nice to Hitler himself. My jaw clenched as tears pushed through. I could burst, I could burst from the sheer inability to move.

I hadn't noticed Abuelo walk up behind us, and I didn't know how long he'd been listening, but no doubt he was already well aware of the news. Abuelo never raised his voice. His disposition was as sunny as the tropical skies he'd lived under for most of his life, but when he spoke this time he seemed a different man. "Don't talk nonsense, old woman," he shot out. "You're talking about your granddaughter and great granddaughter. Don't forget that."

Abuela was about to protest, but he shot her down again. "You turned your back on your own blood and for what? Because you don't believe white people should marry black people. When I told my family in Spain that I wanted to marry a Cuban girl, they tried to talk me out of it. They wanted me to marry a Spanish girl from my village. What if I'd listened to them?"

"It's not the same thing, Antonio. You can't compare it." Abuela waved her hand in the air like she was swatting a fly. "Black people and white people shouldn't be in the same family. It's not natural, and black people feel exactly the same way."

Abuelo crossed his arms. "Not natural? When I held that child in my arms, it felt like the most natural thing in the world."

Abuela's mouth dropped open. "You saw her? Even after you promised me you wouldn't?"

Abuelo stood tall and proud, every bit the man I remembered at Varadero and at the airport all those years ago: "I did, and I don't mind telling you that Lucinda is the most beautiful of us all."

# 18

WE'D BEEN MEETING FOR WEEKS.

Jeremy arrived at eight o'clock Wednesday mornings without fail and insisted on buying my coffee even though I protested. For an instant, when he approached balancing the tray with two large coffees and his briefcase slung over one arm, I could pretend he was mine. I wouldn't dare pretend when he sat so close. At those moments I had to concentrate on remaining friendly and light, and avoid looking at him for too long for fear that my eyes would turn into two adoring hearts.

Our favorite subject for conversation was Cuba. Jeremy had always wanted to visit, but hadn't been able to because of the travel restrictions. I spoke freely about how going back was a forbidden topic with my family. This was the unspoken rule because the suffering and regret such talk would bring was too much for Mami and Papi to bear. Oh, we could talk about the beauty of the beaches, the unsurpassed quality of the seafood, and shopping at El Encanto. It was the sense of having lost our souls we had to keep quiet about, the pain of our transplanted roots craving their native soil. Nobody else would probably ever notice because we Cubans were so good at adapting and accommodating, but I told Jeremy that if you looked really close, you could see it, like invisible Scotch tape on a beautifully wrapped package, or the strings on Peter Pan when he's flying across the stage.

"Why can't you go back?" Jeremy asked.

I pulled my backpack up to my lap and zipped it closed. It was getting late. "My parents wouldn't hear of it. They vowed they would never set foot on Cuban soil until Castro was gone."

Jeremy placed his hand on my arm. "We're not talking about your parents, Nora. Did you make any promises like that?"

"I guess not."

"Well, then."

"It would destroy them if I went against their wishes . . . I know it's hard for you to understand."

Jeremy removed his hand from my arm leaving a cold spot that missed his touch. "It just seems to me that if you want to go back and see your cousin who's going through such a hard time right now, it shouldn't be the end of the world."


By our third meeting, I was in love with Jeremy all over again. And every day, ten times a day, when my mind invariably wandered to him, I reminded myself that he was a married man.

I contented myself with our once a week coffee meetings. Starting Monday I agonized over what to wear, how to do my hair, what book to be reading when he approached with his tray of coffee. When we went our separate ways, I replayed every second of our time together and filtered each word that came out of his mouth, every subtle expression on his face for the possibility, however fleeting, that he might consider me as something more than a friend who reminded him of his fascination with the Latino culture.

My life revolved around Wednesday mornings from 8:00 to 9:00 A.M. And I was quite happy with it.

\* \* \*

Dear Nora,

Forgive me for not having written in so long. I received your last letter, and it's given me unimaginable comfort during these trying times. I thank you with all my heart for offering to help, but I don't know what you or anyone could do now. After many nights of endless tears and self-torture, I've come to accept that I can only wait and see what happens with my precious Lucinda. I put her name on the waiting list at the Havana Eye Clinic.

In the meantime, I try to be Lucinda's eyes. When we go to the beach I describe the sand and the ocean and the palms that sweep the sky clean. I've learned how to keep my voice clear and bright while tears stream down my face. How to find the words to describe the beauty of our home? I struggle with this every day and feel like I'm trying to paint a masterpiece with a box of broken crayons. But Lucinda appreciates my effort; I know she does because she smiles more these days, and she tells me she loves me, as she touches my face and feels for my smile. Everyday she calls for her father and asks when he'll return. For now I can only hope that soon she'll feel his arms around her and hear his deep reassuring voice telling her how much he loves her. Tony knows nothing. As far as he's concerned, our daughter is a normal and healthy three-year-old who's saying the most adorable things as she runs around discovering her world.

Instead of looking forward to seeing Tony again, I worry. I can no longer imagine his joyful face at the sight of his wife and daughter, but the horrible pain I know only too well. As strong as he is, I'm afraid this will destroy him. I can only hope that the love we have for each other will help him through this as it has helped me.

The only time I feel free from my worries is when I go to the church on the corner of our street. Perhaps you remember it, La Iglesia del Carmelo with a little fountain in front where we used to throw coins as children and make our wishes. Abuela would scold us and say we shouldn't make wishes to a fountain when we could be praying to God. I go to this place every day. It's always empty, except for a couple of elderly ladies who sit in the shadows with their veils, lighting candles off to one side. Mass hasn't been said for years.

Hunger is growing, and many people have become starving hawks who take any opportunity to strike for a meal. I try to watch out for the desperate ones and most of all avoid becoming one of them myself. Desperation steals up in the night like a disease and creeps into the heart. The most honorable of human values is crushed under the weight of it, and when it's taken complete possession of a person you smell it on them, like the putrid filth that collects in the alleys of Havana. This filth flows out to the streets and collects in the gutters. If you're not careful you can step in it and carry it home on your shoes. I know it breeds most in the hearts of those who've lost all hope in the revolution and the ideals of change. Tony reminds me in his letters that we have to remain strong and understand that even for a single person to change, it takes an enormous amount of effort, so for a whole country to change . . . well, you see where I'm going with this.

I'm closing my eyes now with happiness in my heart and thoughts of you and Jeremy finding a way to make the love you have for each other grow. I'm not advocating adultery, but I believe all things happen for a reason, and I hope the reason Jeremy is in your life is made known to you and him very soon. I pray for you every day.

Alicia


Marta and Eddie announced they were going to have a baby at about the same time I began my last year of college. Jeremy was fascinated to hear how Mami went to Marta's new house almost every day to help with the details of her home and her preparations for motherhood. And I almost began to get used to the fact that I was in love with a married man, but he rarely spoke of his wife. The only thing I knew was that her name was Jane, they'd met in Peru, and that she suffered from bouts of malaria. I believed he was trying to spare me painful details, but he didn't understand that I'd learned to manage my secret obsession for him very nicely. Whereas before it might've been painful, now I wanted to know everything about him . . . even his choice for a spouse and all that went along with it.

Even so, I managed to meet somebody else. He was a business associate that Papi invited to Marta and Eddie's house-warming party. His name was Greg, but Papi called him Gregorio. He was nice-looking with reddish hair, and a hard worker with a good future, which Mami and Papi liked most of all. What I liked best was that I could look him straight in the eyes without blushing, as I could never do with Jeremy.

During the whole party, Abuela watched me talk to him. But her eyes were far away, and I know she was thinking about how it would be if we were still in Cuba. I don't know if it was the wine, or the bougainvilleas blooming outside the window, but it was as if we'd never left.

We were at a garden party at the ocean's edge, not quite on the sand, but close enough to see the breeze sweeping translucent swirls out to sea. Everyone was vibrant with laughter and warmed by a good-natured sun that knows its place in the blue expanse above.

The surf didn't pound, it was the tempered beating of our hearts. The wind didn't blow, it was the resonating essence of a lilting flute. All our worries dissolved in rainy intermissions that evaporated up to heaven three or sometimes four times a day.

My hair was pulled back in a sleek bun at the nape of my neck. I wore coral lipstick and my face required no other adornment. I was not obsessed with being beautiful. I preferred to languish in the unequaled feeling of belonging to the beauty that surrounded me.

Greg poured me another glass of wine, and I knew I must resist the temptation of another daiquiri. A lady does not drink too much. Mami and Abuela have always told me that a lady must be able to think on her feet and balance on slender heels while strolling, arm in arm with the man of her destiny.

While I was imagining all of this, Greg asked me out to dinner. We began to go out most weekends and sometimes during the week as well. I had no choice, but to break a few coffee dates with Jeremy, saying I had to study for an unexpected quiz, or some such excuse. Although I knew I shouldn't be, I was afraid to tell him about Greg, but soon I knew I'd have to find the courage.

I saw Jeremy stretched out on a warm patch of grass with two coffees steaming next to him. But he hadn't seen me yet, and I thought about walking away before he did. I was embarrassed for him to see me, not in my usual jeans and sandals, but wearing a new coordinated outfit with matching shoes and bag. I was planning to meet Greg after class for a drive along the coast, and dinner at our favorite seafood restaurant. He was expecting me to be at the university entrance in five minutes.

I was stepping away when Jeremy turned and spotted me. Now I had no choice but to join him, and I felt my cheeks flush as I approached. He gave my new look a curious glance, but said nothing as he turned his face back to the sun.

I patted the grass to make sure it was dry and sat down next to him. He handed me my coffee, but we didn't say anything for several minutes. This was customary for us. We were like a couple that had grown comfortable with our silences over the years.

My eyes swept over him and I tried not to notice that he was still beautiful to me, nor did I want to feel the profound sense of belonging I felt when I was near him. I cleared my throat, breaking the warm buzz between us. "I'm afraid I don't have much time today."

His eyes fluttered and he grunted his acknowledgement low in his throat. I knew that sound well. It usually made the lower half of my body grow warm and tingly, but I fought the sensation this time, and tightened my stomach.

"I have a date," I said. "And I need to be at the other side of campus in five minutes."

He sat up slowly and rubbed off the blades of grass that were stuck to his palms. He hardly looked at me, when he spoke. "You should probably go then."

I stood up and backed away as though it were some kind of trap. "Yes, I probably should."

He glanced up at me, his eyes kind and mild as I retreated. "Have a good time, Nora."


Dear Nora,

My angel is home! It's only been two weeks since Tony returned, but already our life has changed in amazing ways. He found us an apartment two blocks from the sea. In the middle of the night we hear the waves like distant sighs. And there's so much more to eat. He brought boxes of dried milk and bananas with him that we trade for meat and toilet paper. You have no idea how long it's been since we've had toilet paper. I think it's far too fine for its intended purpose, so I'm saving it to barter with later if necessary.

Lucinda loves bananas just like we did and she eats one every day now. The very sun shines brighter than it used to, Nora, and color is returning to a city that was fading under its glare.

I heard him before I saw him, asking the neighbors which room was ours. I bolted out the door leaving Lucinda spinning on her feet and so confused about my sudden departure that she started to cry, and Lucinda hardly ever cries.

I saw the outline of his broad shoulders coming up the stairs. His eyes were searching for me, wild and hungry with the pain of too much loneliness. I ran into his arms and we clutched at each other's hair and clothes, and I pressed against him so hard that I almost disappeared into him and the tears poured out of my eyes and every part of me it seemed. If that moment had lasted for more than a few minutes I probably would've died from too much happiness. Is there such a thing?

I never saw Tony cry before, not really cry, until he looked upon his daughter with the knowledge that she couldn't look back. For several days he held her like she was an infant and not a three-year-old little girl. He kept gazing into her face and passing his hands across her eyes over and over. I know what this is. I used to do it myself hoping she'd blink at just the right moment and give me that little bit of hope to comfort me for a couple of hours until I was forced to accept her blindness all over again.

Almost every night at sunset, Tony and I go down to the beach. We lie on the sand without clothes, and it's the most wonderful feeling. The breeze is cool, but the sand is still warm from the sun. We play like children, naked and free and we make love the same way until we are too tired to move. Now in our new apartment, we fall asleep in each other's arms like we used to. To open my eyes and see him by the open window fixing our morning coffee is like waking up in heaven every day.

Just yesterday, I sneaked away to the church again. I had to go back to thank God for answering my prayers and bringing my husband back safe. I lit a small white candle at the altar like I always do and stayed for only a few minutes watching the flame. It gives me such peace to see it waver and dance in the darkness. I have only one prayer left: that Lucinda's blindness be cured. God heard me, because at that moment the windows lit up and filled the church with streams of colored light when it had been dark for more than an hour.

Don't laugh; you know I'm always looking for miracles and if they don't find me, I'll find them, even if they're in the headlights of a passing car.

Alicia

# 19

SUMMER WAS ONCE AGAIN UPON US, AND MAMI HAD BEEN bustling about the house with nervous anxiety for almost a week. Visitors were coming from Miami and it was important that the house be in perfect order. She hired a window cleaner and carefully selected blooms from the garden to arrange throughout the house. The bathroom was equipped with new brightly colored guest towels and bowls of potpourri. Mami and Abuela cooked into the night making *croquetas* and stuffed potato balls, and Papi readied the pit outside to roast the pork.

Mami was at her happiest when preparing for guests. She'd thrown dinner parties as Papi advanced in his career and she enjoyed those, but with Cuban friends and family she rolled up her sleeves and dove into the process with abandon. She played her favorite *danzón* on the stereo and gyrated her hips to the music as she dusted. She could be persuaded to have a glass or two of wine and enjoy the sunset out on the porch even though it was Wednesday night and there was still so much to do before the guests arrived.

"Do you remember your cousin, Juan?" Mami asked me.

"Of course. I was fifteen when we left. I remember everything."

"He's an attorney in Miami. Quite successful I hear and he's coming out with his mother, your Tía Carlota, for some kind of conference."

Mami proceeded to inform us of all the recent gossip about the family. I listened with half an ear while Papi read the paper not even bothering to appear interested. Mami spoke vehemently about Juan's foolishness for having joined a Cuban Brotherhood association aimed at hastening Castro's demise. "I don't want him talking about that nonsense in my presence. All it does is make me upset and get my hopes up for nothing."

Juan and Tía Carlota showed up that Friday in a black limousine from the airport. Tía Carlota wore the Cuban uniform of success—an elegant beige linen suit with a designer handbag and pounds of gold jewelry dripping from her hands and neck. Her red-toned hair (I remembered her as a brunette) was stiffened with hairspray and it almost scratched my cheek when I gave her the obligatory kiss on the cheek in greeting. Juan was twice the size I remembered him, contained within the tailored perfection of an expensive gray suit. But he had the same flush about him that I remembered when he spoke about his life and his work with the Cuban Brotherhood.

Mami put hands over her ears, although still smiling. "Please, Juany, I don't want to know."

Tía Carlota shot Juan a stiff look and he obliged as the good son that he was. It was no secret that he took care of his mother (his father had died of cancer soon after exile) and that she'd been able to resume if not surpass the lifestyle she'd had in Cuba because of him. Even so, she hadn't lost her authority as a mother.

We sat in the living room amongst the blooms of the garden, sipping wine and nibbling on Cuban delicacies when Juan leaned over, straining his impressive girth, to speak only to me. He addressed me in Spanish, and I realized how long it had been since I'd spoken my native tongue with someone of my generation. Marta and I had been speaking English with each other more and more, and now I spoke Spanish only to my parents and grandparents. Speaking Spanish with Juan made it feel as though what we had to say was more important somehow.

"Have you heard from Alicia?" he asked.

"We keep in touch through letters."

"Then you know she's a Communist and that she married some Communist who's literally brainwashed her."

"I know she loves Tony very much. They have a daughter, Lucinda."

"I heard she's blind."

"They're hoping for an appointment at an eye clinic in Havana."

Juan popped a potato ball in his mouth and chuckled as he chewed. It seemed like he was swallowing all joy and hope along with the potato. "They'll never get in there," he said and took a swig of wine to clear his throat. "It's well known that the better clinics serve the needs of foreign dignitaries and high-ranking party members. Ordinary citizens aren't at the top of the waiting list."

I didn't know what to say. Juan was confident about his information. He lived in Miami, and with his ear to the ground and his heart fully engaged in the struggle, was steeped in the latest news. We were removed from such concerns in California where Latino issues focused on problems with migrant workers from Mexico and bilingual education in the inner city. I wanted to argue otherwise, but I had no ammunition and Juan had quite an arsenal available to him.

"You can help her, Nora."

"How?"

"Convince her to apply for a visa. I'm sure I can do something on this end if she does."

"She won't leave, Tony. She won't leave Cuba."

We could've been in Tía María's backyard. "Just play one game of baseball with me Nora," he'd say, squeezing his chubby hands together as if in fervent prayer.

"You always throw the ball too hard," I'd respond.

"I promise I won't this time." He'd toss his glove at me and I'd try it on. It was about three sizes too big, but I'd give in because I was the closest thing Juan had to a male companion at the moment and because I knew he wouldn't give up until I did. We'd play in the yard until the shadows lengthened and engulfed us, until I could no longer ignore Mami's complaints about getting dirty, or until Alicia came and lured me into something more interesting.

"She's the only one of us left over there," Juan added, perhaps remembering that I always gave into his pleas.

"She is?"

"Of our group she is. The only others who stayed were the old people."

"Like Tía Panchita."

Juan furrowed his fleshy brow and glanced at his mother who'd been listening to our conversation without meaning to look like she was. She mirrored his confused expression and turned back to Mami who was rearranging the *croquetas* and potato balls on the tray.

"Tía María said she'd call you," Carlota said.

"About what?" Mami asked, dropping a potato ball on her foot.

"Panchita died two weeks ago. They say she died while smoking a cigar even though the doctor told her she couldn't smoke cigars, and that the best thing that happened to her was the shortage of tobacco in Cuba."

Mami's eyes watered as she leaned back, with the potato ball still resting on the tip of her brown pumps. "May she rest in peace."

"She was a good woman," Tía Carlota added with a solemn nod of her stiff auburn head.

"She cared about the black people like they were her own flesh and blood."

"Sometimes to the detriment of her own people . . ."

"If she'd guided Alicia differently she'd be free and not in the grip of this communist lie . . ." Juan offered.

"They say that before the revolution the plantation would've gone much better if she hadn't given her black friends control of it."

"They say Lola's the one who got her smoking every day like

she did and that Panchita spent money she didn't have to maintain their cigar habits."

Mami picked the potato ball off her foot with a napkin and carefully wrapped it up. "She may not have been very smart, but Panchita was a good woman."

"She was a good woman," everyone chorused.

The doorbell rang and Mami opened the door to find a smiling Greg standing on the threshold. Mami proudly introduced him as my *novio* which I still wasn't too sure I liked hearing. After a robust handshake with cousin Juan he sat in the chair next to me. Although we'd had sex a half dozen times already, he wouldn't dare kiss me or even place a hand on me in the presence of my family. I ignored him, still upset and confused about Tía Panchita's death.

I stood up, knocking a glass of red wine off the table and onto the white carpet. Mami gasped and Greg hurriedly began to blot the stain with his napkin.

"Tía Panchita was a great woman. She was the only one who didn't turn her back on Alicia when she married Tony," I declared to a bewildered group.

"Calm down, Nora," Mami said.

"You're criticizing Tía Panchita because she helped black people, because she loved Lola better than most people love their own sisters and brothers . . . This is why the revolution happened in the first place."

Mami stood up. "You don't know what you're talking about, foolish girl."

Tía Carlota cleared her throat. "Maybe we should leave, Regina. Nora's upset."

Mami held out a firm hand in her direction. "You're not going anywhere," she said, taking a step toward me. "You watch what you say, young lady. While you're in this house, you show respect."

I marched out the front door and heard Greg's strained explanation as I left. "She's very stressed with her job hunt . . . She's been getting upset easily . . ." I could picture his face, red as the stain on the carpet he was blotting.

"She's spoiled," Mami said. "She thinks she's smarter than everybody."

"She definitely has the García smile," Papi said, peering into the crib.

"Don't be silly, José. She can't smile yet."

"I'm telling you, I saw her smile just a minute ago when you weren't looking."

We'd grown accustomed to Mami and Papi's good-natured arguing since the baby was born. It seemed their entry into grandparenthood had momentarily caused them to forget about how to get along. Mami could talk of nothing else but the baby and how Marta was doing and whether or not she and Eddie were dealing well with parenthood. Anyone would think that Marta and Eddie had contracted an exotic and incurable disease that required everyone's constant vigilance. And for the first time in years, Papi was coming home early from work so he could accompany Mami on her daily visit before the baby was put down for the night. We'd hear him whistling a tune as he came in through the back door with a smile from ear to ear.

But Mami's joy over Marta's domestic good fortune wasn't enough to distract her from the disappointing developments in my life.

"I don't understand why you let that nice young man go, Nora. He had a good job and very decent sensibilities. Even more than that, I'd say he was quite in love with you."

I wondered if Mami was suffering from premature dementia when she brought the subject up as if we hadn't already talked about it at least twenty times. Several weeks earlier I'd spoken to Mami and Papi separately and explained that I was no longer seeing Greg. Papi accepted the news with a blend of surprise and curiosity and then made a simple statement that reflected his acquired American ideals more convincingly than his evolving preference for American football over baseball. "As long as you're happy, Nora. That's what your mother and I want for you more than anything." He thought for a moment. "If you haven't told your mother, I suggest you do so as soon as possible. She's grown quite fond of Greg."

Mami stared at me as if I'd told her I'd become an astronaut and was leaving for the moon the next morning. "Was this your decision?"

"Yes. I just didn't feel comfortable with him, Mami." I could've told her that his touch had begun to repulse me and that the last time we made love I found myself thinking about a back pain I'd developed and the dreadful fact that I'd plucked out my first gray hair the day before.

She smoothed out Papi's shirt on the ironing board, but the crease between her brows deepened and began to glow pink. "I hope you thought carefully about this. Greg's a good man. He has a good job and a very promising career and you can't find that every day you know."

"I know, Mami."

"And he understood things . . ."

"Yes, Mami."

"About our culture and respect and . . . I'm telling you right now, I think you're making a big mistake." She began to iron furiously. "Oh, I know the American way. Parents aren't supposed to interfere in their children's lives. They're just supposed to smile and nod and say, 'That's fine dear. Whatever makes you happy dear.'"

"Actually, that's exactly what Papi said."

Mami stopped ironing and glared at me. "Your father's a man, and he doesn't understand that the older a woman gets the fewer her choices."

"For goodness sake, I'm barely twenty-four-years old."

She nodded and resumed her ironing as though she'd been ironing for twenty years without a break and couldn't possibly stop now. "When I was twenty-four, I was married, I had two children, a house, and a servant to help." She looked back up at me from her task, her eyes round and accusing. "What do you have?"

"A college education."

"A lot of good it's done you," she muttered. "You don't even know a good man when you see one."

Dear Nora,

I'm sure you must know by now that Tía Panchita is gone. I thank God that Tony was here when it happened because I know I wouldn't have survived it alone. Before she died, I took her to Güines one last time. The bus was three hours late and the road had so many pot holes I thought it was going to fall apart piece by piece, but Tía didn't notice. She just looked out the window through her big glasses and sighed the whole way there. It actually seemed she was getting better with every mile we got closer.

When we finally arrived at the house, she didn't say a word. The roof over the porch had partially caved in and crushed most of the front stairs. I tried to talk her out of climbing up, but she insisted so we sat on a crate as I prayed the roof wouldn't fall in and kill us both. We looked out upon the forest, the only thing that hasn't changed.

She'd hardly spoken all day, but at that moment she said that this was the only place she could look out at the world and understand it. "When I sit here in my place, I know who I am," she said.

Later she tried to persuade me to let her spend the night right there on the porch. It took a lot of arguing, but finally she understood it was a bad idea or maybe she was too tired to keep arguing. She fell asleep on the bus, and when we got back to Havana she was gone.

I still go to church when I can. I haven't seen the elderly ladies for months, so I sit in the corner by myself and pray until my heart runs dry. Mostly I pray that Lucinda will be given her appointment at the eye clinic soon. Tony tells me it'll be any day now because party members have priority and he's been invited to join. He believes in the revolution as much as he ever did. He reads his books and listens to Castro's speeches on the radio as if it were food that grows scarcer every day. He wants me to read to him sometimes when he's tired, but I hardly listen to the words coming out of my own mouth.

Before, Tony could say things had to get worse before they got better, and I believed. He could say capitalism is the religion of the rich and powerful, and the pure heart of socialism will triumph in the end, and I believed. He continues to say these things and I listen because I know he needs me to listen, but I no longer believe.

We walk along the wide boulevard of the *malecón* every Sunday with Lucinda between us. I look into the eyes of others doing the same, walking past buildings that were once sparkling and beautiful and are now like enormous tombs haunted by hungry rats. The sun has become a bare glaring lightbulb that accentuates the ugliness of our lives. Only at night does pretending hold any comfort. I look at the lights blinking on the *malecón* and remember. Was it all a dream, Nora? Did we ever laugh together on the beach without a care in the world, certain our lunch would be ready with plenty left over for the servants to take home? I could feed my family for a month with the food I left on my plate. I could live for a day on the crumbs that fell to the floor.

Forgive me for complaining, but one of the few comforts I have left is to know that you'll read these words and understand me as no one else can. I know you're thinking that I've become one of the desperate people, but I assure you my sadness no longer consumes me like it used to. Strangely enough, it has become my strength as it reminds me that I can no longer get lost in fanciful dreams if I hope to survive. I don't know if I'm growing up or simply getting tired. Perhaps a bit of both.

Before I close, I must let you know how proud I am of you for breaking things off with Gregorio. It took courage that your mother doesn't understand. Your heart will guide you to your destiny, and you must write me soon and tell me where it leads.

Alicia

I found a job teaching first graders in East L.A. who were just learning English. I loved the children and kept myself busy with work and school and spending as much time with my niece as I could. Time passed quickly with barely a thought about men or dating. I forced myself to accept a couple of dinner invitations, including one from a friend of Eddie who Marta insisted was a match made in heaven just for me, but I declined second invitations from them both.

Marta and Mami warned me that I shouldn't be so picky, but I didn't feel I was being picky at all. I was simply waiting for what felt right. Waiting for hope to find me as I always had. Once again my thoughts turned to Sister Margarita's invitation so long ago. Perhaps she possessed the wisdom to look into my future and see the romantic calamities I might avoid if I only followed her holy example. Perhaps Sister Margarita had been right all along.

My academic efforts had always proven successful, and by the fall I was beginning my preparations for graduate school. It was necessary for me to return to the University on a few occasions to gather documents in order to complete my application. I was surprised by how good it felt to be back, and I was even more surprised to find myself standing outside of Jeremy's office door one afternoon, holding two cups of steaming coffee. I could hear him on the phone, his calm voice trying to reassure one of his students who was obviously unhappy with his grade. I didn't wait for him to finish his call before knocking and peeking in. He seemed surprised to see me and stumbled a bit as he found a way to end the call. I placed the coffees on his desk, and sat down next to him. We gazed at each other smiling and not speaking for almost one full minute.

"How's it been going?" he finally asked.

"Fine. And you?"

"Good, good."

We smiled a while longer and then he shook himself and began to rearrange some papers on his desk. "Let me guess," he said. "You came by to personally invite me to your wedding."

I laughed, strangely delighted that he should say such a thing. "What makes you think that?"

"I got the distinct impression you were involved with somebody and on your way to blissful matrimony last time I saw you. How long has it been?"

"Almost two years . . . I think."

"A lot can happen in two years," he said still fussing with his papers and hardly looking at me.

"Yes, well . . . I'm definitely not getting married. I may never get married."

Jeremy folded his arms and nodded slowly, but his dimples flickered as though he was trying not to laugh. He sat back in his chair, still studying me.

"What's so funny?"

He shook his head. "You sound so American when you say that."

"Is that bad?"

"No, it's not bad," he said still smiling.

The glow had begun in my middle again, and I was feeling a bit delirious. "What's been happening in your life?"

Jeremy uncrossed his arms and leaned back in his chair. "Nothing much." Then his fingers floated up to his face, and he began to stroke his chin as he did in high school when he was working out his translation. His eyes wandered about the ceiling and then landed resolutely back on my face. "That's not really true . . . Jane and I got separated a while back. The divorce should be final any day. I thought of calling to let you know, but it just didn't seem . . ." He stopped himself short and leaned forward to place his hand over mine that were folded on my lap. This time it was no accident. His voice was gentle and clear as he spoke to me. "There's no reason I shouldn't tell you now, and I may not get another chance." He squeezed my hands as though to gather courage before going on. "Ever since the first day I saw you all those years ago with your ponytail and knee-high socks I . . . I loved you, Nora. I looked for you when I got back from Peru, but you'd moved and I figured you'd gone back to Cuba like you said you would. Then I met Jane and I thought it best to get on with my life, but when I ran into you again, I knew I'd made a mistake."

Tears floated to my eyes so that his image became blurred and dream-like.

"I didn't mean to upset you . . ."

My heart pounded harder than it ever had in my life, and I felt I might faint if I didn't concentrate on inhaling and exhaling one breath after the other. "Years ago I told you that when you lose hope it's worse than hunger because you have to wait for hope to find you, remember?"

"I remember."

"I was wrong, Jeremy. I was so wrong. I wasn't supposed to wait for hope to find me, I was supposed to go out and find it for myself. And Sister Margarita was wrong too."

"Who's Sister Margarita?"

"Didn't I tell you about her?"

"No, but I'm listening."

I began to tell him about Sister Margarita, but my words were a jumble, and every time I looked at him, smiling so tenderly, it became impossible to make any sense at all. Still trembling, I reached for the coffee, hoping that it might calm me, but Jeremy took the cup from my hand and placed it back on the desk. He scooted his chair forward so that both our knees were touching, and leaned forward, his eyes awash in peaceful longing.

"I've always wanted to ask you something," he said.

"Of course."

He inched closer still. "How do you say, 'May I kiss you?' in Spanish."

"You know how," I responded, blushing like a high school girl.

"But I like how you say it. Won't you say it for me?"

He was so close, I could feel the warmth of his breath on my lips. "¿Te puedo besar?" I said.

He touched my cheek and repeated in perfect Spanish. "Nora, ¿Te puedo besar?"

"Yes, Jeremy," I said. "For you the answer will always be yes."

I wrote Alicia of the good news about Jeremy and me immediately, but months passed without another word, and I was frantic that something might have happened to her and Lucinda and Tony. As Juan had pointed out, Alicia was the last one of the family left in Cuba so there was no one to call or write to find out. The only way to calm my fears was to tell myself that if she were in serious trouble I'd know it. We'd always been able to guess what the other was thinking and somehow I'd feel the truth underneath everything in the same way I knew in my heart of hearts she'd survived her father's death years ago.

I convinced myself she was well and pictured her digesting my letters like little snacks of my life that kept her going in the midst of her difficulties. But the letters were more for me than for her. They reminded me of who I was. They were my psychological trip home, and I felt incomplete without them. And so I wrote again and again even if she didn't write back.

Dear Alicia

Jeremy and I bought a little house in Santa Monica Beach. It's not on the ocean like Abuelo and Abuela's house in Varadero, but if I stand on the toilet in the bathroom on tiptoes I can just catch a glimpse of it over the rooftops. We take frequent walks regardless of the season as Jeremy believes the ocean is beautiful in any kind of weather. He's convinced me to take a few months off while I get my teaching credential, so we've had more time to spend together.

Mami's teaching me how to cook too. Most mornings

after Jeremy leaves for the university, I drive to her house for a lesson. So far I've learned how to make *arroz con pollo*, *picadillo*, *quimbombó*, *plátanos fritos*, leg of pork with *mojo* sauce, and flan. I remember spending hours in the kitchen helping Beba cut onions, and tomatoes and garlic until we reeked of the stuff, but we never talked about cooking. Beba liked to talk about the spirits that lived out in the forests and evil that befell foolish people who didn't respect them as they should. Mami pretty much acts the same way, so I have to pay careful attention to what she does while she gossips about Eddie's sister who's on her second marriage.

I know now how you felt years ago when you wrote that if your life didn't change from that moment on, you'd die happy. Every day is a perfect flower that begins with Jeremy in my arms and ends the same way.

I don't know if you felt this way as well, but I'm a little scared to feel this happy. I'm afraid that one day I'll wake up and find that I've lost Jeremy and our little house and our afternoon walks and everything. I tried to explain this to Jeremy, but he doesn't understand. He just says, "I'm not going anywhere. You're stuck with me."

I lay awake at night long after Jeremy's fallen asleep and worry anyway. I realize how silly I'm being. Jeremy hasn't given me any reason to doubt him. He's as kind and thoughtful a husband as he was a friend, even more so. But my worrying has nothing to do with Jeremy, it's a part of who I am and it doesn't fade away like my accent did.

One day Mami asked me about my tense expression, and I told her about my crazy fears and how childish I was being. She told me what I guess I knew all along. "That's not childishness," she said, as certain as if I was showing her a mango mistaken for a banana. "When your father got his first job over here, I was sure he'd lose it in a week. And when we bought the house, I constantly scanned the street expecting to see some American man in a dark suit walking up the drive to tell us there'd been some mistake and we'd have to give it back. When you lose everything once in your life, chances are it will never happen again, but it's impossible to forget and it's natural to worry."

So now that I have permission to worry, let me tell you again how worried I am about not receiving a letter from you in so long. I'm certain you must have my new address by now. Perhaps you moved again and forgot to forward your mail? Please know that no matter how much time goes by, I always keep you and Lucinda and Tony in my prayers.

Nora


Dear Nora,

Forgive me for taking so long to write you back. I've read every one of your letters over and over. I wept with joy when I read about your marriage to Jeremy, and I'm so happy to know of your wonderful life together. It is as I always knew it would be.

I don't know where to begin or where I left off in my last letter. My life is like a complicated recipe where you can't remember if you already added the sugar or the salt, and just go ahead because it doesn't matter, it's ruined anyway.

You see, Tony is once again gone from my side. It's not his love for the revolution, but his growing hate for it that is the culprit this time. He didn't change one day to the next. His enchantment began to erode as his anger grew steadily across time like the undying beat of a drum that grew louder and louder until he was screaming with agony as it tormented him with a string of broken promises. That hopeful light that always danced in my man's eyes was replaced with a black rage, seething and unpredictable.

Tony had been going to the eye clinic every week to inquire about the list and to make sure that Lucinda was still on it. He was always told the same thing; that Lucinda's appointment would be scheduled as soon as possible and that a notice would be sent to our home. One day he was told that Lucinda's name was no longer on the list, and he had to be dragged away from the clinic by two police officers. He would've been arrested if one of the officers hadn't been an old friend of his from Angola.

Tony was a different man after that. He sat for hours at a time staring out the window at nothing. He reminded me of myself after Papi was killed, except I couldn't reach him the way he reached me. Only Lucinda was able to bring a faint smile to his lips and then only sometimes.

Then his policeman friend returned and told Tony that a neighbor had seen me going to church with Lucinda and that this was the reason her name had been removed from the list. You may ask how ten or fifteen minutes a day spent in an empty church can ruin your life, but in the Communist party, religious inclinations of any kind are considered a weakness that violates the integrity of communism and threatens the revolution. We tried to go on with our lives as usual, but our desperation grew. Lucinda sensed it too and she cried for the little things.

One night, Tony slipped into bed and whispered in my ear. He was out of breath and his voice trembled as he spoke. He said he couldn't wait around and watch the world fall apart as the life drained out of Lucinda and me. We made love with such passion that night, as if it were the first time—as if it would be the last.

Tony was arrested a few weeks later along with other demonstrators and journalists at the Plaza José Martí. It's been over six months and nobody can tell me if he's dead or alive or if I'll ever see him again. I go to church in the day now and I don't care who's watching. Lucinda comes with me and she sits very still in the light of the windows and prays with me. She prays for her father and for her country out loud in a voice as sweet as an angel's.

This may sound strange to you, but even with all that's happened, I'm hopeful again. Although Tony and I are physically apart, our hearts and minds are more united now than they were during these past months when we were within arm's reach of each other.

I was allowed to take Lucinda out of school because she is still too young to go to the government school for the blind. I'm teaching her myself with the help of a new friend, Berta. She works in a hotel and is very funny. It is more important now than ever to laugh when we can.

I promise to write more often, for both our sakes.

Alicia


Christmas was approaching, and we scrambled, as we did every year, to find a place that would sell us a whole pig for roasting. Jeremy was fascinated with this holiday tradition, and it could've been our most joyous Christmas in a long time if Abuelo hadn't started to experience heart trouble, requiring his third hospitalization in six months.

I visited him daily, and we spent time watching his favorite Spanish soaps and he laughed and complained about the outlandish behavior of the actors as if they were his neighbors and friends. As soon as the programs were over his somber mood returned. He told me this time he wouldn't be leaving the hospital, and I reminded him that he said the same thing during his previous hospitalization. He shook his head and sunk deeper into his pillow. His strong frame was slowly decomposing like the beams of a sturdy pier giving way to the constant barrage of the ocean. As I looked upon him I remembered Abuelo's strength in the water, the best swimmer in the world. He laughed in the face of the most serious arguments, and his presence added reverence to everything we did, even if it was just drinking a Coke together.

I was getting ready to head for home and start dinner when he asked, "Have you heard from Alicia?"

We hadn't spoken about Alicia for some time, but he asked me to update him, and he made it clear he wanted me to spare no details. When I was finished relating the contents of her latest letter, he nodded slowly. "What are you going to do?"

"I'm going to send her more money."

He nodded again. "What else?"

"I don't know what else I can do, Abuelo."

"You can go to her, can't you? She needs your help." His words stung me, and I squirmed under the heat of his glare.

Abuelo had heard the arguments and Mami's outbursts at home. He didn't like conflict, and it wasn't like him to make a suggestion that could create more of it. "But Mami and Papi, you know how they feel about it . . ."

"You and Alicia are as close as sisters. She's alone again, and I worry about this new friend that works in the hotels." He sighed and reached for my hand. It felt as fragile as paper. "You haven't changed, Norita. You think too much when you would just do better to dive in and do what you know you must."

I smiled and held his hand in both of my own. "Last time I followed that advice, I almost found myself on a permanent vacation at the bottom of the sea."

"I was right there, Norita." His eyes were round and serious. "I never would've let you drown, and you know it."

"I never doubted you, not for a second, Abuelo. I knew I was safe."

He closed his eyes. "And I'll be there with you next time. Just dive in. You're a wonderful swimmer."


On the tenth day of his hospitalization, soon after he'd finished watching his favorite soap, Abuelo took his usual nap and never woke up.

I like to think that he was dreaming of the warm blue seas of home, and relishing the way he slipped into the water and propelled himself through it, so smooth and perfect—the best swimmer in all of Cuba.

# 20

SUNDAYS BEGAN TO REMIND ME OF SUNDAYS IN CUBA SO MANY years ago.

Marta and I were married and settled into our lives with our American husbands. Mami and Papi were able to count their brood on more than one hand and set the table using almost all their good china. The meal began at around noon. Marta was pregnant again and liked to sit outside on the deck under the tree in Abuelo's favorite spot, while Eddie chased after Lisa who was quite fond of picking the fresh buds off of flowers and handing them to Papi who was not quite so delighted. We nibbled on Cuban delicacies mixed with our growing fondness for American upscale cuisine. Jeremy had taken to cooking a bit himself on the weekends and thoroughly enjoyed surprising my family with some new dish out of an obscure ethnic cookbook he'd found during one of his travels.

We drank wine and beer into the afternoon. We listened to Benny Moré and Celia Cruz, alternating with new age elevator music, the opium of the yuppie generation, Jeremy liked to say, although he owned and listened to quite a bit of it himself.

Mami and Papi marveled at their grandchild and how fair she was. "Who'd think she had any Cuban blood in her at all," Mami said smiling, obviously quite pleased at the fact.

"You know who she looks like, don't you?" Marta said gazing lovingly at her daughter who was scrunching her nose at the olive she tasted.

"She looks like Alicia," Mami said nonchalantly. She hadn't brought up Alicia since her outburst, too long ago to think about anymore. "Alicia was a beautiful girl. I'd say she was even blonder than Lisa." The unspoken question hung in the air like a black cloud, but nobody dared say anything lest it burst and soak us all. I knew they were wondering if I'd heard from her and how she was doing. And what of her blind racially mixed daughter who Abuelo had believed to be one of the most amazingly beautiful children he'd ever laid eyes on?

Jeremy brought in a tray of Greek hummus with neatly sliced wedges of pita bread on the side. He winked at me when he set the tray down, then made himself comfortable at my feet, his head on my knee. "Nora received a letter from Alicia just a few months ago. It was a long one wasn't it, honey?"

I felt my back bristle and was immediately annoyed with Jeremy for bringing it up even though I knew he wasn't being thoughtless, but very deliberate. I coughed and reached for the pita, flicking Jeremy's head as I did so. "It was a very long letter."

Mami reached for some pita and hummus as well. "This looks so interesting, Jeremy. I always want to try it when I see it at the store, but I'm afraid I'll bring it home and nobody will like it." She popped it in her mouth and nodded approvingly. Papi opened another bottle of wine and poured himself a glass, swishing it around and holding it up to the light.

"How is she doing?" Mami asked as she fished around for another pita wedge.

"Who?"

She looked up from the tray, her face flushed and anxious. "Alicia, of course."

"Not so well. There are problems."

Mami sat back in her chair with a huff. "That doesn't surprise me at all. They're finding rafters every day trying to escape. They say the prisons are full of people who try to leave illegally. The very same people who supported the revolution are now being thrown in jail for trying to get out."

Jeremy squeezed my ankle. He wanted me to speak, but I stayed silent. He sat up and away from me. "Alicia and Tony have renounced the party. Tony's in jail for taking part in a demonstration against the government. Nobody knows when or if he'll get out."

Mami gasped and dropped her pita and humus on the ground. "Oh, dear God." Now she was full of questions, and I began to answer them as she began to cry. Papi tried to calm her down, but she continued to grow more nervous, and trembled as she spoke. "We must send her money, José," she kept saying over and over again.

Dear Nora,

I light a candle at the church for Abuelo every day, may he rest in peace. And as I watch the flame flicker in the darkness I thank God he died in freedom, near you and the family. I pray the years he lived in abundance and joy, erased the years of hunger and fear he knew here.

I must extend my gratitude to you and your family. You don't know what a difference your generosity has made for us. Tony is still in jail, and I use most of the American dollars you send to bribe the guards into allowing me to bring him food. There is one guard with kind eyes who tells me he delivers my packages to him personally, and I have no choice but to believe him.

It was necessary for us to move out of the apartment Tony found and into a smaller one on the first floor. At least we're still close to the *malecón*, and Berta has moved in. She was with a horrible man who beat her black and blue almost daily. When he came around looking for her I told him she moved to Russia with a soldier. I even supplied the name of one of Tony's old friends who I knew had recently gone in case he bothered to check. Berta was very grateful and she's turned out to be a marvelous friend and very resourceful as well. We've been able to eat regular meals and find meat at least once a week since we met her. She works in tourism at the hotels and promised to find me a job soon. I now wish that I'd taken my English classes more seriously, but Berta assures me I don't need to know English and that working in tourism is the surest way to leave Cuba. I won't go without Tony, but I need to have a plan ready so we can leave as soon as he's out. Ricardo, the guard who gives things to Tony, tells me he's been hearing rumors about Tony's release and I want to believe him because when I do, I feel I have two hearts pumping bravely inside my chest instead of one squeezing out its weak existence.

Time is running out for many reasons. Lucinda's been out of school for so long, I'm afraid soon they'll come looking for her and force her to attend the educational camps as they do to all the children. She'd be away from me for weeks at a time, and they'd program her mind and her soul to give up our hope for freedom and build tolerance for the unrelenting frustration we live with.

I wonder sometimes if I shouldn't leave with Lucinda as soon as I can. When I think of how I'd suffer if my daughter were taken from me, ninety miles in a raft doesn't seem like such a risk. I hear that if you leave at the right time when the currents are flowing south and the wind is behind you, you can make it in two days. Two days to freedom Nora, what a beautiful thought.

I must bring this letter to a close, as I've run out of paper. One last thing, you wrote that Abuelo's last words to you before he died were of me, but you didn't tell me what they were. I would like to know when you get a chance to write back, and I'll write again soon. I feel so much better when I do.

Alicia

I awoke with the image clear in my mind. Two white and wavering faces, ghostlike and tranquil, emerging from the sea. They walk hand in hand across the ocean bottom to reach the shores of freedom. They pass through the horror of a thousand deaths to reach me, and I'm waiting on the shore when the tops of their heads emerge from the water like two rising moons. Their bodies glisten with the ocean, but there's a brittleness about their souls, a dried-up misery that calls to me more poignantly than any cry or complaint. Their bare feet sink into the sand as they stand on the water's edge.

Lucinda walks towards me, takes my hand and calls me Tía Nora. She tells me I look beautiful just as she knew I would, and she blinks every time I pass my hand over her eyes. I turn to see if Alicia is amazed by her daughter's miraculous recovery, but she is well accustomed to miracles and I decide to leave this one to its own enchantment.

I take them home to my house that is right on the beach, so close that the waves wash over the threshold of my front door. We eat fruit growing on trees that lean into my windows with such familiarity that I need not even get up from my chair to pick ripe sweet apples and oranges. We chew more than we talk. And when we do speak it is only to say that the weather is good and that the fruit is sweet and that the water in these parts is far too murky for swimming.

# 21

Dear Nora,

Ricardo tells me Tony will not be released as soon as he thought. I didn't want to believe him when he first told me. I preferred to think he'd become confused with somebody else or that he'd been drinking, but then he gave me the note from Tony himself. It was very brief, but I wept with joy at the sight of his lovely writing that still looks like that of a little boy. He wrote that although prison life is harsh, there are a few guards who make his imprisonment tolerable and that Ricardo is one of them.

I realized I had to do something to thank Ricardo for his kindness and to ensure he continued taking care of my love. I began bringing him food I buy with the dollars you send. One afternoon I brought him a fresh mango. It was so ripe and sweet I could smell its perfume in the bag. There was one for him and one for Tony. He took the bag from me and stared at me as he never had before. To be honest, Nora, it's been such a long time since anyone's looked at me that way that at first I wondered if I might have something stuck in my teeth.

I'm not such a fool as I used to be. I didn't for one minute believe Ricardo had fallen in love with me, but I understood that how I responded to his declarations had everything to do with whether or not Tony ever tasted the mango that hung between us.

Did I mention that Ricardo's face is rough and scarred and that with his hairy fingers make his hands look like two giant spiders? The kindness in his eyes grew into a glare, and I soothed him with a light stroke over his spidery hands. That was enough for the moment, but the next week I allowed him to touch my hair and whisper silly things in my ear while he peeked down my blouse. On that day I brought Tony a loaf of fresh bread that Berta had taken from the hotel.

Ricardo informed me that Tony was being moved to another section of the prison and it would be difficult for him to keep taking food to him, but if I allowed him to slip his hands under my blouse, he'd arrange for a transfer.

I've been paying the ultimate price for my peace of mind for months now. Once a week at eleven after Ricardo's shift we meet at the north end of the malecón. He tells me not to be late because his wife is very ugly and very jealous, and if he's late she'll wonder where he is and probably eat his rice and beans because she's fat too. He tells me that having me is worth going hungry for one night, but if he can have me and a plate of food, why not?

I wrote before that desperation changes people. Hunger, like alcohol, has a way of lowering inhibitions so that what was once impossible to do suddenly becomes not only possible, but likely. I know now that I'm capable of doing anything to protect Lucinda and Tony. The problem is that there are fewer and fewer desperate acts to choose from and we're left with nothing, but the most common degradations.

I consider the offer you made me so long ago, to apply for visas and that Juan would help in whatever way he could. Then I believed I'd die if I left Cuba, but today I'd leave on a floating tree trunk if I knew Tony would be safe. I'm a prisoner with him, and the only peace I get these days is from knowing that Lucinda is with me and not in the educational camps. I received word just last week that she's excused for now, but I don't know how long this reprieve will last.

I will leave this place. I promise you with all the love and strength I have in my heart that, even if my daughter never knows what it is to look upon the royal palms or the beauty of her own face, she will know freedom.

Alicia

Jeremy held me as I cried.

"You must go to her," he said with a firm grip on my shoulders. "Maybe you can convince her to stop what she's doing to herself."

"All she cares about is keeping Tony safe. It doesn't matter if I'm there."

Jeremy and I never quarreled. If I had a tendency to raise my voice to the altered Cuban pitch I was accustomed to in my home, his steady rational responses always smoothed my ruffled feathers.

This time he was the one heating up. "Other Cubans go visit their relatives, why can't you? Just tell your parents you're a grown woman, and you've made up your mind."

I turned away from him and felt the numbness creep over me as it always did when I thought about going. I saw my mother's face twisted in agony when Castro declared Cuba a Socialist state. I saw my father curled up like a baby on the bed, sobbing when he learned of Tío Carlos's death. "It's not that easy," I said.

"It is, but you make it difficult."

I turned to face him. "You don't understand because you never stepped out of your life like you were stepping out of a pair of comfortable shoes only to find yourself banging around in heavy boots that don't fit and never will."

Jeremy cocked his head to one side. "You're right, I don't understand, Nora. I don't think I ever will."

\*    \*    \*

We first heard news of the *balseros* on TV. Desperate Cuban men, women and children flinging themselves into the sea hoping that the tires and scraps of wood they tied together with rope would transport them to freedom. We talked about it during Sunday dinner and as usual, Mami was leading the conversation.

"Nobody here cares about what happens to those wretched souls," she insisted. "The Americans have forgotten about Cuba. What is it after all? Just a little island in the middle of the ocean that makes no difference to anyone. It matters to us, but nobody else."

Papi, Marta, and I had learned over the years to keep our mouths shut whenever Mami went on in this way. There was no convincing her of anything that was even slightly hopeful when it came to Cuba and Cubans. She was hopelessly pessimistic and became offended if one attempted to offer a slightly sunnier view. Eddie caught on years ago, but Jeremy either didn't know or didn't care.

"I think there are some Americans who care. I do," he said while dismembering the roasted chicken before him.

"Of course you do, you married a Cuban woman," Mami said as she waved a fork in his direction, but he wasn't finished.

"I cared even before I married Nora." Jeremy placed his fork down and cleaned his hands on his napkin, considering his words carefully. "I wish Cubans could experience the freedom of democracy, Regina. I'm just not sure that the way to bring it about is to keep distancing ourselves from Castro."

If I'd been close enough to pinch Jeremy's knee I would have. As it was, I wanted to dive under the table for cover.

Mami's rage was red and profuse, and it traveled up from her belly making itself seen as flames peeking up over her blouse, engulfing her neck, her ears, until finally her whole face was ablaze. "Distancing ourselves? Did you say distancing? They've been inviting that murderous criminal to European summits and South American meetings all over the place. Meetings attended by American politicians, including our president. Meetings in which that man is officially acknowledged as the president of Cuba.

Have you ever heard of anything so stupid in all your life?" She spit the words out this time like venom.

"President. As if he were elected, as if they had more than one name on the ballot during the circus they called an election. Did you know that people who didn't go out and vote were denied their ration books for God knows how long. Did you know that?" Mami pushed herself away from the table. She was still steaming. "This government has taken a hard stand against communism everywhere in the world, but right next door it does nothing. Cubans have died alongside Americans in Vietnam because of this country's hatred of communism. But can they go next door and get rid of that raving lunatic that uses Cuba for his personal playground?"

Her eyes were bulging at Jeremy who stood silent and unflinching. Only I could see the shadow of disappointment on his face. And I alone knew that his disappointment was directed at himself and his own insensitivity.

I cleared my throat. "Don't get so upset, Mami. There are lots of ways to look at it . . ."

Jeremy interrupted me. "That's OK. You don't need to defend me. Your mother's right."

"Of course I'm right," she huffed, not easily swayed into a truce.

"Please forgive my rudeness." Jeremy directed his apology to both Mami and Papi. Papi nodded although he hadn't said a word.

Mami looked around at all the faces sitting at the table obviously relieved that the explosion had passed without any fatal casualties. She turned somber eyes back toward Jeremy. "Of course, you're allowed to have your own opinion, Jeremy. I'm just telling you what I think. It's not like we're in Cuba, you know. You can think what you want."

Jeremy nodded and Mami smiled as she went into to the kitchen. She returned in less than a minute carrying a beautiful golden flan, dripping with caramel sauce. She placed it in front of Jeremy, knowing that flan was his favorite and cut him a huge piece. Then she kissed him on the top of his head and left to start on the dishes without cutting pieces for anybody else.

Jeremy held me close and whispered in my ear and the base of my neck until I was giggling like a child. We made love by the moon-light that glowed through the open window. Sometimes the ocean breeze found our little house through the maze of neighbor-hoods and houses between us. We breathed in the cool freshness and allowed it to dry the perspiration on our skin.

Jeremy fell asleep with his arms wrapped around me, and sud-denly we were floating out in the middle of the sea in a small sturdy raft. The ocean was rolling pleasantly while the mist sprayed over the sides caressing us. I saw the stars blinking over-head. This was the most beautiful night of my life. My fortune was determined by the strength of my faith and my dreams. It was the wind in my sails, the circular force of the currents, the beat-ing of my heart. What an amazing feeling to risk all that I was and all I believed in for this sense of hope. The growing pitch of the sea didn't bother me. It would calm soon and the sun would rise out of the sea as it always had. We're on our way to a better life.

I woke Jeremy so we could see the rising sun together. It started as a tremulous light that spread in soft ribbons against the dark of the passing night. The ocean glowed deep and warm as it smiled up at the sky. Another day had begun.

"We're part of this now, Jeremy," I said and his face was golden with the sun. He held my hand with loving delicacy, as if it were a flower. A sliver of land floated on the mist beyond. It would be difficult to see if not for the hint of brown contour im-movable against the flow of the sea. We were headed right for it and as we got closer the mist burnt away to reveal the solid hills, the swaying palms, the broad calm harbor that destined the land for greatness in the new world. Once again I gazed upon the beauty of my beloved Cuba.

# 22

Dear Nora,

 I'm proud to say that I now have a job at the Hotel Nacional. They've renovated it beautifully, and as I walk on the marbled floor and smell the rich food coming from the restaurant, I can pretend everything is as it used to be. But I can't pretend for long because the hotel is full of tourists from many countries like Canada and Germany. Nobody speaks Spanish, but thankfully, my job doesn't require that I say much. I just smile politely and show them the way to the lobby and sometimes take them to their rooms. I wear a lovely uniform. It's blue with gold trim on the sleeves and the bottom of the skirt and I have matching shoes too.

 Lucinda stays home by herself when I work. I don't know what else to do. She is young, but she's very mature for her age and knows where everything is. During blackouts, that come very often these days, I rely on her to find things in the dark. I don't want to waste the few candles we have, so we sit for hours in the dark, and I tell her about you and your life. She knows all about Jeremy, and she wants to learn how to speak English to impress you. I've begun to teach her the few words I know, like "Hello, my name is Lucinda," and

"Can you tell me the time?" She's very good at remembering these phrases, but I'm afraid her accent is terrible, even worse than mine.

She tells me stories too. Last week she heard that one of our neighbors left the country in a small boat. He applied for a visa years ago, but he got tired of waiting. It's amazing the things people say to my Lucinda, as if they believe her blindness will keep their secrets safe. Normally, plans to escape aren't shared openly because anyone caught trying to leave can go to prison for many years. But more and more are taking the chance. Life for them here is more frightening than the possibility of jail, drowning, or even being eaten by sharks.

People here have become desperate for things like soap and toothpaste and aspirin. A stash of soap under the bed is the best cure for insomnia. Last year I was able to get hold of a box. It was rose-scented and each piece was wrapped in very thin, almost transparent paper; so delicate. I used to count them every night, and feel the heaviness in my hand as if they were gold bars. I was forced to exchange the last few bars for medicine when Lucinda was ill recently, and then I knew how a millionaire must feel after he loses everything. It is a feeling perhaps worse than hunger; an emptiness that sours the heart.

There are some who find this situation thrilling. The woman across the street leaves her house every morning with a straw bag hanging from her arm. You can see the excitement and spring in her step, like a hunter heading out for the kill. Her husband is not quite so animated. He hasn't left the house for months and slumps around the front steps waiting for his wife to return. When she does, he sniffs out her bag as if he were an old hound dog looking for a bone. I'm not lying to you when I tell you that a few times I've actually seen her smack him on the nose when he gets too close to her bag, and he paws her all the way back into the house. It's very sad to see.

I sit in the dark after Lucinda has fallen asleep and think of how easy it would be, Nora. How easy to float to freedom . . . to paradise. I remember the splendor of my life before the changes. I had a new dress almost every week and the maid would brush my hair in the morning until it shone. The bread was always fresh and warm and the butter dripped off of it onto our plates, and there was meat every day and fish until it was coming out of our ears. There was a new bar of soap by every sink and bathtub. There was lilac water to splash on our hair after a long warm bath. There was music on every street corner, and the musicians were plump and merry and laughed along with their melodies. The children were as crisp as paper dolls new out of the box. I remember how good it felt right after a bath when I was going out to dinner with my parents. My skin was just a little tight from the soap, and my scalp felt cool in the breeze.

If all of this was possible then, then isn't it just as possible to find my way into a raft and float to freedom now?

Enough. Tomorrow is a working day. May God bless you and Jeremy in many ways. Remember I love you.

Alicia

We were late for Sunday dinner because Jeremy had many papers to grade.

Expecting to see everyone sitting around the table, we were surprised to find Mami still in the kitchen wearing her apron and sniffling into a tissue as she worked. She lit up when we walked in, and she almost dropped the salad in her excitement. She grasped my shoulders. "You'll never guess who called."

I looked to Jeremy who shrugged, just as bewildered as I was, eyes still red from hours of reading term papers.

"Aren't you going to guess?" she asked, giving me a little shake as well.

"I have no idea."

"Alicia. It was our little Alicia!" Mami dropped her hands, raised them, dropped them again, and then wrung them nervously. "And you could hear her clear as a bell, the connection was so good."

"Alicia . . . you actually spoke with her on the phone?" I felt Jeremy's hand on my back.

Mami nodded and swallowed hard. "We talked for several minutes about so many things. She asked for you. I gave her your number, and she said she'd try to call you at home."

"Does she have a phone?"

"Apparently she does at the hotel where she's working, but it sounded like she couldn't talk for very long." Mami didn't seem to know whether she should continue with the salad or stir the beef stew. "She sounds just the same, Nora, just the same. She has the same little voice and . . ." Mami leaned on the counter and began to sob. I ran over to her, my own eyes watering, and held her as she spoke. "I could see her so clearly. That last time we said good-bye to them at Varadero, remember? She was a beautiful girl and so sweet and smart." She turned to Jeremy and sniffed loudly. "She had golden hair, beautiful and curly. Nobody would think she was Cuban. And her eyes were green."

"Her eyes are probably still green, Mami. You're talking about her as if she were dead."

Mami returned to her cooking. "People I know who've gone back to visit, describe it like a cemetery full of walking corpses, a living death." She sniffed loudly.

We spoke of little else during dinner. Mami recounted her ten-minute conversation with Alicia at least twenty times. Each recounting seemed to uncover one more detail or nuance of how her life was, and what she would do next. Of course, I already knew all these things, but I didn't share what additional information I had. What Alicia had written in her letters was sacred and meant just for me.

"She's working in a fancy hotel," Mami said. "Tony won't get out of prison for a couple of years, but she's hopeful it could be sooner. It seems she has a friend that watches out for him. She's saving the money we send and that tourists give her. She says that with this money she'll be able to leave once Tony gets out."

"So they're definitely planning to leave?" Marta asked as she attempted to feed her new son, Michael, who was spitting out his black beans, behaving as American as he looked.

"It certainly sounds that way."

"Are they planning to get visas?" Papi asked.

"She says they're going to try, but if they can't they'll get out however they can."

The table was quiet at these words. More reports of drowned rafters were being confirmed every day.

"Did she say she'd call me?" I asked for the tenth time at least.

"She took your number down and repeated it twice. She said she'd call you as soon as she could."

Papi was quiet during dinner. He couldn't hear about Alicia without thinking of his brother. He ate very little and left the table early saying he needed to finish some reading before Monday. Mami apologized to Eddie and Jeremy. "You see, he had a terrible loss. Actually, we all did . . ."

"They know, Mami," Marta said. And Mami was silenced, relieved to be spared the recounting of Tío Carlos's death. We all were.

I waited for days and then weeks. Every time the phone rang I snatched up the receiver hoping to hear the thin crackle of static and Alicia's distant voice balancing precariously on the wire. Would I recognize it after so many years? I heard a child's voice when I read her letters, a lovely flowery voice full of clear light and possibilities. The kind of voice that could only belong to a beautiful girl. But she was now a grown woman, and she'd suffered so many things. It would be different; it had to be.

Jeremy teased that my desperation to hear from Alicia was starting to make him feel like a jilted lover. And my desperation fueled my dreams that came almost every night. I'd wake up clutching Jeremy, his tee shirt moist with my tears. I was looking for Alicia with Tony at my side. We were walking along the beach and he told me how much he loved his wife and his green eyes glowed as he stared out at the sea wondering where she might be. We were both saddened by her absence, and I placed my hand on his shoulder to express my compassion. Suddenly, we were both naked and twisting into each other like snakes embracing in the sand.

Jeremy always wanted to hear about my dreams, but I didn't share this one. He'd never been a jealous man and he'd probably turn a curious smile if I told him. In the darkness his eyes would penetrate me and he'd smile and hold me with a chuckle because I looked so damn guilty.

"I love you so much," I said as I laid my dampened cheek on his chest and felt the comforting rise and fall of his breathing.

"Don't worry. She'll call," he whispered, half asleep.

# 23

Dear Nora,

Your last letter was tucked unopened in my purse for many weeks before I had the heart to read it. Please forgive me, but my life has taken another drastic change. If I'd written to you earlier you would've wondered who that strange person was signing my name. Perhaps you'll still wonder, but I have no choice but to be honest with you. I know now more than ever why Tía Panchita needed to sit on her porch before she died. It is the same for me when I write to you.

I go to church, and I talk to God amidst the silence of the statues covered with dust and cobwebs. Lucinda and I pray together, and I suppose our prayers make it to heaven, but it's been a long time since I heard God's voice. I used to hear Him all the time, loud and clear in the wind and in the roar of the sea. Now all I hear is noise, noise that keeps me from my sleep.

Berta has been teaching me about her work. She comes home with beautiful things almost every day. Last week she had a bottle of lemon-scented shampoo. The week before that, a big square box of tissue paper for blowing your nose. The week before that, two pairs of brand new stockings as sheer as glass. We laughed as we threw them up in the air and watched them float down to the ground like feathers. You put just one toe into them and you feel like Cinderella when that beautiful feeling travels all the way up your body.

For some time now I've known that Berta is one of those ladies Abuela wouldn't let us talk about. She wears her best clothes and sits in the lobby of the hotel or in the bar smoking cigarettes and crossing and uncrossing her legs until a man buys her a drink or asks her for the time even though she doesn't wear a watch. I often see her working from my place at the door. She throws her head back and laughs the way I used to remember doing when in the company of admiring young men. She tugs on her tight skirt so the men can't help but stare at her legs that are bare all the way up her thigh. Before long she leaves on the arm of one of them. Sometimes they go to a restaurant and a show, but the younger ones take her straight to their rooms.

Berta says this is the only way to make real money. Did I tell you she has a degree in engineering? She studied in Russia for a while and can order a drink in three languages, not including Spanish.

About three months ago, a man approached me and whispered in my ear. A week ago I would've stormed out and left him with his words hanging in his mouth, but on this day they sank into my soul. I've become the worst thing a woman can become. And I do it as easily as I swam to the platform so many years ago. I just close my eyes and dive in. I don't feel the men touching me, I don't hear the ridiculous things they say. I'm doing my job, taking advantage of an opportunity that allows me to go home to my Lucinda at the end of the day or night with a bag full of milk and toothpaste and soap and meat and cans of vegetables and fresh fruit.

I still love only Tony and nothing changes that. Others may possess my body for a short while, but it's only with Tony that my spirit has danced. I continue to send him packages every week with Ricardo, but I'm thankful he no longer requires additional payment as I believe he's taken up with someone else.

I'm now able to save money to escape, and when we leave I'll erase everything from my mind and heart. This is the one thought that keeps me alive.

I will wait for your letter as I wait for news from Tony every day, with one hand on my heart and the other raised to heaven.

Alicia

Mami collapsed on the couch sobbing, and Papi stood glum and stoic beside her. It was exactly as I expected, but still my palms were sweaty and I felt a new fear gurgling in the pit of my stomach. Jeremy stood next to me, a few steps back. Even after more than five years of marriage, he wasn't used to these emotional outbursts, and he'd learned the hard way that it was useless to respond like an objective anthropologist studying a strange tribe somewhere in the jungle. Whether he liked it or not, he was one of us now, a bit more cerebral and contemplative than the rest, but one of us nonetheless.

"Do you know how I feel?" Mami asked, lifting her tear-stained face from the cushion. "I feel like my country was taken away from me and now my honor as well because my own flesh and blood is going back to pump American dollars into that criminal system. Every penny you spend will end up in the pocket of that man."

"Regina, please calm down," Papi said placing his hand on her arm and she flinched it away, but shifted her gaze downward like a scolded child.

Papi cleared his throat. His eyes were unwavering, but as sad as they'd been during the worst moments of his life. "You know how we feel about this, Nora, but you're a grown woman now and we can't tell you what to do. Maybe one day you'll have children and you'll . . ." Papi stuffed his hands in his pocket and shook his head as tears swam in his eyes. "One day you'll understand."

We left Mami and Papi without our Sunday meal warm and heavy in our bellies. Instead, we had sushi at a little place near the oceanfront and took a walk on the pier afterward. Few words passed between us, and Jeremy held my hand snugly in his coat pocket while the wind blew cold.

"So are you still going?" he asked when we'd almost reached the end of the pier.

"I'm still going." We stopped for a moment and leaned against the railing as we gazed at the sea beneath us. The wind was full of mist and filled our noses and eyes, washed us clean and blew us dry at the same time.

"Good," he said, wrapping his arm around my shoulder and pulling me toward him so that I was standing only on one foot. "You're sure you'll be all right alone? I can try to get away, but it's just hard in the middle of the semester."

"I'm sure I'll be fine."

We stood watching the waves rolling forward in rounded symmetry, continuous bands of unimaginable strength pounding at the foundations of the pier. It was a deep and ominous green, opaque and glossy, like very thick glass, its edges sharp and pointed, lifting huge crags up toward the sky and swallowing them up again in violent spurts. How different from the ocean I'd soon be seeing in my homeland. I tried to explain this to Jeremy as we stood covered in the mist, and as I spoke, it was as if the sea's jealous roars were trying to drown me out.

"It's quiet for one thing." I said. "The waves don't pound, they glide over you like a soft breeze. And you can see all the way down to your toes even if you're standing in water up to your shoulders. Sometimes when you're suspended in perfect warmth, a rain cloud will float by out of no where and it'll start raining thick warm drops of water right on your head. Alicia and I liked to pretend we were washing our hair in the middle of the ocean like mermaids. Or we'd dive under the surface, thinking ourselves so clever to escape the rain for the few seconds we could hold our breath. Just as suddenly as it started, the rain stopped and the sun would shine even more brilliantly than before. In this way we experienced several mornings and nights in a single day."

He was watching me, smiling that curious smile that makes my heart melt every time. "Really? So then you only need to go for one week instead of two. After all, if you have several mornings and nights in one day . . ."

I threw my arms around his neck and whispered in his ear that was chilled from the wind. "I'm going to miss you too, Jeremy. I'm going to miss you so much."


Jeremy passed the phone to me half asleep, and when I heard her voice on the line I bolted straight up in bed.

"Listen to you answering the phone like *una americana*," she said.

"Alicia, is it really you?"

She laughed. "Of course it's me, silly."

"I don't believe I'm actually talking to you. I don't believe it's you."

"I can see you haven't forgotten your Spanish. I was afraid I'd have to talk to you with the little English I know and that would make for a very boring conversation."

"You sound just the same, Alicia. Your voice is . . . is the same."

She sighed. "If only everything was the same. You know me, I have a tendency to wish for the impossible, but then some of my wishes do come true. Are you really coming home?"

"I'll be there in a few days, just like I said in my letter."

"It's too wonderful to imagine." I heard noise in the background, and then a pause. When she spoke again, Alicia's voice was muffled. "I hear someone coming, and I shouldn't be using the phone."

"Is there something wrong?" I asked, sensing the fear in her voice.

"Not a thing. All that matters is that you're coming home. I'll be waiting for you at the airport. I love you, Nora."

"I love you too, Alicia."

# HAVANA

# 24

TWO HOURS INTO THE FLIGHT FROM LOS ANGELES TO MIAMI, I forced myself to drink a glass of red wine to calm my nerves. Liquid tranquility and finally sleep overcame my anxiety, and I found myself standing with several others in a circle of light.

The fire is brilliant, almost licking our toes and caressing our bodies as we move into and away from it like the shifting of the tides. Our hips jerk to the rhythm of the drums. It's Beba who plays them and she smiles with big beautiful teeth, even whiter than her snowy turban. She beats the drums so hard, I'm concerned she'll grow tired, but she's glowing like an angel.

"I've been waiting for you, little girl," she says, without skipping a beat. "Where have you hidden yourself all these years?"

"I was far away, but now I've come home." I move closer to her. I want to see the polished smoothness of her skin up close. I want to smell the onions and the peppers on her hands and hear the deep and golden timber of her voice that is more reassuring to me than my own mother's.

I look into her eyes and she stops playing. They are as I remember them, alive with the knowing of a secret joke, poised on the verge of tears and laughter. She can make all the hurt and fear of childhood disappear with a single embrace, a wave of her hand, the wink of an eye.

"Everything's going to be OK, little girl. Don't be afraid."

"Do you promise?"

"Has Beba ever lied to you?"

"No, Beba. You never lied to me or anyone. That I know as surely as I know my own name."

Satisfied with my response, she begins to play again and moves her enormous head to sway and dip to the rhythms floating around us, and through us. She's no longer paying attention to me. She knows I'm here. She knows I'm safe.

Lucinda takes my hand and brings me back to the fire. She leads me closer and closer to it. "It's OK, Tía Nora. It won't hurt." She steps into it herself to show me.

Flames shoot through her body, and she lights up from the inside out with the fire curling up in her eyes and her mouth like an oven of hot embers burning and smoldering. Her hair is golden light floating on the heat. She smiles a brilliant burning smile and holds her small hand out to me. It glows gently from the inside out so the veins are clearly visible. I reach out to take it, and the darkness sweeps me away like a quiet storm that silences the wind and the whispering of my mind.

I trembled when the plane touched ground in Havana and when I stepped onto Cuban soil the prayers I remembered as a child formed on my lips. I was not alone. Many other passengers wept for joy, and thanked God and all the saints for allowing them to return to their homeland before they died. One older woman collapsed on her knees and buried her face in the earth. Her young companion, who looked like her granddaughter, was embarrassed by this emotional display, and attempted to raise her by one arm, but her grandmother refused to move.

I walked past them and was preparing to tell the girl she should be patient with her poor grandmother when the tropical fragrance of the air forced me to stop dead in my tracks as well. After so many years of empty remembering, my heart jumped. Like words to a song I'd long forgotten, it was suddenly upon me, every chord, every phrase, every turn of the melody was singing to my spirit, "You're home, you're finally home where you belong." I felt the petals of my heart shift and loosen; another breath and they'd be open completely. A few more seconds of warmth from the sun that hits this land from its unique angle and distance in the sky, and I would be as I was meant to be.

My feet shuffled forward and I heard the sounds of Cuban Spanish spoken all around me, with its dropped s's and slurred consonants that make every word sound like the erratic beating of a drum. Rhythmic and alive, broken with laughter and wild gesticulations, it said more to me than a thousand words.

My head spun with the whirl of commotion. Entire families were at the airport to welcome their Americanized relatives. In their haste to get to them, they stumbled over each other, heavily laden bags of soap and toilet paper tumbling to the dirty floor, and quickly recovered by eager relatives whose emotions were momentarily suspended by the sight of such rare luxuries.

I scanned the crowd, sniffing and waving my handkerchief in the air for Alicia to find me. Several people bumped into me as I made my way through the throng, looking into my eyes searching as I searched their faces. Although I didn't know them, the expression of longing and hope was one I was all too familiar with.

I spotted them leaning against the very wall where I'd waited to leave my country so many years ago. Alicia's face had hardly changed. Her fine and perfect features, her almond shaped eyes dancing with intelligent light, full of inspiration and wonder. She was still a child. Her golden hair, back in a ponytail, wisps of curls framing her face like the most delicate lace. But she was thinner than I remembered and her shoulders slumped beneath her crisp shirt. Her skirt would've fallen to her feet if not for the belt cinched tight around her tiny waist.

My gaze shifted down and I beheld one of the most beautiful children I'd ever seen. She was quite literally a golden child. Her hair was arranged in ringlets of dark gold and her skin, although lighter in tone than her father's, still retained the burnished warmth that filters through the trees at sunset. Her turquoise eyes gazed straight ahead, but they were not vacant. They were mysteriously calm as though she were in constant prayer and meditation. She smiled brilliantly in response to something her mother said to her. Mesmerized by Lucinda, I hadn't noticed that Alicia had spotted me in the crowd, and they were walking toward me.

We stood for a moment, and I was in Tía María's garden again. I was looking to Alicia for guidance or at least a funny joke that could transport us into a trance of endless giggles that irritated everybody but us. Yet this close up I could see that she had changed. The once fine texture of her skin had been degraded by time and although still beautiful, it was far from the porcelain perfection I remembered. Her hair that could once capture every beam of sunlight was dull and dry, and as she pulled me into an embrace, I realized that it was none too clean either.

We held each other for a very long time, and in her arms my shock melted into tears that streamed down my face dampening Alicia's hair. She was crying too, and her skinny shoulders trembled against mine.

"You're here," she kept whispering. "You're really here."

We stood at arm's length, holding hands. Memories had been much kinder than this moment, for as I looked upon this fatigued woman approaching middle age, I was suddenly faced with a stranger. This wasn't Alicia unless I looked at nothing but her eyes and their golden light that wavered with the shifting grace of the ocean.

"You've grown into such a beautiful woman," she said. "Such a beautiful and elegant woman."

Lucinda stepped forward, and took my hand. She stepped closer still so that her head was next to my heart and hugged me tight. I let go of Alicia's hand, wrapped both my arms around Lucinda and kissed the top of her head. I loved her instantly.

"Tía Nora, you smell so good," Lucinda said, and I held her even more tightly.

*   *   *

Berta waited outside for us in a borrowed car. She was a large, attractive woman with thick black hair and full lips painted hastily in fuchsia. She wore a tube top that barely covered her ample bust and the smooth roll of honey colored flesh that escaped over her skintight athletic shorts. She drove a 1955 powder blue Chevrolet with a visor, just like Papi used to have, and she handled the oversized steering wheel and yelled profanities out her window at offending drivers with the same dexterity.

Between shouts and crazy maneuvers, she managed to glimpse at me and my clothes and shoes. Her questions were pointed and not in the least bit apologetic. "I bet you paid more than twenty dollars for those shoes, didn't you?"

"I think so."

"So, what do you do to make money?"

"I'm a teacher. I work with young children who are still learning English."

She flung her head out the window for the tenth time and her raven hair streamed out like a flag, nearly blinding her in the process, not that this prompted her to slow down. "Get out of the road, you worthless piece of shit!" she shouted to another driver.

"So, you have to go to school for a long time to do that or what?"

"A little bit. It's not that bad."

"How much do you get paid?"

Alicia leaned forward from the back seat and placed a cautious hand on my shoulder. "I may have forgotten to tell you how forward Berta can be."

Berta cackled behind the steering wheel, and I couldn't be sure if she hadn't just spat out the window as well. "That's right," she said, grinning from ear to ear and displaying a remarkable set of large and perfect teeth. "But you can tell me to shut up, and I won't be mad at you, not even for a minute."

"We wouldn't make it without Berta," Alicia said leaning back again, obviously exhausted. I noticed perspiration lining her mouth.

Berta yelled out the window again, this time at a group of

young men standing idly in the street and blocking the flow of traffic. "If you don't move your butts, I'm going to serve them up for dinner and your balls for dessert!" This brought a series of even more colorful comebacks from the young men and a sparkling eruption of giggles from Lucinda in the back seat who, until then, had been silent.

I heard Alicia exhale from behind me. "I told you things had changed, Nora." I knew what she meant. Never would vulgarity of this sort have been tolerated openly on the streets, but it now fell from the windows of once elegant buildings, like confetti. It was obviously the order of the day and fully available to women as well as men. Perhaps it was even necessary for survival, for Berta used it as one would wield a huge rifle, and her efforts cleared her path as well as if she'd strapped one to the hood of her car.

We drove through the potholed streets of Havana, dodging young and old alike. Many rode on rickety bikes, sometimes two and even three at a time, their limbs splayed out in an effort to balance like a circus act on a high-wire. The majority of the buildings we passed had fallen to ruin and gave the impression of enormous wedding cakes decomposing in the sun, their former glory strewn about the sidewalks like so many crumbs. Colored glass that once graced the most elegant of windows, fell upon those below like heavy tears.

I had walked this street as a child many times. The driver often dropped us off at the far corner near the pharmacy, and I had held on tight to Mami's hand as we crossed the busy road. Could this be the same place? Yes, it was. And around the corner was the Woolworth drugstore where Alicia and I loved to sit at the counter and order our favorite avocado and shrimp salad. When Mami wandered off to look at this or that, we'd spin on the seats so that sometimes we were too dizzy to eat. Or we watched elegant ladies strolling in their high-heeled shoes with matching bags swinging from their crooked arms. We dreamed of how we would dress and walk when we were old enough to shave our legs and wear stockings. We listened to the street vendors who called out their wares with a dignity that blended nicely with the musicians serenading us.

But now the skin was being stripped off my beautiful memories. People didn't stroll anymore; they shuffled in ill-fitting shoes held on to their feet by a fraying strap. Many children were barefoot. They were at the age when feet grew quickly, and I imagine they were lucky if the one pair of shoes they received once a year lasted more than a few months.

I studied the faces of my countrymen as they ambled about the decomposing city, their eyes turned inward as if they were lost in a dream from which they did not want to wake. They stepped over the garbage and debris without noticing. Perhaps they were, as I was, trying very hard to remember the way their city used to be so they didn't have to see it falling down around them.

I turned back to look at Alicia who was smiling a small sad smile. "Things have changed," she said again with a slight nod of her head. "Don't cry, Nora."

Was I crying? Were the tears on my cheeks my body's reaction to the thick tropical weather so unlike the dry California climate? I rubbed my arms with both hands at once. I could feel the damp softness already, the sensuous experience of mild humidity that makes my skin feel as soft and smooth as the finest silk. I felt the creases around my eyes, and the corners of my mouth, even my scalp, begin to loosen and smooth out like glass. The air was heavier, but fragrant and soft.

Lucinda was leaning toward me, and a smile had drifted across her face like the sun peeking out behind a cloud. "Mami and I have been dreaming of this day for so long. We talked about it since I was a little girl." She reached out her small hand and began to stroke my hair. "Tía Nora?"

I took her hand that had become tangled and kissed it. "Yes, my love?"

"Don't ever leave us."

At this Alicia straightened up and placed a gentle hand on Lucinda's shoulder. "We talked about this. Nora has a husband and a job in the United States. She's only coming for a visit."

"He can live here too. Jeremy even speaks Spanish doesn't he, Tía Nora?"

I smiled at the way Lucinda pronounced Jeremy's name, with the J sounding like an H. I rather liked the sound of it. I took hold of her hand once again. "If there were any way we could live here with you, I would stay. But I'm afraid your Mami's right. I'll have to go back soon."

Lucinda settled back in her seat with a solemn nod.

At this moment, the ocean appeared between two buildings like a jewel set inside two dry and molding pieces of bread. It sparkled and winked its turquoise perfection, and the waves rolled in graceful and gentle bands on to the beach beyond the *malecón*. I gazed at the sky and ocean as they floated together where heaven meets the earth. This point along the horizon where my Cuban soul lives, this place had not changed at all. It was exactly the same, and all the depressing ugliness I'd just seen faded away.

"Stop the car, Berta," I said and she nearly careened into the sidewalk of the *malecón*. I got out of the car and walked to the wall that held back the sea. The wind blew back my hair, and the ocean spoke to me as it rolled forward. The warmth of the sun reached in past the heat of the day and touched my heart and soul so that they glowed. "Welcome back to the only place your heart can ever truly call home. Go ahead, breathe us in. With every breath it becomes more and more difficult to deny that you're a daughter of the island. The passion in your heart belongs here."

My knees were weak when I walked back to the car, as though I'd been administered a strong drug.

"We'll have time to spend at the beach," Alicia said soberly. "Now you're tired and we should go home to rest for a while. Berta and I made you some good Cuban food. You must be hungry."

I realized suddenly that I was. "I don't think I've ever been hungrier in all my life," I told them as Berta burst away from the curb and back into traffic.

# 25

THEIR HOME WAS ONLY A FEW BLOCKS FROM THE SEA. IT WAS actually a two-room apartment within what once had been a lovely town house with rose-colored walls and terraces spilling over with geraniums and lacey banisters of intricately worked wrought iron. With time and neglect, the walls had peeled off in large curling strips exposing the powdery flesh beneath, but the iron, like the teeth of a corpse consumed by fire, was true to its past.

What Alicia referred to as the kitchen was in reality a small broom closet. It contained a double burner hot plate and a small refrigerator barely big enough for a couple of cartons of milk. Several boxes were arranged against the wall and served as shelves in which they kept two bags of rice and a large bag of black beans, a few onions, and a box of powdered milk. The only window, in the upper corner, had no screen and could only be opened during cooking so the kitchen wouldn't be overcome by insects. The effect was a room so stifling hot that it was a wonder the rice and beans didn't cook all by themselves.

When Alicia and Berta disappeared into the kitchen to finish my homecoming meal, I sat with Lucinda and listened to her sweet singsong voice. She sat on the couch that also served as a bed and looked at me with such tenderness that I felt she could not only see my skin, but all the way through to my soul.

"I always took care of Mami when she worked," she said plainly. "Now that she doesn't work, I still take care of her."

"Your Mami isn't working anymore?" My delight at hearing this made me sound almost shrill.

"Mami's been too tired to work lately, but I make sure nothing disturbs her when she sleeps because rest is what makes her feel better. When she's had a good night's rest, we go to the beach and that's my favorite place in the world."

I nodded my agreement. "This country has the most beautiful beaches in the world. Back in California the beaches are beautiful too, but very different."

"Aren't all beaches the same?"

"My goodness, no. Over there the water is cool, even cold. And the color is dark green and so deep that the sun can't light up the waters and warm it like it does here. If you could give the sea emotions, the sea over there is a somber and serious sea, but here it's playful and rather vain. It's in love with its own beauty reflected in the sky. But who can fault the ocean, when there is none who can even come close to her?"

Lucinda nodded eagerly, and I thought sadly of how she'd never be able to look upon the blessing of beauty that was her own face. She showed me the books she kept underneath the couch. They were obviously her pride and joy, and she ran her fingers over the pages tenderly. She read to me her favorite passages from *Jane Eyre* and *Oliver Twist* with feeling and maturity. But I soon realized she had most of these passages confined to memory because her fingers no longer touched the pages as she spoke but hovered at least two inches above.

With a call from her mother, Lucinda put the books away and set the small table in the center of the room, with no difficulty whatsoever. She knew exactly where the dishes were kept, every spoon and fork as well. It was quite amazing and for an instant, I doubted she was blind at all. Perhaps, I thought, she could see just a little out of the corners of her eyes, but when I studied her movements closely I noticed that her hands hesitated briefly to be sure they'd touched what she intended before she took firm hold of the object. In these three dreary little rooms, Lucinda wasn't blind at all, but completely in control, and it was a joy to watch her.

She whispered to me as we waited for the meal to be served. "Mami's happy because she found three fresh tomatoes yesterday."

"That's wonderful. I love tomatoes."

"I'm lucky that I love bananas best 'cause they're easier to find than tomatoes. Is it hard to find tomatoes in California?"

I took her hand. "Not as hard as it is here."

Alicia and Berta emerged from the tiny kitchen beaming and dripping with perspiration. Between them, they brought a meal that was simple, but delicious. A whole chicken had been slowly stewed in its own juices with onions and garlic. The black beans were the best I'd tasted since leaving Cuba, and the rice was fluffy and perfect, with lightly salted tomatoes sliced on the side in thick rounds.

Berta turned on the radio, and we listened to the crackling sounds of Mambo music as we ate. The breeze from the ocean circled the apartment and settled upon us like an old friend. I closed my eyes. We could've been at Abuelo and Abuela's house at Varadero eating *arroz con pollo* after a long swim. After the meal we'd take a leisurely stroll and reward ourselves with coconut ice cream or a freshly cut mango.

I opened my eyes to find Alicia studying me. She appeared more tired than worried, and although dark circles were evident beneath her eyes, she was still beautiful. The weight she'd lost only accentuated the chiseled perfection of her cheekbones, the perfect line of her nose, and the delicate sweep of her jaw that flexed as she chewed. Seeing daughter and mother side by side was quite astounding. Lucinda resembled her father, there was no doubt about that, but her aquiline features were almost an exact replica of her mother's.

"You've come so far and this is all we have to offer you," Alicia said, setting down her fork as her eyes filled with tears. "I'm ashamed to tell you how long it took us to find this chicken . . ." She shrugged off her sadness and winked in Berta's direction.

"Well, I sure don't mind telling you," Berta countered with a flick of her head that swung a shock of black hair across Lucinda's startled face. "What we should've done with this chicken was dress it up in new clothes and take it dancing for the evening. It's almost a shame to eat it."

We all laughed and I realized that Berta helped Alicia with much more than her talent for finding chickens and toilet paper. In some ways, she reminded me of Beba. Her no nonsense humor seemed to beckon hope and forward thinking as resolutely as a good strong heat could boil water. There was no time or energy to worry, when you knew that day would follow night and that you had to continue breathing and living and laughing and crying today just like any other day.

After dinner, Alicia collapsed on the couch while Lucinda did the dishes in the bathroom sink. I offered to help, but she refused with a casual wave of her hand as though she were a middle-age lady quite territorial about her work in the kitchen. Berta retired to her room with complaints that she would need to get up early the next morning. The radio was hers and she took it with her.

Alicia insisted we go for a walk while Lucinda finished the dishes and in less than a minute we were walking arm in arm toward the *malecón*. We were silent as we walked, listening to the sounds of the city, children being called in from the streets for the night. Pots and pans clanging as they were washed after dinner, the scuffling of brooms sweeping the grime of the day out into the streets. Few cars could be heard or seen. Alicia explained that it was next to impossible to find headlights for them so they couldn't be driven at night. If you saw a car at night, it was almost always a taxi or a Russian-built government car.

We reached the *malecón* in a few minutes, at almost the same spot where I'd stood earlier that day, but the difference was dramatic. A blinking necklace of lights spread out before us, tracing the line of the shore. The exact curve and sweep of the lights conforming perfectly to the memory I cherished. The music of the sea, the mist against my cheeks, Alicia's voice speaking to me, telling me whatever came into her head, as she was prone to do. I held on to the concrete wall for support. My eyes were aching from the effort of crying and trying not to cry as tears sprung to my eyes for the third time that day.

I heard Alicia's voice carry on the breeze behind me. "This is what I wanted you to see."

"We shouldn't have come when you're so tired. We could've come tomorrow."

"I wanted to see it tonight."

I turned to Alicia who was gazing and smiling at me. "You can see this every night, silly," I said.

"No. I wanted to see the expression on your face when you saw it." She shoved my shoulder playfully. "Silly."

We walked on a few blocks further and crossed the street arm in arm. Hardly speaking, she guided me past the corner where the pharmacy had been and on toward the street that I knew we must visit. My senses became enlivened, and I felt like an old horse heading back to her stable. We stopped suddenly, my eyes lifting seven stories up to our apartment, and the years swept away as if we had just been sent on an errand. I expected to see Beba's white turban out on the balcony at any moment and Mami watching and waving like she did when we went to the corner for an ice cream. "Bring back some coconut for after dinner," she'd call. "And be careful crossing the street." My eyes strained against the shadows hoping to catch a glimpse of a ghost or anything that could make it all come back again. Perhaps if I looked at it hard enough and long enough.

"Who lives there now?" I asked, trying to keep my voice steady.

"Nobody. The building's been condemned for years."

I looked more closely and saw the windows boarded up and other balconies stripped of their railings. I felt a sudden urge to run up the seven flights of stairs and see it all again; my room, the kitchen, and the chair where Papi used to read his paper. I might even find my Elvis albums where I'd left them by the window. I began to walk forward to do just that, but Alicia held on to my arm. "It's not a good idea to go in, Nora," she said softly.

"Why not?"

"It's very dangerous," she said, leading me away. "More than you know."

We walked back home slowly, and Alicia leaned more heavily on my arm. "Have you seen a doctor yet?" I asked.

"A doctor? For what?"

"You're obviously not feeling well, and you've lost a lot of weight. . . ."

"I suppose you're going to tell me next that a woman should be round and plump with a big butt if she wants to look good."

I laughed, remembering the traditional Cuban abhorrence of skinny women. "I'd never say such a thing, I just think you should see a doctor. Maybe he can give you an antibiotic or some kind of medicine. . . ."

"Doctors here don't have much medicine to give, Nora. Besides all I need is rest and now that you're here, that's medicine enough for me."


I called Jeremy from a pay phone down the street the next morning. Alicia said it served most of the neighborhood and that I should get up early if I didn't want to wait in line for too long. Lucinda asked meekly if she could accompany me, and this surprised and pleased Alicia.

She held my hand tightly and matched her steps precisely to my own, and she never stopped chattering away about her books and how she wanted to be a teacher for blind children one day. She stopped in the middle of the sidewalk next to the phone before I'd spotted it and stood close to me, under the shadow of the phone booth, as I dialed and spoke to the international operator. Lucinda smiled when she heard my English, and I believe she was proud.

It was still very early in the morning, but Jeremy answered the phone before it had a chance to complete the first ring. He seemed delighted to hear my voice, and said many times that he missed me, and asked even more times how I was and how I'd found everything.

"Have you talked to my parents?" I asked.

"They called last night wanting to know if you'd made it OK, but I told them I hadn't heard from you."

"How are they doing?"

"They seemed a little worried about you, but they'll be fine. The important thing is that you take care of yourself and come back soon. I miss you, you know," he said for the tenth time, but I didn't get tired of hearing it.

I felt Lucinda tugging at my sleeve. "Can I say hello to Heremi?" she asked with a shy smile. I passed the phone to Lucinda. "Hello. How are you?" she asked in her best, most carefully pronounced English. Then her eyes flew open and she giggled as she answered Jeremy's questions in Spanish and gave him a blow by blow account of all we'd done since I arrived.

"And we're taking her to our special beach today or tomorrow. It all depends on how Mami feels." Lucinda nodded. "No she's been sick for a long time and she needs to rest all the time, but I take very good care of her. She tells me no one can take as good care of her as me." She nodded again. "Yes, I'll take good care of Tía Nora too. I'll make sure she's always with me, except when she takes a bath or goes to the bathroom. Even then, I won't be very far away at all." After several good-byes, she handed the phone back to me quite satisfied with herself.

"Looks like you have an able little bodyguard there," he said, still chuckling.

"She's precious, Jeremy. I feel as though she's been with me all my life. I really don't know how I'll manage to leave her."

"Are you trying to scare me? You said you'd be back in two weeks, and I don't believe I'll be able to stand it for a minute more than that."

I held Lucinda close to me as I answered him. "I miss you too, and I'll be home very soon. I promise."


As it turned out, Alicia did feel better and we managed to get to the beach several times that first week. Alicia and Lucinda called it their secret beach, and it took some doing to get there. It was at least three miles further than the beach we had frequented near Havana, and we needed to arrive between nine and ten in the morning and enter through an opening in a the barbed wire fence that ran for at least three or four miles further down the road. We took a picnic of bread, cheese, and ham, all items I purchased at the tourist market without difficulty. I was also able to find a beach umbrella, ridiculously priced, but worth the expense, because the secret beach provided no shade whatsoever.

Alicia eased back on her elbows with an audible sigh. The shadows under her eyes had grown more pronounced, and I wondered if she'd become even more tired since my arrival.

"Why don't we just go to the usual beach? It's so far to come all the way over here."

Alicia shook her head and sputtered a dry laugh. Her eyes were on Lucinda who waded in the warm water without a worry in the world. Whenever she stepped on something interesting, she reached down to pick it up and held it to her cheek.

"That beach is closed to us," Alicia said matter-of-factly. "You can go if you want."

"What do you mean?"

Alicia allowed fists full of sand to slip through her fingers one after the other before answering. "Ever since they started building the hotels, they closed the best beaches to the people, the Cuban people that is."

"That doesn't make any sense."

Alicia kept pouring her piles of sand. "This beach is technically closed as well. That's why they have the fence up. They'll start building the hotel in a few months and then we'll have to find somewhere else. Right now they don't really enforce it, but they will."

I was silent while I thought about this. "It's hard to believe that when we left here they called us *gusanos* and traitors to the revolution. Now they let us have the best."

"Ah, well . . . You may have been worms when you left, but now you're butterflies and better than that, your wings are made of American dollars. That's all the Castristas care about."

Alicia spoke with little emotion. She'd obviously accepted this reality long ago. But I was angry and had a good mind to march straight to the nearest hotel and complain. I told Alicia this and her eyes flew open in alarm.

"That's the worse thing you could do," she said. "I don't care about all that. All I care about is Lucinda and Tony and leaving here when we're able." She turned to me, her eyes alive with fear. "Promise me you won't make any trouble at the hotels."

I nodded and she relaxed.

Lucinda called out from the water's edge that she was collecting perfect shells to give to each of us. Alicia smiled and laid down in the sand. She wore an old smock shirt and a pair of baggy shorts. She looked like a pubescent girl, with barely the suggestion of breasts. Her once shapely legs were knob-kneed and thinner than Lucinda's, and her skin was so fragile and pale that I could see the delicate tract of veins pulsating in her throat.

Alicia's eyelids fluttered. "I wish we could look up at the palms like we used to. Remember?"

"I remember," I answered, still startled by her appearance.

She opened one eye. "Lie down next to me, Nora."

I laid down and closed my eyes, feeling a chill despite the warmth of the sun and the sand beneath our bodies. It came from somewhere deep inside me, but I dared not examine it any further. Better to listen to the sigh of the ocean and Lucinda's giggles floating above it.

# 26

THE HOT WIND CAME IN THROUGH THE OPEN WINDOW AND
moaned. I had difficulty breathing as I waited for morning. Alicia
was sleeping on the couch, and Lucinda slept peacefully next to
her on a roll of blankets.

It had been three days since I'd spoken to Jeremy. Had he forgotten me? What silly thoughts popped into my head on sleepless
nights. He couldn't possibly forget me in a week. He loved me
and had pledged to be with me always, and I was painfully aware
of a desire to be with him in our little house. I looked out the
window at the stars, the same stars I'd gazed at as a child from this
particular angle in the sky. I'd be home in less than a week. I'd be
lying with my sweet Jeremy in our king-size bed, his arms wrapped
around me as he liked to do before he fell asleep. If it was Satur-
day we'd go for our morning walk and return to our house for the
eggs and bacon we only allowed ourselves on weekends. Weekdays were dedicated to healthier breakfasts of low fat cereal and
fruit, with maybe a sprinkle of sugar.

The little hand on my forehead startled me. It was Lucinda
crouching next to me. The moonlight illuminated her angelic
features and reflected off her small teeth. She appeared to be
looking into my eyes. At first I thought she was smiling and playing a trick on me, but then I realized it was agony I saw on her
face, a mature pain not appropriate for someone so young.

She inched closer to me and whispered in my ear: "Tía Nora, are you awake?"

"Yes, my love. I'm awake."

"I must tell you something, Tía Nora."

"What is it, sweetheart?"

"Mami is very sick."

The elbow on which I supported myself threatened to give way. Perhaps I was still sleeping? I blinked, but Lucinda remained as she was with her little hand on my shoulder, her corkscrew curls catching the moonlight through the window, her wondering gaze quite at home in the dark.

"Lucinda, you must be having a bad dream."

"No, I'm not. They don't think I know."

"Know what exactly?"

"Mami has a disease." Her face contorted in pain. "I heard Berta and Mami talking when they thought I was asleep."

Her hands reached for my face as she tried to read my expression, her fingertips gently exploring my eyes for tears. Relieved to find them dry, she continued. "They take people who have it far away. They're keeping it a secret so Mami doesn't have to go away from me."

I sat straight up in my cot and held Lucinda close to me. "Don't worry. I'll help your Mami, Lucinda."

Her arms reached around and I felt her tremble with sobs, but she quickly recovered and smothered the sounds of her pain for fear that she'd wake up her mother. As I held her, I was hardly able to breathe, as if I'd been kicked in the stomach.

"Can I sleep with you, Tía?"

I threw the sheet back and made room in the narrow cot for her. She nestled into me like a warm kitten, and fell asleep in less than a minute.

Alicia explained she'd been making this short trip out of town on a weekly basis for almost five years and for the last year or so, Ricardo hadn't required any special favors. She'd told me about it in her letters, but I sensed she had a need to tell me about it again. We walked slowly through narrow streets trying to stay on the shaded side, as the heat was suffocating.

The drying laundry swinging in the hot wind above our heads was the only movement, and our own pace was slow.

Alicia spoke while looking down at her feet. She allowed me to carry the bag of provisions containing items that were difficult to find such as aspirin, a box of saltine crackers, and the inevitable tube of toothpaste with nothing but the world "Dental" written on it.

"It gives me so much peace to do this," she said. "To know that these items can keep Tony more comfortable and safe. Maybe he'll have a letter for me." She brightened up at the prospect.

"Does he write you every week?"

"No. I wish he did, but it's not easy to get paper and I suppose that sometimes he's just too tired. They take prisoners out to work in the fields you know, especially the strong capable ones. One day I sat out in the sun for almost half a day watching a line of men working in the field. I picked one man out of the group and pretended he was Tony. His shoulders were broad and he swung his arms the way I imagined Tony would, and he held his head up high as I hope Tony still does. Then he spat down at his feet and I knew it wasn't Tony. He'd never do that."

We walked for another half-hour in silence, our feet pounding the broken sidewalk like hot pancakes on a griddle. My throat was dry, and I suggested we stop at the next market for something to drink. We sipped lime sodas under the shade of a tattered awning while sitting on the curb. The road was bright with heat, and I wondered if even the ocean was boiling.

"How long have you been sick, Alicia?"

She stared straight ahead at the empty road as if in a trance. Her soda was getting warm, and the condensation of the glass moistened her fingers. "Is it so obvious?"

"It's obvious that you're very sick."

She nodded, still not looking at me. "I've known for a few months now."

"And you haven't seen a doctor?"

"A doctor can't do anything for me now. Nothing that will do me any good."

Alicia finished her soda with long slow swallows, the muscles in her thin neck rolling with every gulp.

"Are you just going to wait around to die? You have to do something. We have to find a way to get you out of here now. Tonight!" My empty glass slipped out of my hands and rolled into the gutter. "Damn it, Alicia. You should've left on the freighter with Lucinda when you had a chance."

"I couldn't leave Tony."

Alicia stood up and I followed her. She was walking down the street, calm and slow, with me weeping like a baby next to her. It had cooled off a bit and some people were venturing out of their crumbling houses. By now I was hysterical as I begged Alicia to do as I said. People threw me incurious glances. They'd seen despair grow into hysteria as often as they'd seen the dawn grow into the glaring scorch of midday. There was nothing unusual in my emotional display, and it did little to move Alicia. She nodded and patted my shoulder as we walked, much as she would do to a child crying over an ice cream.

I stopped and sat down on the curb with my head in my arms. I stared at the dust covering my feet, my tears streaking water trails down to my ankles.

Alicia sat next to me with a sigh. I was tempted to tell her that Lucinda knew everything. That in trying to protect her precious child she was actually torturing her.

She whispered in my ear as she had when we were children and she wanted me to follow her in some childish antic. "I'm not afraid to die, you know." I turned to see her peeking at me through my arms. "I knew the risk I was taking, but I was so crazy to make money I didn't care. I always considered myself to be lucky, but I guess this time my luck ran out."

"Are you sure you have it? It could be something else . . ."

Alicia shook her head resolutely. "Berta and I have seen it too many times. Many people we know, and many more we don't, have been sent away. We're not sure where they go, only that they never return. Alicia stretched her thin legs out in front of her so they were poking out into the narrow street. I remembered how her legs had looked at fifteen, shapely and strong, the legs of an excellent swimmer.

"Perhaps there are treatments. . . ."

"Not here, not for me. The only thing that matters is that my Tony and Lucinda are safe. The rest will take care of itself as it always does." She placed her hand on my knee. "Let's go or Ricardo will be gone, and I'll have to come back tomorrow."

He waited at the end of the path leading to the side entrance of the prison, his greasy face contorted as he tried to make out who I was against the glare of the sun. He cocked his head to one side and rested his right hand on his pistol. In his left hand, he held a white envelope that flashed like a mirror. As we got closer I could see his heavily pock-marked face and that his eyebrows joined in the middle to form a perfect V. His smile revealed yellow teeth and thick swollen gums speckled with tobacco.

Alicia greeted him like a sister with a warm hug and kiss on the cheek. She was genuinely happy to see him and presented me as the cousin from the United States she'd been telling him about. We shook hands, and I handed the bag of provisions to Alicia who promptly turned it over to Ricardo.

"I brought him an extra roll of toilet paper this time," she said, happily eyeing the letter that was still in Ricardo's hand, but he was busy inspecting the bag and his eyes widened when he saw the soap I put in. Irish Spring.

"Oh, I almost forgot. Here you are," he said, handing her the letter. "He finished it this morning."

Alicia took the letter and tucked it inside her blouse. "How is he this week? Have you heard any news?"

He wrenched his head out of the bag. "I hear rumors all the time, but who knows? They might let him out tomorrow or maybe next year." He shoved his head back into the bag.

"There's a letter for Tony at the bottom," Alicia said.

Ricardo peered at us both. Sweat was creeping into his eyes, causing him to blink nervously. With the bag slung over one arm, he took several steps back toward the shade of the guardhouse. He pointed to me with his thick hairy finger. "How long you staying?"

Alicia answered before I had a chance to. "She'll be leaving next week, so I might send Berta with next week's package."

He nodded his approval upon hearing this, and waved us off.

Alicia walked back home with renewed vigor. She was delighted to have a letter from Tony over her heart, pounding new life into her, but the meeting with Ricardo was holding me back from my usual pace.

"Do you think Tony gets the things you send him?" I asked.

Alicia smiled. "You must think I'm pretty stupid, don't you?"

"I would never think that."

She laughed and patted the letter to her heart. "I know Tony gets some of the things because he's written me so, though I'm sure Ricardo keeps the best for himself. But even if he kept it all I wouldn't care because I know that, if nothing else, he keeps an eye on Tony for me."

"Has it ever occurred to you that Ricardo might never want Tony to leave so he can keep getting his packages?"

Alicia stopped in her tracks. "I never thought of that." Then a smile shot across her face. "What if I offer him a reward when Tony is released?"

"I didn't mean you should do that . . ."

"Of course. It's a splendid idea. If what you say is true, then my Tony will be out very soon. And I have the money, Nora. I'll give Ricardo his reward. I've given him everything else."

When we arrived home, Alicia closed the curtain of the only window, went directly to the couch and pulled it back. In the wall behind the couch was a small hole stuffed with wadded napkins and tissues, discolored yellow from the constant moisture in the air. She quickly picked out the paper and shoved her hand inside. After very little probing she retrieved a small metal box. Beckoning for me to come closer, she opened it. It was filled with banknotes, mostly American, but some Canadian and German as well. She insisted I count them, and I estimated there was close to five thousand dollars.

"I told you I could afford it," she said proudly. "Aside from Lucinda, you're the only person who knows about this money."

"How about Berta?"

Alicia shook her head, looking a little ashamed. "It's not that I distrust her, but I've seen desperation do things to people. I can't take any chances with this money."

Carefully, she put the box back in its place and restuffed the hole. I helped her push the couch back against the wall, and she promptly collapsed onto it.


By the time I finished helping Lucinda prepare a supper of cheese and crackers, Alicia had fallen asleep. We ate quickly, and I covered her with a light blanket before tiptoeing out into the balmy evening.

The music from the hotels reached us soon enough as we walked arm in arm along the *malecón*. Lucinda skipped next to me when she wasn't shuffling her feet to the rhythms. The mist of the ocean reached over the wall like a soft wave of wonder and enveloped us. My feet began to follow Lucinda's and soon we were dancing together by the light of dim street lamps that illuminated the mist like tiny crystals suspended in air. From a distance we could see the arched windows of the Intercontinental Hotel, with guests dancing on the polished floor to the same music.

I pictured Alicia arriving to work at a place like this, turning the eye of every man in the room as always, tolerating their disgusting caresses for the hope of escape.

"What's wrong, Tía Nora?" Lucinda was tugging on my arm. Without realizing it, I'd stopped dancing.

"I'm sorry, honey. I guess I'm a little tired too."

We strolled back with our backs to the lights along the *malecón*. Soon we heard only the crashing of the waves and the occasional cry of a seagull.

"Tía Nora?"

"Yes, my love."

"Is Mami going to die?" She asked the question so lightly that it almost floated off on the breeze coming in from the sea.

I struggled to find an answer that would be honest, but not cruel. "We all have to die sometime."

"I know. That's what Mami told me when Tía Panchita died, but Tía Panchita was old and Mami isn't old yet, and she wants to go to the United States even more than I do."

My throat tightened with sadness as I tried to find my voice. "Why do you want to go there?" I asked.

"Because Mami says hope died in Cuba a long time ago. She always says it's possible to live without soap and toothpaste, but you can't live without hope."

# 27

I SLIPPED OUT IN THE EARLY MORNING TO CALL JEREMY. HE'D BE in a dead sleep, but I couldn't take the chance he wouldn't be home. During our last phone call he said he missed me so much he was almost driven to writing poetry, and that I should spare the world this tragedy and get home soon. I pictured him in our king-size bed, sleeping with one arm under his head and the other clutching the pillow where I should be. He wouldn't like my phone call; in fact, he'd hate it.

"You're staying how long?"

"I'm not really sure. All I know is I can't leave Lucinda like this to take care of Alicia by herself. And I'm afraid they're going to take her away and lock her up somewhere. If they find out Alicia is sick, God knows what they'll do to her. It's crazy, Jeremy. It's crazy what they do. And . . ."

"OK. Calm down, sweetheart. Let's just think about this for a minute."

My heart was racing as I waited for a solution to spring from the silence on the other end of the phone. The sun had risen from the sea and a brilliant ray of intense heat was burning the top of my ankles, and it wasn't even 7:00 yet. The phone was sweaty in my hand. "Are you there?"

"Yes, I'm just thinking . . . What if you come home as you

planned, and then go back when it seems that Alicia is . . . When it seems that she needs your help more than she does now?"

A sob exploded from the back of my throat. "I want to be with you more than anything, but I can't leave them. Please understand. I'm all they have. I can't let them take Alicia. I can't let them take Lucinda."

As I spoke, a line was forming behind me and I was reminded that this was the only working phone for several blocks.

"Please, Nora, call me tomorrow or as soon as you can. We have to talk about this."

"I will. I promise."

"I love you."

"I love you too."

I hung up and turned around to find a group of tattered Cubans watching me through the fog of a poor night's sleep in stifling heat. They studied my new sandals and clean clothes. My slim watch flashed in the sun, and I could sense them wondering what this foreigner with plenty of money for a hotel room with its own phone was doing using the public one. Why wasn't I frolicking on the best beaches with my oversized beach towel and a chilled fruit salad waiting for my breakfast? Why wasn't I smiling like all the other tourists they saw stumbling about the streets after a night out, throwing change at the street musicians like they were skinny little birds? Instead, I stood before them whimpering like a child.

An older black woman approached me. She'd been waiting in line with the others, and I could see that she was going to scold me for taking so much time. I began to search my purse for something I might give her. I'd left my money at the house, but even a pack of tissue paper or a stick of gum would be better than nothing. I produced a pen and a roll of mints and held them out for her, but she made no move for them. She was gazing at my face and looking me up and down and shaking her head in disbelief. I waited for her reprimand and hung my head to see her bare feet and bony ankles, swollen and flea bitten.

"If I weren't looking at you with my own eyes I wouldn't believe it." The golden voice flowed like honey into my ears; warm sweet honey that makes everything taste better and makes all the cares of the world float away on a soft current.

I looked up and stared into the crinkled black face and black shiny eyes that were already alive with tears. I clasped the large rough hands held out to me and buried my head into her shoulder as her arms came around me and patted my back reassuringly as they had so many years ago.

"Oh, Beba," I cried. "Where have you been?"

"Right here, child. I've been right here all the time."


Beba lived only a few short blocks from Alicia's house in a small one-room apartment that overlooked a narrow alley. She was on the third floor and as we climbed up past the second floor the heat became suffocating. Because of the continuous heat and humidity, mold stained the inner corridors, an earthy blend of green, brown, and rust, like the moss that grows in the deepest regions of the jungle; it was the color common to most old buildings that hadn't been painted since the revolution. Finding Beba was a miracle I didn't dare hope for since we'd left, although I still thought of her when I felt most alone and afraid. How many times I'd imagined myself with her at the sink, slicing onions and humming one of her exotic African tunes, I did not know. By the time we reached the third floor, I felt a calmness I hadn't felt since I was a child.

She told me to have a seat on one of two metal folding chairs and busied herself at the single burner by the window. Her hands trembled as she measured out the coffee and sugar for our *café con leche*. As she worked, she told me that for the past ten years she'd been living in this apartment, observing the neighbors that came and went like noisy spirits through her one window to the alley. She had a good job rolling cigars in a factory just outside Havana until three years ago when the factory closed down. But she added that her arthritis would've forced her to quit anyway, and now she got by on a measly pension and her monthly rations that amounted to barely five dollars a month.

"I thought of your family often," she said in a shaky voice that I didn't want to hear.

"We thought of you all the time, Beba. I know Mami tried to find you during the first few years after we left, but nobody knew where you were."

"People get lost here very easy," she said with a sober shake of her head.

She walked slowly across the small room with a cup in each hand, careful to give me the one that wasn't chipped. I accepted it gratefully, knowing that the coffee and the sugar and milk were difficult to come by and greedily rationed. She didn't skimp at all on the ingredients, however. The *café con leche* was thick and rich and perfectly balanced as I always remembered it to be when she made it. Tears welled in my eyes. This was the home I remembered; sitting with Beba and waiting for her to tell me what was on her mind as I'd always done. Her way was as direct and delicious as the hot cup of milk and coffee that I held in my hands. It cleared the head and the heart more efficiently than the strongest caffeine.

"You're a woman, Norita," she said gazing at me with misty eyes. "A beautiful woman, like I knew you would be. How's Martica?"

"She's married now and has two children. She gave us a hard time during her teenage years."

Beba laughed and slapped her knee. "And how about you? Did you give anyone a hard time?"

"Oh, no. I was a very good girl all the time. You wouldn't have recognized me."

Beba was thoughtful. "I imagined it the other way. Maybe something in that new country made you trade places? Maybe it confused you in your head a bit like it does when you hit strange weather? When it's too hot like today I can't think. I can't think at all." Beba sipped at her *café con leche* peering at me over the rim of her cup all the while.

I told her about life in the United States, and about growing up there and Jeremy. I told her how Papi and Mami didn't want me to come, but that all the years I'd been away I'd thought of little else. The morning passed like a tropical storm as I told her all these things, and she listened with the wise nod of her head and a flickering smile that was more sad than happy. Then she told me of her life as she stared out the window at the molding wall. She spoke mostly of her daughter who joined the military and was an avid Communist even in this day when so many had lost faith in the revolution.

"We get along all right these days, but I didn't speak to Hortensia for two years," she said. "And I'm glad too, cause for a while there I was afraid she'd have me arrested. A lot of crazy kids all stirred up by that man betrayed their parents, let me tell you." Beba waved a crooked finger in my direction, and I couldn't help but smile. It amused me that she, like Mami, still referred to Castro as *that man*.

"I should call him that dog." Beba said when I mentioned this to her. "Even that's too good for him. He's shit on this country worse than any back street dog would do."

I told Beba about Alicia and Lucinda and she nodded gravely, not in the least bit surprised. "She's right not to see the doctor. They'll just send her away and God only knows what'll happen to her child. I've seen it many times."

"Their only chance is for Tony to get out of prison soon."

Beba pushed her chair against the wall and leaned back, crossing her arms and locking her gaze onto me as she would when she'd caught me in a lie. "What makes her think he's getting out?"

"Alicia gets letters from him all the time, and she seems to think he has a chance. It's the only hope that keeps her alive, Beba." Just saying her name made me feel like I was ten years old again.

"Could be," Beba said pushing out her bottom jaw. "Maybe he'll be one of the lucky ones. I hope so, for her sake."

I didn't want to leave, but it was almost noon and I knew Alicia and Lucinda would wonder where I'd been all morning. I promised Beba to return soon and to bring her many things.

"Don't bring me nothing. If there's one thing I've learned all these years, it's that I don't need much. Just bring yourself Norita. And the rest of your family if you like. I'll be here."

# 28

ALICIA WAS UNABLE TO GET OUT OF BED FOR THE NEXT FEW days. A mild storm swept in as Lucinda and I tended to her. Berta blew in and out with the gales while wearing her stretchy clothes and her hair a mass of black frizz and curls impossible to tame in the humid weather. She barely glanced at us and muttered a hasty greeting before going straight to her room.

"She gets like this when there's a lot of work," Alicia said one afternoon when she appeared to be feeling stronger. "Bad weather means more work because the . . . clients have less to do . . . more time on their hands." She shrugged and sipped the cup of tea she'd been nursing for the past hour.

With the covers pulled away from her, I had to make an effort not to stare at her emaciated form. If she'd been skinny before, she was now a wisp of smoke, curling and fading as I looked on. We heard Lucinda in the kitchen putting away the dishes and bustling about. I knew better than to try and help her. Only one person could work comfortably in the kitchen at one time, and Lucinda was able to manage much better than I would.

"It's been so much better since you've been here." Alicia said when she finished her tea. "Lucinda's happier than I've seen her in a long time. She smiles more and she sleeps as a child should sleep, all through the night and not waking up every half hour to make sure I'm OK."

"She's an amazing child."

Alicia nodded and looked at me, her golden-green eyes huge in her pale face. "I know you're leaving soon, but you won't tell me because you know I'll be sad. You have to go home to your husband and your beautiful life. I'm happy to know your life is good, Nora. It's almost like it's my own life. Does that make any sense?"

I smiled. "When we were growing up I felt like the wonderful things happening to you were happening to me. Like when we walked down the street and every man alive couldn't take his eyes off of you. I might as well have been your shadow trailing behind, but I was happy too, as I had a taste of what it was like to feel beautiful."

"It's hard to believe that was ever me." Alicia pulled the sweater she wore over her shoulders even though it was well past eighty degrees. "I think I feel well enough to go see Beba. Lucinda would like to meet her, and I'm sure you want to say good-bye before you go."

"I'd love to go see Beba, but not to say good-bye. I've decided to stay a bit longer."

Alicia brightened noticeably. "Are you serious?"

I glanced at my watch. "My plane left an hour ago, and I'm definitely not on it."

Alicia threw her head back and laughed out loud as I hadn't heard her do since my arrival. "What's there to eat? I suddenly feel hungry."


We made our way to Beba's house as I held Alicia by one arm and Lucinda held my other free hand. It was only three blocks away, but it took us almost a half-hour to walk one of them. Alicia concentrated on every step she took and was clearly exhausted by the time we got to the corner. It would be so easy if she had a wheel chair, but of course that would require, at the very least, a doctor's referral and after confirming it with Beba, I was convinced that this was an option to be avoided at all costs.

Alicia's breath was deep and labored and she suddenly chuckled. "I feel like I'm learning to walk all over again."

"Maybe this isn't such a good idea. I can ask Beba to come over to our house instead." I shivered in the heat at the term "our house". Had this become my home? Wasn't my home in Santa Monica with Jeremy? That sweet yellow house with white shutters that captured the afternoon breeze. What did a cool breeze feel like? I felt suddenly nostalgic for my uncomplicated life in California.

I felt Alicia's grip tighten on my arm. "It's good for me to get out of the house," she said. "Maybe we can just rest for a while."

We stopped in the shade of an abandoned building that appeared to have once been a bookstore. Inside I could see empty shelves draped with cobwebs and holding nothing but empty bottles of rum. Most likely men sneaked in to drink and gamble after curfew. Some of the bottles looked new and shiny clear next to the soot of more than two decades. The back door was open a sliver, but wide enough so an overgrown patch of yard was visible. Through an entanglement of weeds I noticed a small wheel.

"Lucinda, wait here with your mother. I'll be right back."

It was some time before I could uncover the mysterious item hiding in the weeds. It was rusty and needed a bit of adjusting, but it was exactly what I hoped it would be.

I made my way back to the front of the building, rolling my prize before me triumphantly.

Alicia cocked her head to one side, amused. Lucinda did the same. "What's that funny squeaking sound?" she asked.

"What in the world are you doing with that old wheelbarrow, Nora? You don't think I'm getting into it do you? I'd rather walk to Tres Pinos and back on my knees than be seen in that."

Lucinda jumped up and down excitedly. "I'll get in. I'll get in," she cried, nearly bursting with excitement.

"Maybe later, sweetheart. Right now your Mami needs to be reasonable and let us push her in this. Isn't that right, Mami?"

Alicia crossed her arms and pouted. "It's dirty."

"That's true, but we can clean it up later. And look how well it works." I rolled it back and forth. "We can go lots of places with this."

"People will laugh at me."

"Nonsense. Nobody laughs at five people hanging on to a bicycle for dear life, so why would they laugh at this. Besides, I wouldn't mind seeing a few smiles from time to time."

Alicia hobbled over to the wheelbarrow, touched the rim, then felt down to the base of the barrow where she would sit. "Filthy, just filthy," she muttered as she turned around and carefully lowered herself to sitting position. Lucinda stroked the wheelbarrow, the sides, the handles, the wheels and finally her mother's form tucked inside like a baby chick.

She giggled with delight. "Can I help push, Tía Nora?"

"Of course. We can push together."

"Take it easy, you two. We don't need to go very fast. It's not like we have a train to catch."

The wheels caught and wobbled as we made our way down the sidewalk. It had a tendency to veer toward the right and the broken wood of the handles splintered the flesh on my palms, but it was much easier for all of us to travel this way. We passed the *malecón*, and the breeze rising off the ocean was surprisingly cool. Alicia dropped her head back slightly and let the wind brush through her hair. Her eyes were closed, and a serene smile was on her lips. Alicia's tight grip on the sides of the barrow loosened, and her hand slipped down to her sides.

"It's a nice day isn't it, Tía Nora?"

"It's a beautiful day."

Lucinda had stopped trying to help push after a few minutes. She slipped her little hand around my elbow and kept in step perfectly while her face pointed straight ahead like a soldier.

When we arrived to Beba's apartment building my hands were aching, but our spirits were shining. We parked the wheelbarrow safely within the dark narrow passage that lead to her door so no one from the street could see it.

Beba was startled to see Alicia in her current state, but she recovered quickly and almost carried her to the couch near the
window. She rattled about her sparse cupboard for some crackers
and a little coffee to offer despite our protests. Of course she
wouldn't hear of not offering her guests a little something, and
she was able to come up with a plate of stale crackers spread with
a thin layer of strawberry jam and coffee with a little sugar, but no
milk. Lucinda enjoyed them immensely and it was clear that
Beba was taken with her. As Lucinda hugged her and touched her
wrinkled face, Beba scooped her up and insisted she sit next to
her. We talked and laughed for hours.

"Oh yes, I remember hearing about that boy," Beba said with a
sly smile. "I never met him myself, but Doña Regina told me
about him when it all happened. They say he was one of the most
handsome men around, black or white." She chuckled and shook
her head so that her once full cheeks wiggled a bit. "You," she
said pointing her finger at Alicia, "were something else. When I
heard about what happened I thought to myself, now that girl is
either a fool for love or just a plain fool. I don't know which is
worse."

"Why were people mad at Mami and Papi?" Lucinda de-
manded.

"Now you have to understand, little one," Beba said, lightly
stroking Lucinda's hair. "The world was different then. Today colored people and white people get together and get married or
don't get married, and nobody says much if they even notice, but
in those days people had a lot to say."

Beba delighted us all, especially Lucinda, as she rocked back
and forth on her little stool and laughed with her mouth so wide
we could see all the spaces where her gleaming white teeth used
to be. Her smile was radiant as ever and her piercing gaze just as
persuasive. "It was a good life, wasn't it?" she asked, gazing out
the window and smiling past the cracked and peeling plaster. We
answered her with a silent, but collective sigh.

"Why don't you come with us?" Lucinda asked, jumping up to
the center of the room.

"Where are you going, child?" Beba was still looking out the window.

"We're going to *Los Estados Unidos*. Just as soon as Papi gets out. We have the money all saved, don't we, Mami?"

Beba tore her gaze away from the window, focusing on Alicia with questioning eyes. Alicia smiled sadly at Beba and shook her head just a little. She hadn't yet explained to Lucinda how her illness changed all the plans they'd been making.

"Mami?" Lucinda took several steps towards Alicia. "Mami why don't you answer me? Are you there? As she moved forward, she stumbled on the leg of a chair and fell to the ground. Alicia attempted to go to her, but Beba still spry for her age, picked Lucinda up and swiped the dust off of her knees with her arthritic hands, while she muttered that she should be careful because she was too old and tired to keep picking children off the floor. How many times she'd done the same for me as a child, I couldn't say.

"I wish I had straight teeth like you, so I don't have to wear braces, Beba," I'd tell her as she brushed my hair out in the morning and made the simple pony tail I preferred to Marta's fancy braid.

"Now, don't you start complaining so early in the morning." She'd stop brushing, and stare at me hard in the mirror. "You know what they say about complaining, don't you?"

"What, Beba?"

"Complaining gives you a hard heart and soft bones. Just the opposite of how they should be." She continued brushing my hair so hard that my head pulled back every time she took a stroke, but it felt so good, as if she was brushing all the bad thoughts out of my head. "Try gratitude instead. It'll make you strong," (stroke) "wise beyond your years," (stroke) "a lover of life," (stroke).

Lucinda nestled herself next to Beba again. "I want you to come with us," she said, hugging both her legs.

"Beba's too old to go anywhere."

"Don't you want to see what it's like? Markets full of any kind of food you want, hot water and soap every day of the week, and some people have more than three pairs of shoes."

"I'd sure like to see that again," Beba said with a solemn nod of her head and a wistful grin that eased across her face. "Believe it or not, I used to have six pairs of shoes, every one of them bright white. Most of them were gifts from Doña Regina. She was a good and generous woman, God bless her."

"Six pairs of shoes?"

"That's right."

"Why would anybody need that many shoes?"

Beba shook her head, lost for an answer. "Many years ago I could've told you, but the truth is I forgot."

The next morning Lucinda and I scrubbed the wheelbarrow on the inside and out until not a fleck of rust or dirt could be seen. We lined it with a blanket and two pillows and thought hard about how we might create some shade. I attempted to attach an umbrella to the wagon, but I couldn't figure out a way to have it open without restricting the driver's view. We finally concluded that whenever possible we'd walk in the shade.

The problem with the wheels proved to be the trickiest part. We borrowed tools from the neighbor, Pepe, and I busied myself with trying to straighten them as Lucinda stood by. Pepe peered at us through the window as I banged at the wheels with the hammer, but my efforts resulted in very little progress.

Before I knew it, Pepe was standing over me. He was a small thin man with skin the color of ripe olives. The nostrils of his aquiline nose flared wildly when he inhaled giving him an intense and angry appearance. Yet, his eyes glowed the color of soft amber and always appeared to be swishing with tears. He shook his head disapprovingly. "That's not gonna work, cousin Nora."

"Why not?"

"You got to take the whole thing apart and put it back together again. It's the only way."

Pepe was an expert on the subject of wheels because he'd worked at a bicycle factory for many years. Now he worked one or two days a week if he was lucky, and he spent the rest of his time sitting on the stoop of his front door, watching the comings and goings around the neighborhood as he smoked his rationed cigarettes as far down as he could. The fingers of his right hand were permanently stained with nicotine.

"I don't know how to do that." I rolled back from my hunched position and sat with a plop on the ground, stretching my sore legs out in front of me. I picked up the wrench and dropped it with a start. How could it get so hot in less than a minute under the sun?

Pepe clicked his tongue and flicked his head indicating that I should get out his way. He picked up the wheelbarrow with one hand, scooped up his tools with the other, and settled down on his stoop, a spot that was significantly shadier than what I'd chosen. I took Lucinda by the hand and we hovered about as he worked.

"It's very nice of you to help us," I said.

He grunted. Pepe was not a man of many words, although when he looked at Lucinda it was the closest I'd ever seen him come to a smile.

"Señor Pepe, Mami says you know how to fix everything. Is that true?"

He'd already removed the wheels and was resecuring them by turning bolts with quick and dexterous hands. "I can fix most things, I guess."

We brought him a glass of cold water flavored with fruit powder mix that turned the water to a blood red color. He accepted it without a word and drank it down very fast, his nostrils flaring like fish gills gasping for air. He set the glass down and grunted his thanks again. After a while he stood up and stretched his lanky frame. He rolled the wheelbarrow back and forth to test it and then passed it over to me. It rolled smoothly and perfectly.

"It's like new. Thank you so much."

Pepe shrugged and his mouth flickered into the suggestion of a smile.

That evening after our meal, Lucinda and I took Alicia out for a stroll in her new wheel chair. The sky was scattered with gold ribbon clouds and children were laughing and playing baseball in the middle of the street. Rarely did a car drive by to interrupt their game. We headed, as always, toward the ocean to catch sight of the darkening sea and the first twinkle of lights on the *malecón*. The fragrance of night jasmine floated about and mingled with my memories. No one had spoken for sometime and when we stopped I looked down to see if Alicia might be asleep again. But her eyes were open wide and more alive than I'd seen them in days. Smiling, she pointed up toward the curve of the *malecón*. The lights had begun to pierce through the mist of the encroaching evening.

She took my hand. "I'm so happy right now."

"I'm glad."

"When you left, I worried you might forget me. I could never forget you because everywhere I turned I saw things that reminded me of you, girls with long black pony tails and Tía's porch, even the palm trees themselves. This view right here," she said raising an arm as delicate as a wisp of smoke. "Is the one that reminds me of our plans to become chorus girls at the Copacabana, remember?"

"As I recall, that was your idea."

"Perhaps it was, but you went along without too much argument."

I adjusted Alicia's pillows so she could sit up higher. "There was no arguing with you, dear cousin. I tried a few times and I always ended up wrestling with myself while you continued on with whatever little scheme you had going at the moment.

Alicia laughed. "I must've been impossible—a spoiled brat."

"You were amazing. Correction, you are amazing."

Alicia sighed and I heard the pain in her breath. "I wish Tony were here. I believe I'm ready to tell him everything now. I feel strong enough."

The sun had set and the lights of the *malecón* twinkled at full force, like a diamond necklace on the throat of the most beautiful woman in the world.

# 29

WE LEFT EARLY THE NEXT MORNING, BEFORE THE HEAT OF THE day had a chance to dig its nails into the concrete and broken earth. Alicia was so tired she bounced along in the wheelbarrow with the letter clasped firmly in her hand as though it were a ticket she had to show at any moment.

She'd dictated it to me the night before, after Lucinda was asleep in whispered words that sometimes got lost in the whirl of the fan. It was more of a declaration than a confession. Although this was the first time Tony would learn of her work at the hotel, she expressed guilt only about not staying healthy. Her one regret was that she wouldn't join him on his escape to freedom.

> . . . I respect the choices you've made now more than ever. I hope you can forgive me mine and remember me as I was when we first fell in love. That is how I always picture you, a handsome young man sitting in Tía Panchita's rocking chair and giving me such a smile that I thought my heart would stop beating. What a blessing to know that the only man who makes me feel this way is also the man I call my husband, my most precious love.
>
> Although we haven't slept in each other's arms for years, I can't close my eyes without whispering my good night to

you and remembering that nothing, not even the sinking of this beautiful island, can destroy our love for each other.

Nora is still here with us. She hasn't gone home as I mentioned in my last letter she would. Everything is better with her here. Lucinda smiles more, and sometimes behaves as a young girl should and not like a middle-aged woman with a thousand worries. What should I do, my love? How should I talk with her? Can I tell her that her Papi will soon be home to take care of her . . .

Ricardo eyed the wheelbarrow with a frown as he stuffed the letter Alicia held out to him in his pocket and took the plastic bag from me.

He shoved his face into it without a word and sniffed loudly, sweat dripping into his eyes. "Something wrong with your legs?"

"I've been tired and Nora found this wagon to help me get around."

He took a step back. "Are you sick?"

Alicia laughed dryly and even attempted to swing her legs out of the cart, but she was only successful at propping herself up straighter on her elbows. "Not to worry, Ricardo. Anything I have I got long after you and I decided to be . . . friends."

Ricardo relaxed and dropped his hand from his holster. He took a more studied look inside the bag. "Tony likes fresh fruit. I don't see any fresh fruit here."

"It was impossible to find this week, but maybe next week."

Ricardo grunted and began to saunter back toward his post.

"I'll pay you good money when Tony gets out," Alicia said abruptly.

Ricardo turned slowly and squinted in the heat. "What do you mean?"

"I've been saving money for when Tony gets out so we can leave this place."

He nodded pensively, while chewing the inside of his cheek. "I'll let you know when the time gets close."

"Don't you have a letter for me?" Alicia asked.

He didn't turn around when he answered, "Not this week."

"Why not? Is something wrong with Tony? Is he sick?"

Ricardo stomped his feet, creating a cloud of brown dust about him. It was obviously taxing him to get up the hill, and he resented having to turn around again. "There's nothing wrong with him that a doctor can do anything about."

"What's that supposed to mean?"

"Look, woman. Have you ever been locked up?"

"No . . ."

"Have you?" he asked pointing a hairy finger at me. I shook my head.

"It changes a man. They can go dead inside after a while."

"My Tony would never go dead inside. Tell him I expect a letter next week."

Ricardo turned on his heels and kept walking as he waved us away with one hand. "Bring some fresh fruit and maybe he'll feel like writing. Some cigarettes wouldn't hurt either."

"My Tony doesn't smoke."

"Your Tony's been smoking for years."


Alicia worried about Lucinda all the way home. We had planned a surprise trip to the beach and a picnic as well, but when Lucinda heard that her Papi hadn't written, she was very disappointed. It was only at the suggestion that Beba join us that she brightened a bit.

Beba was happy to come when we appeared at her door, and Lucinda insisted on holding her hand on the short walk to the public beach. Nevertheless, her head hung low and she stumbled more than once.

"I should've written a letter myself and pretended it was from her Papi," Alicia whispered.

"She'll be fine when we get to the beach, you'll see."

I was right. Once Lucinda was able to dig her toes into the sand and feel the course heat sliding between her toes and the cool dampness beneath the surface, she raised her head toward the ocean and walked confidently toward the sound of the waves. Beba wasn't able to keep up with her and had to let go of her hand or risk falling face first in the sand. Lucinda walked on, and Beba helped to maneuver the wheelbarrow toward a shady spot beneath a squat palm tree. We spread out a blanket and assisted Alicia out of the wheelbarrow and on to the sand where she settled in comfortably.

Her eyes were on her daughter, and they glittered with love and fear. "Anyone who saw her right now would think she was a beautiful young lady spending time with her dreams, her whole life ahead of her."

"That's exactly what she is," Beba retorted as she fluffed the pillows behind Alicia and covered her feet that were always cold.

"She doesn't have girlish dreams, Beba," Alicia said with a quiver in her voice. "She has adult worries. She worries about me and her Papi and about being taken away."

"Nobody's going to take her away," I reminded her.

Alicia's eyes were grateful. "I know you'll do everything you can to see that that doesn't happen, but you've only been here a short while. Soon it'll wear on you as it does on all of us. The power this government has to stop your throat and steal every breath you have is something you haven't experienced yet and I'm afraid that when you do . . ."

"I won't let them take her away," I repeated.

"And what about Jeremy? What about your husband who's missing you every minute you're here with us?"

"He understands."

Alicia scowled as she did when she thought I wasn't being honest. "If I knew my Tony was waiting for me somewhere, what I wouldn't do to go to him! A man who really loves you is a blessing you shouldn't play with. What if he gets tired of waiting?"

"If he really loves me, he won't get tired of waiting."

Alicia rolled her eyes and coughed. "He's angry with you now, I know he is."

Beba was listening to us while keeping an eye out for Lucinda who was walking along the water's edge, carefully feeling her way with her toes. Beba placed a hand on Alicia's knee. "Rest now, child. Nora knows her man better than you do, and you can believe what she tells you about Lucinda. Beba's going to see to it that nobody ever takes her anywhere she doesn't want to go."

This was enough assurance to calm Alicia, and allow her to doze under the shade of the palm.


This was the third attempt I'd made to contact Jeremy. The voice on the message machine I listened to was mine, but it didn't sound like me anymore. The woman requesting I leave my name and number reflected a light hearted innocence that came from too few worries and an overabundance of solutions. The voice of the woman leaving the message was heavy and restless and brimming with the kind of anxiety that weighs on your heart and mind so heavy that your feet ache to their soles.

Again there was no answer and I calculated the hours quickly. In Los Angeles it was eleven in the evening. Where was he? He wasn't one to stay out late. I contemplated calling my parents. Surely they'd be over their anger by now and able to speak to me in a reasonable manner. I thought about this with my hand on the receiver of the public phone.

Thank God for the light of the moon that illuminated the streets after the lights had long gone out. It was a dangerous time to be out. Crime was increasing, especially in Havana, and theft was not as uncommon as it used to be. Tourists were told to be particularly careful, but I comforted myself with the knowledge that I didn't look like a tourist anymore. I'd given away most of my clothes and was saving one good dress for my return home. I now wore stretchy shorts, a long T-shirt of Jeremy's, and plastic flip-flops on my feet. This was the uniform of the Cuban woman who'd resigned herself to the fact that there was no reason to be elegant anymore. She wasn't going to be invited to the parties she heard bouncing off the *malecón*, and glittering like a distant universe.

Everyone was sleeping comfortably when I arrived home. It was the first night we hadn't needed a fan in a week. I heard the dripping of the faucet in the kitchen, and reminded myself that we were lucky to have running water in the house, that there were many who lived in apartments where the plumbing had corroded after years of neglect, and where inhabitants relied on public water mains in the street. Did I really have a dishwasher in my kitchen that I rarely used because it was just the two of us? Was it true that I'd been known to take two showers a day? Since I'd arrived, I'd managed to wash myself every two or three days with cold water while standing in the tub.

I pulled back the thin sheet of my cot and lay down quietly so as not to disturb the soft cadence of sleep in the room. The next day I'd get up early and heat water on the stove for a proper warm bath. Then I'd do the same for Alicia and Lucinda. We'd be fresh and ready to go wherever the day dictated.

# 30

IT TOOK FOREVER FOR THE WATER TO BOIL, BUT ONLY THREE large kettles converted the tub of cold water into a pleasant and frothy warmth in which I submerged myself with incredible delight.

"Why are you doing that, Tía," Lucinda asked, a curious expression on her golden face. Her eyes still reflected the soft swelling of a peaceful night's sleep.

"It feels good to have a hot bath. When I'm done I'll make one for you."

She giggled and shook her tangled head of curls. "Mami says she used to give me a bath when I was a baby, but not lately."

"You'll love it. Is your Mami still sleeping?"

"She just woke up, and I made her some breakfast. Do you want some?"

"In a little while."

Lucinda closed the door behind her, and I soaked for a while longer. The peeling paint in the bathroom curled down in long moldy ribbons that reminded me of the moss that hung from the trees on the way to Tía Panchita's house. Perhaps that would be an interesting trip to take on this day. I'd ask Berta, who'd been home for the last couple of days, to give me the name of the person who lent her the car. We'd stop by the tourist market on the way out, and I'd pack a picnic. I hoped that Alicia was feeling up to the trip. The fact that she was eating breakfast was a good sign.

Lucinda soaked in the tub even longer than I did. She held on to the sides for a long time as she experienced the soft silky feeling of the bubble bath I'd brought with me from the States for the first time in her life. She smiled with wonder at the sensation and her turquoise eyes flashed with life. It was still hard to believe that eyes so beautiful couldn't behold the world around her.

"Tía, this water is even warmer than the ocean."

"Isn't it wonderful?"

I gently placed my hand on the top of her head so she knew I was near. "Now tilt your head back a little and I'll wash your hair."

Lucinda did as she was told and shut her eyes tight. Washing her thick curly hair was a formidable job, and my knees were aching by the time I was finished rinsing. I imagined that Lucinda's neck was also sore, but she never complained.

Alicia was feeling better and allowed me to help her into the bath and wash her hair as well. I tried not to shudder as her golden locks slid down the drain. She had half the hair she used to, and I twisted it into a tight and fashionable knot at the back of her head so it would be less noticeable.

We were all dressed and ready to go when Berta emerged from her room, her thick black hair grizzled into a mane of unbelievable proportions. She blinked and propped her hands on her generous hips. "What's this? Are we all ready for Catechism?" she chuckled to herself as she sauntered to the bathroom.

"Berta, we want to rent a car for the day. The car you used to pick me up at the airport would do well. Could you tell me how to find it?"

Berta looked momentarily confused. She tried to remember as she examined her cuticles. "It's this guy who lives down at the end of the street. I had to pay him . . . You know . . . not with cash."

I blushed. "I understand, but I imagine he'll take cash."

"Probably. It's the house with the blue door," Berta said and she disappeared inside the bathroom where she would undoubtedly remain for most of the morning.

Lucinda and Alicia waited for me while I ventured out to find the house with the blue door. It was easy to find and as I knocked I realized I hadn't asked Berta for the name of the car's owner. After a few seconds the door was opened by a tired looking woman in her mid to late thirties missing a tooth in the very front of her smile. Eyeing me suspiciously, she shrugged her thin shoulders. "Carlos went out last night and he hasn't been home. He's probably drunk as a skunk and sleeping it off somewhere. I don't know when he'll be back."

"Can you help me?"

The woman waved me into the house and beckoned me to follow her through dingy rooms, cluttered with broken furniture and tools, out to the small backyard. Without looking to see if I was following or not, she kicked open the back gate to reveal the shiny blue Chevrolet that had transported us all from the airport on my first day here. It looked freshly polished and the chrome shone in the morning light making it look like a bright cartoon in the middle of an old black and white photo.

"This car is my husband's heaven and my hell. If you want to take it and drive it into the ocean, I couldn't care less."

"Actually, I just wanted it for the day to go to Güines. I'll have it back before nightfall."

"I don't care," she said.

"I'll pay you for the use of it."

"I said I don't care." She walked back into the house with me following close behind and rummaged through a drawer before producing a set of keys and tossed them at me. "Finding gas is a lot harder than finding a car, you know."

I looked down at my plastic flip-flops, almost identical to hers and my stretchy shorts and tank top. My hair was pulled back into a ponytail and I wasn't wearing a drop of makeup. "How did you know I was visiting?" I asked.

The woman smiled for the first time. She'd once been lovely, and I imagined her, elegant in her matching shoes and purse, sauntering down the avenues as men craned their necks to catch a glimpse. Carlos had no doubt been one of them and had pursued her with a vengeance.

"I can always tell the Cubans that come back," she told me. "First of all, they always have cash to spend on things like a car or prepared food. A Cuban would offer me soap for the car or a bag of onions, or . . ." She sniffed the air with a sour expression, "other things too. But how I can really tell is by your hands. May I?" She took my hand and held it next to hers. "I don't think I'm much older than you, but see?" The difference was dramatic. Hers were swollen and cracked, with thick knuckles and nails that were gray and moldy near the base. "It's from using cold water and bleach to wash the clothes and dishes. When I run out of soap I have to use bleach or nothing at all. The only women who don't have hands like this are visitors and prostitutes."

The woman told me her name was Lourdes, and we talked for a bit about her two children who were away at school and came home only one weekend a month. She wanted to know about the United States and said she had friends who had escaped on a raft several months ago. "I don't know if they made it."

I was ready to leave with keys dangling from my fingers like a prize. All I had to do now was find gas. How hard could that be? "Will Carlos be mad if he comes home and finds the car missing?"

Lourdes threw both hands up in the air. "His anger doesn't scare me. Besides, he didn't remember he was supposed to show up for his construction job at the hotel this morning. Why should he remember he has a car?"

Lourdes told me of some people in the neighborhood who might have gas for sale and suggested I find it before taking the car as I could easily waste the quarter tank left trying to find it. I agreed and set out on my quest. Immediately I discovered that Lourdes was not exaggerating. The first two men promptly informed me they wouldn't have gas until the middle of next week, but if I paid them in advance, they'd give me a discount. I declined their offer and continued down the list toward my next lead. It was almost noon when I resigned myself to the fact that our plans would have to wait until next week, and I considered returning to the one person who seemed the most decent and least likely to cheat me if I paid in advance. I could ask Lourdes if this was customary.

I decided to drop by the house first and inform Alicia and Lucinda of the situation, but I was surprised to find nobody home. Even Berta was nowhere to be found although the door to her room had been left open and her radio was blaring. In the kitchen I noted the dishes had not been washed. Lucinda always washed the dishes before leaving for fear that ants would find their way in.

I walked outside and spotted Pepe sitting on his front stoop, squinting out into the perpetual haze of endless summers while smoking a cigarette stub. He barely glanced at me as I approached, already knowing what I was going to ask.

"They went down the street that way," he said flicking his free hand in the general direction. "Right after a man I never saw before was knocking on doors asking about a blind girl. I sent him that way." He pointed the opposite direction to the apartment. "And then I told them it would be a good time to go for a walk."

My heart constricted with fear. Had they come looking for Lucinda? Or perhaps Ricardo had informed the authorities that Alicia was ill, and they'd come to take her away. I was almost choking, my throat was so dry. "Did he look official?"

At this question Pedro looked somewhat dazed. "Official? He had good shoes and a clean shirt."

My worst fears confirmed, I dashed down the street in the direction Pepe indicated they'd gone. I peered down narrow alleys piled high with garbage, almost tripping on my flip-flops in the process. I imagined how frightened Lucinda must feel, how desperate and confusing this must be for Alicia. Berta was probably doing her best to help, but she didn't know how to deal with people like this. She was probably making matters worse by offering sexual favors to set them free. I was in a near hysteria when I reached the *malecón*.

I heard Lucinda's voice first. A soft sweet melody, floating as if

from the sky and when I turned to the sound of it, I almost fell to
my knees. She walked confidently, smiling to herself as she chattered, holding onto the handle as Berta wheeled Alicia in the
wagon. Berta was the first to spot me and she looked grim.

When I reached them I held Lucinda tight. "We climbed out
the window of Berta's room," she said excitedly. "It was so fun,
Tía Nora. Berta just made up this game and we were pretending
to be secret spies and we had to escape the bad man. Mami said
she used to play this game with you when you were little girls.
Maybe next time you can play with us too?"

I studied Alicia's expression. She seemed relieved and grateful
for my understanding, but there was a resignation settling into
her I'd never seen before. I turned my attention back to Lucinda.
"Guess what? I just saw Pepe, and he told me the bad man is gone
so we can go home now."

Later, when Alicia was sure Lucinda wouldn't hear her she
whispered to me, "I saw the man when he was down the street.
I'm sure he's from the Ministerio de Educación and he was coming to take her."

"Don't worry about that now," I said, startled by how much
she'd weakened practically overnight, her eyes shadowed and hol-
lowed with fatigue.

Alicia awoke later that afternoon to the company of Beba
who'd stopped by to see how she was doing. Beba was concerned
to hear about the day's events, but even more so to see Alicia's
physical deterioration.

She spoke with gentle authority. "If you come to my house tomorrow I will help you with your pain."

I could see Alicia ready to protest that she felt fine, but Beba
raised her long bony finger to silence her. "Your eyes are full of
pain. Come see me tomorrow and you will feel better."

# 31

LUCINDA AND I SAT IN METAL CHAIRS AGAINST THE WALL. THE thin curtains were drawn and, since sunlight had difficulty making its way down the alley into Beba's window, the room was almost as dark as it would've been in the middle of the night. Numerous candles provided the only light necessary. Beba wore a white turban, the one she'd worn before the revolution, twisted high on her head, and colored beads of red and yellow clacked around her neck as she moved about the small room.

She'd placed a large metal tub in the very center of the room where Alicia now sat. Eyes lowered, Beba passed her hands over Alicia's head and body without touching her. This went on for several minutes before she began to chant softly as she poured fragrant oil on Alicia's head.

At first, Alicia had been reluctant to participate. When she'd woken up she said she didn't feel well enough to do anything but lay in her bed and look out the window. Every breath caused her to wince with pain and she looked like someone waiting, simply waiting because there was nothing else she could do. Lucinda sat next to her in the bed and tried to persuade her to eat, but Alicia refused even a little water and a few crackers. In just one night she seemed to have slipped further away from life. Her skin was yellow and tight over her beautiful cheekbones, the skin on her shoulders like gauze.

"You should go," she said with a cough. "You should go out and enjoy the day." She said nothing about Lucinda joining me. It was clear she wanted to keep her daughter by her side. She closed her eyes and lay very still. Then she opened them wide and looked at me with sudden alarm. "Why do you say that Beba is always right Nora?"

"She's always been right. She knows things; she sees things."

Alicia closed her eyes again. "I'll go see her then. I'll go and see if she can make this pain go away." It was the first time Alicia had admitted to feeling any pain at all.

Beba scooped warm water out of the tub in a perfect pink seashell and poured it over Alicia again and again. Alicia closed her eyes, and Beba chanted a song deep in her throat that seemed to emanate deeper still from the pit of her belly until the music filled the room and all the spaces within us. The words weren't Spanish, but Yoruba and the sounds were round and liquid and beautiful. We began to sway with the flickering candlelight until we were all quite relaxed. I had closed my eyes, but opened them every now and then to check on Alicia who was crouched in the tub, shoulders stooped, looking as if she had drifted off to sleep which she tended to do more and more. Suddenly she sat up straight as though a current of electricity had shot through her spine, but Beba didn't change the pace or rhythm of her chanting. She didn't even seem to notice this profound change.

I sensed Lucinda shiver next to me and took hold of her hand. It was warm and dry, not sweaty and clammy like my own. Beba's eyes opened a sliver, and she sprinkled a variety of sweet smelling herbs into the tub. Her chanting grew more intense, and her face began to contort as though there were invisible hands pushing at the loose flesh of her cheeks and forehead. Producing a butcher's knife from the pocket of her skirt, she held it out so that the blade gleamed in the flickering candlelight. She then proceeded to slice away at Alicia's dress one piece at a time until Alicia was quite naked, with strips of wet fabric clinging to her, to the tub, and to Beba as well.

Even in the dim light it was difficult to look upon Alicia's emaciated body, and I was grateful that Lucinda couldn't see her. She was a whisper of human form, a fragile collection of bones spotted with sores the color of raspberries. In that instant, my once beautiful cousin became aware of her nakedness, and covered herself where breasts had once graced her sensuous figure. She glanced shyly at me and saw my eyes filled with tears.

"The pain will leave you, child," Beba said in her singsong voice, eyes closed once again. "Ask me what you want to know."

I had no idea what Beba meant by this, but Alicia did. "Will I see my Tony before I die?" she asked, her voice full of courage.

"Not as you hope to see him."

"I hope to see him healthy and well."

Beba began to sway and then she knelt and placed a hand on Alicia's shoulder. "He is well. You will see him well, and you will see him free."

"How about Lucinda? Will my Tony and Lucinda live together free in America?"

"It is not mean to be; it cannot be," was Beba's quick reply. Too quick for the cruel blow it delivered.

"Why can't it be, Beba? I have the money. Why can't it be?"

Beba opened her eyes and stared straight through Alicia. "Tony cannot be free with both you and Lucinda."

Alicia began to whimper and tremble and I stood up to go to her, but Lucinda squeezed my hand and I held back.

Beba raised her gaze to the ceiling. "Tony has been waiting for you for a long time. Almost two years. He sees you now and he's waiting for you to cross over and be with him."

"That can't be. Tony's here and . . ." Alicia let her words and thoughts float and dissolve in the warm water that surrounded her. "Tony is already dead."

"He's been waiting for you, my child," Beba said.

Alicia slept soundly as Lucinda and I hovered about Beba's apartment whispering for the rest of the day. We were both shocked by Beba's revelation, but when I questioned her, she was vague.

"When I'm in trance I don't plan what I'm going to say, Nora."

"But what if Tony isn't dead?"

Beba was not in the least bit concerned about this possibility. She blew out the candles one by one and shook her head resolutely. "What is done is done," she said.

I turned my attention to readying Alicia for our short walk home. With blankets tucked in and pillows adjusted, the three of us headed down the hall for the street.

"Let her sleep as long as she needs to," Beba said, her white turban gleaming in the darkened hallway. "She'll wake before midnight, and things will be better."

Alicia woke up at precisely 11:45 P.M. Her eyes opened suddenly and they were bright, as if she hadn't been sleeping at all, but engaging in the most animated of conversations. She placed her hand on Lucinda who was lying next to her, and Lucinda woke up as well. She'd refused to leave her mother's side since we arrived and asked constant questions about her father and if he was really dead and what the whole thing with Beba meant. I hardly knew how to answer her.

"I'm thirsty," Alicia said. "May I have some water, please?"

Lucinda sprung up from the bed and scuffled to the kitchen.

Alicia beckoned for me to come and sit next to her. "I feel as light as a feather. The pain that used to tightly wrap around me, squeezing the life out of me, is very far away, like a little star that blinks at me, but can't do me any harm."

"I'm so glad, Alicia."

I took hold of her hand, and she squeezed it with amazing strength. "And Tony's eyes are closer than the pain. I know he's there, and I can see them. I dreamt about him just now. We were dancing on the sea together. We were floating up above the palm trees, and we saw Cuba down below us flowing like a fragile leaf in the river. She was floating toward a giant waterfall and then she rushed over the top and landed at the very bottom far below." Alicia smiled and closed her eyes. "She was fine when she landed, just fine."

"Rest more, Alicia. That's what you need to do right now."

Her eyes flew open and she was a child again, bright and amazing with a mind as quick and agile as a tiny *zunzún* bird flittering among the flowers. "Everything's going to be OK, Nora. Don't worry anymore."

The next morning I set out early to find Ricardo. It wasn't the usual meeting day and I had no idea whether or not he'd be at his post, but I decided that if he wasn't there I'd inquire about Tony at the prison office myself. I had nothing to lose, and nothing to hide.

When I arrived, I saw no one at the guard post, but then Ricardo emerged from behind the building zipping up his fly. I shuddered to think of how many times Alicia had seen him in a similar situation. He straightened when he saw me, sniffed loudly and flicked his hairy hand over his revolver to make sure it was still there.

"This isn't the entrance for visitors," He informed me gruffly. "You have to go around the other side."

"I'm not a visitor. I'm Alicia's cousin. We met before."

Ricardo eyed me closely under bulging sweaty brows. He rolled his tongue over something in his mouth and spat it out, leaving a wad of spit glistening on the dirt. He spread his legs, his hand firmly on his revolver. "What do you want? This isn't the day to come."

"I have reason to believe Tony Rodríguez is dead and has been for some time."

Roberto blinked the sweat out of his eyes, but said nothing.

"You can tell me the truth yourself, or I can go inside and find out myself, but I don't think you want any trouble."

Ricardo bared his big yellow teeth and his lips twitched. "What kind of trouble can you make for me?"

I stepped forward. "I can tell them you've been extorting a helpless widow, and forcing her to bring you food and perform sexual favors."

Ricardo's grin widened into a dry laugh. "How are you going to prove that, huh? Nobody gives a shit about things like that. They won't do nothing to me."

I had no doubt he was right and the helplessness I felt in combination with the hate I had for Ricardo was almost too much to bear. Suddenly a thought occurred to me, prompted by my memory of Ricardo's face during our last visit when Alicia mentioned Berta might be making the next delivery.

I lifted my head high. "I believe the prison officials will be interested to know you may be sick as well."

"What are you talking about?" Ricardo's black eyes ricocheted in their sockets. "Alicia said she was sick after . . ."

I took another step forward and captured his darting eyes in my steely gaze. "I'm not talking about Alicia . . ."

His beady eyes flew open, and he stammered for the first time. "Berta's healthy, like a young cow and I . . . I feel fine."

"Then how do you explain the sweat running down your face, and the yellow color of your eyes?"

Ricardo's hands fell limp to his side as he considered the possibility of detainment and death and he leaned on the guardhouse, a man suddenly aware of his impending doom. "Tony Rodríguez died about two years ago. He was caught trying to escape and they shot him."

"Don't they send notices to the family?"

"It's easy to intercept the mail. I paid a friend to help me out."

I clenched my fists hard upon hearing this and my nails bore deep into the palms of my hands. "You took advantage of the love and faith of a good woman. You're worse than a rat in the sewer."

"It was a good thing and I didn't want it to end," Roberto said, pumping up a bit. He licked his lips. "She got something out of it too."

"You're a pig."

"I'm a survivor," he corrected, glaring at me from head to toe. "Look at you standing there with your plastic shoes pretending to be one of us. You don't know what it's like. In a few days you'll go home to your easy life, but the rest of us will still be here rotting away. We do what we have to do, just like you would."

My eyes became blurry and hot, and my ears began to hum and pop to the erratic pace of my heart. I wanted to run and beat my hands against a wall until bloody, I wanted to feel the pain Alicia had been suffering. Most of all, I wanted to kill Ricardo.

I reached down for one of many stones that lay on the rough road, but Ricardo had already turned away from me. He believed that he too was dying, that before long he'd be carted around in a wagon, if he was lucky. I threw the stone at him with all my might, but it landed several yards away, not causing enough of a stir to prompt him from his torment.

This time I was successful in finding gas and Lourdes handed me the keys after we'd shared a quick cup of very strong coffee. "Don't drive at night if you can help it. The lights don't work," she warned.

The blue Chevy lumbered down the broken road like an old man with a cough. The gas was cheap and the tires worn, but it would get us where we had to go. Alicia had weakened since the previous day, and it was becoming more difficult for her to find the energy to speak. Mostly she watched Lucinda, her impossibly large green eyes trying to take in as much of her as she could. Lucinda was always nearby, within touching distance of her mother. More than once I saw her smile back when Alicia smiled at her.

Alicia stayed awake once we got on the road, but she asked no questions about where we were going. The three of us sat in the front seat and Alicia clung to her daughter's hand.

It took almost two hours along the coast road to get there, but when we did, there was no mistaking where we were. The royal palms welcomed us like old friends, the white expanse of talcum sand fanning out toward the sea. There was a new sparkling hotel crawling with tourists in brightly colored suits and towels slung about their shoulders or wrapped around their waists like sarongs. It was obvious we were not tourists.

I parked the car a few blocks away from our final destination and settled Alicia into the wagon. Lucinda took her post next to me, one hand on the handle, her eyes straight ahead and unwavering.

They'd built an impressive fence along the perimeter of our beach with thick curving poles that looked like inverted ribs of a whale. It would have been very difficult to climb by myself, but with Alicia and Lucinda in tow it was impossible. Our only hope was to wait discretely near the entrance of the hotel for a moment when we might pass through unnoticed. We waited on a nearby bench for almost an hour, but the moment never presented itself. I surmised that it was probably easier to escape from prison than it was to get onto our beach. I reminded myself that no matter how many new hotels, or regulations prevented Cubans from using them, Varadero belonged to us, and it always would.

I was starting to feel that our situation was hopeless when I noticed a group of workmen passing through the gate loaded down with building equipment and supplies. One fellow even carried his bricks in a wheelbarrow very much like mine. The guard never asked who they were and hardly blinked as they passed. I gave Lucinda explicit instructions not to move from that spot next to her mother until I returned, and I ran back to the car. Never was I more grateful to see a pile of dirty clothes in my life. It was obvious that Lourdes's husband had finally shown up to work, and lucky for us he'd forgotten to take care of his laundry. I threw on a pair of his baggy pants covered in grease and paint and a large tee shirt stained deep yellow under the arms. There were even two hats to choose from. I chose the one with the widest brim and grabbed as many greasy towels as I could hold.

I bundled Lucinda into the barrow next to Alicia and covered them up with the towels, arranging them this way and that until I was satisfied they could pass for a pile of lumber or bricks. It was then a matter of waiting for the right moment to step in line behind the crew of workmen. My opportunity came soon enough, and I lowered my head and hunched my shoulders up to appear bigger. Momentarily distracted by a group of scantily clad female tourists, the guard waved us by with a flick of his hand.

We were on the sand almost immediately and the wheelbarrow became extremely difficult to roll, but I couldn't take the chance of having Lucinda get out from under the towels until I was sure we wouldn't be seen. Once we were several hundred yards from the gate, I gave Lucinda the word and she scurried out from beneath the towels, surprised to feel the warm sand on her feet.

"Where are we, Tía?"

"This is home, *mi cielo*. This is where your Mami and I grew up. Where we learned how to dream and how to pray."

Slowly, we made our way toward the water's edge where it would be easier to roll the wagon.

"The sand is so soft here, Tía. Much softer than at the other beach we go to."

"This is the best beach in the whole world. Even though I haven't seen all the other beaches in the world, I can tell you it's true."

Lucinda smiled and tossed her hair to the wind. Her springy curls bounced as she kicked at the rolling waves. Her hearing was so precise that she caught the crest perfectly every time with the tip of her toe.

Alicia spoke for the first time since we'd arrived, and the clarity and strength of her voice surprised me. "Have they cut down our trees, Nora? I'm afraid to look."

"I see them just as they were. Don't worry."

Lucinda stayed near the water as I carefully placed Alicia on the sand directly under our palms. Beyond Lucinda I could see the platform, to which Alicia and I swam as children, bobbing peacefully, the curve of the pure white sand spreading out like two loving arms reaching towards heaven.

Satisfied that Lucinda was safe and that we wouldn't be discovered as trespassers, I lay down next to Alicia. We looked up at the impossibly blue sky as the sun bathed us and winked through the palms.

Alicia sighed, shifted in the sand, and turned towards me, her green eyes reflecting the crystalline sand like jewels embedded in her skeletal face. She was lovely still and the tenderness in her expression was so fragile and intense I could hardly bear it. I knew she was watching me and loving me with her last ounce of energy.

The corners of her mouth flickered into a faint smile. "You know, Nora. If you stare straight at the sun without blinking, you can see God." Alicia opened her eyes wide at the sun and then shut them tight. She turned to me again, her eyes glistening.

"What did you ask Him for?" I asked.

She smiled and closed her eyes. Her breathing grew shallow and rapid and her words escaped through her tangled breath like tiny butterflies. "When you're with me I'm not afraid."

I held her close. "I'm here with you Alicia, I'm right here."

Above us the royal palms swayed, their shadows drifting over us as quickly as the time which had passed with such ruthless indifference across our island and through our lives. We were little girls again with our hearts set on an afternoon swim, tingling with the thrill of the warm clear waters. We were learning how to skate over the cracks without falling down and scraping our knees because scars would be unseemly on a young lady's legs. We were pressing our hands against our chests, afraid and curious about the painful little buds that grew with each passing day. We stared at the movie stars on TV and saw how they kissed with their mouths barely open. Soon we would discover for ourselves that sex is much more than kissing, and kissing is much more than sex. We were grown women lying on the sand between heaven and earth, broken by the incomprehensible effort of trying to understand our friendship and the love that slips from life into forever.

I moved closer to whisper in her ear. "I'm glad we're here together, Alicia. It's just how I remember it."

Eyelashes flutter over eyes that are fading to a quiet, somber green, and I was not sure that she'd heard me. "Take care of my Lucinda," she whispers back. "Promise me. . . ."

"I promise."

Her eyes close and I feel I should be quiet now, but I want to tell her how much I love her, and about everything in my heart and all that she means to me. As I start to speak, she releases my hand and turns her face to the sun. I see her let go and lighten with the peace of the warmth all around us. Never has she looked more beautiful than she does at this moment and I realize that she's gazing into the face of God, and that this time He's taken her home.

# 32

ALICIA WAS BURIED IN A SMALL CEMETERY ON THE OUTSKIRTS
of Havana. Aside from Beba, Lucinda, and I, there were only a
few neighbors gathered at her graveside. Berta complained her
work made it impossible for her to attend the simple funeral and
that she didn't believe in them anyway. "I said my good-bye's
when she was alive. That should be good enough for anybody."

The somber mood contrasted sharply against the glorious
tropical sky. When she was healthy, Alicia would've insisted a
day like this should not be wasted, and she would've organized a
trip to the beach or the countryside or anywhere she could to
soak up the beauty around her. I only had the strength to sit on
the wall of the *malecón* and stare out at the sea. I had never felt so
lost, so incapable of understanding what I should do next. Alicia
was gone, and this immutable reality crept over me like a slow
freeze so that even the warmth of the sun couldn't reach me anymore.

Beba was a rock of strength and compassion. After the burial
she came to the house every day to check on Lucinda. We both
feared for Lucinda's health and general well being. She'd hadn't
spoken a word for three days after Alicia died. She hardly ate and
she slept fitfully, waking suddenly and calling for her mother. I'd
go to remind her gently that her Mami was gone. She'd lay back

without a word, no longer requiring any comforting, at least not from me.

In the house, she began to stumble into furniture and tripped several times, once bumping her head hard enough to produce a black and blue lump on her forehead. Beba kept ice on it most of the day. She was the only person Lucinda allowed near her. When I tried to get close she flinched and turned away from me every time. This is how it was since she heard I was planning to leave Cuba without her.

I went to the American Interests Section to inquire about the status of Lucinda's visa, hoping I'd be able to take her with me. I was confronted by a middle-aged woman with sagging cheeks and teeth stained dark yellow from too much coffee and smoking, a sure sign of someone who'd had steady employment for a while.

"When are you leaving?" the clerk asked as she shuffled through a stack of papers that looked as though they'd been weathering on her desk since before the revolution.

"In five days."

She stopped her shuffling and stared at me in disbelief. "Five days? You better pray for a miracle."

I tried to explain that I was Lucinda's closest living relative and that I wanted more than anything to adopt her, but the clerk wasn't impressed and waved me off with a well rehearsed click of her tongue.

I phoned Jeremy for the third day in a row, hoping he'd help me find a solution to what was becoming an impossible situation, and he remained calm and logical in the face of my growing hysteria. I clung to his every word. "Lucinda will come live with us when her visa comes through. It's not going to happen now, the way you'd like, but it'll happen. We can even get your attorney cousin to help us."

"It could take a year, maybe more. What about the promise I made Alicia?"

"You promised you'd look after her and you still are. You've made arrangements with Beba."

"It's not the same."

Jeremy's sigh was lost in the static of the connection. "Do you think Alicia wanted us to be separated so you could look after her daughter?"

"I know she didn't want that."

"Do you trust Beba to take good care of Lucinda?"

I laughed in spite of my turmoil. "Beba will do a better job than I or anybody else could do."

"There you have it then. Beba will look after Lucinda while her visa is being processed. And you'll come home with me because . . ." he paused for a moment, " . . . because I love you and need you with me."

"I love you too, Jeremy."

"Promise me you'll come home."

"I promise."

"Promise me you'll come home next week and that you won't let this plane leave without you."

"I promise, my love."

It all seemed so clear and sensible after I spoke with Jeremy. I tried to explain this to Lucinda as she sat on the couch where Alicia had spent her last days. She barely raised her head to acknowledge I was speaking to her and her hair, which she refused to let anyone comb or wash, hung down like overgrown ivy. She kept her hands folded tight in her lap so her nails lit up like bright little crescent moons. Tears splashed on her wrists as she nodded her understanding, but she wouldn't accept a hug.

"I've started the paperwork to send for you. You'll be with me as soon as possible," I said.

She nodded and reached out a probing hand for Beba who had left the room. "Where's Beba?"

Beba appeared soon enough to comfort her.

Even though I believed what Jeremy said to be logical and sound, there were brief moments when I resented him, and I felt an uneasy distance building in my heart, the same as I'd felt with my parents before deciding to go against their wishes. And Lucinda was beginning to hate me as well. I could feel it thick and heavy in the air whenever I came close to her. I only reminded her of the agonizing loss of both her parents. The best I could do was to keep a distance and spare us both anymore pain. Never in my life had I felt so alone.

Beba spoke to me plainly on the day I announced the date of my departure. She'd finally coaxed Lucinda into the bath and had her soaking in my lemon-scented bubbles. "You're doing what you have to do so you don't break in two, Norita. You're only one person and you can't be in both places at once."

"I wish I could be here and go, Beba. I wish I could more than anything. Now Lucinda hates me."

"That sweet child isn't capable of hate. She's doing what she has to do to stay whole just like you are. It's too much grief for one person to take."

Beba was right as always, and I tried to remember her words when Lucinda asked me if she could go home with Beba for the night. I was so happy she'd spoken to me that I wasn't able to respond to the question or understand that it meant yet another rejection. She'd been staying with Beba ever since.

I preferred sleeping on the couch that still smelled of the body lotion and perfume I'd given Alicia on the day I arrived. It seemed like a lifetime ago, several lifetimes. She appeared one night in my dreams, her hair floating on the wind like golden clouds suspended in air. She was as beautiful and vibrant as I remembered her before I left Cuba, and she danced with Tony above the palm trees that tickled their feet. They laughed as they looked down on me, and I was angry they should be so careless and free when I was so shackled to my problems.

There was a knock on the door the day before I was scheduled to leave. My large suitcase lay on the small living room floor so it was difficult to open the door completely, but when I finally did, I stood face to face with a small man wearing black rimmed glasses. They seemed to do little to improve his eyesight, for he persistently peered over my shoulder to see who or what was in the room. As he did, I took note of his clean shirt and good shoes.

"It's been reported to me that there's a child here. A . . ." he consulted his notebook more carefully. "A Lucinda Rodríguez."

I stepped this way and that so he couldn't see into the room. "Is there a problem?"

The man continued to consult his notes. "It says here that the child has been recently orphaned. It's the obligation and authority of the state to evaluate the care-taking and education . . ."

I opened the door wider so I could stand outside the threshold. "I'm Lucinda's aunt, and I'm caring for her just fine."

He glanced at the suitcase on the floor. "But you're leaving."

"The child will be well taken care of."

"May I ask by whom?"

"A close family friend."

The man jotted down something in his notebook and shook his head in the process. "I will report this to my superiors. However, I must inform you that it is not customary for orphaned children to reside with non-relatives. Our reports indicate that the child is blind and has had no formal education to speak of."

"I assure you that she's been very well educated, even if she hasn't attended the state school."

The man's grimace became a thin smile. "We have schools for disabled children."

"I'm sure you do."

"Where is the child now?"

"I'm afraid she's not here at the moment."

The man jotted some more, ripped a leaf of paper out of his notebook and gave it to me. "Her whereabouts must be reported to this office. If I don't hear from you in a couple of days, I'll be back."


Beba listened gravely as she measured the sugar for our coffee. "Did you tell them she was here?"

"Of course not."

"Good." She handed me my coffee and the cup rattled on the saucer. "She can never go back there now, and we have to stay indoors for a while, especially in the day."

I showed Beba the paper the man gave me, and she promptly crumpled it up into a small wad and tossed it in the trash. "I never did learn to read."

Next I handed Beba the box of money Alicia had been saving in the wall. When she saw how much there was, she placed a hand over her chest and collapsed on her stool. "Good Lord, child, are you walking around the streets with this? They'll slice your throat around here for ten dollars."

Lucinda had been asleep on the floor on a bed Beba made for her. As she stirred I whispered, "Alicia was saving this money for when Tony got out so the three of them could find a way to the States. Use it for whatever you need to take care of Lucinda, and I'll send you money every month. For you and Lucinda."

"You don't have to pay me to take care of that child."

"I know I don't."

I told Beba I'd be back later in the day to say good-bye because the next morning I was leaving very early. As I hugged Beba at the door, I saw Lucinda's small face reflected in the cracked mirror, leaning against the floor next to her. Her eyes were wide open, and her face was tight with the strain of trying to muffle the sound of her own weeping.


Berta came to see me that afternoon, taking the opportunity to say her final good-byes, as she'd be gone for work before the end of the day. I'd been meaning to thank her for helping Alicia with Ricardo, but didn't quite know how to bring it up.

I offered her my shoulder to lean on as she removed her bright pink high-heeled shoes. "I know how you helped Alicia with Ricardo."

"How'd you find out?"

"I figured it out by the look on Ricardo's face when Alicia mentioned you'd be making the next delivery."

Berta cackled and collapsed on the couch. "If it weren't for Alicia, I'd never let a man that ugly get near me no matter how much money he had." She raised her painted eyebrows. "Well maybe . . ."

"I think you should know . . . I told him a little lie. I was so angry for what he did to Alicia that I told him . . . you were sick too. You see Alicia had already said she got sick after she and him . . . and I had to do something to get back . . ."

Berta was still and thoughtful for a moment and then she looked at me with all sincerity and said, "Alicia always said you were smart, but that was brilliant. If I know Ricardo he'll be crapping his pants for the next ten years." She broke out in a fit of laughter. "And he deserves to suffer, that bastard."

"But it could jeopardize you . . ."

"He may be a devil, but he's no fool. He won't say anything." Berta thought for a moment longer. "Besides, it might be true. Alicia took a lot better care of herself than I ever did." She shrugged off the few seconds of doubt, and stood up to give me a strong hug, almost drowning me in her jungle of hair, stiff with sprays and potions that did little to calm it down.

I'd already told her three times before, but just to make sure I told her once more that no matter who came to the door she was to tell them Lucinda had moved and that she didn't know where. Each time, Berta agreed, but I worried. In spite of her generosity, she wasn't immune to bribery, and she'd succumbed to the illness caused by desperation long ago.

I decided to take the longer walk up the *malecón* to Beba's house. The temperature had cooled and the ocean swelled its turquoise perfection against the cobalt sky. This was the Cuba I had dreamed about. For an instant I envied Alicia for having lived all her life in the midst of such beauty. She was more a part of Cuba than I could ever be and her sweet-hearted music was leaving me, slipping away as surely as the tide.

At this time tomorrow I'd be back in Los Angeles. I'd wake up and take a steamy shower as American coffee brewed in my automatic coffee maker. I'd settle into my tidy Honda and drive down smooth streets lined by manicured lawns. I'd park in my reserved parking space and work for exactly eight and a half hours and then drive home and order Chinese because I was too tired to cook. And Jeremy would come home to me as he always did and fall asleep in my arms.

Lucinda was sitting primly in her chair when I arrived. Beba had taken special care to comb her hair in ringlets and dress her in one of the dresses I'd brought for her. It was the yellow one with delicate embroidery on the collar. She looked like one of those collectable dolls you place high on the shelf because they're too beautiful to play with.

I chatted with Beba as I watched Lucinda by the window. She slowly turned to face the sound of my voice. Her eyes were soft and beamed with a lovely light. She hadn't looked this open since before Alicia's death, and my throat was tight with hope and emotion. Without thinking about it I went to her and knelt before her so we were at eye level. Immediately, her hands floated up toward my face and she smiled.

"Tía Nora," she whispered and I hugged her so tight that this little china doll could break, but she hugged me back every bit as tight. "I'm sorry, Tía Nora. I'm sorry I've been so mad at you."

"No, *mi cielo*, don't apologize for anything. Please don't . . ."

"I want to because I truly am sorry and because Mami said I should."

"Mami?" I looked to Beba who shrugged while squinting at the paper on which I'd written my home address and phone number. It was then that I spotted the metal tub in the corner of the room and became aware of the faint smell of sulfur.

"Beba gave me a bath today like she gave Mami, to take away the pain, and it worked, Tía Nora, it worked. I don't feel mad or sad anymore because I know Mami and Papi are happy together in heaven and I know you'll come back for me. You won't forget me?"

"Of course I won't forget you, my love. How could I ever forget you?"

I held her as Beba looked down upon us. For the first time, I felt unsettled by those eyes that seemed to know and see so much, but I decided not to ask her what she felt, or exactly what happened with Lucinda. I didn't want to taint the moment with doubts for any of us.

Beba pressed her beautiful dark hands against my face, and I breathed in the fragrance of coffee and lemons and salt crackers and deep abiding wisdom. Then I kissed her on both cheeks and said good-bye.


I tried to sleep, knowing I had to be up early to catch my flight that was scheduled to leave José Martí airport at eight in the morning. I gazed out the window at what had been Alicia's view during the many months of her illness, as she dreamt of being with Tony again, and as she prayed for Lucinda once she accepted she'd never recover her sight. I could see a once elegant apartment building and in the evening light, its former glory was almost restored, its wrought iron banisters adorning the balconies like curling eyelashes heavy with paint and glitter.

I saw the glowing light of a cigarette floating about on one of them and just made out the figure of a young woman sitting in a chair and leaning back with legs crossed as she gazed up at the night sky. Even in the dim light I could see she was lovely. Her slender limbs caught the light of the moon in narrow ribbons, her hair was awash in golden light and she began to glow as if a stage light had been placed on her and was gradually starting to intensify. I blinked hard. I was tired and needed to sleep, but I couldn't tear my eyes away from this young woman. I tried to discern what she was doing, but as the light grew brighter I realized she wasn't smoking at all. In her hand she held a candle and she moved it up and around, trying to get my attention. She was motioning, beckoning to me. Was there something wrong? Was she stuck up there?

I remained in my bed watching the young woman, transfixed by the circular movement of the candle and the way her hair floated away from her face as though there was a breeze stirring about her. But the night was still. The motionless curtain against the open window confirmed this.

I concluded that she thought I was Alicia and was trying to communicate something to her as she had in the past. I should go out and tell her that Alicia had died. All the neighbors knew this. Why didn't she?

I got out of bed and threw on another shirt over my shorts and tee shirt. The girl was only three floors up on the other side of the street. It would be an easy thing to shout up to her and see if she was OK. I opened the door and went out into the road. She was still there, holding her arms out toward me as though she was in trouble.

"I'm coming," I yelled up to her and rushed to the main door of the building. It was not only locked, but bolted with layers of boards that appeared to have been rotting there for years. Then I remembered the building was condemned and hadn't been occupied for some time. The girl must have found her way inside and didn't know how to get out. I was about to call to her again, but when I looked up, she was no longer there.

I tested the main entrance and concluded she couldn't possibly have entered or exited through there. I walked around the building several times, but all the windows and doors were hammered shut with layers of old boards.

Perplexed about her disappearance, I began to circle the building once more when I caught sight of something gleaming out of the corner of my eye. Perched on the frame of the gate was the white votive candle the girl had been waving about on the balcony, its delicate flame still flickering in the night. I walked closer to examine it and finally picked it up. How, I wondered, could she have come out without my noticing? The windows and doors were boarded up from the outside. She would've had to jump down three floors.

I took one final look down the street before heading back to my bed. It was already late, and I tried to put any thoughts about the mysterious girl out of my mind and focus on Jeremy who'd be expecting me in less than twenty-four hours. Would it be the same for us after so many days apart? I was giddy with anticipation, and yet my heart sank with the realization that this was my last night in Cuba—my last night at home.

# 33

I ARRIVED AT THE AIRPORT AT SIX IN THE MORNING, KNOWING IT would be a mass of confusion. I carried my one empty suitcase and wore the only dress that remained of the clothes I'd brought. I decided to leave my other suitcase outside Berta's bedroom door as a gift.

I'd been in such a rush to get to the airport that I hadn't had time to think about the events of the previous night. And there was a part of me that didn't want to think about them at all. It was time to get on with my life. I was the wife of a wonderful and loving man who was waiting for me. I should've been thinking about how much I wanted to make love to him instead of what had happened to that girl on the balcony. I'd tucked the candle safely in my purse, and now I poked my hand inside to make sure it was still there. If only I'd had time to talk to Beba. I was sure she'd have an explanation involving the "call of one's dreams" or the "power of the lesser known spirits". However far-fetched, I longed to hear something that would make sense of the lingering doubts that had preoccupied me all morning.

I was near the front of the line and was preparing to hand over my passport for its third or forth time since I arrived. I closed my eyes and forced myself to picture Jeremy waiting for me, so happy to know that soon I'd be there with him and all would be well with the world. We'd take care of Lucinda's papers, of course we would. She'd be with us in no time. Beba was more than capable of making sure she was safe. She was more ingenious and savvy about life since the revolution than I could ever be. And Lucinda didn't hate me. She knew I'd be back for her, Alicia had told her so herself.

My head and my stomach jolted, and my feet refused to move forward in the line. Sweat erupted on my brow and everywhere else, dripping down my body and the backs of my legs. I thought I might faint.

The young man expecting to receive my passport sounded concerned. "Is there something wrong, miss?"

"I . . . I don't know."

"Step up and lean on the counter," he offered as though he was quite accustomed to managing fainting spells.

I did as I was told, but didn't feel any better. My head was swimming and a faint humming vibrated through my ears as though I had two large shells glued to them. I couldn't hear anything at all.

The young man reached for my passport, but I held it to my chest as if to still my heart. "I can't go."

He didn't hear me correctly. He was transfixed on the computer screen with one hand still open and waiting. The passengers who'd already cleared were taking anxious little steps toward the open door and the plane that awaited us. "There's a bathroom on the plane, miss."

I staggered backward onto the shoes of the person standing behind me. "I can't go," I said again and collapsed into the nearest chair. How could I forget how Alicia had looked when she first became a woman and fell in love? I reached inside my purse for the candle. She had lighted countless candles over the years to keep hope alive when her world was crumbling around her. And now she wanted me to stay and see to Lucinda's freedom myself. I knew that as surely as I knew Jeremy wanted me to go back to him and our wonderful life in California.

I took a deep breath and tried to focus on the fact that I had to get on that plane. Perhaps Beba was getting to me with all her *Santería* and rituals, but all I could think of was my vow to Alicia that I wouldn't abandon her child. I had promised her as she died in my arms.

I managed to stand and make my way to the window, smeared with the remnants of squashed mosquitoes and sweaty palm prints, to watch the plane bake in the heat as the mechanics milled around checking this and that. I had plenty of time to change my mind if I wanted to and the passport in my hand reminded me of this. Sweat accumulating on my fingers caused it to slip and fall to the floor. I didn't bother to pick it up until the plane had rumbled down the runway and lifted off Cuban soil.

Lucinda hugged me and laughed with joy. "Tía Nora you came back so soon. I didn't think you'd come back this soon, but I'm so glad you did." Her hands fluttered over my face.

Beba wasn't at all surprised to see me standing there in my last good dress, an orange linen shift with matching sandals and purse. She leaned in the doorway leading to the kitchen with arms crossed, chuckling, and shaking her head. She promptly disappeared to prepare coffee and returned with two chipped cups. As we drank our coffee I explained what happened the night before and showed her the candle I found.

Lucinda took it from me and pressed it against her cheek, already convinced that her mother had left it. But Beba, munching on her cracker like a chipmunk with her one front tooth, appeared unmoved. I was waiting for a supernatural explanation that would set me straight, anything that might help me justify my decision to not go back to Jeremy as I had promised I would.

"It doesn't matter what you saw last night, whether it was a ghost from heaven or hell or just your wild imagination," Beba said finally. "What matters is that you did what you thought was right."

This was not what I wanted to hear. I needed something more substantial; assurances that I'd done the right thing. I pressed her about Jeremy and how she thought he'd take the fact that I wouldn't be on the plane. I pressed her like I did when I was a girl, insisting that she tell me yet another story before turning out the light.

"For God's sake child, I can't give you what I don't have to give. All I can tell you is that time and happenings will let you know if you did right."


Time and happenings, as Beba said, spoke to me soon enough. I spent the night at Beba's apartment and the next morning we were awakened very early by a knocking at the door. By the solid sound of it, it was clear that whoever was on the other side was using some sort of object. And it wasn't just one person because we could hear conversation. Beba, who always slept fully dressed, complete with handkerchief on her head, slipped on her sandals and headed toward the door while shooting a look in my direction that said, "I'll handle this; just keep quiet."

I pulled the sheet over both my and Lucinda's head. From where we slept on the floor, the person at the door would have to pass Beba and enter the room to see she wasn't alone. I didn't have to tell Lucinda to stay quiet. We held each other tightly and hardly breathed.

Beba coughed and opened the door. I could easily imagine her sizing up the intruders. She had a stare capable of turning blood to ice water when it was at full strength. I had been victim of this and benefited from its protection on many occasions in my life. At that moment I never felt more grateful to have Beba in my corner.

"We're looking for a child," the man said, and I recognized the voice as that of the bespectacled man from the *Ministerio de Educación*. "Her name is Lucinda Rodríguez. And we were informed she's living here now."

"What do you want with her?"

Another voice spoke up, a woman's voice strained and high pitched as though she had her vocal cords tied in a very tight knot. "Are you a relative?"

"Yes, I am," Beba replied without hesitation.

"That's funny, we were informed the child had no living relatives."

"You got your facts wrong."

Silence followed. They were staring each other down now, I was sure of it. They'd be no match for Beba. Their bones were probably already turning to jelly. I had to fight the bizarre temptation to giggle, and I held on to Lucinda more tightly.

"Your name please," the man asked.

"Beba."

"And your last name?"

"It's just Beba."

Silence again and the shuffling of feet. Not Beba's feet. "Your lack of cooperation won't help you or the child, let me assure you," the woman said in a superior tone. "Unless you have documents indicating you have legal custody of the child, she'll be placed in the government orphanage for her own protection. Is that clear?"

"Oh, very clear. You put your words together real good."

It was the man who spoke this time. "We'll be back . . . Beba."

Beba closed the door behind them and went to the kitchen window. Once satisfied that they'd left, she lifted the sheet from over us and stood with hands on hips and a funny smile on her face. I knew she was afraid, but she didn't want Lucinda to notice and it was too hard for a woman as honest as Beba to look one way and sound another.

"I think now's a good a time," Beba said to Lucinda and I as she fixed our breakfast. "Now's a good time to take that money and find a way out of here."

"You mean not wait for the visa?"

"With the money you have, you don't have to wait for anyone or anything."

It was an option I'd never considered. I always imagined we'd leave legally with my American passport and Lucinda's visa in order, and hadn't thought of the possibility of escape. I remembered what Alicia had written to me about securing passage on a banana boat a few years back. Perhaps we could find something similar now? Suddenly, I wanted to run to the nearest phone and call Jeremy to tell him all was well and not to give up on me. I'd be home soon.

Lucinda informed us that it was Pepe, the neighbor, who was known for helping in these matters, so I told her and Beba that I would go and see him. I found him a few hours later sitting on his front step unraveling a fist-sized ball of thread. He explained that his wife had paid pennies for it because it was all knotted up, and it was very difficult to find thread. He didn't seem particularly excited about having thread, but he appreciated having something to do that didn't cause him too much anxiety.

When I told him what Lucinda and I needed, his long brown fingers that were moving like spider's legs stopped and he looked straight out in front him. With lips barely parted he asked, "How much have you got?"

When I told him, his fingers started moving again and he nodded soberly. "I can find you something with that. In a couple of weeks there's a shipment coming in and . . ."

"I don't have that kind of time. I need something for tomorrow or the next day at the latest."

His brow furrowed. "Ships come and go every day, but the people coming in a couple weeks, I know them. I know they'll be fair. I can't be sure about anyone else."

"I'll have to take my chances. The authorities will come back any day and if they find Lucinda, I'll never see her again."

Pepe nodded his agreement and I pulled the envelope of cash out of my purse and handed it to him, but he refused it saying he only needed fifty dollars or so to secure an agreement. The balance I could pay myself. We agreed to meet later that same evening.

I told Lucinda and Beba that Pepe might find a way for us to leave the next day and that we'd know by this evening.

"How should we spend our last day in Cuba?" I asked Lucinda.

She was sitting on the couch reading, where she'd been most of the morning. "I don't think we should go out Tía Nora, in case they see me. I think we should stay here and wait," she said after a pause.

"You want to stay here all day?"

She nodded and turned back to her reading.

Beba sat with me by the window, her arms crossed over her chest. The thought occurred to me that we might have enough money so Beba could leave with us too. Maybe there was enough time to inform Pepe? I mentioned this possibility to Beba who grinned at the prospect.

"Could you see Beba in such a big fancy place?"

"I could easily see you there, Beba."

She shook her head and pressed her lips together as if she'd tasted a sour lemon. "It's too late for me, Norita. Maybe ten or fifteen years ago I would've gone, but not now. I'm going to die here in my country where I belong."

"Don't you want to live in freedom again?"

"Maybe I don't think of freedom the way you do. There's a freedom I found over the years. It comes from discovering I don't need much to be happy. It comes from living past misery and fear and finding hope in your own tears." Beba laughed that deep golden laugh that filled the room. "I feel freedom standing in line all day with my ration card, only to learn they've run out of bread before it's my turn. I feel freedom when I pray at the water's edge and ask the Good Lord to feed me with the wind and the sun and the sky." Beba readjusted her handkerchief and tucked stray strands of hair underneath it. "That's my freedom, Norita, and I don't have to escape anywhere to get it."


There was no one at Pepe's house when I arrived in the evening, so I sat on his usual spot on the stoop. The breeze swept down the narrow street and when I leaned over to my left I could see a portion of a plaza where children played in an old fountain long since dried. I remembered this plaza when we drove to church on

Sundays before the revolution. It was bordered by white and yellow roses, and the fountain always flowed with the melody of soft water. Children were allowed to throw pennies for a wish or two. And, at least in my case, this was usually followed by a treat of coconut ice cream. No wonder Pepe loved this spot. For a moment it was possible to dream of the days when Cuba was young and carefree.

He approached with his loping side to side gait. It was impossible to guess by studying his face whether or not he'd been successful in his quest. Pepe always looked the same. He barely nodded his head when he saw me and when I stood up to greet him he handed me a folded piece of white paper.

"It leaves tomorrow at seven in the morning. You have to go meet the man tonight and pay him in advance."

"How much?"

"Two thousand. And the rest when you get there. The ship's going to Jamaica first. That's where you get off, and it's easy to get a flight from Kingston to Miami."

I couldn't help myself. I grabbed hold of Pepe and gave him a hug. He endured my affection without a word, although his stoic expression was rippled by a curious half smile.

"I need to pay you for your help, Pepe, please." I reached into my pocket for the wad of cash that had felt thick and sticky against my thigh all day.

Pepe raised his hands slowly to stop me. For him this was the equivalent of an emotional hurricane and I froze. "Don't pay me yet, Cousin Butterfly. If it all works out you can send me some cash from home or a box of American cigarettes. I know you won't forget.

# 34

LUCINDA AND I PACKED OUR FEW BELONGINGS IN THE MESH BAG we used for our picnic lunches when we went to the beach. We took just the few T-shirts I'd bought weeks earlier and a couple pairs of shorts. The rest of the bag was filled with crackers and fresh fruit.

Beba brought out another bag of fruit and placed it next to our bulging sack. "Really, Beba, we'll be in Jamaica in a short time. How many bananas can two people eat?"

Beba placed her hands on her hips and wagged her head knowingly. "You may not eat them, but a ship full of men will make quick work of that. Better they keep their minds on mangos and bananas. You'll need all the distractions you can handle." She flicked her head toward Lucinda who was napping on the couch. Her golden curls caught the light of the setting sun, and her heavy lashes barely fluttered against rose-tinted cheeks. Her long limbs were beginning to assume the curvaceousness of womanhood and she was looking as Alicia had when she was at her most beautiful, except that Lucinda would be taller and her face, although equally sweet in expression, was more exotic in form and color. There could be no doubt that she was destined to be a beautiful woman. I put the thought of potential trouble out of my mind. I had other things to worry about.

\* \* \*

It was just as Pepe described. A tall thin bearded man with a red shirt was fishing at the end of pier 17 in the warehouse district. I was to hand him my plastic grocery bag filled with any food items I wanted as long as amongst it was a coffee can stuffed with half of the money. The other half would be delivered when we arrived in Jamaica.

I walked up to the man and held the bag out to him, but, with a furtive nod of his head, he indicated that I set it down at his feet. I did so and worried for a moment that the bag might tumble into the sea, but I steadied it well away from the edge before stepping back.

"Stay and talk for a bit," he said without looking at me. "It looks strange if you just walk away without a word."

Looks strange to whom? Was somebody watching us? "Of course," I muttered.

"I understand there's a blind girl traveling with you?"

"My niece."

"Getting out of the dinghy and onto the ship could be tricky. Do you think she can handle it?"

"I'll make sure she can."

He studied the water and pulled on the line. "Almost had it." He reeled the line a bit and turned half way to face me, still avoiding my eyes. "I expect you here tomorrow morning at five and not a minute later or we'll miss the connection. We have two hours to paddle out towards the ship and I can't be sure how rough the waters will be."

Until that moment, this had never occurred to me. It was what I had to do to get home and keep Lucinda from becoming a ward of the state. It was what I had to do to see Jeremy again as soon as possible and save my marriage. "Will it be dangerous?"

"Only if we get caught and they don't believe our story."

"Our story?"

"We've gone out for a day of fishing. You're my wife and the girl is our daughter. It's her birthday and we wanted to catch some fish for a party and she'd never been fishing before. If any boat comes toward us you immediately throw whatever you have in the ocean. And put something in the bag so it doesn't float."

I studied the man's long European nose and glossy brown hair. His skin was darkened by the sun, but it was obvious he didn't have a drop of African blood in him.

"I'm afraid my niece would never pass as your daughter or mine, and especially not yours and mine together. Her father was mulatto and she looks a lot like him. We'll have to come up with another story."

"OK. We'll go over it tomorrow at five sharp."

"May I know your name?"

The man choked on a smile in spite of his efforts to remain serious and to the point. He looked me directly in the eyes for the first time. "My name is . . . José Gómez. What's yours?"

It took me a moment to understand. "María Gómez," I replied.

He nodded approvingly and returned to his fishing without another word.

Lucinda wanted to know every detail of my conversation with the man at the dock who'd help us escape, and I told her what I knew which wasn't very much. She listened as though we were planning a day's excursion. She hadn't been so animated since before her mother's death.

"I've never been on a boat," she said, while holding on to the edge of her chair for the sheer joy of it. "Mami never let me because I can't swim very well. But now I have to, don't I, Tía? Now I have no choice."

The question caught me off guard. Of course she had a choice. She could stay here and go to the state school. She certainly wasn't the only blind child on the island. Maybe the school wasn't as bad as Alicia said. Would she have wanted me to risk Lucinda's life rather than let her go to a state school for the blind? Because I was risking her life, wasn't I?

Beba listened calmly to our conversation, her face devoid of expression as she picked something out from under her nails. I wanted to talk to her without Lucinda present. She'd been short on answers lately, but this time I wouldn't let her get away so easily. Why was she suddenly so careful about giving her opinions on things? In the old days she always shot them out at whomever was nearby without worrying about their impact.

Telling Beba that I needed her to help me select more food for the sailors, we left Lucinda resting in bed. I lead Beba by the arm down the street, toward the sweet breeze of the ocean. The *malecón* was still several blocks away, but its whispering mist seemed particularly lovely, if only because it would help disguise our voices.

"What do you think, Beba? Am I making a terrible mistake? Is this risk worth it?"

I'd bombarded her with questions before we were even half way down the street. I whispered them in her ear and felt I was having trouble breathing and walking at the same time.

Beba didn't answer, but sat me down on the fountain of the plaza with a firm hand on my shoulder. Together we looked out upon the maze of streets from which we'd come, at this labyrinth of crumbling buildings with rusted gates and laundry dripping from the balconies. Children ran in and out of the open doors barefoot and happy to be children. They paid no notice to the grim faces of their parents too fatigued to be amused by their play and too consumed by their hunger to notice that some of the babies were getting close to the stairs or ambling out into the street.

Teenage girls strolled together swinging their stretchy hips this way and that, and walking so their young breasts bounced under tube tops and threadbare T-shirts. Young and old men alike called casually after them, offering vulgar comments about the particular body parts they found most alluring, as if the breasts of one girl and behind of another might jump off their respective torsos and find their way to them.

One particular drama played out before us. A girl, no more than fifteen, had been persuaded to exchange more than glances with a significantly older man. A few seconds later they walked off, the girl trailing behind like a puppy straggling on a short leash.

Beba turned to me. "She's probably been whoring since about twelve, maybe younger." She waved a hand at the group of girls left behind. "They're just the same, and I happen to know they all finished high school. The government saw to that all right."

"Are you saying Lucinda could be like them some day?"

"I'm saying that hunger makes you do things you thought only the devil could do. Lord in heaven, I never thought an ugly face and a big belly would be such a blessing."

"So you think I'm taking a necessary risk with Lucinda. Is that what you mean, Beba?"

Beba looked a bit exasperated to be put on the spot again. Then taking my hand in hers, she spoke to me as clearly as she ever had in all my life. "The decision you make is not as important as the heart that's behind it. Stand by your decision and it will stand by you."

Lucinda was dressed and ready when I opened my eyes in the faint haze of morning. Beba was in the kitchen preparing our coffee and toast, our last meal in Cuba. We hardly spoke as we ate and I glanced frequently at the noisy plastic clock on top of Beba's TV.

"We have to go in a few minutes," I said.

"Do you want me to walk with you?" Beba asked.

"I don't think it's a good idea because the man is expecting only Lucinda and me. I don't know if it makes any difference . . ."

Beba put up her hand to let me know she understood. She took the breakfast dishes back to the little sink, but she didn't rinse them immediately as she always did. She came back to the room to be with us for every minute she could. We stood up from the table and Lucinda reached out for Beba, and when she found her, buried her head into her bosom and wept openly.

"I wish you were coming with us," she said as Beba stroked her hair and patted her back.

"Now, don't you worry about me. I'm going to be right here like I've always been. One day we'll see each other again. That man can't live forever."

At the door, I hugged Beba long and hard. "You'll keep trying to call Jeremy for me, won't you?"

"I'll be at that phone so often, people will think I'm a spy. And when I get a hold of him I plan to tell him a few things I got on my mind."

I kissed her on the cheek. "I think you should."


After twenty minutes of brisk walking, we were half way down the *malecón*. Lucinda stumbled a few times, but I didn't slow my pace. We couldn't risk being late and I'd long given away my watch. Lucinda didn't complain. In fact, she didn't speak at all. She knew we had to concentrate on not appearing suspicious. Perhaps we already looked suspicious because we were walking so urgently. Better slow down a bit and point towards the ships on the ocean like sightseers. But what would sightseers be doing out at dawn? Of course we looked like we were trying to escape. What else would a woman and her child be doing out at this time of morning? The only people out at this hour were vagrants sitting on curbs and young prostitutes dragging home with tired faces and high heels dangling from their fingers.

I pointed to the ships and told Lucinda that our ship was out there somewhere. So eager to appear the unlikely tourist, I forgot that Lucinda couldn't possibly see where I was pointing.

"Tía Nora?" Lucinda was slightly out of breath. "I feel so sad inside. I never felt like this before, not even when Mami died."

I slowed my pace slightly and struggled to push my mind away from the nervousness I felt. I remembered the first time I had said good-bye to my country so many years ago. Although I wasn't sure exactly what she meant, Beba's words made all the difference to me then and I knew they'd help Lucinda now.

"The sadness of leaving home is like nothing else you'll ever know," I said slowly. "And it comes in strong waves that can knock you off your feet when you think you're standing on solid ground. Everything can be just fine and then you'll hear the chords of a song or smell onions frying in olive oil and your heart will break all over again into a million pieces, just like that. You'll want to sell your soul to be home again or just to belong some- where . . . anywhere. That's when you have to hold on most to who you are. And don't ever give your true heart away, as broken and bleeding as it may be, because when you do, you've lost something you may never find again. Better to give away your ghost heart, and then you'll always know who you are."

"What's my ghost heart, Tía Nora?"

"It's the heart inside you that can never be hurt by broken promises or the pain of too much longing. It goes right on beating no matter what happens, because your ghost heart has many lives. But your real heart has only one precious life, and you must al- ways keep that one for yourself."

The mild glow of dawn had begun to intensify on the horizon, causing both of my hearts to beat erratically. There was no time to waste, and I picked up my pace again. "We'll talk more about this, but for now you must remember everything I told you."

"I won't forget," Lucinda said, running to keep up with me. "Mami said I had the best memory of anyone she ever knew and that I'm rich because of it, because memories are like jewels that can never be stolen."


We arrived at the designated dock flushed and slightly out of breath, but the man in the red shirt was nowhere to be found. I was certain this was the right place, and I turned in circles several times in confusion and panic. My God, where was he?

"I hear something in the water," Lucinda whispered.

I looked over the side of the dock to see José Gómez sitting in a small, battered looking dinghy that bobbed up and down in the receding tide. He was watching us anxiously as he motioned for us to get in quickly. We carefully climbed down the steps and Lu- cinda dropped into the boat without any fuss. José didn't wait for introductions. He hurriedly untied the boat from the mooring and started to row away from the pier with strong thrusts of his arms and legs. Lucinda and I huddled together on the other side of the boat with our small bag of provisions between us.

The sun had begun its glowing ascent in the sky, turning the water into pink and gray ribbons of light. All was still except for the rhythmic splash of the oars in the water. It was amazing how quickly José moved.

Satisfied that we were far enough out, he rested the oars on his thighs and began to instruct us between gasps of air. "We're husband and wife, José and María Gómez. This is our niece and we're taking her fishing to celebrate her birthday."

"My birthday isn't until July. And what about Tío Heremi?"

"No, honey, this is what we say if somebody stops to question us."

José nudged the fishing pole resting at his feet toward me and resumed rowing. "Better start fishing."

I'd never been fishing in my life, but I knew better than to ask for instructions. I took hold of the pole, untied the line from its tip and dropped it into the water. I looked out toward the shore and gazed upon the *malecón*. It too was pink and wavering in the morning light. The skyline cut a clear edge along the sky, and the windows blinked with the reflection of the pale light. A few early risers were making their way on foot near the shore. Some were also launching boats closer to shore with their fishing poles cast.

It was then that I saw her standing at the very end of the pier. She held one hand up to shield the morning sun that peeked over the horizon. The light caught the brilliant white of her turban. It was Beba, and she was waving to us frantically. Perhaps she changed her mind, and she wanted to come with us after all.

"You have to turn back," I said to José standing up and rocking the boat. Lucinda gasped.

"What are you doing? Sit down before we tip over."

"It's Beba. You have to turn back."

"Is Beba here?" Lucinda asked.

"Who the hell is Beba? What are you talking about?" José

stopped his frantic rowing and looked toward the pier. "It'll take me almost an hour to get back there against the current, and we'll miss the ship."

The waves had grown taller, and we could see Beba only at the top of the swells. She was still waving. Then she wasn't waving anymore. And then she was gone.

José was drenched in sweat and his T-shirt clung to him. He observed Lucinda for a moment with certain curiosity. She was holding on to the side of the boat, keeping her eyes lifted toward the sky. He reached under the seat and threw a tattered life jacket at me. "I brought this for the girl."

I put the jacket on Lucinda quickly and tied the buckles tight. "What is this, Tía?"

"It's a special jacket that floats in the water so if we fall in, you'll float just like the best swimmer in the world."

Lucinda smiled as she passed her hands along the orange plastic and coarse ties. Then her eyes grew somber. "How about you and Mr. Gómez?"

"We're good swimmers, honey. You don't have to worry about us."

José began to row again, looking over his shoulder from time to time to see how far we'd gone. He told us that we needed to reach the far ship with the red stripe along the side. It was docked out further because of its immense size. The waves continued to roll higher and splash over the sides of the boat. Although José rowed harder than ever, it seemed that we moved more slowly and sometimes not at all.

"The current is crazy here," José shouted over the roar of the wind and the ocean. "It was working for us closer in, but now it's pulling us back." He was exhausted from rowing and his face grimaced with the pain of his effort.

"Can I help," I shouted, but he didn't hear me. He just kept rowing with all his strength. At one point the swells got so high that one of the oars came completely out of the water and José almost lost it for lack of resistance. Lucinda held on to me tight. I could only imagine how frightening it felt for her. All she could hear was noise that sounded like thunder. Ocean water splashed over the sides of the boat so that soon we were all quite drenched. Lucinda's foot slipped in her plastic sandals as she braced herself against the lurching movement of our small craft. The only comfort was the sight of the huge white ship with the red stripe along the side. Once we got on we'd be safe and very easily hidden. Pepe had assured me those ships were never searched because government agents were bribed to look the other way. "A lot of money for passage goes toward the bribe," he'd said.

"Our ship is very close, honey," I said to Lucinda who nodded her head against my chest.

After another rolling wave that completely obscured the sight of the white ship, José told us to lean against the direction of the waves. We followed his instructions and the boat stabilized significantly, while José rowed with renewed energy. I looked behind us. The *malecón* still visible in the morning sun, fully revealed in a cloudless sky. We were too far away to see people on the shore, and it was impossible to know if Beba was still watching us. I felt safer believing that she was and I told Lucinda that Beba was there praying for us and making sure we were safe.

We'd been on the water for well over an hour and the ship was close enough so I could make out the small portholes just above the painted red line. Perhaps one of those portholes would be our quarters for the trip to Jamaica. We'd be stashed in there with a load of bananas or raw sugar. It suddenly occurred to me that I didn't know whether or not José was escaping as well. Last night I figured he was taking a cut of the money in exchange for getting us to the ship, but he seemed to be interested in more than money. He was like a man possessed.

"Are you coming with us?" I asked during the brief instant he rested his arms.

"Of course," he replied. "No matter what happens I'm getting out."

I didn't bother to ask what he meant because he was pumping his arms and legs with amazing concentration, and we were making significant progress again. I was glad to know he'd be joining us. We could continue to present as husband and wife and that would keep inappropriate attention from the crew at bay. I'd mention this to José before we boarded the ship. The waves had calmed down and he was rowing with greater ease, but I couldn't bother him with questions now even though one loomed large and heavy in my mind. How were we going to board the ship?

As we approached, its enormity was more apparent than ever and our little boat was barely visible next to it. There was certainly no door or hatch so far below through which we might enter. And the portholes were several stories above the water level. The only way was to pull us up by some sort of rope. I shivered at the thought of it, not for me, but for Lucinda who was already shaken enough.

"There should be someone watching out for us on this side," José said looking up at the giant towering above us.

"Do you think they can see us?" I asked.

My question was answered when a thin rope was flung over the side of the ship. Far too thin, it seemed, to support the weight of a small dog. But when it got closer to us we saw that the rope was actually quite sturdy. The problem was how to grab hold of it without hitting the side of the ship. The waves, although calmer, still had the strength to slam us against it if we weren't careful, and it was obvious our weathered dinghy couldn't take much abuse. If the waters had been calmer it would've been an easy matter to swim out for the rope and bring it to the dinghy, but I'd never swum in such water and I didn't want José to leave us alone on the dinghy.

Although we hadn't spoken since the appearance of the rope, I was sure José's hesitation stemmed from the same concern. He held the oar static and dripping over the water as we bobbed and rolled closer and then further from the ship with every passing wave.

"I can hear waves hitting the metal ship, Tía. It is very close."

"It's right next to us, sweetheart. They'll pull us up as soon as they can."

José rowed us in closer still. We were only a yard or so from reaching the rope and every time the waves threatened to push us in too far, José held the oar out to keep us at a comfortable, if not stable, distance. He motioned for me to take hold of the rope, while he held out the oar. Lucinda would be first. I tied the rope securely around her waist and instructed her to hold on to it as tight as she could. She nodded and blinked the water spraying up from the waves out of her eyes.

"They'll pull you up a very long way, but I'll be right below you."

Lucinda took hold of the rope with both hands and waited. José pulled hard on the rope two times, and it started to pull up slowly at first until Lucinda's feet were dangling off the ground. Her plastic shoes fell off, one falling into the boat and the other into the ocean, floating off on the waves before I had a chance to make a grab for it. I was afraid this might disorient Lucinda and that she'd fidget and the rope would loosen, but she didn't move. Her hands gripped the rope and her little face pressed against it. She swayed to and fro over our heads as she inched higher and higher still, three stories up, almost to the portholes. We were craning our heads as she went, but José was vigilant with the oar, although from time to time I thought he might get thrown off the dinghy because of the force he had to withstand against the ship.

Lucinda was up to the portholes now, too far away to hear my voice. I could only imagine the fear she felt, and I began to shiver and pray.

"They've stopped," José said.

I looked up. Lucinda was still dangling, but not moving up or down. Then she started to move slowly down, and then up again, before she jerked to a stop. The rope shifted up her waist so that it was hidden by the life jacket. Suddenly she started to move down very rapidly. The rope was like a wild, vibrating snake, and I realized she was free falling. Paralyzed, I watched her feet swinging wildly as she screamed, then disappeared into the waves about fifty yards from the boat.

I dove into the water and began to swim toward where I'd seen Lucinda fall. The waves rolled over me and I was barely able to gasp for air, such was the force of the water pushing me down and then up again. I caught sight of Lucinda's head bobbing beyond the crest of the next wave, eyes closed and chin resting on her life jacket, but I was unable to find the rhythm that would propel me to her. That familiar heaviness that I knew was brought on by my own fear was creeping into my limbs and making it almost impossible for me to stay above water, let alone swim. "Fear doesn't float," Abuelo always said during our lessons. "It sinks straight to be the bottom every time. But courage," He said, his eyes shinning. "It not only floats, it flies."

Suddenly, Abuelo was swimming alongside me and urging me on. "I'm proud of you, Norita," he said. "You jumped in without thinking about it, and now you will know what I have always known." I felt his strength surging through my muscles, and I became as sleek as a dolphin, my legs pumping like pistons and my lungs filled with pure oxygen. I swam for my Lucinda more surely than I had ever done anything in my life, and when I reached her I pulled her toward me by the strap of her jacket. She was breathing, thank God she was breathing, and I held her to me while José brought the boat close enough for us to get in. He pulled Lucinda in first, and then I followed collapsing in heap onto the floor of the boat.

Exhaustion took hold of me and everything became dark and silent as a dreamless sleep, but not before I heard Abuelo whispering, "You are an excellent swimmer, Norita."

# 35

JOSÉ WAS FISHING AGAINST THE BACKDROP OF A PERFECT BLUE sky. A pair of small bare feet were just below where he sat and the toes wiggled like little crabs peeking out of their shells. I turned with a start and my head exploded with pain. I settled back on my elbow and turned more slowly.

Lucinda lay next to me, and she was breathing. I saw her little chest rise and fall, and it wasn't the movement of the boat because the boat was hardly moving. It was very still. We were both completely dry, and Lucinda's corkscrew curls shot out from her lovely face like fire works.

I placed my hand lightly on her cheek. Her eyes fluttered and rolled as if in a dream and then she smiled. "I can see the light, Tía Nora, and it's so beautiful."

José heard us talking and turned only half way around to look at us, but said nothing. He caught two fish one right after the other and threw them onto the small deck between us. They flapped for a short while as their lives quickly evaporated in the hot sun. Apparently convinced that he wouldn't catch anymore, he gutted and skinned the fish and promptly handed us each roughly cut strips of raw fish flesh. The other fish he cut into even thinner strips and laid out on the narrow wooden seat to dry. He did this all without speaking or looking at us.

I encouraged Lucinda to take the warm white flesh into her mouth and chew it quickly before swallowing. It was a tasteless mass of hard jelly going down my throat, and I realized then how thirsty I was and that my shoulders ached when I sat up higher on my elbows to see over the side of the dinghy. I don't know exactly what I was expecting to find. Perhaps the Havana skyline sitting up on the Caribbean like a rusty crown, a few other fishing boats, Beba waiting for us on the pier with her hands on her hips because she had other business to get to and had been waiting long enough. It was a shock to see the vast blue ocean spreading out in all directions. I turned to where I thought Cuba should be, ignoring the ripping pain that shot through my shoulders, but there was nothing but the thin line of the horizon, unwavering and distant, circling us like an enormous ghostly ring.

"Where are we?" The air was so humid and thick that it was almost possible to drink from it.

José was chewing on fish as he carefully rewound the fishing line. "On our way to freedom . . . María." He smiled revealing small even teeth, teeth that had been well cared for. "My mother's name was María. Whose wasn't?" He chuckled.

"Freedom," Lucinda murmured as she chewed obediently and swallowed her fish.

José informed us that, although he couldn't be certain, there must have been government agents aboard the ship. After Lucinda was dropped into the water, the rope had been quickly cut. He was keeping an eye on the two of us in the water while watching out for another rope, but it never came.

"If I hadn't been so tired from rowing earlier, I would've gotten to you sooner," he said before stuffing his mouth with more raw fish. "You were both so tired, I just let you sleep."

"Why didn't you row to shore?" I asked.

"I told you I was getting out no matter what. Today was my last day on that island."

"What about water and provisions?"

"I brought water and citrus fruits. With what you brought I figure we have two or three days if we're careful."

I felt a terrible jolt of fear as I remembered hearing about Cubans who'd spent many more days in the channel because of shifting currents and storms. Many had drowned or died of dehydration before reaching freedom. I said this to José, who cast a wary eye toward Lucinda. "That won't happen to us. I haven't come this far to lose it all now."

José passed me a Styrofoam cup filled one third with water. This was to be mine and Lucinda's ration of water for the morning. We'd have another at midday and another in the evening. I noticed that José poured his ration out exactly as he had ours.

"Stay under the shade," he instructed and I became aware of the makeshift tarp made out of an old blanket strung over half of the boat and held up like a V with the oars.

"Don't we need those for steering or something?"

"The current will take us where we need to go. Now get some rest."

"How about you?"

He leaned back on the seat and stretched out his legs between Lucinda and me. He pushed his wide brimmed straw hat over his face and crossed his arms in front of him. He muttered something under his hat and fell asleep.


"I won," Alicia says. There's a contest to see who can find the most perfect shell. Abuelo always makes up games like these when he wants to take a nap or relax and not deal with our continual demands that he play with as in the water. Alicia holds up her palm-sized prize that swirls with delicate pinks and yellows from base to tip. It is indeed perfect.

I consider my own growing pile of shells. There were some interesting ones. Even a blue oyster shell that I never saw before, but it's chipped in several places. It'll be hard to find one that compares to Alicia's. She's standing over me and I see her pink toes wriggling in the sand, digging in against the gentle current that scoots her along the edge. She holds the shell down closer to my face so I can get a closer look. It is truly spectacular. What looks like yellow from a distance is really fine threads of gold and the surface is polished and smooth like china cups for show in Mami's dining room. This is no mere shell, but a work of art.

"I want you to have it," she says and drops it down to the sand before I have a chance to break its fall. I hold my breath and pick it up. Thankfully, it hasn't been damaged.

"This is the most beautiful shell in the world. You should keep it for yourself."

"I want you to have it, Nora. I want you to sleep with it under your pillow every night and think of me."

"It'll break if I do that."

"It won't break, silly." She snatches it out of my hand and dances along the shore tossing it in the air and turning and catching it at once. I chase after her, and try to catch the shell while it's still in the air, but it eludes me. Alicia is much quicker, and she's able to jump much higher and every time she catches the shell she laughs like a wind chime. Sometimes she catches it with just one finger and this delights her even more. Skipping in the water, she tosses it higher every time, so high that it pricks the sun with it's swirling tip and returns to earth glowing even more than before.

I'm very upset now. She's jumped and played with my shell long enough, and I know that it's only a matter of time before she breaks it. I try my hardest, and jump with all my might, catching the shell in mid air with both hands. I hold it to my heart, but when I'm back on the sand, I realize that I've crushed it. I watch the pieces, tiny bits of gold and rose colored loveliness, float out to sea. I look up to apologize to my cousin, but she is gone and not even her footprints remain on the sand.

I awoke this time to an amazing panorama of stars, a dome of blinking lights against a midnight blue sky and a familiar sound against the stillness of the night. José was rowing differently this time, easing into each stroke with the gentle eloquence of a dancer. His refined features caught the fragile light of the stars making him appear as though he were outlined by a fine dusting of iridescent powder. Lucinda was already awake and sitting up next to me. Her hand was on my arm and probably had been for hours because I didn't feel it until I sat up myself and felt the cold emptiness where it had been. She reached for me and I quickly took her hand into my own.

Without a word, she passed me an orange and I saw the broken pieces of orange skin in a neat pile next to her. I was thirsty and hungry, and the warm, sweet juice exploded in my mouth like little pricks of acid pain. I watched José as I ate. He appeared relaxed and quite satisfied with the progress we were making.

"We couldn't ask for better weather," he confirmed. "And it's better to row at night. I don't perspire as much. Anyway, I only need to row until we get back in the current that takes us toward the straits. Many cargo ships pass that way and one is bound to find us."

José explained that he'd been studying the tides for months just in case he needed to leave the island on his own. If we stayed with the proper current, we'd keep on track toward freedom with very little difficulty. If we strayed too far, we could drift indefinitely and not be found for weeks if ever. What was left of us, anyway. Of course, this didn't bother José at all. He spoke of the possibility of perishing without so much as a blink or a shrug. It was a possibility he considered with the same cold analysis he'd applied to his study of the tides.

He pulled the oars into the boat, and I felt the pull of the tide moving us along like an invisible hand beneath the sea. The water was slick as glass and even reflected the stars making it appear that our little boat was afloat in a vast universe of stars above and below us.

"Tía Nora?"

"Yes, Lucinda."

"Mr. Gómez knew my Papi in jail."

José nodded as he pulled the oars into the boat. "She looked familiar to me the moment I saw her on the pier. Her eyes are just like her father's. But I didn't put it together until she mentioned her mother's name. For almost three years all Tony ever talked about was Alicia. I asked myself if any woman could be so many things . . . so beautiful and clever and strong. I think I fell in love with her myself."

"She was all those things," I said, sitting up in amazement at the coincidence. "And you're in good company. We all loved her."

I was eager to hear his story and, as he rowed, José told me what he'd begun to tell Lucinda. He was trained as a journalist, had traveled extensively to Europe and South America, and had been a loyal revolutionary, writing fervent articles supporting Castro's position as a socialist in the world. These articles had propelled him into positions of greater intimacy within the upper echelons of the government. His final and most prestigious assignment was as a television reporter who had the honor of regularly interviewing Castro on television. He knew what questions to ask so his leader appeared well informed and balanced and yet he asked them with the pointed indifference of a ruthless reporter in search of the truth.

"As close as I was to the inner circle, I became increasingly aware of the glaring disparities between their way of life and that of ordinary citizens. After a tiring day of endless speeches about the need to sacrifice for one's country and the honor of an empty belly, the powerful elite would retire to a life of royalty. Their homes are sumptuous and they dine on imported foods and wines of every kind. They laze over long elaborate meals as they discuss domestic and international concerns as their mistresses serve them."

"Of course, I ate these beautiful meals myself and laughed along and offered my sage and objective opinion when I could. For a while I fooled even myself into thinking I was beyond the desperation that motivates men and women to sell their bodies on our streets. It's the same for everyone. Some people sell their bodies and others sell their souls."

"Soon I came to see that my place in the inner circle was no different than it was for every Cuban who sits down to a meager bowl of rice and beans with a bit of meat if they're lucky. The promise of a sandwich is enough to entice them to wave flags as if their lives depended on it. My mother attends Communist rallies whenever she can, not because she believes the government is doing right or wrong anymore, but because she's tired of rice and beans and wouldn't mind tasting a little meat and fresh bread for a change. It wasn't a sandwich I was selling my mind and spirit for, but a seven-course meal complete with cigars at the end."

José folded his thick forearms and shook his head slowly. "I began to hate myself. Every time I smiled and agreed, it felt as though I was swallowing my own bile. I turned down dinner invitations and came to know other writers who weren't afraid of the truth. They were using their writings to educate people and light a fire under those shackled by the day to day challenge of survival. We felt we'd become like Castro's poorly kept pets, chained to the fence out back and fed on the crumbs from the master's table."

"Together we wanted to urinate and defecate all over the polished floors and fine carpets of Castro's new hotels that were popping up along the beaches. We wanted to bark and howl like wolves when he insulted the people with his droning, meaningless spectacles of absolute and thoughtless power. We did this by writing articles, brief and to the point. Just as I'd misled the people with my writings before, now I intended to tell them the truth."

"They took some of us from our houses at night, and others boldly by daylight. Tony was in the cell next to mine. He was a man of amazing strength, a natural leader, and because of that I knew they'd never let him out. He talked to me when I decided to take my own life before Castro took it from me. But Tony spoke of God and what we'd do when we got out of prison and how we had to keep ourselves strong. I used to tease him when he talked like this and ask him what kind of a revolutionary believes in God. Tony always said that even in the early days he was only a revolutionary from the neck up. From the neck down he'd always been a good Catholic boy." José shuddered in the warm air and looked out at the open sea all around. "I owe him my life."

Lucinda's small voice came from the far corner of the boat. "Did Papi miss us, Mr. Gómez?"

"Every day he told me how much he missed you and your mother. He'd been planning to escape since the day he was imprisoned. Nobody knew it except for me and he persuaded me to join him. Our plan was to wait until we were assigned to work near an area of dense vegetation where we could slip away and get lost in the jungle. The guards were disorganized and lazy and we had a good chance if they didn't notice our absence for an hour or more. It was almost a year before the perfect opportunity came. We were to repair a road up in Matanzas, and Tony said he knew the area well. The group of men assigned was large, there was well over a hundred of us, and the road bordered the jungle."

"We didn't have time to think about it too much. When they slowed down so we could climb down from the back of the truck without falling over each other, I took my place in line and Tony motioned I should go first. I stepped back into a ditch in the road. The guard assigned to our detail was the laziest of all. I was sure I'd be able to make it into the trees before he noticed I was gone, but I wasn't so lucky. He saw me and was raising his gun to shoot when Tony was on top of him in an instant, and I ran as fast as I could into the jungle. I ran for hours and hid inside the hollow of a tree for three days and prayed like I'd never prayed before. Then I hitched a ride into Havana and found some friends who took me in. For two years, I've been hiding."

"What happened to Papi?"

"Any aggression toward a guard is punishable by swift execution." Manuel paused and considered his audience before speaking more gently. "I have no doubt your Papi met his death with honor and that his last thoughts were of you and your Mami."

Lucinda nodded and her sweet child's voice spoke with a depth of knowing much more appropriate to an older and wiser person. "Mami always said Papi would find a way to take care of us. And now you're here to take care of Tía Nora and me because Papi can't be."

"You better believe I'll take care of you. And you'll live in freedom just like your Papi wanted you to," José said, clearly moved.

As if to toast to his resolution, José poured out an even ration of water for the three of us, and I sipped mine tentatively as if it were the finest champagne. I felt euphoric. Was it the expanse of stars over our heads? Was it the sugar in the orange still dancing on my tongue? I had no doubt we'd make it to freedom with little difficulty. We were miles from the Cuban shore by now. Beba would have called Jeremy and he would be expecting us home. He'd be wondering why I hadn't called, but within a day or two I'd be calling from somewhere in Miami to tell him that we were safe and that we love him so very much.

Lucinda was dozing, her head resting on her arm. It was only slightly chilly and I pulled the blanket that shielded us from the sun in the day up over her shoulders. Would Jeremy have remembered to prepare her room? How wonderful it would be to lay safe in his arms knowing that Lucinda was safe and sound with us in her own little room. It would be a yellow room, the color of the sun. I'd find her a good school right away, and the family would fall in love with her instantly as everybody always did. Of course, we'd have to adopt her as soon as possible.

José wasn't sleepy and his eyes shone as they searched the waters around us. He was watching out for huge ships and tankers that moved with silent speed through the water. The same ships that could rescue us in the day might destroy us by night.

"What's your real name?" I asked him after a long silence.

"Manuel Alarcón. And yours?"

"Nora García-McLaughlin."

"Ah, married to an American, are you?"

I nodded and smiled at the thought of Jeremy, Tío Heremi, as Lucinda called him.

"He's a good man. I love him very much."

"He'll be waiting for you then."

"Yes." I thought of Jeremy's easy smile and kind hazel eyes. Even after we were married I couldn't look at him too long without feeling a hot blush spread all over me.

José asked no more questions. He was a practical and focused man, and he scanned the ocean with a disciplined eye as he wound and unwound the fishing line around his finger.

"Are you married?" I asked.

"No." he answered, without removing his eyes from the sea.

"Why not?"

He pressed his lips, the first sign of anxiety I'd seen cross his face. "Perhaps one day I'll have the time and the energy to find a wife."

"Do you want her to be Cuban?"

"I hadn't thought about it." And it didn't seem that he wanted to think of it now. "I always imagined she would be, but right now I'd settle for an American wife."

We talked for some time, although I did most of the talking. I told him of Alicia and how we'd grown up together and the promise I'd made to her before she died. We watched the stars rotate slowly through the night and I told him about how difficult it was to leave Cuba, and of my early struggles in the United States and with the American way of life. He agreed with me that the romance of Cuba was hard to resist, but that it had died for all Cubans, even those who remained in their homeland. Now all we had were memories and stories to keep the romance alive and that would have to be enough.

We talked with long spaces in-between until the faint and delicate light of morning began to glow upon the horizon. "This is the direction we must go," Manuel said. "Towards the rising sun. We're doing well."

He repositioned the oars with the blankets draped over them as I dozed with Lucinda next to me. How could I feel so relaxed and positive about my life when we were out in the middle of the ocean with only a couple of days worth of water and just a little more food? Was I going crazy? And then I realized that it was probably the relief of having escaped and knowing that no matter what happened now, nobody was chasing us or trying to take Lucinda away. Perhaps death was just as close as the creaking boards beneath us, but we were free and it was a beautiful feeling.

I told Manuel this and he stopped his work for an instant and stood up carefully in the dinghy so as not to rock it. Cupping his hands around his mouth, he yelled into the fresh morning air. "One day Cuba will be free and returned to the people who love her most, and Castro's lies will choke him like a noose around his neck!"

I stood up next him. "And when they bury him in the ground we'll dance on his grave!"

Lucinda awoke and yelled above us both, catching us unawares. "He's a son of a bitch!"

We laughed so hard that the boat rocked and we almost lost the oars. Then we observed the silent, undulating sea, unperturbed by our declarations.

"I guess you're right," Manuel said. "No matter what happens now, we're free."

# 36

MANUEL MANAGED TO CATCH SEVERAL MORE FISH DURING THE next two days and the flesh dried quickly in the hot sun so we had plenty of food, but we were down to three oranges and our fresh water was running low. We decided to reduce the ration to only a quarter cup three times a day. If another day passed without spotting a ship we'd drink only twice a day. It wasn't that we hadn't seen any ships because we had, but they were too far away to see our little dinghy that, with the glare of sun on the water, probably looked like another piece of driftwood. If they'd been looking for us it might've been different, but they weren't and we grew hoarse from yelling at these metal giants and weary from waving our arms when they passed.

We made a flag from the blanket and one of the oars when the last ship came into view, but as we began to wave the blanket came loose and it fell into the sea. We spent most of the time the ship was in view trying to fish it back out of the water. This wasn't just our flag, but our blanket at night and our protection from the sun in the day. It was hard to imagine surviving without it. Manuel was not discouraged. He was certain that before long another ship would pass shortly, and we'd secure our flag to avoid a similar accident.

On the third day, not even one ship was sighted and an ominous wave of desperation hit us all. Manuel didn't say it, but I knew he feared that we'd passed the channel where most of the ships passed. We began to worry that we were off course and drifting aimlessly. Every horrible outcome took shape in our minds, and we hardly spoke to each other for the next day and a half. The only thing that was exchanged between us was pieces of dried fish meat and cups of very little water. Manuel had further reduced the rations so we were barely able to moisten our lips. I noticed that he refused to take any water during the last round, and he'd suffered severe sunburns on his arms and neck because there wasn't room for him under the blanket.

Without thinking about it, I stripped off my shirt so he could wrap it around his neck and face. I was past any self-consciousness I would've normally felt. I was past worrying about anything but survival.

The only thing that hadn't turned on us was the weather. The sea remained mild in the day and night. Occasional swells gradually lifted our little boat before bringing us down, like a gentle mother placing her babe in its crib to sleep. One day when the sea was the stillest it had ever been and the only thing moving was the sweat rolling down my torso, I took off my shorts and slipped into the water. The ocean was cool and still and marvelous. I was smiling and refreshed when Manuel helped me back into the boat. He was angry, afraid even.

"You shouldn't have gone in. There are sharks all over these waters."

"I didn't see any sharks."

"They see you."

I filled an empty bottle with ocean water and rinsed Lucinda's hair and the rest of her with cool water. She closed her eyes and smiled. She'd stopped asking about the United States and about Tío Heremi, but now she asked if it was true that everyone in the United States had hot water for a bath. I assured her everyone did and that most people took showers every day and sometimes more than once if they felt like it.

Manuel had stopped rowing in the day or night and we drifted with the tides. Most of the time he didn't answer if we asked him a question unless it required only a one word response.

"Would you like a piece of fish?"

"No."

"Do you think we're still in the right current?"

"Yes."

"Do you want me to pour some water over you to cool you off?"

"No."

"Do your shoulders hurt?"

"No."

"Will it be long now?"

"No."

I started to whisper to Lucinda without realizing it because I had the impression that speaking in a normal tone of voice was beginning to irritate Manuel. Sometimes he grimaced in pain while he slept. At others he laughed out loud. He continued to refuse water and to say that he was no longer thirsty. There was no arguing with him.

That night I put two rations (the two that he had refused) in the cup that was already brown and stained. He slept with his mouth open and snored as loudly as a bear. Ever so slowly, I poured a thin stream of water a little at a time so that he couldn't possibly choke. His mouth was hot and dry and absorbed the water immediately. Then I took the last orange and split it between Lucinda and myself, giving most of it to Lucinda who ate it without a word. Except for one dried fish, she knew as well as I, that this was the last food we had. We both knew Manuel would probably not fish again. In the last two days, he'd changed radically from a sober, self-assured man into a petulant, moody little boy. And there was a dryness creeping into his eyes, causing him to look rather like a lizard and I suspected I looked very much the same. Nevertheless, I wished I'd paid better attention to how he'd fished on that first day. What had he used for bait? How did he prepare the hook? He wouldn't answer these questions in his present mood.

I took the fishing pole that lay next to his sleeping form and inspected it closely. The only thing we had for bait was our last remaining food source. Would a piece of dry fish attract anything? I consulted with Lucinda in hushed whispers, and she agreed that it was worth a try. I took a fairly large piece of dried fish from the bag behind the seat and pierced it with the hook. Slowly and carefully, I lowered it into the water as I'd seen Manuel do that first day. I waited with my back against the opposite side of the boat.

Manuel woke up an hour or so into my fishing and he stared at me with glassy eyes as though he couldn't be sure if he was dreaming. It seemed the water I poured into his mouth had revived him a bit. That and the cool night air. Lucinda could hear he was awake; I knew by the way she repositioned her body slightly to face him.

His voice was hoarse. "What did you use for bait?"

"A piece of dry fish. That's all that's left."

"I'm sorry. I have no strength to help you." He lay back down with eyes gaping open at the darkening sky. "I believe I may have failed you, Nora. You and Lucinda."

I moved the pole back and forth and up and down as I'd seen him do before. The bait was supposed to look lively. Our dried piece of fish should be looking spry and happy to be alive in the tropical sea if another bigger fish was ever going to go for it.

"I know Tony would forgive me because he was that kind of man." He went on with a droning voice and I realized that he didn't care if anyone was going to answer him or not, he just needed to hear himself talk, but I didn't want Lucinda to hear his fatalism. She had buried her head in her knees for most of the day and hardly spoken a word. Her head was up now and she was listening intently just when I would've wanted her to be asleep.

"Don't talk like that, Manuel. It's not over yet." I said.

"Tony always said the same thing. He'd always talk me out of these hopeless moments. There was something about the way he talked that always made me listen. I used to tell him that he'd make an excellent preacher when he got out."

"Tony would want you to be strong and not lose hope. If you

can't do it for yourself, do it for his daughter. She needs you, Manuel, we both do."

"I know, but it should've been Tony here, not me. I can take fair knowledge of that to my grave."

I jerked hard on the pole. "Lucinda can hear you."

"She might as well know the truth," he droned on. "I've always heard that before a person dies, there's a certain premonition, a sense that it's coming. If that's true then . . ."

"Shut up! Do you understand me?" I hit the pole hard against the side of the boat, making a sharp flat noise that would go nowhere in the thick humid air. We might as well have been in a padded cell. Manuel was silent and slowly turned on his side. I was worried that I had made him angry, and I didn't know what he was capable of in a rage. What if he went insane? Would I have the strength and the will to push him overboard if he threatened Lucinda's and my safety?

He crossed his ankles and rolled up into a fetal position under the seat. I saw him watching us under the moonlight and caught the glint of one eyeball. It closed when I looked and opened when I turned back to my fishing. I could pretend I didn't notice he was staring at me and he'd stop, but I couldn't resist the temptation of turning to look because he reminded me of a rat waiting underneath the cupboard for the right moment to make his move, whatever that move might be.

"There's something in the water, Tía." Lucinda's voice caused me to jump and almost lose the fishing pole. "I hear it, and it's swimming all around us."

I pulled in the pole and sat up straight to look around. The water was still calm and rolling away from us in gentle swirls, but I saw nothing, only a sliver of moonlight and the cloud cover almost obliterated that.

Lucinda sat up straight as well, her expression electrified and almost twitching with concentration. "There it is again."

"I don't hear anything, honey. Maybe it's your imagination." But just as I said this I heard a soft rap on the bottom of the boat very quickly followed by another.

"They're everywhere," Lucinda said turning her head side to side as if she were equipped with some kind of radar. I stared into the ocean once again, and this time I saw it. There were shapes in the water that rose and fell in the shadows of the sea. They could be anything I wanted them to be: the Miami skyline, a huge air craft carrier, or a little pleasure craft close enough to touch with my fishing pole.

Manuel inched out from under the seat and sat in the middle of the boat. "They're sharks," he said dryly.

Suddenly I could see the dark silhouettes of razor sharp fins rising and falling out of the sea, circling us, gliding beneath us in strange and fantastic formation. I could see them perfectly now. If I looked more closely I'd be able to look into their black and barren eyes searching for food in the night. There were several more sharp blows under the boat. The sharks were powerful and focused.

"Why are there so many?"

Manuel was sitting up now and holding on to his knees as Lucinda had done most of the day. "They must be feeding." More knocks came rapidly this time. It sounded as though a very large man was punching the bottom of our boat with bare fists. The boat would not handle much more of such abuse.

"Why do they keep hitting the boat, Tía?"

"I don't know. I'm sure they'll stop soon."

"Because they think we're food and they won't stop until they're convinced we're not, or until we are," Manuel said.

"We have to do something, Manuel, please," I pleaded.

At that moment, one of the larger sharks rammed the side of the boat propelling it toward a gathering of fins several feet ahead of us. They had their strategy for the kill, and their bodies near the surface of the water were like sleek submarines parked all around us. I wondered if these sharks had already acquired a taste for human flesh. How many rafts had been overturned by sharks such as these?

Manuel looked about with simple curiosity. "There's nothing we can do except hope that something more appetizing comes along. But I don't think that's likely."

I grabbed the oars that had lain dormant for almost three days. I'd never handled them and I wasn't sure what to do now, but I assumed the rowing position Manuel had before and directed Lucinda to sit away from me. The oars were heavy and awkward, but slowly, I began to row. The blows continued on the sides of the boat from both directions. Manuel was stoic and unflinching even when one of the blows was strong enough to cause the frame of the boat to splinter. Lucinda screamed and I would've screamed too if all my energy had not been concentrated on rowing. The oars hit the sharks' backs on several occasions, backs as solid as steel. They were trying to bite at them, hoping that someone had been foolish enough to dangle arms and legs over the sides.

"Forget it, you can't row fast enough." Manuel said. "They aren't feeding on anything else. They want us."

The boat would splinter into nothing. I knew it was just a matter of time. I pulled in the oars and stood up in the boat to look around. Lucinda held on to my legs and sobbed, crying out for her mother. The blows came more rapidly and evenly. It was as if the sharks were lining up in formation to demolish the boat like a well-trained regiment of soldiers. I took one of the oars and began to whack the sharks when I saw the fins approaching the boat. I remembered reading somewhere that sharks were particularly sensitive on their noses. So this is what I aimed for. With what strength I had left, I brought the oar down on their backs over and over as I screamed at the top of my lungs for God and the saints to help us. I hurled blood-curdling screams into the night to give me strength to scare away the enemy, the evil spirits and death itself. Death by drowning or dehydration I could imagine if I had to, but please God, not to be eaten alive by sharks, anything but that. As I shouted I whacked them on their tails and their backs and their noses. I slapped the water on both sides with a surging rhythm as though possessed by the spirit of the jungle, the black spirit that conquered all.

It was then that the sea rose up in all directions, and we became covered in blood and water and the saliva of hungry sharks.

Suddenly, there was complete and utter silence. Only the slipping sound of the sea and the soft murmuring of the breeze. I scanned the ocean with my oar still raised and then brought it down slowly. All the sharks had gone. Not a fin could be seen anywhere.

I looked about the boat. Lucinda was still crouched down and holding on to my legs. Manuel was back under the seat. I wasted no time and took up the oars once again and began rowing until fire was burning through my back and arms, until the agony in my muscles overcame my fear of a repulsive and horrible death.

I collapsed on to the floor of the boat and turned to see if Manuel was still watching me like a little rat. I wanted him to be so I could gloat at the little rat and say I told you so, and why didn't you help me save our lives? He wasn't there. I turned my head the other way, but Manuel was nowhere in the boat. Manuel was gone.

I took hold of Lucinda by the shoulders and shook her. "Where is Manuel, Lucinda? My God, where is he?"

In my frenzy to get away I hadn't noticed that Lucinda was crying and pulling at her cork screw curls so hard that there were chunks of hair in her fists.

"He whispered in my ear that freedom is for the living," she said between sobs. "Then he left and everything was still."

# 37

I BEGAN TO UNDERSTAND HOW TIME IS MEASURED IN DIFFERENT situations. In the normal world, Manuel's sacrifice would've ground into our psyches for weeks and months before we could focus normally on the matter of living. On the boat, we were making our next plan for survival in less than an hour.

By the time the sun had risen, it was as if Manuel's death had occurred a couple of year's ago and not a few hours ago. One hour of survival was worth months in real time, and we had to make every second count or we would be lost. We had no water or food, and by midday our mouths were sticky as we huddled under the blanket, no longer bothering to tent it over the oars.

In the delirium of heat, my mind turned constantly to Jeremy. He was drinking American coffee at the kitchen table. Or was it dinnertime? He didn't cook much. Maybe Mami made him his favorite chicken stew and packed it for him in layers of plastic because she didn't trust the Tupperware alone. He's sleeping in our bed and reaching for me in his sleep. He could be sleeping with somebody else by now because he didn't think I was ever coming back. He'd think my Cuban life swallowed me up whole.

Nobody knows we're out here. We could be drifting in the Atlantic. But the Atlantic waters would be dark and rough, and these waters remain a royal blue at their deepest and sometimes fade into swirls of turquoise.

Lucinda, your eyes are the color of the ocean. When you open them and turn to me, it's as if your eyes are giant round windows to the sea. I should be telling you this, but I can't open my mouth, it is so dry. Did I tell you that Jeremy brings me coffee in the morning? He knows I like it with a little sugar and cream and he knows I have a favorite cup. He'll probably bring you coffee in the morning too. Would you like that? You don't answer me, but that's because you're conserving your energy just like I am.

Isn't if funny how we don't sleep or wake? We're asleep and awake at the same time. But I know when I'm more asleep than awake because for an instant I'm not thirsty anymore. I'm dreaming of swimming in drinking water. I'm pouring soft drinks over ice cubes that crack and swish in the glass like maracas. There is a strong gush of water pouring out of my mouth. It's so strong I can't close it. It pushes out my teeth and hurts my throat if I try to swallow against it. This is worse than the constant thirst I can understand and fight against with my mind. I cannot take this anymore. I hope you don't feel this, I hope to God you don't.

Dark clouds gathered as the sun set. Another day passed like a universe of time forgotten. The waves deepened and peaked in their shadows and a grayish gloom surrounded us when we came out from under the blanket. I felt a rain drop on my nose and then another. Tiny droplets perched on Lucinda's thick eye lashes causing her to blink curious eyes. The torrent of rain came all at once. I scooped the water out with Manuel's shoes and directed Lucinda to drink from the bottom of the boat. I did the same. Thank God we hadn't lost our empty water bottles and I was able to fill one half way before the rain stopped, before Lucinda vomited the water she'd gulped in a frenzy. I vomited too. We'd been drinking water thick with the filth of our bodies for almost a week. We lost all the water we drank and maybe more, but it had absorbed into our skin and washed off the hazy salt film. Our blanket was wet and so were we, but we slept deeper than a trance that night. We sipped sweet water from the bottle little bits at a time and watched the stars circle above us.

Lucinda, did I tell you about the time your mother and I planned to run away from home? She wanted to rescue me from becoming a nun. We were certain we'd have much more fun as showgirls. The showgirl idea was your mother's. In fact, most of the ideas were hers, but she was always looking out for me. She was very brave and I always wished I could be more like her. She was the most beautiful and smartest girl I ever knew. When she walked down the street, every eye was on her, every word of praise, every second glance. She walked with eyes forward, back straight, neither proud nor ashamed, just happy to be who she was and where she was.

Lucinda, listen to me. If Jeremy doesn't want me anymore, will you be happy living just with me? There's a chance, a big chance, that he won't, you see. Yes, he loves me, he just doesn't understand that I had to stay longer. I couldn't leave you and now we may both die here together. I'm not afraid to die, Lucinda. Your Mami died so easily in my arms that afternoon on the beach. She took a deep breath that quivered just a little and then she just died as beautifully as she lived. I miss her so much.

Take my hand, Lucinda. I want you to hold this. It's the candle your Mami left for me. I brought it in the bag with the oranges. I have matches and if they're not wet I can light it when it's night. I knew you'd want to see it too. I can put it right here on the bench so we can both look at it when we lay down. Isn't it so beautiful? I knew you'd like it. Now we can sleep here and feel safe. The light will protect us from all harm.


Somebody's pushing on my face and rubbing at my eyes and stretching me backward and forward. I reach for Lucinda, but she's no longer next to me. I try to sit up and many hands hold me down against a rough surface like sandpaper that smells of plastic and bleach. Men are speaking around me, soft muffled words that drift in and out. I must find Lucinda. She may have fallen in the water and she's blind and she can't swim. Don't you understand what I'm telling you? I have to find Lucinda!

"Lucinda is fine. She's very dehydrated, but she's sleeping peacefully below deck." I can hardly open my eyes, but I know Jeremy's voice and those are his hazel eyes gazing down on me. "And you're fine too, my love. Thank God."

I want to speak to you, I want to speak to you, Jeremy, but I can't make the words.

He runs trembling fingers across my forehead and I look more fully into eyes swollen and tired from lack of sleep and weeping. Mine want to close, but I'm afraid when they open again, he'll be gone.

He whispers in my ear. "Beba called me the morning you left. She said you weren't able to make it onto the ship and that I should search for you at sea. We've been searching all week and we found you both this morning, right before the sun came up. We were turning back when we saw the smoke. The boat was burning right underneath you. We would never have found you if not for the smoke."

Jeremy cradles me in his arms as he weeps and kisses my face again and again. "All that matters is that we're going home, my love. You and me and Lucinda, we're going home."

# 38

IT IS AS IT HAS ALWAYS BEEN, THE SEA A TURQUOISE BLUE FADING
into a sky bluer still. Alicia and I wonder whether we should disturb the calm waters with a swim or whether we should stay right
where we are, sitting on the sand side by side, our eyes half closed
to the sun. One of us will soon break the silence with a thought
about this or that. Usually it is Alicia, so I wait for her to draw in
her breath and speak to me, and all the while it is the whispering
sea I hear, and the wind calling my name . . .

"She opened her eyes. I'm sure she did." Mami's voice rever-
berated in my head with such clarity that if I hadn't opened them
before, and they flew open to look at her now. She was almost
falling over the railing at the side of the bed, peering at me with
swollen eyes, a handkerchief clutched between her fingers. Papi
was next to her, calming her as best he could, but his voice was a
bit shaky as well; neither of them looked quite as I remembered
them. My eyes focused beyond a mild haze of pain and I realized
they'd both lost a bit of weight and their faces were drawn from
lack of sleep. I could only imagine how I must look to them.

The fear in their eyes flared anew when I attempted to move
my mouth to speak. I felt an enormous boulder pressing down on
my diaphragm squeezing the breath and the life out of my lungs,
but I managed to squeak out a question just the same.

"Where's Jeremy?"

Mami released herself from Papi's arms and lunged across the bed before he could stop her. "He's here, Nora. Oh my God, my baby, my sweet Nora," and she collapsed in a chair and began to sob as she had been for days, no doubt.

Papi leaned forward, trying to contain his emotion for my sake, but his hand trembled on my arm and he squeezed down in such a way that betrayed his own quiet desperation. "Jeremy's fine, Lucinda's fine and so are you."

I tried to reach for Papi's hand, but felt the discomfort of a foreign object in my nose. I went to remove it, but Papi gently stopped me. "The tubes are there to help you breath, but they'll take them out soon enough, you'll see."

I nodded and allowed him to guide my hand back down to my side. "Where am I?"

Mami had regained her composure and pulled her chair forward so she was almost at eye level with me. She slipped her hand through the bed railing and squeezed my shoulder. "We're in the hospital in Miami. Lucinda is here too in the pediatric ward. Jeremy's with her now, but I'm sure he'll be back down soon. He hasn't left your side for two days."

"As soon as we heard you were found," Papi continued, "we took the first plane we could get. We arrived yesterday and we'll stay as long as you need us, Norita."

Tears slipped down my cheeks and I felt like a child again, as frail and vulnerable as one who'd been caught in a terrible lie. But I had to ask the question and be rid of the burning anxiety I'd felt ever since I'd gone against their wishes and left for Cuba. "Are you still angry with me?"

Mami was the first to speak, as I knew she would be and the strain in her voice was palpable and thick on her tongue. "What you did was a foolish thing, Nora. For a child who was never prone to foolishness it was beyond understanding and I can only say . . ." Her eyes began to steam, and Papi placed a soothing hand on her back as if reminding her of something they'd spoken about earlier.

"Nora's not a child anymore," he said gently.

Mami sniffed, and the recollection of their previous conversations cooled her considerably. "No, she's not a child anymore." She released her anger with a sigh and looked upon me with such hope and love, that I could only smile back at her, my face stiff with what felt like the first smile I'd been able to manage in weeks.

In the evening when we were alone, Jeremy climbed into bed with me, careful not to disturb the various tubes and lines attached to my arm and face. He rested his head on my shoulder and settled himself in as best he could.

I closed my eyes and tried to imagine that the humming of the equipment all around us was the whispering surf or the wind in the palms, but I was unable to conjure up a vision that might calm me. The dread I'd felt before we were rescued came upon me in waves as though we were still at sea fighting for our lives.

"I have exciting news," Jeremy said softly in my ear. "The doctors believe there may be hope for Lucinda, that she could regain some of her vision. It's not certain and I haven't said anything to her yet, but they're already making inquiries at UCLA."

My heart beat furiously upon hearing this, and I longed to rip out all the wires attached to me and go to her. "When can I see her? I have to see her, Jeremy."

"Tomorrow. I promise that first thing in the morning I'll look into it. And she's doing well, my love. She's an amazingly strong child, and when she sees you it'll make her all the stronger."

His breathing grew deep and relaxed and I thought he'd fallen asleep when he spoke. "Don't leave me again, Nora. Don't you ever leave me again."

Back in California, Mami arrived daily with Cuban casseroles and desserts of all kinds to help us recover from our ordeal. Lucinda could hear her car down the street before Jeremy and I heard her in the drive. She'd open the front door before Mami had rung the doorbell and follow her into the kitchen full of delight and awe at the feasts that revealed themselves out of brown paper bags and layer after layer of aluminum foil and plastic wrap. In spite of packing that would put the NASA space program to shame, Lucinda was able to clearly detect the delectable aromas of *ropa vieja, carne con papas*, and *arroz con pollo*.

Mami presented her meals on TV trays for us in bed because I was too tired to sit at the table. She stood back and waited eagerly with arms crossed until we took our first bites.

"This is delicious, Abuela Regina," Lucinda declared and Mami beamed with satisfaction at both the compliment and that Lucinda had called her Abuela.

I remembered how distant Mami had been with Lucinda when they first met in Miami. I expected as much. Mami had always been stubbornly loyal to her traditional values and in matters of the heart and life and family, she did not easily accept defeat. She'd been openly critical of Alicia's marriage to Tony for too long to accept Lucinda right away, especially with everybody looking on. I think she blamed her too for putting me at risk. In fact, for those first few days, Lucinda seemed to be the embodiment of all that was wrong with Cuba since before and after the revolution.

The day before Lucinda and I were scheduled to be discharged, the family was gathered together in my room. Lucinda sat near me as she preferred to do, listening to the chatter back and forth of new voices intermingled with familiar. Mami was particularly animated as she considered the prospect of going back to California. Papi even spoke of throwing a party to celebrate my homecoming. The thought prompted tears of joy which began to flow down Mami's cheeks for the third or forth time that day.

Only a foot or so away, Lucinda reached out and gently touched Mami's cheek with the tip of her finger. "You're crying again, señora Regina."

Mami nodded, but said nothing.

Lucinda thought for a moment. Her eyes were shining as she turned fully to face her new relative. "Mami always said it was good to cry as much as you want, as long as your tears fall on someone you love."

Mami's face writhed with agony as she attempted to swallow her distress and battle with that reflex for blatant rejection she'd perfected over the years. She might just as easily have told Lucinda to keep her thoughts to herself. Instead, she swept her up in her arms and wept openly, moistening the top of her curly head with a cloudburst of tears. She did not let her go for a very long time, and ever since, insisted that Lucinda call her Abuela Regina. Now she wouldn't tolerate any degree of criticism directed toward her precious Lucinda from anyone. When Papi commented on how naive Lucinda was for her age, Mami thrust out her chin and let him have it.

"José, how you could raise two girls and know nothing about children is beyond me. This child is advanced in every way, and I won't be surprised if they discover her to be some sort of genius when she gets to a proper school. You mark my words."


Mami glowered over me, watching me move the food she'd so carefully prepared around on my plate with growing concern. She and I and everyone else knew I hadn't eaten for days. The truth is I had no appetite whatever and Cuban food was particularly unpleasant. The richness of the spices and sauces and onions and peppers I once loved so much now caused my stomach to turn with revulsion. I slept most of the time and complained about a heaviness about my chest and stomach that hadn't left me since my stay in the hospital.

Mami spoke to Jeremy in hushed tones when he returned from work in the late afternoon, and Jeremy came and sat next to me as I lay on the couch. I'd hardly moved since lunch, being interested only in the way the sun filtered through the trees at sunset creating a wild and lacy pattern on the wall opposite me. I'd been staring at it for what seemed like hours.

"You're not going to get well again if you don't eat, Nora."

"I know."

"You haven't put on any weight like the doctor said you should. In fact you've lost weight and . . ."

"I said I know!" I had never before raised my voice to Jeremy and the hurt and confusion in his eyes startled me for a moment, but when he left the room, I didn't have the energy to do or say anything more about it. I was transfixed once again by the shadows of the encroaching night and the lovely pattern playing in the corners of the darkening room.

A psychiatrist friend of Jeremy's from the university came to see me some time after that. He was a nice man with a double chin and thick-framed glasses who insisted I call him Peter instead of Dr. Mills. This was one of the privileges of being an academic's wife, I thought, and answered his questions as best as I could. Yes, I had very little energy, and there were few things I could think of doing that made me want to get out of bed and get dressed. No, I had no trouble sleeping; in fact I preferred to sleep over anything else because only then was I released from the bitter nothingness that ate at me like a hideous worm. No, I had no appetite, and the sight and smell of food, especially Cuban food, was nauseating to me. No, I hadn't thought of killing myself, but I had thought about death a lot lately and how peaceful it sounded.

Peter had been listening to me, nodding his head, seeming to understand it all. With a pudgy finger he nudged his glasses back up his nose so his eyes were clearly focused onto mine. "What do you think is causing your depression?" he asked plainly.

Should I tell him? Could I tell him? I gazed at his kind bespectacled face. He was a psychiatrist after all and had heard things from his patients more bizarre than anything I could ever say.

"It's my heart," I ventured.

"Your heart? What's wrong with it?" he asked, quite curious.

"It feels like I gave it away or lost it and that now I'm trying to live with a . . ." I glanced at him to see if he was still following me and was encouraged to see his expression as intent and kind as before. "I'm living with a ghost heart instead of a real heart." Tears slipped down my face in quiet streams.

"I see. A ghost heart," he repeated, still nodding.

"Beba would know what to do, but she's very far away in Cuba, and I can't even write her a letter because she doesn't read."

"Beba?"

"She was our maid in Cuba and she knows so many things, things that ordinary people don't know."

"I see," he said, and thought for a moment. "This ghost heart you mentioned, tell me more about it."

"I'm not sure how to describe it. It's the part of yourself you can give away without losing who you are, but somehow I did it wrong and gave away the part that's real and that's why I don't feel anything anymore, not even hunger and I care nothing about getting better. I don't even care about Jeremy or Lucinda anymore." I covered my face ashamed by such a horrible disclosure I hadn't dared admit even to myself until that moment.

He gave me time to compose myself. "I can see how upsetting this is for you, Nora. I think for now it's best that you rest as much as you can. Can you do that?"

I nodded obediently, and Peter left with assurances that he wouldn't say anything to Jeremy or my mother about how I felt. I knew this would only cause them to worry more. But he said he'd have to talk with Jeremy about his recommendation that I get a good rest.

Peter hadn't been gone for five minutes when Jeremy came in the room to sit with me. Lately, he didn't mind sitting with me for long periods without saying anything if he thought I didn't feel like talking, but I knew he was the one who needed to talk this time. The little lines around his eyes had deepened, and his mouth was tight with a worry that had grown into an agitation he could hardly contain.

"Peter thinks you should go to the hospital for a while."

"The hospital? Do you mean a mental hospital?"

"He thinks you've been through a lot, much more than most people can take, and that getting some special care might help you."

"Do you think I should go too?"

Jeremy lowered his head and teardrops fell on his hands, thick semi frozen blotches of pain. "I don't know what to think, Nora. I used to dream of spending the rest of my life with you." He looked up at me with eyes that had always been so confident and serene, my perpetual sanctuary. Now they were helpless and pleading. "I don't want to lose you." He choked down a sob. "I thought I had lost you once and then . . ." He took hold of my hands. "I just want you well again. I want my Nora back."

"Give me until after Christmas," I begged. "If I'm not better then, I'll go to whatever hospital you and Peter want me to go to. I promise."

Christmas was less than a week away.

The dream I'd been waiting for arrived during one of those rare nights in Southern California when the temperature dips down below forty degrees. I am a child again. Alicia and I are holding hands by the water's edge and watching the tide dance upon the shore. We laugh as our feet scoot along the soft sand and we feel the writhing ribbons between our toes. Alicia is urging me forward into the surf, laughing and teasing all the while in her playful way that means no harm. Her fingers lock like a vice on to mine and I am unable to break free as she pulls me into the deeper water, until we're floating loose like jellyfish, breathing memories and faces through our gills. I look into the ocean depths and see Tony's mild green eyes glistening with the vision of his beloved, Manuel's burnt shoulders hunched over the boat as he fishes, Tío Carlos playing his guitar on the porch, Tía Panchita's curious smile flashing through a haze of cigar smoke and Abuelo, standing at the water's edge after a long swim.

Alicia's fingers loosen and the surf lifts me back to shore as I watch them disappear beyond the sea, receding into an oblivion of peace.

\*   \*   \*

I woke up on the morning of Christmas Eve to an unusual and noisy commotion. The plan was for Mami and Papi to arrive early and help Jeremy prepare the meal for later that evening. Marta and Eddie and the kids weren't due to arrive until 5:00 P.M. or so. I dreaded the feast of roast pork and plantains, black beans, rice, and yucca that lay ahead of me, and my stomach churned as I imagined the contents of the grocery bags I heard rustling in the kitchen. The talk between Jeremy and my parents sounded nothing like the good-natured banter typical of them when planning a holiday gathering. It was agitated and strained. Voices were being raised and I distinctly heard Mami's above the rest. "The doctor said not to upset her. That much I know."

The argument continued and I wondered if at the hospital there might be some peace. I'd made little improvement, and I hadn't forgotten my promise to Jeremy. Surely that's what the argument was about: when and how to get me to the mental hospital. I tried to garner the strength necessary to get out of bed and begin packing and wondered what to say to Lucinda about my absence. Jeremy had managed to find a school for her even as he juggled his schedule around her medical appointments at UCLA. She'd be starting classes after the Christmas break. She knew I wasn't able to help Jeremy with this because I wasn't well, but she attributed my illness to what we'd been through and seemed to understand that talking about it was not in my best interest.

They were just outside the bedroom now and they were trying to be quiet, but the fear in their voices, caused me to shudder. They burst through the door, their faces flushed.

"Jeremy, don't do this," Mami said, puffed from her agitation.

"We should talk about this a bit more," Papi added firmly.

Jeremy shook his head. "I've never kept anything from Nora before, and I don't intend to start now."

"But she's not the Nora we knew," Mami implored. "Don't you realize that? Nora is sick and if she reads this she could get worse."

"What's wrong with Tía Nora?" Lucinda's small voice from the doorway forced everyone to pause.

"Nothing, sweetheart." Mami led her into the room with a protective arm. "Your Tía Nora is a little weak now, but she'll be fine."

Jeremy held out an envelope to me. "This came for you yesterday. It was postmarked a few days before Alicia died. Perhaps it was lost in the mail, or got rerouted or something." He glanced back at Mami and Papi who were tight with fear as they held on to Lucinda. "Your parents are upset because they believe Alicia's letters did you more harm than good. They say you're too vulnerable to read another one right now." The letter dangled in his fingers between us. "What do you think?"

With a deep breath I took the envelope from him and turned it over in my hand. The three postmarks printed near the Havana address confirmed Jeremy's suspicion that the letter had been lost, and I recognized Alicia's delicate script on the outside of the envelope as well. I stared at it for several long seconds as I imagined Alicia during her last days on the couch.

"I think I'd like to read this by myself," I said without looking up. They all turned to leave and I held my hand out to Lucinda. "Stay with me, Lucinda. Your Mami would've wanted you here."

Lucinda made her way to the bed and nestled in next to me. I felt her head on my shoulder as I tore open the envelope and slowly unfolded the pages of the letter.


Dear Nora,

When you read this I want you to imagine that you're relaxing under our palms at Varadero and looking up at the sky because that's where I imagine myself at this moment, and you're next to me listening and smiling as you always do so my worries float away on the breeze. Although I'm tempted, I won't write you of my worries right now. I'll write instead about something you always wanted to know ever since we were girls playing on the beach. Even now I can hear your voice asking me as we stare up at the sun through the trees, "Did you see God? What did you ask for?" I guess it's OK to tell you now that I asked Him for a guardian angel to watch over me always. For years I didn't think He was listening because the angel didn't appear as I expected, over my bed with soft feathery wings and a silk gown like I saw in the paintings at church. I know now that you, dear cousin, have been my guardian angel and comfort during the worst moments of my life. Even now I wait for death with peace in my heart knowing you will look after Lucinda with all that you are and for that I would gladly give my life and more.

In truth, you have not only been my guardian angel but my confessor as well, and I'm afraid I have yet another confession to make. For almost two years I took the American dollars you so carefully folded inside your letters and set them ablaze by the flame of my candle one by one. I didn't want to admit how much I ached for your American life, your nice house, your hot running water, and twenty-four hour supermarkets, and ranting reporters who hate all politicians and aren't afraid to insult them on television. I resented your personal telephone ringing off the hook and six brands of toothpaste, and sleeping in a clean bed after a full meal and waking to a strong cup of coffee in the morning and so many things.

I tried to escape my jealousy by convincing myself that you and everyone like you had betrayed Cuba and that I betrayed her too with my envy. I ask your forgiveness. But I don't feel guilty anymore and I don't think you should either, because we did not betray our country, Nora. Our country betrayed us. You and all who left are orphans just like Lucinda. And just as she'll embrace you as her new mother after I'm gone, so must you embrace your American life with all your heart and soul even if the tears of grief and parting are still moist in your eyes. Because if you wait for your tears to dry, you'll be waiting forever.

But never forget, Nora, never forget the Cuba we knew, and tell it to Lucinda and your children before they're old enough to understand so it becomes a part of them as it has become a part of us. Tell them how we swam in the blue-green waters of the Caribbean and how we ate sweet mangos as the juice dripped down our faces. Tell them about the chaperoned dances and white linen suits and about the way musicians played their music to coax even the moon from its quiet place in the sky.

And always remember the dream that was . . . the sounds of enchantment . . . the breezes that caress the soul . . . our palm trees in the sky.

All my love,
Alicia

Jeremy knocked softly and, not hearing a response, peeked in to find Lucinda and I embraced and weeping after having read Alicia's letter three times over. He wasn't sure about whether or not he should enter, but I held my hand out to him, and he crossed the room swiftly and took us both in his arms.

"I love you, Jeremy," I whispered, feeling my strength return-ing as our tears flowed. "Please, forgive me."

# Epilogue

ALMOST A YEAR LATER ALICIA GARCÍA-MCLAUGHLIN WAS BORN. When I brought her home from the hospital, Lucinda gazed at her through triple thick glasses that made her eyes appear as giant emeralds.

"She smiled at me, Tía Nora. I saw her smile at me." Lucinda was bursting with delight.

Later that evening Lucinda laid her head on my lap as I rocked Alicita in my arms. In a few minutes, when he finished grading midterms, I expected Jeremy to poke his head in the nursery and remind Lucinda it was time for her eyedrops and that she needed to brush her teeth before bed and that it didn't matter if she'd already brushed them once that day. Lucinda would complain she wasn't tired and try to squeeze a few more minutes from him. These he almost always obliged her knowing, as did I, that it was wonderful she was behaving as a normal thirteen-year-old girl should.

"Tell me the story again, Tía Nora," she said with a little squeeze to my knee.

"Again?"

"Yes, but this time start at the part I like; right at the beginning."

I cleared my throat and stretched my legs out slowly so as not to wake my little girl, but I gazed into her sleeping face as I spoke, knowing she heard me through her dreams. "What I most love about Cuba is the warmth. The way it spreads out to my fingers and toes so it feels like I'm part of the sun, like it's growing inside me . . ."

"Tía Nora?"

"Yes, Lucinda."

"Will we ever see Cuba again? Will we ever go home?"

I was tempted to answer her with the same variations of "maybe" that I'd received from my parents after leaving Cuba for the first time all those years ago. "Perhaps if things change" they would say, or "We can't know for sure what will happen." These hopeful crumbs did little to satisfy my soul's longing for home.

I tugged lightly on one of Lucinda's springy curls and the silhouette of her cheek plumped up with a smile. But I realized she was anxious for my reply, and I knew I'd have to answer her honestly as I answered everything else.

I inhaled my own fear, and forced myself to exhale through a heart more resilient than resolved. "Yes, Lucinda," I told her. "I'm sure that one day we will see Cuba again, but until then and perhaps afterward too, this is our home."

# Acknowledgments

I could not, in good conscience, put my name to this work without acknowledging the people who've made sharing it possible: my agent, Moses Cardona, of John Hawkins & Associates Inc. I am ever grateful to him for his intelligent guidance and unceasing support; my editors Johanna Castillo and Amy Tannenbaum, who have infused this publication with an enthusiasm and energy that have given new life to the book. With professionals such as these on my side, I can't possibly lose.

I also wish to thank my husband, Steven Myles, without whom I would be unable to live my dream.